# WAVELORD

## DAUGHTER OF VANRIS
## BOOK THREE

NIKKI McCORMACK

ISBN: 978-1-969616-04-4
First Edition 2025

Published by
Elysium Books
Bellevue, WA



Written by Nikki McCormack (https://nikkimccormack.com/)
Cover Design by Robert Crescenzio (https://robertcrescenzio.artstation.com/)
Map Design by Melissa Nash
Typesetting and Design by Brian C. Short
Editing by Alexander Lockwood

•

*To everyone who has accompanied me through the many tales of Vanris, I am honored to have gone on this journey with you. You are all amazing, and I hope to encounter you again on the next adventure.*

•

*Content warnings can be found at the end of the glossary or on my website at elysiumpalace.com.*

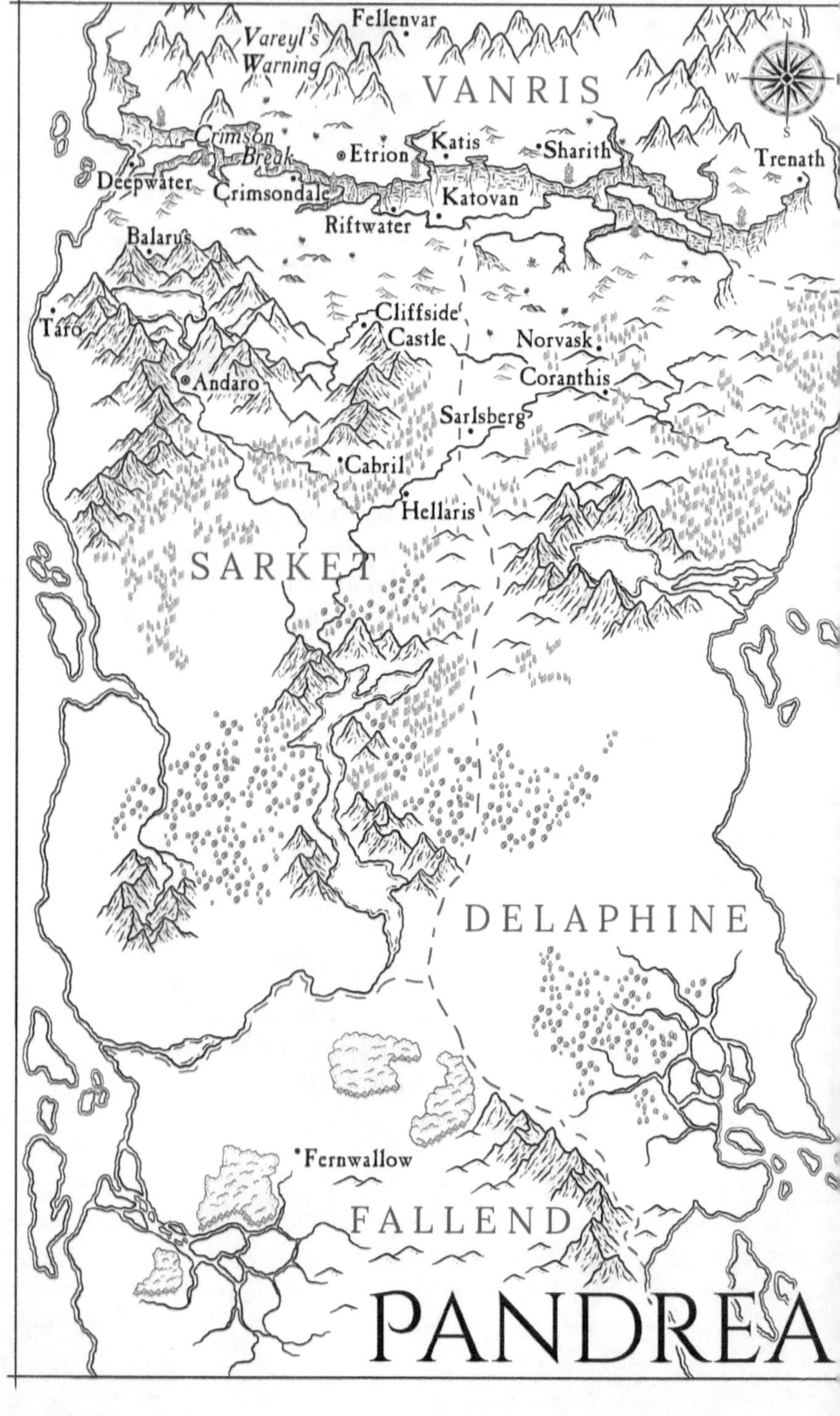

N
W
S
VANRIS
Fellenvar
Vareyl's Warning
Crimson Break
Etrion
Katis
Sharith
Trenath
Deepwater
Crimsondale
Katovan
Riftwater
Balarus
Cliffside Castle
Norvask
Taro
Coranthis
Andaro
Sarlsberg
Cabril
Hellaris
SARKET
DELAPHINE
Fernwallow
FALLEND
PANDREA

THAELIS ISLANDS
N
E
S
PANDREA
Deepwater
Crimsondale
Balarus
Taro
Dagony
Mukyeny
0 100 200 300 kilometers

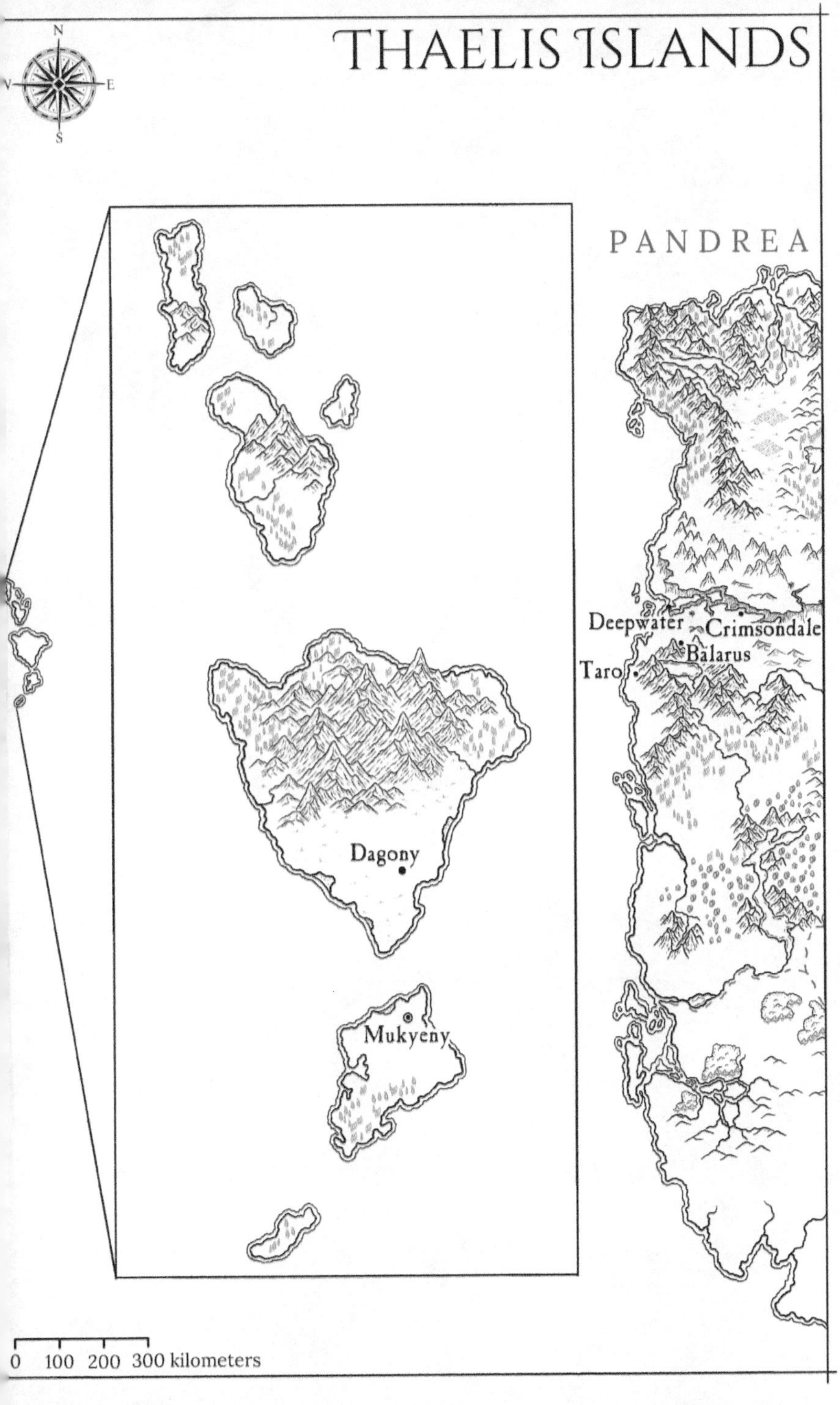

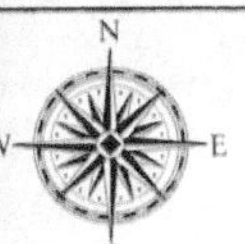

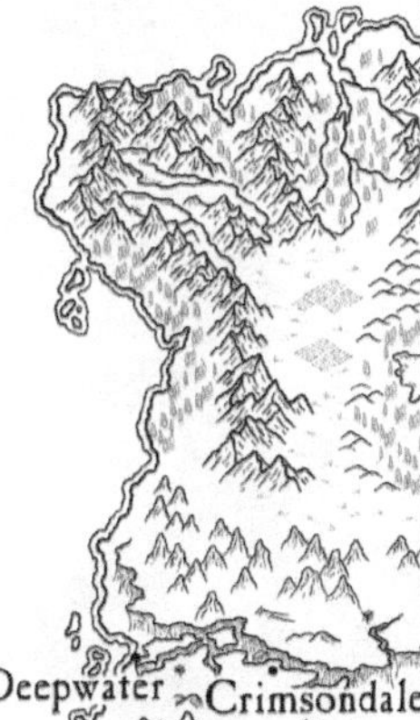

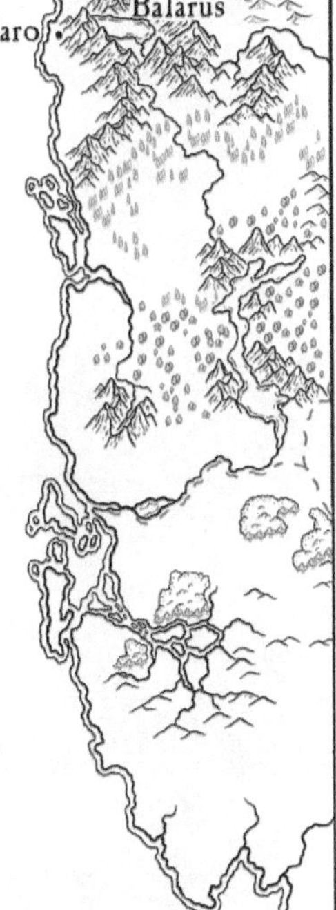

nren Ahrin." Kyril's commanding tone pulled the younger man's attention abruptly away from a conversation with his brother.

Now the new leader of their fledgling unit, the Thaelian Feral was only a few inches taller than the twins, but something about him demanded immediate respect. Perhaps his long black hair, with the early morning light calling out stained streaks of deep blue in it. An unusual color in Vanris, where Veyl's blood-red hair, like her mother's, was uncommonly dark for her people. Or maybe his silver-blue eyes, bright and piercing within rugged features. He had gained a few scars since the first time Veyl encountered him on that awful night in Deepwater, but they took nothing away from his predatory allure, as of some powerful, untamable beast.

And yet, none of those things, as much as they enhanced his presence and pleased the eye, were what ultimately captured her affection. Beneath the surface, he possessed a deep sincerity and kindness, along with a desire to help those in need. Those parts of his nature led him to protect her on that first unfortunate journey to Thaelis and to sail to Vanris when she asked him to warn her people about Thrasser, despite the risk to himself.

Then there was the connection that had drawn her

to him the night she nearly kissed him on his ship. An inexplicable link that had only grown stronger with time... until now. Did that still exist for him, somewhere beneath the emotional and mental scars from Jaysen's cruel abuse?

She startled when Iyvalin bumped her with her elbow.

"Watching his lips move is not the same as listening to him," her friend whispered, stifling a giggle.

Veyl's cheeks warmed, and she forced herself to focus on what Kyril was saying. Today was their first day of training together as a unit after he had spent most of the last two weeks with her father and some other Ferals learning to handle groups of tethdraks. During that time, the rest of them had worked with some of the other officers to learn their roles in the unit. To say that she found this opportunity to spend more time around the Thaelian Feral emotionally trying would have been understating the issue. Why did her need to be close to him have to be so intense while he still struggled with the mess Jaysen's Evoker had made of his memories of their relationship?

"What would you consider your strongest combat skill?" Kyril demanded of Ahrin.

"I'm a decent hand at mounted archery," Ahrin answered tentatively, brushing a lock of light auburn hair away from his eyes and looking at Veyl as if seeking confirmation.

Kyril arched a brow at her where she stood leaning against the fence that encircled one of the training rings.

Unsure of what either of them expected of her, she simply nodded.

He picked out his sister Kitria with his gaze, not giving her a chance to speak before saying, "Yours is the light crossbow." Then he turned to Gannon and Iyvalin.

"What about you two?"

Like Ahrin, their attention drifted to Veyl as they answered.

"Melee with a shortsword, I guess," Iyvalin said, her gaze turning back to Kyril as she spoke. "Though I'm equally comfortable with a light axe."

"Also melee," Gannon answered, never looking away from Veyl, "but I prefer a longer sword. I can make do with a shortsword or a mace in a pinch."

Veyl was standing close enough to hear the deep, frustrated exhale Kyril let out before he spoke. "I get the impression the first point we need to establish is that *I* am the commanding officer of this unit. When we are training or on duty, Veyl is not your khesran. She is another inren like the rest of you. Are we clear on that?"

The other three glanced at her again as if seeking her endorsement of his statement, and she couldn't hold back a small laugh.

Kyril turned a stern gaze her way, though for an instant before he reined it in a hint of amusement tugged at the corners of his mouth, flaring a spark of hope in her. "Are we clear on that, Inren Veyl?" he asked, his tone softening a little.

Forcing a serious expression, she straightened and faced him. Seyn stood up from where she lay beside her and assumed an alert stance, as if attempting to present a unified front with her bonded companion. Veyl set a hand on the wave dancer's shoulders, a gesture that had already become habitual. "We are, Ahninveth."

He no longer looked as uncomfortable as he had just a week ago when someone addressed him using his new title. In Thaelis, he had been an ahnkreth, commanding a fleet of ships, and she suspected that was still how he saw himself. But ahnkreths didn't lead ground troops, so her parents officially made him an ahninveth in Vanris to support the new role they had given him.

When he turned his gaze on them, the other four echoed Veyl's confirmation. The words came easily enough, but how long would it take them to adjust to the idea of following orders from the man who had taken them prisoner aboard his fleet not so long ago?

"Then we can proceed." His troubled look didn't quite match the conviction in his tone. "Today we will focus on archery, since some of us are still recovering from injuries. Kitria and Ahrin, assuming you truly are the more skilled archers, you may also provide pointers to the others as needed." He gestured to an array of bows and crossbows laid out for them.

When Veyl moved to join the others in selecting a weapon, he stopped her with a hand on her shoulder, the contact making her pulse quicken. How frustrating it was that he could do that even with an impersonal touch.

"Not you."

Irritation subdued the pleasure of the contact. She spun to face him. "I'm as skilled with a bow as anyone else here."

"I don't doubt it. However, drawing a bow requires a strong, stable core. I know how serious the wound over your ribs was. I will wait for approval from the healers before I allow you to put undue stress on it. For today, you can help me assess their performance."

Under different circumstances, she would have been delighted to do so, but being close to him was unfairly tormenting now, knowing he no longer shared the memories that made her feel more alive and complete whenever he was near. Still, she couldn't argue with him when he was right. Drawing a regular bow would put strain on the healing injury, and the healers hadn't given her permission to do so yet, but there were alternatives.

"A light crossbow won't hurt it."

The long look he gave her made her feel as if she had

missed something important. Then, his gaze returned to the others. "I want to see how each of you works with every type of bow out here. Except Veyl," he added with a hint of a sigh in his tone, "who will stick to the latchet crossbow."

Could assigning her to help him have been more than just a way to avoid aggravating her injury? How she wished she could read him better, but he had grown so much more guarded around her since they escaped Taro.

Pushing aside her uncertainty, she joined the others to gather their weapons and approach the practice range. Merrin was busy training a couple of newer recruits in one of the nearby sparring rings. Kince, who had been offering occasional feedback throughout the process, abandoned any pretense of being involved and moved closer to watch their unit. His angular features gave an extra sharpness to his cynical gaze, the stacked dark blue symbols of his ke'hanoath tattoo on one cheek adding a touch of asymmetry.

The interest he took in them wasn't unexpected. His tehnaak Darro's sons were out here training to work under the command of the man who had abducted them. He would judge Kyril's skill and leadership ability and report back to Darro whether he felt they were safe with him. The best thing she could do to influence that was to focus on the task their ahninveth had given them. She turned to loading the crossbow and fired her first shot, setting an example for the group that they were quick to follow.

The bolt struck about two inches from the center of her target. Kyril watched as she released another with similar results. Then he walked down the line to observe as each of the others loosed a few arrows. He offered some feedback to each before making his way back to her, by which time she had three more bolts in about the same area.

He stopped next to her. "Excellent grouping. Now, let me see you fire it with your dominant hand."

She changed her stance and switched the crossbow to her left hand. It was harder to focus with him standing by her shoulder, but she had grown up learning these skills under some of the best instructors in Vanris. The first ranged weapon her father taught her to wield was a light crossbow, not so different from the latchet she was using now. She drew a breath and let it out, allowing the tension caused by Kyril's presence to depart with it, then fired. The bolt struck the center of the target.

"Not bad," he allowed. "You're wasted as a khesran."

A glance at him caught the faint, teasing smirk that curved his lips.

"I bet she could beat you with any bow here," Gannon boasted.

Though flattered and more than a little surprised by the pride and confidence in his tone, Veyl shook her head at him and picked up a bolt, passing it and the crossbow over to Kyril when he held out his hands. After loading it, he raised the weapon and fired in a single smooth motion, not even pausing to take aim. The bolt shifted hers as it dug into the center of the target next to it.

Gannon shrugged. "A decent shot."

Kyril handed the crossbow back to her. "My father insisted I learn on a ship at sea before he would allow me to shoot on land. I suspect Veyl might find that more of a challenge than you suggest." He glanced down at her, his expression turning thoughtful. "With a sword, however, I'm not confident she wouldn't win, but we won't be testing that until she's had more time to heal."

Ahrin eyed the distant target. "You must have lost a lot of bolts learning that way."

Kyril chuckled. "Anytime an arrow or bolt went overboard, my father made me dive in and try to retrieve it. I became an exceptional swimmer by the time I got proficient enough not to miss."

Veyl smiled to herself. "I can't help imagining your father dragging you out to sea in a storm, handing you a crossbow, and telling you to hit the target."

His unreadable gaze drifted back to her. "I don't have to imagine it. It might surprise you to hear how often he did exactly that."

For a few seconds, he considered her, mouth opening slightly, as if he might say something more. His gaze shifted to her lips for one heartbeat, moving to her eyes with the next, and his brows pinched. She let those silver-blue eyes draw her in, forgetting that they had an audience. Had he recalled a memory of their connection that the Evoker failed to strip from his mind? Could some of the passion they had shared still be there, lurking behind that carefully restrained countenance?

Gannon loosed an arrow, the *thunk* of it hitting the target snapping them back to the surrounding reality.

Kyril looked away. "Gannon, swap bows with Ahrin. I suspect you'll find that one suits you better."

Veyl turned and fed her frustration into the target, landing a cluster of bolts around the two in the center while she listened to him offering advice to the others and swapping out weapons to check their skills with each. She had made a veritable pincushion out of it by the time he returned to her.

"Whatever it is you're at war with, it looks as though you killed it."

How could he not see that it was him she was at war with?

She drew a deep breath and set down the crossbow. When she glanced over at the practice rings to avoid looking at him, she noticed Kince perk up and start walking toward the palace. Turning farther to see what had caught his attention, she spotted an attendant heading their way.

"There's news," she said.

They stood in silence for a moment, waiting and watching as Kince spoke with the woman. When they finished, he turned and beckoned to them.

"Ahninveth Kyril, Khesran Veyl, you might wish to join me."

Kyril glanced at the other four. "Keep practicing. If I'm not back in an hour, you can leave, but make sure you clean up the targets and put the bows away first."

"Yes, Ahnkreth," Kitria answered.

The other three echoed her with notably less enthusiasm.

"Ahninveth," he corrected before turning away.

"What's going on?" Veyl asked as they fell into step with Kince behind the attendant heading toward the palace.

"A scout arrived to report on developments in Sarket. Kasiel summoned the closed council together to hear what news they bring."

The closed council consisted of her father, some core members of his tehsheyn, her mother, and her grandfather, Arhk. Limiting attendance made sense, since they would want to find out what they were dealing with before bringing it before the larger group. It surprised her a little that she and Kyril were being involved in the initial gathering this time.

"Were we included in the summons?"

"No." Kince glanced back and pointedly met her eyes, making it apparent he was addressing just her. "After what Jaysen put you through, you deserve to be part of this."

Ceris nosed her right hand where he walked between her and Kyril, opposite Seyn. "Put both of us through, you mean," Veyl prompted.

A crooked smile curved Kince's lips before he faced

forward. "I only asked Ahninveth Kyril along because I enjoy finding opportunities to judge him."

Kyril let out a soft, weary breath, but he held his silence.

"You're a calloch, Uncle," she muttered.

Kince merely chuckled.

They made their way toward the towering, expansive structure of the palace, with the sharp angles of its black stone and metalwork construction presenting an aggressive exterior designed to intimidate enemies. The attendant led them through the main entrance and down halls with black stone walls and dark marble floors.

Instead of stopping at one of the meeting chambers, they turned down another hall and entered a large sitting room. It surprised her to see the soldier reporting in was not a Vanrian scout, but rather a dark-skinned Delaphinian woman with long hair split out into several braids and bound back out of her face. Her brown eyes widened a fraction when they walked in, awe and curiosity crossing her features as she stared at the two wave dancers.

Veyl's father stood. The members of his tehsheyn remained seated, the casual bond they shared making it acceptable somehow in this less formal setting. "Captain Annora, this is my daughter, Khesran Veyl, and our new Thaelian ahninveth, Kyril, along with their companions, Seyn and Ceris."

The two wave dancers stood at attention, taking seriously the acknowledgement given them.

Veyl recognized the name. "Annora? The one who acted as a messenger for you back when you ended the war?"

Her father smiled at the woman. "The very one."

Veyl executed a respectful bow. "It's an honor to meet you, Captain Annora."

Annora reciprocated the gesture. "You as well, Khesran Veyl. And you, Ahninveth Kyril." She smiled at the amphibious creatures and offered them each a nod. "And your two remarkable companions."

Ceris and Seyn both cracked broad canine grins, their tails swishing back and forth a few times.

After Kyril returned the greeting, her father had two of his guards bring over some chairs set against one wall and bid them join the group. When everyone had settled, he turned his focus back to their guest.

"Our attention is yours, Captain," he said. "What news do you bring?"

"Thank you, Khemron Kasiel. I've been stationed in northeastern Sarket for several months, running a group of scouts to keep track of the situation there. The Sarketi people have grown angry of late. They've lost faith in King Regent Thrasser now that Crown Prince Jaysen has reemerged and is spreading word of the king's underhanded attempt to remove him so he might keep the throne. Many are calling for single combat in the Sarketi tradition. More recent rumors that the crown prince is working with mind-crafters from another country have sparked unease as well. Although a fair number seem to assume they are Vanrian and are less concerned, since Vanris hasn't abused Sarket's oath of fealty in the years since the war ended. More importantly, we thought you should know the king regent has reached out to Delaphine and Fallend in search of allies to support his claim to the throne against the crown prince."

"But not Vanris." Darro dropped the comment as more of an observation than a question.

"He is panicking." Arhk's brow furrowed. The harsh burns on his face still made it uncomfortable to look at him, though they had healed considerably. "He assumes Vanris will stand with Jaysen, given that we have had close ties with the crown prince in the past. If he cannot find other allies, he knows he will have a difficult time keeping his position should Jaysen secure the support of the Thaelians, the Eydarith, and Vanris."

"Except Vanris isn't supporting him," Veyl remarked, hoping they hadn't made some decision otherwise without her knowledge.

"No," her mother confirmed. "And we are unlikely to after what he did in Thaelis, among other things, though we must keep it on our list of options for now."

Veyl's stomach turned at the thought that they might consider backing Jaysen after all he had done. If the council made that choice, how was she supposed to reconcile with it? Would they keep her out of negotiations with him? Would she want them to? Not knowing what he was up to might almost be worse than having to face him again. Yet, could she do so without suffering that nauseating swell of black hatred and fear that accompanied the memories of his unwelcome touch, his possessive kisses?

Seyn nosed her hand, pushing calm and reassurance to her. Out of the corner of her eye, Veyl caught Ceris bumping his muzzle up into Kyril's palm too. Was the Feral having a similar reaction to that possibility? The idea of working with Jaysen couldn't sit any better with him than it did with her, not after how Jaysen had tortured him and ordered his memories torn apart. The urge to take his hand was nearly too much to resist, but even if he might welcome it, she didn't dare do so here.

"Our current stance in Delaphine," Annora continued, "according to the most recent missive I received, is one of deference to existing allies while our leadership considers the situation. Jaysen is the rightful heir. As such, they are more inclined to support him, but they are aware of the significant conflict between Vanris and the Thaelians he returned with, so they look to you to take the lead. We have not yet gotten word from Fallend that I know of, but a messenger was sent from Dekingham to advise them of Delaphine's position on the matter."

Her father nodded. "We sent a messenger of our own to Delaphine several days ago. Jaysen and the Thaelian council were behind an attack on the combined Delaphinian and Vanrian fleet we sent to Thaelis. He also took Khesran Veyl prisoner and attempted to coerce her into marriage to force an alliance. She and those taken with her were fortunate enough to escape." Annora's eyes widened as he spoke, and her jaw visibly tightened. It was possible she knew people in that fleet, or perhaps it simply appalled her that Jaysen would commit such crimes. Either way, the attack on the fleet was an attack against both their countries. "The crown prince would have to provide an extremely compelling argument to gain our support now, but we have not yet decided to grant it to the king regent, as his recent actions suggest intentions to turn against Vanris."

"It sounds as if you don't find either option appealing, Majesties." She bowed her head in a gesture that would encourage an appearance of deference, though Veyl caught the edge of burning curiosity in her tone. This was information the Delaphinian king and queen would want to know. "If I may ask, what other possibilities are you exploring?"

Arhk and her mother regarded the young woman with the same careful reservation. Her father considered Annora as well, but with a fondness that spoke positively of the brief time she had served under him at the end of the war.

"We could wait to see who emerges victorious and approach them while they are still recovering from that conflict and vulnerable, or..." he paused, an invitation in the glint in his eyes.

"Or you could launch an attack while they are fighting each other and install someone else on the throne,"

Annora speculated.

Arhk gave his son a look that somehow rode the line between fondness and mild reprimand. He had told Veyl more than once that he thought her father was too trusting. "These are matters we have yet to finish discussing with the full council." He stood. "I will have one of our guards show you to where you can rest and refresh yourself while we deliberate, Captain."

Annora bowed deeply to the khemron and khevarin of Vanris, then allowed Arhk's appointed escort to usher her from the room. When she was gone, Veyl's mother's attention shifted to her, and the skin tightened on the back of her neck before that silver-eyed gaze.

"We would like to revisit the subject of Wavelord Kronach. You spent a little time around him, Veyl."

"You don't mean... Not as..." She paused, gathering her thoughts, the wavelord leaning in uncomfortably close in her memories, his lips brushing against her ear, his fingertips biting into her jaw. Those moments were nothing compared to the torments Jaysen had seared in her mind, but the man did not respect physical boundaries, and his harsh manners made it hard for her to trust him. She shook her head. "No. Kronach is not someone I would consider putting on the throne. He may have aided me, but I believe it was more for his own amusement than out of any sense of kindness or justice."

"I think he would consider taking the throne if offered it," Kyril added, "but he would want more than that. You would need to offer him something he considered of great value to make it worth his time and effort." His gaze shifted to her, any accompanying emotions well hidden beneath the coolness in his silver-blue eyes. "Something like the hand of a wave-touched khesran."

Anger flared in her so powerfully that the absence of

any crackling energy in her chest made her more certain than ever that Arhk was right. Her Frightener ability truly was gone. Why would Kyril suggest such a thing? Not ten minutes ago, in the training area, she thought the connection between them might be rekindling. Apparently, that had been the mere fancy of a desperate imagination.

She wasn't sure who in the room objected most vehemently to his statement, but there was comfort in her parents being foremost among them.

"That is out of the question," her mother snapped. "The only suggestion more offensive would be to offer her hand to one of the current contenders for the throne. Such an arrangement is not up for consideration." She stood, casting a frosty glance in Kyril's direction. "We should move this conversation before the full council."

Veyl rose, refusing to look at Kyril, and hurried out with her parents, Seyn staying close beside her.

The council was to convene in mid-afternoon. As soon as they were away from the sitting room and a time had been determined, Veyl excused herself, dodging her parents' attempts to engage her by insisting that she had tasks to attend to before the meeting. The flat looks they gave her as she hurried away told her they could tell she was deliberately avoiding them. Still, they let her go, though she had little doubt they would try to bring the matter up again later. She took an indirect route back to her private chambers, not in much of a mood to deal with anyone other than Seyn, who padded dutifully along beside her.

It was hard not to feel cursed. Her original tehnaak, Jethan and Keyla's first child, died at a young age. Her second tehnaak bond with Jaysen was severed twice before he betrayed her trust, colluded with the Thaelian council to abduct her and set the Ukhen'kya against their fleet, and tried to force her into wedlock. The man she loved had all positive memories of their relationship stripped from him, another miserable development she could thank Jaysen for. That Kyril would put voice to the idea of offering her to Kronach told her their connection was now as broken as her Frightener ability.

Her throat tightened. She swallowed against threatening tears, struggling to hide them from anyone who might look her way at least long enough to reach her rooms where she could indulge her heartache alone.

Veyl rounded the corner, and her stomach dropped.

Kyril leaned against the wall by her door, Ceris sitting beside him. With her parents delaying her by trying to get her to talk to them, he had enough time to arrive there ahead of her. His gaze focused on her the moment she turned into the hallway. Doing her best to keep her strides steady, she gave him a scowl she hoped was discouraging and strode to her door.

He straightened as she grabbed the handle. "I take it you are not planning to rejoin the rest of your unit at practice?"

She gave him a withering look and yanked open the door. When she stepped through and started to shut it, he blocked it with one hand and followed her inside.

Veyl stalked farther into the room and turned on him. "No. I'm not certain I want to continue serving in a unit under your command." She yearned for the satisfying crackle of destructive energy to give her something to fight against apart from her own tumultuous emotions.

Ceris joined them, and Kyril shut the door behind the beast. "I've offended you?"

Desperate to hide the hurt, she let her rage soar above it, rising like a tidal wave in her chest. Both wave dancers sat watching her, heads cocked to one side, their ears perked with curiosity when she stormed up to him, glaring into his unfortunately striking eyes.

"How could you suggest the idea of marrying me off to that man? Maybe they destroyed what you and I had together, but do you honestly believe I deserve no better than that?"

Kyril's expression remained infuriatingly calm. "Wavelord Kronach was captivated by you. A fierce and resolute woman not of his people, yet favored by his god.

If his fascination with seeing what you would do given a chance at freedom had been a little less compelling, I suspect he would have tried to keep you for himself. You know as well as I do, he wouldn't hesitate to make such a demand of Vanris's leadership if they proposed putting him on the throne. The assistance he offered you was not inspired by any desire to court an alliance with your country. You are an enthralling new creature he would love a chance to play with."

"Exactly why such a notion coming from him wouldn't surprise me, but you could at least pretend to have more respect for me after everything we've been through together." Some of which he no longer remembered. Veyl turned and moved away from him, closing her eyes to search for calm in the darkness. "Please leave." She felt him walk up behind her, his presence bringing her love for him into painful focus even now.

"Are you finished, then?"

She said nothing.

"All right, then. Maybe you'll hear me out now." He took another step closer. "I brought up the possibility of Kronach demanding your hand because I wanted your parents to be aware of the potential cost of taking that path. I also wanted to see how they reacted, so I would know if I might have to protect you from your own family."

"You…" Veyl opened her eyes. "What?" She despised that her heart was now beating triple-time, a treacherous glimmer of hope rising in her again as she turned to face him.

"I would never let that man have you. Not even if it meant going up against all Vanris to stop it. You deserve much better." She started to lift one foot, intending to close the distance between them, when he added, "Better than him, and better than me."

She settled her weight back, sinking into a sea of

frustration and disappointment. "It appears I misread your intent in there," she murmured. "I apologize for my outburst. Recent events have unsettled me. I seem to expect the worst, even of people I would normally trust."

"Understandably." He considered her with that unreadable gaze that left her adrift for a few seconds. Then he nodded, as if coming to some decision. "Do you still want to leave my unit?"

She sighed, a yes lingering behind her lips, her gut telling her it was the wiser answer. "No."

A faint gleam sparked in his eyes. "You had best return to practice, then, Inren Veyl." He stepped to the side and gestured to the door.

"You must know how insufferable you are," she said, stalking past him.

Why did his soft chuckle have to create such a rush of giddy pleasure in her?

Kyril and Ceris fell in beside her and Seyn as they headed down the hall, the four of them drawing glances from palace attendants and visitors. The two unusual amphibious canines were spectacle enough. With them accompanying the khesran of Vanris and the Thaelian Feral who had abducted her and was now an ahninveth in the Vanrian army, it wasn't surprising people stared.

By the time they returned to the archery range, the others had turned practice into an archery contest, something Kyril's faint smirk told Veyl he had expected and perhaps even hoped for. Kitria was standing off to one side with a bemused expression, watching Iyvalin and Gannon subject Ahrin to good-natured taunts as he nocked an arrow and aimed, his draw strong and steady. Two braids worked along that side of his head and tucked behind his pointed ear kept his light brown hair from getting in the way. Sunlight drew out the faint hints of auburn in it as he stood there, focusing past the attempted distractions of his brother and Iyvalin.

The twins were both attractive young men, like their father, Darro. Iyvalin, with her pale gray eyes and silver hair, was a bright star next to them, her playful smile a pleasant contrast to Gannon's typical severity. It was still strange to see the three of them together without Lorek. A life wasted for nothing. Gannon's tehnaak, dead because of a chain of events that started with Kyril following the orders of the Thaelian council. Maybe it wasn't so hard to understand why his relationship with her caused him such conflict if the only memories he had left of them were of the awful cruelties he inflicted on her and her people in his efforts to restore the people of Thaelis.

And yet...

She dared a look at him as he watched Ahrin loose the arrow, his slight nod of approval, following the *thunk* of it hitting the target, telling her it had been a successful effort. Even had his fleet not captured them at Deepwater, tumultuous times would have come for all of them. Thrasser would not have been so quick to take advantage of the Thaelians' arrival to dispose of Jaysen if he hadn't already been plotting something. Vanris only learned of that before Sarket could take it further because Kyril risked coming to warn them at her behest. If not for that, they might not have known the Sarketi regent was up to something until it was too late. They would never find out now what might have happened if things had worked out differently, how many lives might have been lost if Thrasser had caught Vanris by surprise with his scheming. Although the path ahead of them still had the potential to lead to war with Sarket.

"Ahninveth." Ahrin spun and stepped to attention, the other two following his lead as they realized their unit leader had returned. "We were only–"

"Turning training into a game?" Kyril arched a

brow, his stern gaze sweeping over them. He glanced at her, gesturing for her to join them with a jerk of his head. Once she had done so, he asked, "That precise grouping on the target was the three of you?"

"Yes, Ahninveth." Gannon bit off his words, his relationship with their new leader understandably still strained.

"Impressive. You all have considerable experience working together, I presume?"

"We have," Iyvalin answered. "The five of us…" she faltered, her apologetic gaze flickering to Gannon, who looked away. "We all trained together growing up and used to run patrols and assist the guards as a group."

"That bond will be extremely useful if we see battle, though I expect you to work toward building something similar with the rest of the unit." His gaze shifted to Kitria, and a hint of pink rose in her cheeks.

"I was being an unbiased observer." She scuffed the ground with the toe of one boot.

"It's difficult being in a strange place where you don't know anyone, but I need you to be more assertive about making yourself part of the group here."

The color deepened in Kitria's cheeks, and Veyl got the sense that some anger joined her embarrassment at being called out. She opened her mouth to come to his sister's defense, but Ahrin was there ahead of her.

"After Kitria's first shot, we decided we would all have a far better chance of winning if she acted as judge." He winked at Kitria, and she quickly dropped her gaze, trying to hold back a pleased smile and failing spectacularly.

"I see." Kyril glanced between the two, his brows rising a fraction. "Retrieve those arrows. I want you all to take turns firing each of the different bows while the rest of us analyze your technique and offer feedback. Let's see what we can learn from each other."

That was how they spent the next few hours. Veyl leveraged her status to have food and drinks brought out from the palace kitchens, so she might prolong what eventually transformed back into a friendly competition.

Gannon finished a round, smirking at the well-placed grouping of arrows. On the ground, he was a little more consistent than his brother. He just didn't have the knack Ahrin did for firing from the back of a fast-moving mount.

"Well done, but your grip is too tight," Kyril commented. "Ease up and relax into it a little. You're trying to kill the target, not the bow."

"That was the best shot any of us made that round." Gannon thrust the shortbow at him. "How about you, Ahninveth? I'd like to see how you do against us."

Kitria sighed.

Ahrin leaned close to her as Gannon stepped back on the other side to watch. "My brother will never stop challenging him," he said in a low voice, and Iyvalin nodded to support the assertion.

"Because of what happened in Deepwater and to his tehnaak?" Kitria asked.

Veyl took a few steps closer to listen and instantly regretted it.

"Mostly, but also because of *who* he did in Thaelis."

"Ahrin!" Iyvalin gave him a startled look, and he shrugged.

Kitria's wide eyes met Veyl's. "I'm sorry, I swear I didn't tell—"

Veyl cut her off. "You're not responsible for any of this. You have no reason to apologize." She gave Ahrin a stern look. "Some things aren't proper conversational subjects."

He shrugged. "Who here didn't know?"

Veyl's cheeks warmed as she heard the *thunk* of an arrow striking the target, fired by the man who had done her, as Ahrin so elegantly phrased it. "That is not the point."

"Break-blasted calloch," Gannon grumbled under his breath as he accepted the bow back from Kyril.

A pang of disappointment ran through her at missing him take his shot. She would have appreciated a chance to observe his form, strength, and unwavering precision. "I apologize, Ahninveth. I got distracted. Could you do that again?" The knowing looks the others gave her brought a hot flush to her cheeks that she wished she could hide. "I simply wanted to see your technique," she added, wincing inwardly at the defensiveness in her tone.

Kitria coughed softly and looked away.

Ahrin clenched his teeth, at war with the laugh she could see trying to burst free.

Kyril stared at her for a long moment before reaching for the bow. Gannon handed it back and crossed his arms, glaring at the weapon, perhaps to avoid doing so to the man holding it.

The Feral faced the target, the slow, steady draw attesting to the strength in the muscles tightening through his arms and back. He released the arrow, and it struck a fraction to the left of center. Then he passed the bow to Gannon again and turned to face her. "Did you have any critiques that time, or do you perhaps need yet another demonstration?"

Her pulse quickened under his intense gaze, and she yearned for some insight into his thoughts. Did her interest annoy him or make him uncomfortable? Might there be a glimmer of connection suppressed behind that carefully neutral regard? "No. It was skillfully done."

She stepped forward, holding out a hand to Gannon. When he moved to pass her the bow, Kyril took it from him.

"I said no. You won't be shooting anything more

than a crossbow until a healer has approved it."

"You had an injured wrist, and you're doing it. Besides, I don't need you—"

He raised one hand in an abrupt gesture to cut her off, his gaze moving past her.

Mouth still partly open, she turned to see a male attendant approaching.

"Ahninveth Kyril. Khesran Veyl." The man offered each a partial bow. "Khevarin Velara bid me bring you word that the council is convening."

Kyril glanced around at the others. "Clean up here and then you're dismissed. We'll meet up again tomorrow."

Iyvalin touched Veyl's arm. "We're going to the Twisted Vine later. If you get away in time, you're welcome to join us."

"I'll try."

Ahrin turned to Kitria. "You're coming too, I hope."

Kitria's gaze flickered to Kyril, and he gave his approval with an almost imperceptible nod.

She smiled at Ahrin. "I'd love to."

They parted ways with the others then. Veyl's status as khesran and Kyril's as a representative of Thaelis earned them both a place at the table for this session. Seyn and Ceris trotted over from where they had been reclining in the shade of the stable entrance. The dry heat of the desert inspired the amphibious creatures to spend a considerable amount of their time outdoors seeking cooler spots.

She placed a hand briefly on Seyn's head when she trotted up beside her, waiting until they were out of earshot to ask, "How is Kitria handling all of this? I know neither of you expected to end up here."

"She's getting more comfortable around your friends. I'm sure that helps. But she's not happy. She wants to go home and see what damage the Unclean did when they attacked the night we were all taken.

Dhomvalen Arhk says the fleet and the Thaelian soldiers worked together to defeat them, but not without cost."

With much of the Delaphinian fleet that had traveled to Thaelis damaged in that attack, most of the ships and their crews had stayed behind to repair the vessels and help protect Thaelis. Arhk informed them that the focus of the assault had been on the Vanrian fleet, and few of the Unclean got past them into the town. Still, reassurance given by people you barely knew could only carry so much weight, especially considering everything the Thaelians had lost to the Ukhen'kya in the past.

"I imagine you feel the same."

He glanced over at her. "I do."

Her ears caught the lack of conviction in his tone. "But?"

"I have personal reasons for wanting to return home and see to my people, but I now have some equally compelling ones for wanting to stay here and aid Vanris in this complicated conflict with Sarket's leadership."

They followed the attendant into the palace, pausing their conversation as they walked through the door. Veyl glanced over at him, wishing he would give up that guarded neutrality he wore like armor now.

"Because of what Jaysen did to you and your sister?"

"Because of what he and the Thaelian council did to all of us. Besides, I suspect Sarket would not remain a benevolent ally to Thaelis once they succeeded in their plans for Pandrea. The hatred they harbor for mind-crafters won't vanish if they defeat the ones here."

Between them, Ceris nosed her hand, and she absently moved to pet his head, not realizing until their fingers brushed that Kyril was already doing so. She abruptly pulled away, averting her gaze.

"I'm sorry."

He said nothing.

When they entered the meeting room, Ahndhomen

Adnar was already jumping into the discussion. "You routed Thrasser twice in the war, Khemron. Would he even accept our support if we offered it?"

Her father nodded in recognition to the two of them as they entered before responding. "He might. He has proven to be something of a coward in the past. I can't imagine he is eager to face Jaysen in single combat, but that is apt to be what the people of Sarket want. It is their way."

Veyl and Kyril sat in the adjacent spots left open for them with extra space provided for the wave dancers. Her father's cliff cat, Irith, was at his side, and Adnar's tethdrak lay on the floor behind him. The reptilian beasts weren't particularly fond of anyone aside from their bonded companions, so it was generally more comfortable for everyone not to have one sitting at the table.

"Perhaps we should offer," Adnar continued. "Jaysen is making use of the Thaelian council and their mind-crafters to help him take back his throne. To the Sarketi people, that will appear no different from allying with Vanris. It will weaken a position that was already compromised by the years the crown prince spent living here."

Allonda, a new Delaphinian representative, the darkness of her skin and her rounded ears making her stand out amongst her Vanrian allies, rested her elbows on the table, folding her hands in front of her. "But wouldn't Thrasser accepting your aid compromise his position for the same reason?"

"It would," Kince said with a faintly amused smirk. As much as Veyl adored him as one of her father's tehsheyn, he always looked to her like he was planning someone's demise and expected to enjoy it. "If we help Thrasser win, the political environment will be ideal for a new challenger for the throne to step forward. We merely need to figure out who we want that to be and try to nudge the odds discreetly in their favor."

Adnar sat back, his expression turning thoughtful. "What about the one whose men carried the prince's missive, Wavelord Kronach?" Behind him, his tethdrak lifted its head, the beast considering them as if it shared its bonded companion's curiosity.

Veyl's mother glanced at her. "There may be difficulties with that option. He remains a possibility, but we would prefer to find a better alternative."

"General Danovan?" someone suggested.

Her father gave an indignant snort. There was a complicated history there.

Her mother answered with a tight smile. "He is as much of a coward as the king regent."

"If you support Thrasser, you will be forced to go up against the mind-crafters assisting Prince Jaysen, will you not?" Allonda asked, leaning forward to look at the khevarin and khemron.

Jethan, seated next to her father, faced Kyril then. "Yes, but how many mind-crafters could they have here?"

Sitting next to him, Veyl could see the tension of anger in Kyril's jaw before he answered. "It depends on how successfully they lied to us. They told us we had no Frighteners in Thaelis, but one attacked Khesran Veyl the night we escaped Taro. I'm afraid no one other than the Thaelian council themselves can reliably provide that information."

A flash of remembered fear swept through Veyl, which she redirected into anger. "We won't have to worry about that Frightener, at least."

Her mother's expression tightened, distress rising in her eyes. "We are merely grateful you had the skill to survive that encounter. It could have ended much differently."

A skill she no longer had. If not for her now-broken

ability, the man could have easily disabled her with his power.

Her father took her mother's hand in a gesture of comfort, then turned his attention back to Kyril. "How many ships did they take from Thaelis?"

"According to Jaysen, they left with Ahnkreth Eavara's fleet. Most of the Thaelian fleets sail with five to seven vessels." His jaw muscles twitched again, barely contained rage trying to break free.

His relationship with Eavara had been fraught from what Veyl saw in Thaelis, but she was the tehnaak of the woman he had loved who died in the Devastation. Did this feel like a betrayal, or had their relationship always been hostile?

"I saw six ships when they took Gannon, Kitria, and me out to the fleet that night," she offered.

"Confronting Jaysen and his new allies carries significant risk." Arhk tapped his fingers on the table, his cool, unreadable gaze coming to rest on Veyl. "But unless we intend to offer him Khesran Veyl's hand, we may have to do so eventually. Having heard the accounts from Veyl and the other three taken to Taro, I do not believe he will ally with us unless we include that promise in the terms of the agreement."

Darro chuckled and winked at Veyl, though a hint of sympathy came through in his gaze. "If you two had a less exceptional daughter, this might be a lot easier."

Adnar's brow furrowed, a low growl coming from the reptilian beast behind him. "That doesn't sound like the same young prince who lived within these walls. Would he really be foolish enough to hinge everything on that?"

Veyl's voice trembled when she met his eyes and said, "He is *not* that young man anymore."

Suddenly, another presence moved into her. Like

Seyn, but different and familiar. With it came the confidence and comfort she had experienced a few times before, when she sat before the council as ambassador for the Thaelians. It was Kyril, with Ceris forming a temporary connection between them.

For the next two days, a rigorous training sched-
ule kept Veyl and Kyril busy between council
meetings. Merrin and Avris took over some of
the unit's instruction, allowing Kyril to spend
part of each day with Kasiel and Adnar in the
canyon habitats, working with tethdraks and
trying to build a connection with the kanodrak that had
shown interest in him. This morning, they were running through sparring sessions with Merrin and Avris.
On Nerith's orders, Veyl had to sit out the full contact
work for at least one more day, which meant she found
herself stuck doing solitary rehabilitation exercises when
she wasn't providing feedback from outside the ring.

When she had gone through her exercises, she found
a spot to observe from until boredom with evaluating
the performance of the others led to leaning on the railing staring at, or rather, through Iyvalin and Gannon
as they went over the same series of maneuvers for the
third or fourth time. They were practicing evasions and
blocks in a dance that both parties appeared to have perfected the steps to. Seyn stood abruptly from where she
had been curled at Veyl's feet, giving her a few seconds
of warning before Jhanik joined her at the edge of the
ring. His tethdrak stood on his far side, the big reptilian beast eyeing the wave dancer with a mix of curiosity
and suspicion.

"You look distracted, Khesran."

She glanced at him, noting the dark lines of his ke'hanoath along the freshly shaved side of his head. He always kept his chin slightly raised in a manner that hinted at arrogance. Not an inappropriate first impression. That he and her father had ever overcome their initial differences enough to work together all these years baffled her sometimes.

"I don't like being relegated to observing."

"Given who your parents are, it would surprise me if you did." His amused smirk tempted her to ask about whatever story of their past played through his mind when he said that, but he continued before she could. "I was heading down to the kanodrak habitat to visit Arkos and speak with your father. Care to join me?"

She gave him a shrewd look. "Did you get lost? This isn't exactly on the way there."

He cracked a grin. "I was talking to Nerith before I came here. She said you were growing frustrated with your current restrictions and thought you might need a break from watching the others practice."

"She's getting increasingly clever in her attempts to keep me from violating my healer's orders." Veyl reflected his grin, a glimmer of better humor sparkling to life with the prospect of visiting the kanodraks. It had nothing to do with who else might be down there. At least she tried to tell herself it didn't. "You know, you're not all bad, no matter what my father says."

He drew back, assuming a mock look of offense. "Wait, what does he say?"

Veyl laughed. "Nothing you haven't already heard straight from him, I'm sure."

She waved to Avris, who was watching from the other side of the ring. When she had the woman's attention, she pointed to Jhanik, then toward the beast canyons. Avris nodded, following the gesture up with a wink and a suggestive grin, her light green eyes sparkling with amusement. The expression gave Veyl a moment's pause. Avris couldn't possibly think there was anything going on between her and Jhanik, could she? He was a little older than her father. But then, did that mean the woman suspected her entanglement with Kyril?

Not that it mattered now. That attraction was something she needed to let go of. Her parents would never approve of them being together, even if she could figure out how to rekindle what they'd had. Still, as foolish as it was to cling to that hope, she couldn't convince her heart to give up on them. Not yet. It felt like there was still a connection there, buried beneath the trauma caused by Jaysen's cruel abuse of the Thaelian Feral. The way he had been linking to her through Ceris during council meetings did nothing to discourage the notion.

She turned away with Jhanik, his tethdrak extending its neck out to try discreetly sniffing at the wave dancer as they started walking. When Seyn twisted to sniff at the reptilian beast in return, it jumped back and retreated to Jhanik's other side.

"They're intriguing creatures."

Veyl glanced up to see him watching the wave dancer as they strode along. "They are." She brushed the backs of her fingers along the side of Seyn's face, and the wave dancer pressed into her touch.

"That she can bond to you even though you aren't a Feral... It's remarkable. And she adamantly refuses to let me in. They may be much smaller than a kanodrak, but they seem to be nearly equal in their intelligence and mental fortitude."

A surge of pride moved through Veyl as she lengthened her stride to keep up with the tall Feral. She wasn't entirely sure if the feeling was her own or Seyn's. Perhaps both. The wave dancer had an uncanny understanding of human speech. Another trait that made them much like the kanodraks. "They can create temporary connections between people as well."

He glanced at the wave dancer again with greater interest. "They really are more like a kanodrak than most other beasts." His gaze moved up to Veyl, perhaps catching the slight hitch in her step. "This pace isn't hurting you, is it?"

"A little, but not in a bad way. It's better to move it. The muscles are stiff and the scar tissue pulls, but I need to work through the pain if I want it to improve."

"You do. I'm glad you recognize that." He faced ahead again, not slowing his stride. "You earned that scar. You'll defeat it as surely as you did the person who gave it to you."

His respectful tone surprised and intrigued her. "Do you think I'm a fool for wanting to be involved in the fighting?"

Jhanik chuckled. "You're asking the wrong person that question."

She pressed her lips together for a moment, almost letting it go, but no, she refused to let him brush it off that easily. "I am asking exactly who I meant to ask."

He glanced over at her, the look in his eyes telling her he approved of her assertiveness. "No, I don't. This is your fight as much as it is anyone else's. More in some ways. Given everything you've been through this year, I can't believe you have any illusions about the risks. Besides, I've seen you in action. You can hold your own."

"Thank you, Jhanik." She focused ahead, his response giving a little more determination to her strides.

"However..." He waited for her to look at him again before he continued. "Believing they had lost you nearly destroyed your parents. They may have hidden it reasonably well when you returned, but your disappearance shattered them. Keep that in mind when you decide what risks you are willing to take. Their stability affects that of this entire country."

"I…" Shattered? Certainly, they were heartbroken by the loss of their daughter, but how bad had it really been? Jhanik wasn't one to exaggerate, nor was he the type to soften it for her sake. It wasn't his way. He was blunt and a bit on the clueless side when it came to navigating other people's emotions. For now, maybe it was better not to dig in deeper. "I will."

They entered the massive building with its open rear wall that overlooked the tethdrak canyon. On the way down on the lift platform, Seyn leaned out over the railing, her long black tail with its peculiar thick hair drifting side to side in a gentle wag as she watched a few of the beasts near the front of the enclosure. When they reached the bottom, she bounded straight to the door of the tunnel that led through to the kanodrak canyon, clearly aware of their intended destination.

A muted presence, similar to Seyn's, touched Veyl.

Ceris? It had to be. Would he alert Kyril to their arrival?

They passed through the tunnel between the canyons, stopping to peer out the window in the far door and check that it was safe to enter. Her father and Adnar were outside the bars that separated the front of the habitat, watching Kyril on the inside where he stood facing one of the vaguely feline kanodraks. Niskenya, her father's kanodrak, lay to one side, resting in the shade cast by the canyon wall. The twitching of her tail was the only sign that the current situation annoyed her, probably because it prevented her from spending that time with her bonded companion. Farther back, Veyl could see the big male, Arkos, lurking, undoubtedly aware that Jhanik was approaching.

The beast Kyril stood facing was the same male that had shown interest in him before, the one with darker shading on his spine and a hint of bronze in his milky white eyes.

"That's one of Arkos and Niskenya's offspring, isn't it?"

Jhanik grunted an affirmation, his intense gaze riveted on the scene outside the door. Veyl moved closer to watch.

Was Kyril truly as composed as he appeared, standing straight and sure before the massive predator? He looked strong and confident, but the beast would know if he held fear in his heart.

Kyril held up a hand in offering. The kanodrak didn't move, his sleek, silver-gray scaled hide picking up a muted glow in the morning sun. The beast stood perfectly still, looking him in the eyes with the intensity of a hunting wildcat. Then, in a flash of motion, he snapped his jaws over the Feral's forearm as he had done with his hand on their first encounter, the elongated canines caging it in. Since the almost imperceptible tightening of Kyril's shoulders was his sole reaction, she had to assume the beast hadn't used enough force to do any damage, though his snarling made it sound as if he wanted to. For his part, Kyril made no move to free himself, keeping his gaze and stance steady.

Outside the bars, Ceris shifted his feet, his hind end rising slightly from the ground as if he wanted to intervene. After a few nerve-wracking seconds, during which Veyl forgot to breathe, the kanodrak released Kyril's arm and lowered his head, presenting the bone-armor plating on top to him. The Thaelian Feral allowed himself a faint smile as he calmly placed his palm against that armor, accepting the offered physical connection. His shoulders rose and fell with a deep breath.

"He's got guts, I'll give him that," Jhanik said, slowly opening the door.

"Yes, and fortunately, they are still in his body."

Chuckling, Jhanik put a hand on her shoulder and steered her out ahead of him. "Come along, little khesran."

Kasiel and Adnar, both grinning at the outcome of the encounter in the enclosure, glanced their way when they walked out. Kyril was moving forward now, stepping calmly up alongside the beast with awe and admiration in his gaze. The kanodrak growled, though he made no effort to move away or more aggressively correct the Feral.

"That looks promising," Jhanik commented.

"It does," Adnar replied.

Her father nodded his agreement and cast a brief glance at Niskenya, a wistful smile curving his lips.

Ceris trotted over to Veyl, exchanging a brief sniff with Seyn before looking up at her expectantly. The tall wave dancer stepped from one paw to the other and glanced out at his companion, then back up at her.

Veyl shrugged. "I'm not a Feral. I have no power over the beast."

Ceris snorted his disappointment at her and trotted back to the bars.

Her father grinned. "I believe he expected more help than that."

"If he thinks I have any influence over his companion, he is mistaken."

"Hm." Her father's expression told her she had not convinced him of that.

She glanced away to hide the warmth that rose in her cheeks, only to see Kyril standing next to the kanodrak, one hand on the beast's shoulder, both man and beast looking at her. The kanodrak cocked his head to one side, considering her for a second, then he snorted and loped off into the canyon. Kyril's gaze followed him for a moment before he strode to the gate, Ceris's tail wagging now as he waited there for him.

"Did you need something, Veyl?" her father asked.

"She looked to me like what she needed was a break from monotony, so I brought her along," Jhanik offered.

"I'm still on light duty for my injury." The complaint came out sounding more petulant than she had intended, though it earned her an amused grin from Jhanik.

"Good. Pushing yourself to do too much before you're ready is a mistake," Kyril said as he joined them. "I'd prefer you not learn to regret your choices."

A flash of irritation swept through her, and she narrowed her eyes at him. "I know plenty about regret, Ahninveth. Though perhaps not as much as you."

Jhanik brought his hand up to cover his mouth and glanced away, clearing his throat in an obvious attempt to hide a laugh.

"Ah." Adnar looked at each of them, then he focused on Kyril. "Well done with the kanodrak, Ahninveth. I suspect you will find it easier to progress from this point forward. Now, I have an injured tethdrak to check on," he said, excusing himself from the suddenly awkward conversation and heading to the tunnel.

While her father considered her and Kyril, Niskenya trotted up to the bars and huffed, not wanting to wait any longer to visit with her bonded companion. Arkos also came forward, hanging back a little farther when Niskenya growled a warning at him. The kanodrak Kyril was attempting to bond with was the offspring of the two, but, outside of mating, the massive predators were solitary creatures, and she was the dominant matriarch in the enclosure. Arkos would yield to her.

"Perhaps it was a mistake to assign you to serve in Ahninveth Kyril's unit," her father said once the door had closed behind Adnar. "There may be too much tumultuous history between you."

"No." Veyl lowered her gaze, doing her best to appear contrite. "I am merely frustrated with my injury. I didn't mean to lash out at my ahninveth."

Her father nodded and walked over to take her hand, giving it a soft squeeze. "I understand that frustration all too well, but you can't let it drive you to say or do things you will regret." He offered her a gentle smile, a hint of wistfulness rising in his eyes. "You should count yourself fortunate that you don't have Nerith trying to massage out the scar for you."

"Oh yes, that reminds me." Jhanik's grin was much too cheerful. "She told me to tell you she would be by later to check on you and make sure you've been caring for it properly."

Veyl scowled at him. "You're a calloch."

He bowed his head a fraction. "I try, Khesran."

Her father breathed a soft laugh and turned his attention to Kyril, releasing her hand. "We're done down here for today, if you want to head back to your unit. We shall see if you can make more progress with him tomorrow."

Kyril offered her father a respectful nod. "Thank you, Khemron."

Veyl took a quick step forward, inserting herself into his line of sight as he turned to leave. "Ahninveth, if I might have a word."

Kyril gave her a long, unreadable look before gesturing to the tunnel. "You are welcome to walk with me to the training grounds."

Her father opened his mouth, and from the slight narrowing of his eyes, she feared he would object, but Jhanik intervened.

"I had something I needed to discuss with you, Khemron."

After a second, her father tore his gaze away, facing Jhanik and setting her free. Veyl immediately turned with Kyril and led the way to the tunnel, hoping to get through the door before he could change his mind and call her back. Once inside, that cool, enclosed space gave them a little privacy, and the wave dancers, as if aware of her discomfort, sent reassurance along to bolster her courage.

Drawing in a deep breath and forcing a calm exhale, she said, "I am sorry for my temper. This has been hard for both of us, but I can't imagine how violated you must feel, having had your memories torn from you that way."

His posture stiffened a fraction, but his stride didn't falter or slow, bringing them closer to the other end of the tunnel much too quickly. "Yes. I imagine it's about as scarring as being taken forcefully from your home or having your tehnaak bond severed against your will and replaced with something designed to control you."

"By the Break!" She stopped. "It was me those things were done to." She waited until he stopped and turned to look at her. "Regret it. Feel guilty if you must, but don't decide for me how I should feel about my own experiences or you, now. That's no better than putting a zenyal bond on me to begin with."

He tensed, and Ceris grew still, gazing up at him. This time, he didn't reach out to the beast, at least not physically. "You're right. I'm nearly blind with rage when I think about what Jaysen had them do to me. I understand I have every reason to feel that way when it comes to my people and their involvement in this, but him?"

He took a step closer. More than close enough for her to see the storm of dark torment in his eyes. "When I think of the nightmare I subjected you all to, I realize Jaysen has as much cause to loathe me as I do him. I despise him for what he did to me, but even more so for what he put you through. And if I hate him for what he did to you, how can I not hate myself for the same reason?"

What he said had a ring of truth to it that brought a bleak wave of despair surging up within her, but she refused to let it win. She couldn't. "What you did to us was awful. I won't spare you that, but don't make it worse now by trying to tell me what I should think and feel. I know your memories don't support my affection for you anymore, but mine do." When she started to take a step forward, he immediately shifted back. She clenched her teeth for a moment, fighting a flash of frustrated anger. Seyn's soothing presence helped her quell it and opened the door for something else. An opportunity, perhaps. She softened her tone and met his eyes. "Dine with me this evening. Just the two of us. Let me tell you what I remember. Trust me to fill in some of those stolen moments and help it all make more sense." She could only hope it really did make sense.

He met her gaze for several seconds, the possibility of someone walking in on them creating an itch between her shoulder blades. Finally, he nodded. "All right."

Tension released in her chest. This could be her chance to help them both. "Thank you. I'll send for you later."

·

When evening came around, Veyl requested an attendant she trusted to bring a meal for the two of them to the sitting area in her rooms. Once that was ready, she sent the man to invite Kyril to join her and drew the curtains so her father would at least have to work a little harder to check in on her. Then she put out a few of the sconces to set a more intimate mood. Seyn lay by the couch and watched her as she paced before the fireplace until the door opened a short time later. Her pulse quickened with anticipation, but it was only the attendant who stepped through, offering her a deep bow. His apologetic look caused a sinking in her chest.

"I am sorry, Khesran Veyl, Ahninveth Kyril was not in his rooms. I learned from one of the other attendants that he had already answered a different summons to dinner."

"From whom?"

The attendant shook his head. "I'm afraid she didn't know."

Crestfallen, Veyl stared at the wasted selection of food.

"Is there someone else you might call on to share this meal, Khesran? It's too pleasant an arrangement to let go to waste." He took a step closer, earnest sympathy in his eyes. "I believe the ahninveth's sister is on her own this evening."

Kitria?

At least the meal wouldn't go unappreciated that way. She nodded. "Yes. Please see if Kitria is free to join me. Thank you."

After a brief wait, Kitria arrived and sat down to dine with her. She also didn't know who had summoned her brother, but Veyl was glad to at least have the distraction of company. That there was a distinct family resemblance between the young Thaelian woman and Kyril made it hard not to dwell on thoughts of him and wonder who had taken up his evening. Kitria kept her black hair trimmed a little shorter than her brother's. Tonight, she had it braided on both sides with the back hanging loose. Her eyes were pure silver without the added blue his had, but she looked every bit like a more delicate, feminine version of her brother. Oddly, it worked nearly as well on her as it did on him.

They made their way through most of the meal with awkward silences between brief snips of conversation. They hadn't been alone together much since the ordeal in Taro, and the emotional scars from that experience were still raw. The things Kitria had seen Veyl do, both to appease Jaysen and to free them from him, hung between them with an unspoken unease. Not only that, but the other woman had gotten dragged into this and was now trapped in Vanris simply because she had tried to help Veyl back when she was stuck in Thaelis. Perhaps it was time to return the favor.

"I think Ahrin is rather taken with you," Veyl ventured when they both appeared about finished with their meals. The sudden burst of color in Kitria's cheeks told her everything she needed to know about that budding relationship. "He and the others should be at the Twisted Vine around now. Would you like to join them?"

"Not after you said that. I'd be too embarrassed."

Veyl grinned. "What? You don't like him?"

"It's not that. I… Wait, I didn't mean to imply that I do like him. Not that I don't." She gave a soft cry of frustration. "Look what you did. Now I can't think straight."

Veyl laughed and stood. "Come along, we're going."

Kitria got up, smoothing down her hair with her hands. "Do I look all right?"

"Trying to impress someone?" Veyl arched a brow at her.

Kitria lightly smacked her arm. "You're terrible. Let's just go before I lose my nerve."

Veyl stepped closer and took a moment to adjust the fall of Kitria's braids over her shoulders, then she nodded her approval. She caught a hint of gratitude shining through in the young woman's tentative smile before she turned and led them from the room.

The Twisted Vine was busy enough that a few groups had spilled out into the street. They stood before a door framed by vertical black stone slabs that had the Vanrian symbols for the establishment's name etched into them. As they made their way inside, Veyl's rank as khesran and her reputation for working with the guards and soldiers earned them easy passage, with several people offering greetings as they moved to let them by, though Kitria, with her black hair, got many lingering looks, some of which were not especially friendly.

None of them knew Veyl had been a mind-crafter for a brief time. Because of the lethality of her Frightener ability and the fact she had become an icon for anti-mind-crafter factions in Vanris, her family opted to keep that information quiet until they figured out how best to handle it. Now it didn't matter. She was the only person she had ever heard of who could say they had *been* a mind-crafter while they still lived.

The observation brought a strange dissociation with it, separating her from the people surrounding her, as if she were a figment of a dream and they were all real. Voices moved around her—music and laughter—as meaningless to her ears as if they spoke an unfamiliar language. Sweat prickled on the back of her neck. The room rocked like a ship at sea.

"Veyl."

She startled at the hand that came to rest on her shoulder, connected to a stranger. They were all strangers.

A calming wave washed over her, and Seyn's cool, moist nose touched her palm. The feeling of disconnection vanished. Sounds and images became clear again. The hand on her shoulder was Gannon's, his brows pinched with concern. Kitria had already joined Iyvalin and Ahrin at their table, the three beckoning them over.

Gannon leaned close. "Are you all right?"

Veyl drew a breath, feeling as though she hadn't done so in a long time. "Yes." Her breathless voice didn't convince her any more than it did him, given the way the lines in his forehead deepened.

"I can take you back to the palace. They'll understand."

"No." She shook her head, sinking her fingers into Seyn's coat. "I'm fine now."

He nodded, his expression still troubled as he turned to walk to the table, his fingertips resting on her elbow as if he worried she might need him to stabilize her. Perhaps she did.

Iyvalin was putting in an order with a serving woman as they sat. Gannon settled beside Veyl, making it clear he intended to continue watching over her, but he didn't press her about her peculiar behavior. He gave her that much consideration, and she appreciated it more than she could hope to convey with mere words.

"I see you convinced the khesran to come visit with us commoners," Ahrin said to Kitria, before giving Veyl a teasing wink.

"Oh, no." Kitria shook her head. "This was all her idea. I still haven't entirely gotten my bearings with how I ended up in this country, let alone this tavern."

They all looked at Veyl as if that had somehow been her doing. Did they believe she had any control at all over Jaysen's actions? If she had, things would have worked out far differently, and he wouldn't haunt her nightmares still.

Kitria's cheeks colored, and she lowered her gaze. "Sorry. I don't mean to be negative. I'm grateful for the chance to get to know all of you, and I appreciate how welcoming you've been. I just worry about what might be happening back home."

The server placed a tray of mugs on the table, and Iyvalin took one, setting it in front of Kitria. "Well, you're here now, and you're part of this unit. Let's make the most of it."

"If you like, we could press Arhk tomorrow for more information about how things were when he left Thaelis," Veyl suggested.

Kitria nodded. "I would appreciate that." She took a mug and passed it to Veyl. "My brother appears to be settling right in. I suspect your father knew exactly what he was doing when he appealed to him with the possibility of working with a kanodrak."

"I'm not certain Kyril is all that pleased with how things ended up, but he appears to be making the best of it." Veyl took a long drink, savoring the robust alcohol with its smooth, balancing sweetness from the evalis fruit.

"Relax." Gannon's dismissive tone lacked the delicacy the subject probably required, but he had always struggled in that area. "You have several ships' worth of Vanrian and Delaphinian soldiers in Thaelis right now who can help with recovery efforts and dealing with any further aggression from the Unclean."

"I understand that." Kitria gripped her cup before her like a shield of some kind. "But you're forgetting that everyone in Thaelis grew up being taught to see your people as oppressive enemies to be avoided and kept out."

Gannon snorted. "Maybe kidnapping us wasn't the best way to accomplish that."

"Gannon," Ahrin snapped, giving his brother a kick under the table.

"Thank you, Ahrin, but he's right." Kitria gazed into her cup, rotating it in her hands now. "What the council had our fleets do to you was foolish and cruel. That makes it worse in a way. Ultimately, our greatest enemy turned out to be our own leadership."

Iyvalin reached across the table and touched her hand. "But we can help you build back something better now."

Kitria managed a tremulous smile. "I hope so."

"How is your brother dealing with the loss of his memories?" Ahrin cast an anxious glance at Veyl after he asked. "Never mind. That might not be a suitable subject right now."

Kitria shrugged. "He refuses to talk about it much."

Veyl peered around the room, not wanting to think of Kyril. The tavern had more Delaphinian soldiers in it than normal. With their country collaborating on the situation with Thaelis, they had sent a substantial number of troops to the city. An internal transition was also in progress. With the influx of Vanrian units from outside of Etrion in preparation for potential conflict with Sarket, many non-military families were retreating to the north, moving away from the border and providing more housing for soldiers coming in. Etrion was gradually reclaiming its wartime status as a military city.

"All right, let's find a different topic." Ahrin leaned his elbows on the table, his gaze locking on Kitria. "If you had to pick one thing you like about Vanris, what would it be?"

For her part, Kitria seemed to become trapped in his hazel eyes, looking into them as if the world outside them had disappeared from her view. "It's something in this room, actually." The slight upturn of her lips and the spark that lit her eyes turned the tables, and suddenly Ahrin was the trapped one, his intense gaze flickering briefly to her lips. Kitria grinned and lifted her mug. "Vanrian Black Mead, of course," she said before taking a swallow.

Iyvalin let out a laugh as Ahrin leaned back and crossed his arms, a good-natured grin slipping past his brief attempt to look wounded.

Veyl broke out in much-needed laughter as well, and Gannon along with her. "You have been upstaged by mead, my friend," she said, her words prolonging the laughter of the others.

Ahrin chuckled. "At least it wasn't just any mead. That might have been insulting." He winked at Kitria and raised his mug to her, getting the same in response.

At that moment, Veyl was certain the two would soon find themselves in a romantic entanglement. It might not last long, given the distance between their homelands, but they could have something for a time, and no one would try to stop them. She envied them that, but she could be happy for them too.

They stayed at the Twisted Vine for a couple of hours. When they left, the other three accompanied them most of the way to the palace, Ahrin and Kitria walking close enough that their fingers occasionally brushed. Neither pressed for more before they parted ways, and Veyl had to resist the temptation to encourage them. Time could be so fleeting, but this was their experience. They could take it at their own pace.

With a pleased little smile that she appeared unable to suppress, Kitria wandered inside to go to bed, while Veyl lingered outside the palace for a few minutes to give Seyn an opportunity to relieve herself. When she went inside to return to her private quarters, a door to one of the more intimate dining rooms opened just ahead of her. Not wanting to speak to anyone, she ducked back into the shadows of an alcove, watching with growing interest as Kyril emerged in the company of four others. The two men she thought she might have seen once or twice around the healer's building, though she had never spoken to either of them. The second pair, both women, she didn't recognize.

"Thank you, Ahninveth." One man inclined his head, and the other, his tehnaak, she suspected, mirrored the gesture. "We look forward to working with you."

"Likewise," Kyril answered, returning the gesture to a lesser degree before the two men departed.

"It has been a pleasure," a tall woman with long white-blond hair stated, her tone perhaps a bit too warm.

"It has," the other echoed. She was a little shorter, closer to Veyl in height, her hair light brown with a slight hint of red to it in the light from the hall sconces.

Kyril faced them. "I know you two are less familiar with the palace. Would you like me to escort you out?"

"Thank you, but you needn't trouble yourself," the shorter one said, earning a scowl from her companion. "A guard can show us out."

"Good evening to you, then. I will see you both in the morning." He nodded to a guard by the door, who stepped forward, ready to escort them.

"Indeed, you will." The taller woman had a dazzling smile that she eagerly put on display. "Goodnight, Ahninveth."

The two lingered as he struck off down the hall, waiting until he rounded a corner to speak. Then the taller one turned on her companion, ignoring the patient guard. "Why didn't you let him walk us out?"

"Why would I? We're perfectly capable of..." The shorter woman exhaled heavily, blowing some of her hair away from her face. "By the Break, Tassa, he's not even Vanrian."

"I wasn't planning to have his children, though I'd be open to practicing a few techniques for making them."

Veyl's anger burst into life. Maybe it was fortunate her ability was gone after all, because she suspected it would be extremely active right then. Seyn nudged her hand with that cool nose.

The shorter woman rolled her eyes. "Come on, let's get some sleep."

The guard nodded in response to a gesture from her, and the trio departed. Veyl drew a breath and struck out for her room. She now knew why Kyril had missed her summons. He had been called upon to dine with the four soldiers selected to round out their unit. Training was about to become more interesting, and not in a good way, at least not in her opinion.

"Come, Seyn, we should also get some sleep. I'm afraid we're going to need it."

●

She was dressing for practice, the conversation she had overheard between the two women about Kyril playing back in her head, when Nerith arrived in the morning. Without more than a succinct greeting, the healer walked over and pulled up Veyl's shirt to check the scar.

"Must you?"

"You were conveniently missing when I arrived last night, so we will do this now," Nerith answered.

"It's healing fine."

"I will decide that."

Veyl jumped, gasping at the sharp stab of pain when Nerith pressed firmly on the middle of the scar. The other woman continued to torture her for a few seconds with her skilled hands before straightening and letting her shirt down.

The healer narrowed her eyes. "You haven't been massaging it, have you?"

Veyl turned away, grabbing her belt. "Sometimes I forget."

Seyn, lying on the couch that Veyl had given up keeping her off, crossed her paws in front of her, the gesture somehow emphasizing her judgmental gaze. It appeared she was going to side with Nerith on this one.

"While you're unlikely to do any damage if you take a hit there at this point, it will be excruciatingly painful, perhaps enough so to create a dangerous distraction for you in actual combat. You have my permission to start full contact training, provided you promise to rub it aggressively at least twice a day. You need to break down the scar tissue if you want to regain flexibility and have less pain in that area."

Veyl faced her and nodded. "All right. I promise."

Nerith pulled a small container from one pocket. "Take this. If it's sore later, rub a little on it. It should help."

Veyl accepted the offering and set it on the table. "Thank you, Nerith. It may be hard to tell, but I appreciate your efforts."

Warmth infused the healer's smile. "I know. You may not be my child, Veyl, but I have always loved you like a daughter. Now go. I can see you're itching to train with your unit."

"Thank you."

Veyl leaned in and gave her a kiss on the cheek before hurrying from the sitting room with Seyn at her side.

Kitria was already in one of the practice rings, moving through a few blade techniques with Avris when Veyl arrived.

Merrin arched a brow at her, quickly catching on to the change in her bearing. "Nerith cleared you for full contact?"

"Yes, and I would love to warm up with someone."

Merrin nodded. "Hand to hand. Get in the ring." She ducked under the railing.

A chill of unease swept through her at the prospect of facing Merrin. The woman was one of the best fighters they had in several forms of melee combat, but Veyl had to assume she wouldn't kill her or, hopefully, even damage her too badly. Resisting the urge to remind the other woman that she was a little out of practice, she ducked into the ring, checked the arm guards on her training armor, and selected a starting stance.

They had become fully immersed in an elaborate dance of avoidance and attack when the twins and Iyvalin showed up. Gannon and Ahrin stopped at the edge of the ring to watch while Iyvalin went to take over sparring with Avris, giving Kitria a break. Kyril arrived a few minutes later with the four she had seen last night. Veyl tried not to notice him or react to the flare of irritation that arose in response to Tassa's presence. It didn't work. She missed a crucial block and took a blow to the shoulder that twisted her torso to one side. Pain lanced through the scar, but she sucked in a breath and did her best to hide it.

"Enough." Kyril stepped in and strode up to her. "Do you have a healer's leave to be doing this?"

"I do. Full contact, so long as I massage the scar out twice a day."

He answered with a curt nod and started turning away.

"I think you owe me a sparring session, Ahninveth."

Kyril stopped with his back partly to her. Then he lowered his head slightly, something unnervingly predatory in his movement when he turned to face her again. "Dual blades?"

She nodded.

Avris and Iyvalin halted their practice and came over

to watch as Merrin retrieved four training swords for them. With her nerves on fire now, Veyl moved into position, remembering the way he fought when they were on the ship. He had been taking it easy on her then, knowing he had the zenyal bond to stop her if necessary. Would he hold back this time?

The moment they both had practice weapons in hand, Veyl darted in, her speed and skill with the swords nearly earning her the first strike, but Kyril was agile and strong. He narrowly evaded the initial swing and struck away the second with enough force to almost knock the blade from her grasp. Veyl darted out of reach of his counter. They traded some more careful attacks, testing one another, then she committed herself fully to the next lunge. Kyril twisted, one of her strikes skimming past his ribs as he caught the other with a block.

The fire in her nerves cooled, the soothing calm of the wave dancer sharpening her focus. Something sparked in Kyril's silver-blue eyes as he faced her. They began a true dance of violence, moving fast enough and swinging with adequate force to cause actual damage, even with practice weapons. Yet somehow, they countered each other's moves perfectly, as if they knew in advance what the other would do. Every block precisely on target, every dodge putting them exactly enough out of the way to avoid a hit. They moved together like the ebb and flow of the tide. A smoothly choreographed display of skill built through the flawless partnership that formed between the four of them—Veyl, Kyril, and the two wave dancers—during the encounter.

Veyl was exquisitely alive. She felt connected to him in a new and exhilarating way, the light in his eyes telling her he felt it too. It was as if they had become one being. One awareness.

"Delicious."

Somehow that single spoken word cracked through

Veyl's focus, and her gaze flickered to Tassa as the other woman licked her lips like she was admiring a feast. The connection broke. She faltered, stepping too close, and a strike that she should have easily avoided caught her in the side. With the amount of force behind it, the pain was excruciating enough to steal her breath away, and she fell to one knee.

Kyril sank down with her, his hand taking hold of one shoulder to steady her. "That was careless of me. Are you all right?"

She struggled for a few seconds to draw a breath before she could speak. When she finally did so, tears of shame and pain stung her eyes. Such an extraordinary experience, and she had allowed the woman's crude, inappropriate commentary to destroy it. "Yes. I just need a moment."

"Seh'hali," he murmured, drawing her gaze up with the softly spoken name he hadn't used in some time. "You are a remarkable dual wielder. The best I have ever faced." He kept his voice low enough that the others wouldn't hear them. "You don't have to prove anything to me."

"You vex me," she muttered, the spears of pain gradually lessening with each breath she took.

He had the nerve to smile at that. "I know."

She became acutely aware of the presence of the two wave dancers watching them, the rest of their audience fading to the background when she met his eyes. With the next beat of her heart, the time she had almost kissed him on his ship swept to the front of her mind. It had been late in the evening, after drinking too much mead and observing the magnificent whales. She had hated him as intensely as she yearned for the comfort of a human embrace, and their inexplicable connection had drawn her to seek it in his arms. For an instant, the memory was so vivid she could feel his arms around her again. A desperate moment full of longing. Searching for connection and compassion in a world turned upside down.

Kyril drew back from her abruptly as if she had startled him, his brow furrowing, confusion in those silver-blue eyes as they searched hers. He gave himself a slight shake and took her hand, pulling her up with him, then faced the others. "That is the level of skill I would like to see from all of you, but first, there are new members to be introduced."

Kitria, Iyvalin, and the twins came to join Veyl, watching the newcomers with a wary curiosity when Kyril introduced them.

"We have two healers in our unit now. Dailan and his tehnaak, Feyd, who is a Dampener as well."

Veyl eyed the second man with more interest now. He and his tehnaak were older, in their early thirties perhaps. The amount of schooling Feyd must have gone through to train as a mind-crafter and a healer would have required exceptional dedication and determination. He had pale gray eyes and silver-white hair partly bound into several meticulous braids, revealing the symbols of his ke'hanoath running down in three narrow columns from his left temple to his lower jaw in the same color as his eyes. There was a certain shrewdness to his gaze as he considered them that made her feel as though they were being assessed, and probably quite accurately. It was uncommon for a fledgling unit to be given a Dampener or Frightener, considering their military value.

Feyd's tehnaak, Dailan, was his opposite, with a warm, friendly smile that lit his dark green eyes and an unruly mane of light red hair that almost entirely hid his pointed ears. His ke'hanoath started at the corner of his jaw and branched, with one line of symbols following his jawline and the other tracking down the side of his neck, as if continuing on him where his tehnaak's left off.

Kyril turned to the two women. "And to round out our unit, we now have Tassa, an Enkindler, and her teh-naak, Leath, who will be our Speaker."

That gave them four mind-crafters, including Kyril. An unusually high number for a single unit, especially a smaller Feral one, where they had fewer actual soldiers than others because the beasts filled in the extra ranks as fighters. Veyl saw her parents' hands in this. Protecting their daughter as best they could if she insisted on being involved.

"Now, I want all of you to pair up, preferably with someone you haven't worked with before, and demonstrate your best melee skills." When Veyl stepped forward, he caught her shoulder, pulling her back. "Except for you."

"But Nerith—"

"I think you've pushed it far enough for your first day back on full duty." He beckoned Gannon closer. "Would you go through some lighter work with her? Low contact. I believe I can trust you to make sure she doesn't get hurt again today."

"You can, Ahninveth."

Kyril nodded and walked away, going to adjust some of the other pairings more to his liking.

Veyl watched him. He was right. The scar still blazed with a fiery pain. That didn't mean she wanted to be set aside again, though at least he was letting her do more than solo exercises today.

She faced Gannon. "Shall we get this over with?"

Gannon chuckled, a faintly bitter edge to the sound. "Don't sound so despondent. It's a little disheartening knowing you'd rather have him hurt you than work on easier skills with me."

Her face grew warm. "It's not like that."

He shook his head and put an arm around her shoulders, steering her toward an unclaimed practice ring. "It is, and it's all right. I can handle being the man who looks out for you when the other one can't pull his head out of his ass."

"Don't be a calloch. He's been through a lot."

"Then you're perfect for each other." He gave her shoulders a squeeze. "And being a calloch is my entire identity. Don't take that away from me."

Veyl laughed, though even that caused more pain. "I wouldn't dream of it."

For the following three mornings, Kyril kept them busy practicing an array of varied skills to assess their strengths and weaknesses. They did archery again, since the new recruits had missed that, as well as melee combat, both unarmed and with a variety of bladed and blunt weapons. Veyl wasn't sure how much to read into the fact that he hadn't allowed her to spar with any of their recent additions, choosing instead to keep her working with her familiar companions, who he was confident would be mindful of her recovering injury. She wanted to believe his reasoning went beyond simply looking out for a member of his unit, but she was afraid to put too much hope in that.

When they weren't training with their ahninveth, he disappeared into the canyon habitats with Kasiel and Adnar, and sometimes her little brother, for long hours. The chance to invite him for another try at dinner remained elusive. By the end of the week, with a free day ahead of them, she was determined to catch him before practice ended. She stood with her companions, doing her best to keep her feelings hidden while they watched Kyril demonstrate a Thaelian sword form with Feyd, who it turned out was a capable fighter on top of his skills as a healer and Dampener. Tassa was less subtle, allowing her hungry gaze to follow him through every movement.

"Enough standing around," he called when he finished. "Pair up."

Veyl moved to intercept him as he ducked out of the ring. Tassa, with Leath close behind, approached from the opposite side, her focus locked on Kyril as well. Veyl quickened her pace, hoping to reach him first.

"Ahninveth Kyril," a familiar voice called, drawing away the attention of their mutual target.

Tavin walked out with Ellaris at his side, the young woman so slender and frail looking that it was no wonder her parents worried about her, particularly after her sister's unfortunate passing. Veyl had seen her fight though, and she wasn't quite the fragile creature she appeared to be.

Kyril walked over to meet them, and Veyl glanced around to see Kitria standing by the railing watching her with a faint smirk, though a hint of sympathy softened the expression. They both knew how hard he had been to get time with of late. A glance back at the twins and Iyvalin found them taking advantage of the moment to engage in some intense, quiet conversation. With Kyril otherwise occupied, there was little point in lingering.

Veyl started toward Kitria, making it about halfway to her before Tassa's voice behind her stopped her in her tracks.

"Hard to believe she's a khesran of Vanris. You know, Leath, she's the eldest child of the strongest mind-crafter family in the country, and yet she isn't one. She must be such a disappointment to her parents. I wonder if that's why they put her out here like a common soldier."

Veyl spun on the ball of her foot, ready to challenge the woman, but her words died on her lips. Kyril was coming up behind the two, apparently having already concluded whatever business Tavin had with him. The dark storm clouding his expression convinced her this was the right time to hold her tongue. Though a newly made ahninveth, he was far from new to the role of leadership, and he clearly didn't find the antics of his new recruits amusing.

When he spoke, his voice was loud enough to startle the two and ensure that the rest of them could hear him. "All of you will treat each other with respect if you want to remain part of my unit." The two spun to face him, Tassa falling back a few steps when his cutting gaze sank to her. "And you would do well to remember that Inren Veyl is your khesran when she is not actively working with this unit, and her memory is as sharp as her blade." He glanced at Veyl as he said those words, a flicker of distress flashing behind his eyes. "She's unlikely to forget the treatment she receives as your peer when she is acting as your leader. She is also one of the single most accomplished dual-wielders I have ever fought, and an excellent archer besides. If there is a problem between members of this unit, she will not be the one I transfer elsewhere. Are we clear?"

Both women bowed their heads, Leath standing with her tehnaak even though she wasn't the recipient of his ire, and spoke almost in unison. "Yes, Ahninveth."

Veyl wanted to be pleased by his defense of her, but the pain that haunted his gaze stole away any sense of satisfaction. If only she could make right Jaysen's wrongs. It wasn't her responsibility, but it was a task she would gladly take on if she only knew how.

That increasingly familiar sensation of soothing moved through her, and she glanced down, unsurprised to find Seyn gazing up at her. Of late, she got the feeling the wave dancer was trying to tell her something, but the limitations of their connection made for a wide gulf to cross.

"Khesran Veyl." She looked up at Kyril. "Your father has summoned the council and would like us there in an hour." He turned his attention to the rest of the group and walked to the nearest ring, where Kitria and Dailan were preparing to spar. "I imagine you can all get in a fair amount of practice in a little under an hour if you start now. I would like to see you break a sweat before we finish. Show me why I want you in my unit."

"Of course, she'll never be the one to go," Tassa grumbled. "Her father wouldn't let anyone toss aside his precious little girl."

Veyl faced the other woman, still riding the wave of Seyn's soothing. "Am I a disappointment to my parents or am I their precious little girl? It's so awfully confusing."

Leath's lips pressed together as she struggled to smother a smile. Schooling her expression, she faced Tassa. "As your tehnaak, can I lovingly suggest that you refrain from picking fights with another member of the unit just because you're jealous of how our ahninveth looks at them?"

Tassa's eyes narrowed more at Leath's words, her glare focused on Veyl, but she didn't voice any of the loud, angry thoughts lurking behind the expression.

Veyl offered the shorter woman a nod of gratitude. "Thank you, Inren Leath. I hope we can all move past our differences and start working together as a true unit. We will need each other if war breaks out with whoever gains control of Sarket."

Leath gave Tassa a warning look, apparently anticipating a negative response, but the woman ignored her. "Don't pretend that we'll ever leave Etrion. With a Thaelian as our ahninveth and a khesran of Vanris in the ranks, we all know this unit is a farce designed to make you look more connected to your people and put forth a front of peace with the Thaelians. It's all for show."

If she genuinely believed that, it could explain why she wasn't taking it seriously. She might even find it insulting being assigned to what she saw as a fake military unit. If that were the case, perhaps her behavior was understandable, to a point. Though her disrespect of Kyril, refusing to see him for more than a potential conquest, wasn't excusable.

Veyl settled her fingers on Seyn's head. "You could be right, but I wouldn't stake my life on that if I were you. And regardless, experience working with any Feral unit could be quite valuable going forward, so what harm is there in putting forth our best efforts?" She nodded to Leath and turned away to find Kyril watching her, a hint of approval in the slight curve of his lips that brought a flutter to her chest.

He gestured to the nearest ring with one hand and beckoned to the Dampener with the other. "Omren Feyd, I'd like you to work with Veyl this time."

The man strode over, nothing in his narrow features offering insight as to his feelings about the assignment or anything else, really. Veyl wasn't sure if the pairing implied that Kyril had decided she could handle more or that he felt he could trust the Dampener enough to let him work with her. Either way, the man's ability made her wary.

"Blades, Khesran?" Feyd asked.

"What is your preferred weapon, Healer… Dampener…" She trailed off. Perhaps she should have defaulted to omren, though his use of her proper title had inspired the attempted reciprocation.

"Feyd is sufficient. Axes."

A man of few words.

She nodded and accompanied him to claim wooden training axes with blunted edges from the rack. Not a weapon she often used, but it never hurt to work on less polished skills. They faced each other, and Veyl lunged in, not giving him time to prepare. Before she could make contact, her axe was gone. She faltered, looking down to discover she still held it in her hand. She simply couldn't feel it anymore. At least that explained why his axe remained at his side. He had used his Dampener ability instead of a physical reaction to counter her. A glance in Kyril's direction found the Feral smirking at her.

He nodded. "Carry on."

Veyl blew out a breath, trying to release her irritation along with it. This would be interesting at the very least. Would Feyd interfere with her other senses? There was only one way to find out.

The answer turned out to be yes. When she finally managed to trust her own instincts and skill enough to follow through on a swing despite being unable to feel the weapon in her hand, she landed a solid strike. After that, he expanded his efforts to manipulate her vision too, reducing it to varying extents at critical moments. The closer she came to another successful hit, the more he took away, limiting her sight or sense of touch, or both, to greater degrees, forcing her to act on memory and instinct.

When Kyril called an end to the practice, frustration overflowed in her, but so did determination, and she had landed several blows despite the Dampener's efforts. After Kyril dismissed the others with a few critiques of their performances, he came to join her. He waited until the rest were gone and she had fallen into step with him heading toward the palace before speaking.

"You adapted well to Feyd's manipulations."

She began unbuckling the practice bracer from one wrist. They wouldn't have much time to change before they were due to join the council. "Were you testing me?"

"There's a significant chance we could end up facing Thaelian mind-crafters in battle. I see no harm in preparing you for that eventuality. I also needed to give him an opportunity to practice his other skills, and I believed you would provide him with the greatest challenge of anyone in our unit."

Veyl caught herself straightening a little at that. How easily his words influenced her. "I broke quite a sweat doing that, and now I won't have time to clean up properly."

"I know."

Something in his tone drew her gaze to the faint smirk that curved his lips. "My stink pleases you?"

Kyril chuckled and looked at her. "Your stink, as you call it, carries the aroma of physical exertion blended with your own unique scent. If anything, I find it enticing enough to be distracting. So, yes, I suppose it does please me."

"Ahninveth, you aren't flirting with me, are you?"

His grin sent a pleasant shiver through her. "That, Khesran, would be inappropriate."

What had changed to bring about this lighter mood? Not that she was complaining. She enjoyed the way he was allowing himself to banter with her and admit some attraction. More than that, she loved having confirmation that Jaysen's abuses hadn't entirely eradicated his desire for her. Regardless of what caused the change, it seemed like an opportune moment to push for more.

"About that dinner we haven't had yet…"

"I am sorry I didn't join you the other night. Your father called on me to meet with the new members of the unit."

"You needn't apologize." She rushed the words out, trying to deflect the flicker of sorrow that returned to his eyes. "I assumed it was something of the sort."

"Let's find out what this is about first. After that, we can arrange our dinner. Agreed?"

Veyl nodded. "Agreed."

They entered the palace and turned down the hall toward the private quarters so they might use the few minutes they had to clean up a little. His fingers brushed the back of her hand, and she noticed this was the first time in a while that he hadn't situated Ceris between them. When she glanced at him, he met her eyes for a second before turning down the hall to his rooms.

"You have three minutes, Khesran."

Veyl all but sprinted to her chambers, a lightness in her chest that she hadn't felt in some time.

When they entered the larger council hall not ten minutes later, she had at least sponged off some sweat and thrown on something clean. The clothes and armor she had worn for practice she had left in a smelly heap on her bedroom floor, but no one else needed to know that.

Several senior officers were in the room today, including three high-ranking representatives from Delaphine, and two ambassadors from the southern kingdom of Fallend. Whatever her parents had summoned them for, it appeared to be a matter of some significance.

Adnar, Jhanik, and Kenna, three of Etrion's Ferals, entered the chamber behind them with their bonded companions, bringing the number of beasts inside up to seven with the wave dancers, Tavin's hound, and Kasiel's cliff cat already there. Once everyone settled into their seats, her mother addressed them.

"We have received an official request from King Regent Thrasser for a meeting with some of his representatives at a neutral location, with the stated goal of securing a public declaration that Vanris supports him over Crown Prince Jaysen. He is leaning on the fact that he, as Sarket's acting ruler, swore fealty to Vanris and has a standing relationship with us. His missive also presented Jaysen's alliance with the Thaelian council as a reason for us to back his claim to the throne over the prince's." Her gaze came to rest on Veyl and Kyril for a second before she continued.

"As we are all aware, Prince Jaysen's claim to the throne is legitimate and one we staunchly supported in the past. However, his new alliance with that specific group of Thaelians and the crimes they have committed between them against our people weaken any argument for backing him in this. Thrasser, however, aided the Thaelians in earlier offenses against Vanris and her people as part of an attempt to have Prince Jaysen eliminated. There is evidence that this was merely the start of a plan for engaging in more significant hostilities toward our country."

She steepled her fingers and regarded the gathering over them. "We currently have two options we could endorse for the Sarketi throne, and both come with substantial counts against them. We are considering granting this meeting the king regent requested. It could help guide us in determining where we want to offer our support or whether we even wish to do so. Granting one contender our assistance now could improve Vanris's position with Sarket's ruler after this conflict resolves, but it could also result in having to go back on our word later should we decide that leadership still needs changing."

"Which is highly probable, given our uninspiring options," her father added.

Her mother took his hand, offering him a tense smile. "Unfortunately."

Emboldened by the wave dancers and an encouraging morning, Veyl spoke into the pause. "It sounds as if we are here to determine who we will send to meet with Thrasser's representatives. Or do we need to waste time arguing pointlessly over whether we shall attend first?"

Arhk made no effort to hide his grin.

Her father gave him a chastising look. "Don't encourage her, Father."

"I stand with Khesran Veyl," Dhomen Nevias stated, settling back in her chair. She was one of Vanris's more accomplished military leaders. The long scar that ran through the symbols of her ke'hanoath under one eye and the limp she walked with were mere allusions to everything she had given in service to her country. "We could learn too much from this meeting, even if we decide not to grant him our support. Besides, Thrasser reaching out to us now tells me he is afraid of the prince and his new allies. He might be open to significant concessions under the circumstances."

"He always was a coward," Jhanik remarked.

Her father tapped the table with one finger. "Yes. But he used to care about the well-being of the people serving under him. I'm not confident that is true anymore."

"Then we proceed with caution," Veyl offered. "As we always should with Sarket."

Arhk leaned in, brows rising a fraction. "You wish to be part of the contingent we send."

Veyl met those eyes that matched her own. "I do." Kyril's soft chuckle beside her told her the declaration didn't surprise him.

Her mother scowled and met her eyes. "All right, Khesran. Tell us what makes you think you are a reasonable choice for this critically important political engagement?"

The intensity of that regard made it almost feel as if her mother had forgotten everyone else in the room, but Veyl refused to let it unsettle her. Her mother was giving her a chance to argue her case. She didn't dare waste it. "Send me with Ahninveth Kyril's unit. Several of us have dealt with Jaysen in his current state, and we possess considerable knowledge of the Thaelians. Not to mention, the mere presence of Kyril and Kitria will show that we can offer him an edge against Jaysen's allies without us ever having to say as much."

"A powerful argument for sending the Thaelians." Her father's unspoken words told her she had a long way to go to convince them she should be there.

Veyl drew a breath and forged ahead. "We know Thrasser will not attend himself. He won't want to leave Andaro for this when his position is under threat any more than the two of you will want to leave here amidst all the conflict Vanris is facing. He will send someone in his stead. General Danovan, perhaps. A man who any member of our family would have an advantage over. And obviously, I would not be going to negotiate alone. With Dhomen Nevias and Ahndhomen Adnar there, we would have more than adequate representation."

"I would rather someone else attended," Adnar stated. "Ahndhomen Jhanik, perhaps."

Jethan scoffed. "Jhanik, at a negotiation?" As soon as he said it, her father's tehnaak gave the Feral an apologetic look. "No offense, but you are not the most charismatic individual."

Jhanik smirked. "None taken."

"Neither is my tehnaak," Nevias commented, giving Adnar a fond smile.

Jethan grinned. "That seems to be a common problem among Ferals."

Tavin gave the Charmer a scowl, but when Veyl cast a furtive glance at Kyril, the Thaelian Feral responded with a slight shrug as if to say he couldn't disagree.

"Charismatic?" Her father turned to his tehnaak. "Jethan?"

Jethan's expression sobered, and he nodded. "I would be honored."

Veyl's gaze lit upon another somewhat sarcastic smirk at the table. "You could send Darro and Kince with us, as well as one or two representatives from Delaphine and Fallend, if they wish it," she suggested.

"Yes, we would prefer to have a presence at the table," General Lucia, an officer from Delaphine, stated, her dark eyes focused on Veyl.

The contingent was coming together fast, but the unwavering reluctance in her parents' regard spurred frustration. "What have you trained me my whole life for if not this? Our family has suffered many hardships this year, but that doesn't change who I am or my responsibility to our people. Why did you bring me to your political meetings if not for this?"

Her mother breathed a sigh and set a hand on her father's arm as if seeking comfort in that contact. "You will accept the guidance your more experienced counterparts offer throughout this process?"

A spark of victory lit in Veyl's chest, followed by a burst of anxiety. Partly because of how critical it was for this venture to be successful, but more so at the idea of leaving the safety of Etrion again. The last two times hadn't worked out well for her.

Accepting Seyn's support, she kept her voice steady and said, "I will."

Her mother turned her shrewd gaze to the man at Veyl's side. "And you, Ahninveth Kyril, do you have any objections to being a part of this and taking your fledgling unit out into the field so soon?"

"If you are comfortable and Ahninveth Kenna is amenable to going as backup, we could send a few tethdraks with your unit as well," her father added.

"I am honored by your trust and confidence," Kyril began, giving a respectful nod to her father. "I agree there is value in having a Thaelian presence at these proceedings. As for my unit, an outing such as this, with little likelihood of combat, could be an ideal opportunity to forge bonds between those who are newer to working together." Nothing in Kyril's voice betrayed any personal feelings he might have about the assignment, which made Veyl itch to ask him.

"Very well. We need to determine the size and makeup of the rest of the delegation, after which we can move on to discussing what outcomes we will and will not consider for negotiating with Thrasser." Her mother's gaze shifted to a guard by the door. "Please have food delivered. We may be here for some time."

It was moving on toward evening when they ended the session, and her father invited Arhk and Kyril to speak with him in the study. Arhk could turn down that invitation if he pleased, though he didn't, but Kyril was in no position to refuse his new khemron. Veyl stopped outside the meeting room and watched them depart with a flare of frustration. Would she never have time to speak with him alone? Not that the development surprised her. Her parents were allowing her to take an active role in the negotiations. They would do everything in their power to ensure she came back unharmed, and Kyril, as ahninveth of her unit, would have a significant role to play in that.

"You too?"

She glanced over to see Kitria walking up beside her. "Me too, what?"

The other woman smiled, though the expression lacked the vivacity that it had when Veyl first met her in Thaelis. "Thwarted again in your efforts to speak to my brother."

"You were trying to catch him on his way out?"

Kitria nodded. "Want to join me for a drink in my room? His is across the hall. We can leave my door open a crack and ambush him when he returns."

Veyl laughed and slid her arm through Kitria's.

"Sounds like a plan. Maybe you can help me puzzle something out."

Kitria's rooms, like Kyril's, were in the guest portion of the private quarters. Well-appointed and comfortable, but somewhat smaller and less opulent than those of the royal family and other elites like the dhomvalen, who resided within the palace full-time. The fireplace was lit, and a welcoming fire crackled in it. Two mugs and a pitcher of mead sat upon the table along with a tray of fruit, cheese, and bread, making it apparent Kitria had made plans for extended company, though not the company she ended up with.

"It looks as if you had a lot you wished to address with your brother." Veyl sank into one chair at a gesture of offering from the other woman. For a moment, she considered telling her about the coming mission, but that was official business. Kyril would handle sharing that with his unit in the manner he deemed best after her father was through with him. "Is there something I might help with?"

Kitria's cheeks blossomed a warm shade of pink. She turned her attention to selecting a grape from the platter, her reaction providing all the answers Veyl needed.

"I'm guessing at least part of it has to do with Ahrin?"

"I can't discuss that with you. He's your friend."

Veyl smiled. "I care about you both. I promise you I can be objective and that nothing you say will get back to him through me."

The look of gratitude Kitria gave her reminded her how odd it must be for the woman being stuck here like this, in a place where she knew almost no one. An experience with which Veyl could relate far too well.

"I appreciate that. The problem is that I genuinely like him, but I intend to return home to Thaelis as soon as the opportunity arises. It feels wrong to encourage his interest under those circumstances." She popped the grape in her mouth, her silver eyes pleading with Veyl to provide an answer.

Theirs was a difficulty that she and Kyril also shared, although without the added complication of one of them being royalty. "Your leaving is a problem, but one you are both fully aware of. Considering how intensely you two appear to be drawn to one another, the right approach may be the simplest. Bring it up with him and see what he thinks. The answer might be that there is value in finding happiness in each other while the situation allows it, so long as you both recognize that it will end sooner than you would probably like."

Kitria finished chewing and eyed the platter to consider her next selection. "That sounds so reasonable when you say it."

"Maybe because it is. It's also a certain path to a broken heart, but the alternative is trying to resist something that could bring you both a bit of joy for as long as it lasts." She took a drink of the mead.

"All right. I'll take your advice into consideration. Thank you. Now what is this puzzle you're struggling with?"

"Your brother."

Kitria laughed. "I'm going to need more than that. He's a complicated man."

"Isn't he?" Veyl sighed and put the drink down, settling her hand on Seyn's head where the wave dancer lay beside her. "The destruction of his memories has been difficult for him to come to terms with. I understand that, and I have been trying not to be impatient with him. I feared Jaysen might have destroyed what we had between us, but when we were sparring the other day, I felt like there was an intense connection there. And today, he actually flirted with me when we were heading to the council meeting. I believe there is something to it, but I'm afraid to expect much, and I don't want to push him. As his sister, maybe you would know if something has changed?"

Kitria washed down a bite of cheese with her mead before answering, the shadow that fell over her causing a spike of anxiety in Veyl. "He's been reluctant to talk about it, but I can tell that being tortured while having his mind violated in that way, particularly by one of our own people, scarred him deeply. Being uprooted from his life like this hasn't helped him recover from that. I do think that having a unit to command has been a useful distraction for him, though. He's always been more at home on the ocean overseeing his fleet. Having a leadership role again seems to have given him some stability and focus."

Veyl took a drink, considering her speculations. "That certainly makes sense. He is a leader at heart. It's something I think I appreciated about him, even back when I hated him."

Kitria shook her head, a hint of amusement brightening her smile. "You know what hasn't changed?"

"What?"

"You, Veyl. You are still the woman he fell in love with before. If anything, I think you're stronger now. Look at all you've endured. Why wouldn't he fall in love with you again?"

Veyl took a long drink of the mead, fighting to keep her emotions in check. There were far more important matters she ought to be focusing on, but she had spent several hours in the meeting chamber discussing the coming negotiations, all of them with Kyril by her side. Now she wanted to let her head have a rest, and her heart seemed happy to fill the time away from responsibilities with its wishes.

Kitria leaned back in her chair with a few slices of apple. "Tell me about Ahrin. Nothing too personal, but maybe a little of what he was like growing up."

Veyl took another drink of the mead before indulging her request. Recalling many stories from their youth in which Jaysen didn't play a prominent role proved difficult. He had been with them for seven years, a fixture in their lives, much to Gannon's irritation. She came up with a few tales from their very early childhood, though the loss of her original tehnaak, Minya, overshadowed most of those. A little while later, as she was recounting one of their more recent adventures assisting the guards in the years after Jaysen returned to Sarket, Kitria held up a hand, turning one ear toward the door.

Footsteps sounded in the hall, one set at first, then a second moving faster and coming from the opposite direction. Seyn's ears perked up as the click of Ceris's claws on the hard floor reached them through the cracked door.

"Apologies, Ahninveth Kyril, but you have a couple of visitors asking for you out in the entry hall." Given the speaker's deferential tone, it was safe to assume the feminine voice belonged to a palace attendant.

"Do you know who it is or what they want?" A hint of impatience gave a sharp edge to his voice.

"Speaker Leath and Enkindler Tassa, Ahninveth. They said part of your unit is going to the Red Dust Tavern and wished to extend an invitation for you to join them."

Part of the unit indeed. She shared a sour glance with Kitria. The two women clearly hadn't wanted to include the entire unit, given that neither of them had heard about it. She held her breath, waiting for his answer, which didn't come for a few seconds.

"Tell them I appreciate the invitation and will join them if I am able, but that I have something I must attend to first."

That ignited another flare of frustration. What else had they dreamed up to keep him occupied? At least he wasn't rushing off to meet Tassa and Leath. She could be grateful for that much.

"Of course, Ahninveth."

"Thank you."

Footsteps retreated down the hall. A moment later, the door to Kitria's room opened. When Kyril stepped through, his eyes lit upon Veyl as if he had expected to find her there. Most likely, he had sensed Seyn with his ability. A slow smile curved his lips, and he shut the door before walking farther into the room. The satisfaction in his expression told Veyl this was the something he had to attend to first.

She didn't recall standing up, but since she was on her feet, she moved around the chair and took a few steps toward him, aware of Kitria and the wave dancers watching. Kyril strode up to her and slid his hand along her jaw, his thumb sparking heat in its wake when it brushed her cheek. He stared into her with those piercing eyes, his unexpected touch making the rest of the room and its occupants melt away.

"Do you truly want to be with me?" His soft voice held a trace of wonder along with something deeper that kindled her desire.

"There is little I want more."

He leaned in, and she met his lips in a kiss that sent a wave of fire rippling out from that point of contact. Despite the softness of the contact, it carried within it a mountain of longing and passion that set the room spinning around her. It lasted for a few seconds of perfect bliss before he drew back and met her eyes.

"After we sparred the other day, when we were kneeling there in the ring, I saw us in my mind. You were in my arms in the cabin on my ship, and you almost kissed me. Only I was seeing myself through your eyes. I felt your fear and hatred, and your longing. A bit too much mead and an intense desire to feel safe and wanted nearly overpowering your aversion to me. I also felt a sensation of you being drawn toward me by something within you. I don't know if any of it was real..." He trailed off when she nodded.

"It was. Is that why you drew back so suddenly?"

"Yes. It surprised me. It also made me wonder even more about how you could possibly want something genuine with me now, knowing the conflict and confusion I inspired in you."

"I recalled that moment in the ring, though I don't quite understand how you could have experienced the memory with me. But I feel far different about you now than I did back then. Hearts can change, you know."

A wry smirk curved his lips. "I certainly hope so, because, no matter what I do, you are on my mind every minute of every day."

Kitria's voice brought Veyl back to the room they were in. "Could the wave dancers you're both bonded to contribute to your connection?"

"It's possible." Kyril's gaze sank to Veyl's lips before he moved away. "It might have to do with who you are as well, Seh'hali. Daughter of the Ocean. Wave-touched."

"Both the Qwilki and Wavelord Kronach see a connection to the ocean in you too, Brother. If there is something to that, it could create a powerful bond between you."

His brows rose slightly, as if he were willing to consider the possibility.

Veyl brushed those ideas aside, ill at ease with where they could lead. "What did my father want with you?" she asked, moving closer to him again.

Kyril breathed a laugh. "To ensure that I would prioritize your safety and to warn me against trying to cultivate any inappropriate attachments between us."

She chuckled. "A warning I see you took to heart."

"I will never know what Jaysen stole from me, but I know I want to be with you. Whether it makes sense to me or not, you've made it clear you feel the same. I'm done resisting that. I intend to repurpose that wasted energy toward discovering ways I can be worthy of you instead."

That was a sentiment Veyl could agree with. She stepped up to him and kissed him the way she had longed to for some time now, flicking her tongue against his lips in search of entry. He responded instantly, deepening the kiss as if he might consume her, and his arms moved around her, pulling her into a firm embrace. A wave of desire and something more rose in her, but before it could crash over them both, Kitria pointedly cleared her throat. They separated, flushed with passion and, at least for her, a hint of embarrassment at becoming so caught up in him in front of his sister.

"Um, could you take this to another room?"

"Sorry, Kit." Kyril gave her an apologetic look, one hand lingering warm and welcome on Veyl's waist. "The khemron did emphatically encourage me to do everything in my power to ensure the unit would protect our khesran from harm on this little adventure, not that I needed much convincing. They are understandably worried about something else happening to you," he added with an unreadable glance at Veyl that made her wonder if he now disapproved of her committing them to the mission.

Kitria set down the slice of evalis fruit she had been about to eat. "What little adventure is that?"

Kyril gave Veyl a puzzled look. "You haven't told her?"

"You're our ahninveth, and she is your sister. I left it for you."

"In that case, meeting up with the rest of the unit might not be a bad idea. Do you think the twins and

Iyvalin will be there?"

Veyl smiled at Kitria's hopeful look, though she would have much preferred to spend the rest of the evening reconnecting with Kyril. "They usually go to the Twisted Vine, but the Red Dust might be less crowded. We could send an attendant to find them."

"Let's do so." He started turning toward the door, then paused, a grimace twisting his lips when he looked at Veyl again. "There are no circumstances under which you and I can be together in public."

She drew a deep breath and blew it out, feeling some of the elation that came with their rekindled relationship fading. "I'm fully aware of the limitations upon us."

He leaned in and placed a soft, consoling kiss on her lips. "We'll figure it out," he murmured, before pulling away and leading them out of Kitria's rooms.

The Red Dust was farther from the barracks, though that had less of an impact on patronage back when most of the city's population had been military or military adjacent, according to some longer-standing regulars. Recently, with the influx of new troops, its business had picked up again, though it still had more open tables than the Twisted Vine did on most days. The wood-paneled walls had swirls carved into them meant to evoke the blowing of the wind, the inside edges of the outer spirals stained red to represent the dust prevalent throughout the Crimson Break. It was honestly quite lovely. A location Veyl might enjoy more if it were only her and Kyril there.

With the modest crowd, it was easy to spot Tassa, her long white-blond hair unbound, her momentary victorious smile twisting to a frown when Kyril entered and turned to hold the door open for Veyl and Kitria. She schooled her expression to a welcoming smile that looked much too forced. Dailan was saying something to her and Leath that she nodded absently in response to.

Kitria nudged in between Veyl and Kyril as they headed toward the table. "Do you think Tassa realizes how subtle she isn't? She couldn't be much more blatant about her intentions if she walked over here and mounted you."

"I'm not a horse, Kit."

"Maybe not, but she would clearly like a ride."

Veyl sucked back a laugh, trying hard to hold on to her composure despite the siblings' banter, especially with how intently Feyd was watching them now, offering a solemn nod to accompany his scrutinizing gaze. It unnerved her how the Dampener could give off the impression of knowing everything about someone with a single discerning look.

Veyl waved to a server, drawing the woman over as they arrived at the table.

"How may I help you, Khesran?"

"Do you mind if we move another table in alongside this one? We have three more coming."

The server bent in a partial bow. "I wouldn't hear of it, Khesran. We'll move one into place for you."

"That's not neces..." She let her objection fade away as the woman hurried off, calling another server over to assist her.

The rest got up, moving out of the way as the two servers arranged the tables. Tassa used the opportunity to move closer to Kyril. When they sat, Veyl and Kyril settled across from each other at one end out of necessity to provide the wave dancers space on the floor alongside them. She got the feeling he didn't mind the positioning any more than she did. Although it made it harder not to stare at him and smile when her thoughts wandered to the distance that had broken down between them earlier. It wouldn't make the situation easier, not considering how her parents would react if they found out, but she refused to let that keep them apart. If he wanted to be with her, they would figure the rest out.

Kitria deftly snagged the seat beside Kyril, blocking Tassa out. With a pout, the Evoker settled for the next place down, with Leath at her side, choosing not to sit next to Veyl. Feyd claimed that spot, Dailan alongside him. When the twins and Iyvalin arrived, they filled in the rest of the table, though both Ahrin and Gannon both looked less than thrilled with the arrangement, if for different reasons.

When they all had mugs in front of them and two stoneglass bottles of Vanrian Black Mead waiting in the center, Kyril offered an appreciative nod to Tassa. "Thank you for suggesting this. I needed to speak with all of you."

Tassa answered with a smile that didn't reach her eyes. "Certainly, Ahninveth."

"Our unit is heading out on a mission." That brought all side conversations to an abrupt halt. "We are riding out with a political delegation in a few days. Because this is not a military action, and I am still learning to work with the beasts here, we will be operating as a reduced unit, with just a few tethdraks and the wave dancers. Khesran Veyl and I are to take part in the negotiations, which means members of our unit could be called upon to act as guards if necessary when we reach our destination."

The slight spark of alarm in Tassa's expression told Veyl the woman truly had believed this unit was merely for show. A rude awakening, it seemed.

"Where are we heading?" Feyd asked, his casual tone suggesting that his interest didn't originate from a place of concern. Perhaps he had experience with such missions.

"Because of the sensitive nature of the situation, I will disclose where we are going and who we are meeting with after we have left Etrion. I need two things from all of you right now. The first is confirmation that you are willing and able to work together as a cohesive unit for this mission. If you have the least bit of reluctance, I expect you to speak with me about it by practice tomorrow morning. The second is a commitment to focus most of your waking hours before we depart to training. I won't have anyone's lack of preparedness putting the unit at risk. We shouldn't need to fight this time, but I would rather be ready to do so and not have to than deal with the alternative." His gaze had the intensity of a hunting predator when it swept over them. "Do you all understand what I'm asking of you?"

"Yes, Ahninveth." Feyd was the first to say it, but the words echoed around the table.

"That's what I wanted to hear." Kyril reached for one of the stoneglass bottles. "Let's crack some stones, then."

"To our first mission." Gannon raised his mug, and the others followed suit.

As they relaxed into the evening, Dailan, Tassa, and Leath engaged Kyril and Kitria in conversation about Thaelis, occupying them with a seemingly endless barrage of questions. Feyd, sitting beside Veyl, followed along for a time, but he soon turned his discerning, gray-eyed gaze to a different target.

"Khesran, as I understand it, you lost your tehnaak at quite a young age. Why have you never chosen to take a new one?"

For a second, she considered telling him she had, but her bond with Jaysen wasn't common knowledge, and it was best to keep it that way, especially now that the crown prince had made himself their adversary. Still, that did not mean she had to accept his assessment of the matter as accurate. She shrugged. "I couldn't merely steal someone else's tehnaak. There were no youths of my age in Etrion who were not already bonded."

His eyes narrowed a fraction, and a distinct edge of

anger sharpened his words when he spoke. "You are a khesran of Vanris. Anyone in the country would have leapt at a chance to be your tehnaak. Your family had but to reach out."

She turned a shrewd gaze back on him. This couldn't be just about her. For some reason, it bothered him on a personal level. "Why does this matter so much to you?"

Feyd held her gaze, a hint of torment in his eyes. Then he stood abruptly. "Excuse me."

Veyl's gaze followed him across the room until Dailan slid over next to her.

The man kept his voice low when he spoke, letting the noise in the tavern act as a privacy barrier. "Feyd's sister died in a riding accident last year. Her tehnaak bonded with someone new not three months later. When he confronted her about how quickly she replaced his sister, she claimed it was her duty as a Vanrian to find a new tehnaak and honor that part of our culture. The whole affair didn't sit well with him. He felt moving on that fast disrespected the bond she'd had with his sister, particularly when our future khevarin has never taken a new tehnaak. Your name came up with some regularity in his arguments with her and in many rants I've listened to."

Veyl glanced in the direction Feyd had gone. His anger came from a very personal place indeed. One filled with heartache and loss. Perhaps she could help him understand her choice without revealing details better left unspoken. "Three months is fast. I can see why that might have upset him, although I have a hard time imagining him opening up enough to rant about anything."

Dailan chuckled. "I may be the only one who has ever witnessed it. He is a man of discipline, and he doesn't believe in wasting effort or words. That discipline and his sister's encouragement got him through all the training he's done. He's had a hard time moving on since her death. I tried to discourage him from bothering you about it, but I don't think he could handle sitting next to you for this long without bringing it up."

Kyril spoke then, having apparently turned his attention to their conversation somewhere along the line. "If his sister only died last year, then her loss is a fresh wound. I imagine being placed in a unit where four of us have lost and not yet replaced our tehnaaks is like rubbing salt into that wound. Do you think it will lead to problems?"

A glance revealed he was looking at her. Asking her. "No. I don't get the impression he would let it stand in the way of his responsibility to the unit."

"Oh, you have nothing to worry about there," Dailan confirmed. "He would never let himself fail in his duty to Vanris or his unit. He may be as fun as a loaf of stale bread, but you can rely on him."

Veyl breathed a soft laugh at his choice of words. Then her gaze drifted to Tassa, who was now engaged in conversation with Ahrin and Iyvalin. If anyone was going to cause problems, it would be the Enkindler, but they needed her tehnaak. A Speaker was an invaluable asset in any unit.

When she let her gaze move back to Kyril, he acknowledged her concern with a subtle nod. They would at least be going into this together with their eyes open.

You're staring at him again." Gannon kept his voice low as he moved his horse closer to Veyl's gelding.

Heat crept up her neck, and she turned her attention straight ahead. They were fast approaching the end of the second full day in the saddle and their destination. Her thoughts needed to be on the coming negotiations, but that wasn't where they kept wandering to. "I wasn't staring. I just happened to glance in his direction."

Her gaze flickered back to Kyril for a moment. He looked more relaxed today despite Kenna, the other Feral, having left him full responsibility for managing the tethdraks and keeping the horses from panicking around them. The big reptilian hounds were even weaving through the company now and then and took turns trotting up beside Kyril's horse to sniff noses with Ceris as if checking in. Was that merely him practicing or was he showing off? Perhaps a bit of both.

"I believe that is the only direction you've happened to glance for most of the last hour." Gannon cracked a grin. "I get it. He looks exceptionally handsome riding in the light of the setting sun. The way it turns the streaks of blue in his hair almost purple…" He gave an exaggerated, wistful sigh.

"You're impossible."

"I'm quite possible. You've just never tried."

Veyl broke out with a short laugh, drawing a few eyes their way. She caught herself shrinking in the saddle as if that might somehow make her less visible and quickly straightened. "Has anyone else noticed my, um… preoccupation?"

"I don't know. I was staring at you."

She blew out her breath. "You really are impos–"

His grin broadened when she cut herself off and gave him a chastising look. "Kyril has been talking with Feyd and Dailan for about the last mile, Tassa hasn't taken her eyes off Kyril long enough to notice you, Leath is sulking because her tehnaak is too preoccupied to chat, and Kit and Ahrin haven't stopped acting like every word the other says holds the answer to life eternal since we rode out of Etrion. Beyond that, I honestly couldn't say." He glanced toward the unit riding to the left of theirs. "Actually, that's not true. I have noticed Lord Jethan watching you and Kyril both periodically throughout the afternoon."

"Fantastic," she groaned under her breath. As her father's tehnaak, Jethan would be sure to report any unseemly behavior back to him. "Obviously, you weren't staring at me the whole time if you noticed all of that."

"I've got exceptional peripheral vision."

She laughed again. "You are full of yourself today, aren't you? What has put you in such a mood?"

"I don't know. After everything we've endured this past year, I like that we're actively engaging in efforts to resolve some of the conflicts facing Vanris. It feels better to be doing something, doesn't it?"

He had a point. It was nerve-wracking going to negotiate with the representatives of Sarket's king regent knowing he must have been plotting against Vanris. The same man who had assisted Kyril's fleet when they came hunting for her people. Still, it was also gratifying to no longer be sitting around waiting for their problems to resolve themselves.

And yet, if they supported Thrasser's claim to the throne, they would be throwing their lot in against Jaysen, possibly determining his fate with a single decision. They would not merely be turning their back on Sarket's rightful king, but on someone she had spent her childhood with. A young man who, if not for the demands her parents made at the end of the war, might never have had the misfortune of falling in love with her. He could have found acceptance among his peers instead of being shunned and abused by them when he returned home after his years in Vanris. Not that she blamed her parents, but they had played a part in the events leading up to this. It was his own people whose stubborn hatred for Vanris made those circumstances far more of a problem for the crown prince than they needed to be.

Her gaze drifted to Feyd. The man who found her lack of a tehnaak so distressing.

Jaysen was the actual reason she never bonded with anyone else. Her secret tehnaak, her best friend, and now, her tormentor. She couldn't tell him that.

"Uh oh, someone's thoughts drifted to a dark place." Gannon nudged his mount closer still. "Are you all right?"

Veyl looked ahead toward Crimsondale. This was the site, near Sarket's northern border, of the incident that started the war between Vanris and the southern kingdoms. A memorial tower rose from the desert landscape, built three years after the war ended with equal parts black stone from Vanris and white stone from the mountains around Andaro, the capital of Sarket. A display of unity between the two countries that was apparently little more than symbolic. The tower was round, centered on a broad circular foundation that had four spear-shaped extensions reaching out from it, one pointing toward each of the four kingdoms' primary capitals.

To the east of the tower, a single-story building sprawled, built primarily of clay and sandstone. It contained living quarters and extensive meeting facilities, designed specifically to host political engagements between Vanris and the southern kingdoms. Local materials used in the outer walls gave a slight reddish cast to the tan structure.

Interestingly, the design and construction were handled almost entirely by architects and builders from Delaphine, with assistance from Vanris. Perhaps that was why Sarket's leadership was reluctant to make use of it. This time, however, it seemed they would set aside their fierce pride for the sake of the king regent's desperation. Thrasser's usual preferred meeting location in Balarus was much too close to Taro, where Jaysen had established his base of operations.

The white sections of the tall tower picked up a vibrant glow in the light of the sinking desert sun, giving the monument a strangely solemn beauty.

"Veyl?"

"Hmm?" She gave herself a small shake, recalling Gannon's concerned inquiry a moment ago. "Yes. I'm fine."

They had pushed to arrive a day early, hoping to reach the location ahead of the contingent from Sarket to ensure there would be no surprises waiting. Even with the internal conflict as volatile as it was in Sarket, they were unwilling to fully trust Thrasser's motivations in calling them here.

The groundskeepers were expecting them, though not so soon, but they had everything in order and rooms ready for those staying in the main building within an hour of their arrival. The Vanrian company spent that time setting up their soldiers in facilities outside the main building. Given that political gatherings were the site's primary purpose now, it included separate barracks for housing the military escorts that typically accompanied visiting dignitaries. Veyl and Kyril fell into the latter category as representatives for Vanris and Thaelis—excluding the Thaelians who fled their homeland to ally with Jaysen. Although the annexation of Thaelis had not been fully realized while they were there, Arhk told them the transition was underway when he left the island nation, so Kyril agreed to proceed under the terms of that original agreement.

Vanris's council had also prepared a political delegation, along with some soldiers and shipwrights, to send to Thaelis to assist with the process of annexation and recovery from the Ukhen'kya attack. Kitria, even more so than Kyril, had seemed distressed at the idea that they would miss that opportunity to return home. Recognizing that, her parents surprised Veyl by offering Kitria the option to go back to Thaelis with them, a choice they notably didn't give Kyril. After a few aggressive sparring sessions with Merrin, Kitria burned through her initial frustration and opted to stay with her brother. A decision Veyl suspected also had a lot to do with her blossoming relationship with Ahrin.

Kitria and Ahrin were standing in front of the barracks Vanris had claimed now, engaged in some apparently riveting conversation, given how intensely they were focusing on one another. Iyvalin had lost interest and wandered off to chat with Dailan and Feyd. Mostly Dailan. Feyd lurked off to one side a little, currently watching Veyl with that flat expression of his.

"It's growing late, Khesran," Kyril said, walking up to her and Gannon. "We should head inside."

"Ahninveth." Gannon acknowledged with a reasonably respectful nod before returning his attention to Veyl. "You know where you can find me if you need me."

He grinned. "Out here with the common soldiers."

"There's nothing common about any of you," Veyl countered, answering his teasing tone with a smile. "Keep your brother out of trouble."

"Yes," Kyril added firmly. "Considering it's my sister he has his sights on, I would appreciate that."

Gannon glanced between them, a smirk twisting his lips, and shrugged. "I'm not convinced they're the ones most in need of supervision, but I'll do my best." He winked at her before walking away.

"Comforting." Kyril turned, heading not to the manor, but out toward the open desert.

Veyl strolled along with him to a spot where the wave dancers could run for a few minutes before going inside. It was nearing full dark. Silence hung over them, but not in an uncomfortable way. Although there was a glimmer of tension there, it wasn't negative. It was born instead of the longing to touch, hands and bodies yearning for contact they couldn't have. After a few minutes, Seyn and Ceris rejoined them, and they wandered inside.

There were guards posted outside the entrances to the section their rooms were in. The primary structure had four wings leading off the central building, arranged specifically to provide the four different kingdoms with their own private spaces. On this occasion, the few representatives from Delaphine and Fallend had come as part of the Vanrian delegation. Since it was a modest contingent, and they wanted to present a united front and avoid giving Thrasser's people opportunities to sow division, they would share one wing.

When they entered the hallway, Dhomen Nevias was just vanishing into her room, leaving them alone for the moment.

Veyl glanced up at him, a sudden reckless anticipation thrumming in her chest, easily drowning out the quiet voice in her head that warned her to caution.

"Might I have a word in private before we retire, Ahninveth?"

The corner of his mouth curled up in a faintly predatory smile. He opened the door and gestured for her to enter ahead of him.

With her nerves aflame, she walked inside, spinning to face him as the door clicked shut behind them. His arms were around her the instant she completed the turn, his lips claiming hers in an ardent kiss, his strength deliciously overwhelming. She slid her hand into his hair, remembering vividly the pleasurable encounter in his house near the port in Dagony. Her first time being with anyone. An act of passion, surrendering her heart and body to the desire he had awakened in her.

Kyril jerked back, not fully disengaging. A flicker of unease tightened his eyes and pinched his brows. "How…"

"Did it happen again?"

He nodded.

She glanced at the wave dancers resting on the floor in mirrored poses, their noses nearly touching, eyes shut. If they were to blame, they gave no indication of it.

"I was remembering our first time together." His taut muscles relaxed a little as she slid one hand around his waist, bringing herself closer again.

"Seh'hali… I could feel your apprehension and longing. No fear that time, though. No hatred." He slid his hand to the back of her neck and applied gentle pressure to draw her into a softer kiss. When he broke that kiss, he touched his forehead to hers and whispered, "I have no memories of our first time together. I don't remember ever having made love to you. There are only a few fragments that might have been… something." An ache of sorrow deepened his voice.

Veyl smiled. She wasn't going to let Jaysen ruin this. "I want you to make love to me for the first time again."

He chuckled, the sound sending a thrill through her, and answered with a deep kiss, his fingers gathering up her shirt and finding their way beneath the fabric to her bare skin. Veyl surrendered to him, leaning her head back to let him do as he pleased with her, simply feeling every caress and kiss as the desire between them burned away the memories of Jaysen's hands and lips upon her. After a few exquisite minutes of letting herself be at his mercy, she turned to undressing him, savoring the feel of his lean, hard muscles under her hands.

He lifted her then, and she wrapped her legs around him, kissing him deeply as he walked them to the bed. Once the last of their clothes were off, he teased her with his touch and started moving kisses down her body, but she caught hold of his arm. When he looked up at her, she shook her head.

"Please," she whispered, a tremor in her voice, "make all of me yours again."

He met her eyes, that Feral wildness rising in his, and moved over her, capturing her mouth in a devouring kiss that cut off her gasp as he entered her.

•

Veyl left a couple of hours later to ensure she would be in the proper room if anyone came looking in the early morning. As she slipped out with Seyn, she heard the click of another door closing a few rooms down, and the wave dancer growled softly. Veyl's heartbeat sped up. Whoever had been out there appeared to have been entering their room when she came out, so it was likely they hadn't seen her, but she didn't intend to press her luck by lingering. She hurried to her room and ducked inside.

A firm knock on the door came much too early the next morning.

"Inren Veyl," Kyril called from out in the hall, sounding unfairly energetic. "We have time to get in some training before Sarket's contingent arrives."

"Have fun." She turned her back to the door and tugged the blanket up over her ear.

"Mandatory training."

She groaned and rolled over to glare at the door. Seyn was standing next to it, long tail wagging, jaws parted in a large canine grin.

"Fine. You win, but only because Seyn's on your side."

She heard his chuckle as she threw off the covers. "I'll see you out there."

Intense memories of the evening, of their sweating, naked bodies passionately entwined, were enough to encourage a thorough sponge bath before she dressed and walked out to find her unit. The original builders had set up a few rings for sparring and a limited range for archery practice alongside each barracks. Ahrin, Gannon, Tassa, and Leath were already out working with bows. Iyvalin and Dailan had paired off in one ring, with Kitria and Feyd in another.

Veyl walked over to where Kyril stood watching the latter two. "You don't need me here. Unless you mean to spar with me yourself."

"Patience. I have plans for you." He glanced down at her, his smile holding a glimmer of something more intimate in it. Releasing her from his gaze, he called a halt to the two in the ring and stepped in. "Kit, you're fighting a different evolution of Vanrian forms than you grew up with. Let me give you a few tips to make it easier."

Veyl leaned on the fence and watched as he walked Kitria through some techniques for dealing with the variations in their forms and for facing the axes Feyd favored. The morning was cool, and an energy moved through her that had the distinct feel of the wave dancer. Being amphibious beasts, the poor creatures suffered some in the desert environs. For them, a cooler morning here was something to be cherished and enjoyed.

Feyd stepped out of the far side of the ring at Kyril's direction, giving the ahninveth room to spar with his sister. His gaze settled on her, but he didn't approach. She had almost decided to walk over and join him when Seyn trotted over and nosed her hand, bringing her attention to someone else coming up beside her.

Kince leaned on the fence, putting one foot up on the lower bar and moving some of his long blond hair out of the way with a toss of his head. "Good morning, Khesran. I trust you had a restful night."

Something in his sharp tone sent unease creeping up her spine, but perhaps it was nothing more than a sign that he hadn't slept well. "I did, thank you, Uncle." Not that they were blood relatives, but he was part of her father's tehsheyn, those she'd called her aunts and uncles since she was old enough to speak the words. It wasn't likely to change now.

Kince stared out at the two in the ring, watching as they exchanged a few attacks and Kyril paused to adjust Kitria's stance. "I hope you didn't just come on this trip looking for a chance to get your Feral ahninveth alone."

Veyl stilled, the cool morning air picking up an unpleasant chill. "I don't—"

"You were seen, Veyl. We'll leave it to your parents to decide how to handle this when we return to Etrion. For now, we will keep it quiet and move you into a shared room with Dhomen Nevias for the remainder of our stay. It was a lapse of judgment that will not happen again." His tone made an order of those last words. "One that could have devastating consequences."

Her gut clenched. What would they do to Kyril? "Who claims to have seen me?"

"It doesn't matter. You aren't like the rest of us." The faintest hint of sympathy in his glance eased a little of the sting from his words. "You can't run around finding pleasure where you will. You are a khesran of Vanris, and you could have hardly picked a less suitable partner."

She pushed back against a surge of frustrated anger. It wasn't his fault that his words were true. "Kince, please. I won't retaliate. I just need to know."

He looked at her, a trace of compassion softening his fierce, angular features. "Omren Tassa."

She drew back, a dark flame kindling in her chest. "But she was out in the barracks. How could she have seen something?"

Kince breathed a bitter laugh. "Apparently, your ahninveth has broad appeal. She admitted to using her ability to help her talk her way past the guards, hoping to find welcome in his bed last night. When she saw you coming out of his room, she ducked through the closest door, which put her in the room Jethan was sleeping in. We will deal with her infraction when we are back in Etrion as well."

He stepped away from the railing. "The contingent from Sarket has been spotted riding in. Jethan asked me to escort you inside to prepare for the meetings, but you are not a child anymore. I trust you to handle yourself properly for the rest of this trip. Your behavior from this point forward could have a significant bearing on how this goes when we get you home."

Veyl nodded, hating that she now regretted something that had made her joyously happy only a short time ago. Not even for what might happen to her, but because of what it could mean for Kyril. "Thank you, Uncle." The words came out flat and emotionless, a reflection of the helplessness that weighed heavily on her shoulders.

He nodded and left her. Veyl watched him depart, a sour taste rising in the back of her mouth when Tassa walked up on her other side.

Seyn growled softly.

"All this time, I thought our ahninveth was treating you differently because of your status. I guess that makes me the fool."

Veyl held her tongue, trying not to let her rising rage inspire her to do something else she would regret.

"Hm. Impressive self-control, Inren Veyl. You should have used some of that when you were deciding how to spend your evening."

Veyl swallowed her pride. She could do that much for him. "Please don't tell anyone else about this. It's already going to do enough harm."

"Oh, I've been sworn to secrecy. Though I suspect your parents will take it even further and put me before an Evoker when we get back no matter how cooperative I am, just to make certain I can't sully their daughter's name. Not a compelling motivation for keeping my mouth shut, now is it?"

Veyl looked at her, noting the tightness in her jaw and her narrowed eyes. She was angry. Angry that Veyl had taken what she wanted and left her feeling embarrassed and slighted. Angry that, because of who Veyl was, she was likely to have her memory of the incident removed. Not a promising place to start a reasonable conversation from.

"I can ask them not to put you through that."

"Oh, and I'm sure they'll be in a mood to grant your wishes when they hear of this." She sneered. "No. I think I'm better off without your help, Khesran." She spat the title, then spun and strode back toward the archery range.

"What was that about?"

Veyl startled. Somehow, even with Seyn watching

out for her, Kyril had caught her by surprise. She avoided looking directly at him and dropped her voice low enough that no one else would be likely to hear her. "Kince came to let me know someone saw me leaving your room last night. That someone." She glanced meaningfully at Tassa. "They're moving me in with Nevias for the rest of our time here. They intend to keep it quiet and let my parents deal with it back in Etrion." Out of the corner of her eye, she saw a ripple of tension move through him.

"How did she see you? She should have been in…" His chest rose and fell with a deep breath. "She came inside intending to proposition me?"

Veyl nodded. "I am so sorry." Her throat tightened around the words.

"Don't be. No matter what comes next, I refuse to regret being with you. For now, however, it might be best if we maintain some distance. Doing otherwise will only lead to more problems."

"Sarket's delegation is arriving. With your leave, I'd like to head inside to compose myself before we meet with them. Be wary of Tassa. I don't trust her not to make this a bigger incident than it currently is."

"Nor do I." He stepped back from her. "I'll see you in the negotiations, Khesran."

Veyl made her way to her room, only to find that they had already moved her few belongings out. Making herself walk down the hall to Nevias's room was like wading through deep water. With a distinct lack of enthusiasm, she tapped on the door.

"Come in, Khesran," Nevias called from within.

Knowing the woman was obviously expecting her didn't make her any more eager to open the door. Glancing down at Seyn, whose solemn gaze conveyed an uncanny awareness of how serious the situation was, she heaved a sigh and walked in.

Her things lay on one of the two beds set against opposite walls. Nevias was sitting on a bench at the foot of the other bed, working a second braid into her hair above one pointed ear.

"Would you like some help?" Veyl offered, unable to keep the ache of sorrow from her voice.

Nevias stopped what she was doing and let her take over the strands of hair. Veyl worked them into the desired weave with practiced fingers.

"Do you believe Ahninveth Kyril will keep this quiet?" Nevias asked.

"Yes. I would worry more about Omren Tassa spreading it around," Veyl answered, reminding herself not to pull the dhomen's hair in her frustration.

"We'll take her into custody if we need to. I would prefer not to arrest him right now, however, not while he could still be an asset to our negotiations."

Veyl cringed inwardly. "Arrest him?"

"You are a khesran of Vanris. It is not as if he could have missed that fact."

"But…" Her cheeks felt like they were on fire. "I invited him."

Nevias gave her a hard look. "That may be true, but he is older than you and your superior officer. Not to mention, he is the man who attacked Deepwater and took you and many others prisoner. This will not end well for him."

Veyl stopped weaving. "I won't allow them to hurt him."

Nevias's lips pressed into a thin line. After a few seconds, during which Veyl resumed braiding, she drew a deep breath. "The best thing you can both do right now is keep your behavior professional and focus on what we came here for." Her gaze drifted to a table on one side of the room. "At least you had the sense to come prepared, a fact that supports your claim to have initiated this."

Veyl followed her gaze, spotting the vial she had brought containing a few doses of the contraceptive preparation they used. They had dug through her belongings. The people she grew up with trusted her so little now that they felt justified invading her privacy in such a way.

What an awful mess she had made.

**V**eyl entered the meeting hall with Nevias and Seyn, every step a struggle, as if her ankles were shackled to heavy weights. She felt trapped. She was trapped. They both were, but Kyril would suffer more for it than she would. Knowing that made it worse, making the invisible weights infinitely heavier. Kyril and Ceris entered through another door with Jethan, the first to learn of their nocturnal activities.

No one so far had pressed Veyl about how long they had been romantically involved or if they had been intimate before this. Perhaps they wanted to leave those details for her parents to investigate. She could only assume so, since she doubted they would give her an opportunity to ask Kyril if they had questioned him about it.

Their two groups converged near where some of the Sarketi delegates were speaking with a few servants, requesting refreshments sent to the hall. They wanted to begin discussions immediately since the Vanrian company was already there. One man turned, and Veyl recognized him instantly. The man whose brother had abducted her father as a child and killed his mother, her grandmother. A whisper of hatred moved through her, intensified by her current distress, but Kyril spoke before she could say anything to him.

"General Kassian Danovan."

Kassian's dark eyes widened as he looked up at the tall Feral, his heavily grayed brows rising. "Ah… Ahnkreth Kyril."

"Ahninveth Kyril now," Jethan corrected. "You two have met?"

How much of the barely contained anger she saw in Jethan's eyes and tight jaw was for the Sarketi general, and how much was for the man standing next to him? How much was for her? At the very least, they would strip Kyril of his rank when they returned to Etrion. What else would they do?

"Well…" Kassian shifted his feet, clearing his throat as if something had lodged itself in the path of his words. Guilt, perhaps.

"Yes," Kyril offered into the Sarketi general's silence. "General Danovan was there when the king regent asked my fleet to head to Deepwater, where we might find Vanrians to take back with us and eliminate his competition for the throne in a single attack." He paused, tilting his head to one side." In fact, I believe you were the one who suggested adding a supply of your firebombs to make the agreement more attractive."

"This is… most unexpected." As Kassian spoke, the other men with him eyed Kyril warily, all of them looking ready to bolt for the doors. Did they fear Vanris had come here to exact revenge for their actions?

Veyl hoped they were terrified.

"Don't worry," Kince said from where he had come up on Jethan's far side, "the Thaelians we are working with do not support those Crown Prince Jaysen brought back with him. But they did have some fascinating information to share about their dealings with Sarket's king regent."

Kassian wrenched his eyes away from Kyril, his gaze settling on Jethan for a moment, a hint of distaste in the slight curl of his lip. They all knew her father's tehnaak was a Charmer. When possible, Vanris avoided sending mind-crafters to diplomatic meetings with Sarket, given the powerful distrust the country still harbored toward them. With all that had happened over the last year, they were less concerned about pandering to Sarket's bigotry this time. Thrasser wanted Vanris's help in this conflict, but Vanris still had other options, as distasteful as some of those might be.

The general's gaze sank to Seyn at Veyl's side, his brow furrowing in puzzlement, then moved up to settle on her. "It is nice to see that you are well, Khesran Veyl."

She answered with a sour smile. "No thanks to King Regent Thrasser's meddling. His actions put him in violation of the fealty he swore to Vanris. I hope you didn't come here believing you enter these negotiations from a position of strength."

"No... Of course not." He lowered his gaze, the hesitation in his words suggesting he had not expected to be confronted with Thrasser's flagrant betrayal.

"We should move on to business, then," she prompted, gesturing to the two long tables that sat facing each other on a raised platform, as if meetings here were intended to be a spectacle.

By the time they had all taken their seats, Kassian appeared to have regained some of his composure, though the strategically late arrival of the representatives from Fallend and Delaphine stripped some of that away again. They did a brief round of introductions. There were several on Sarket's side she hadn't met before, filling in for a few conspicuously missing members. Was it possible some had defected to join up with Jaysen? Or had Thrasser simply held them back to serve him in other ways?

One of the Sarketi representatives spoke first. "With respect, might we know why you haven't chosen to declare your support for the crown prince? King Thrasser was expecting you to do so, but there have been unsettling rumors that Prince Jaysen may have acted against Vanris."

"Hence the sudden eagerness with which your sitting king now prostrates himself at our feet?" Veyl allowed her current mood to sharpen her tone.

Nevias touched her arm below the table. A gentle warning. Kince, on the other hand, sat back in his chair and crossed his arms, a smug grin curving his lips. Not at all the discouragement she needed to rein her in.

"Unsettling for whom?" Nevias asked before he could respond to Veyl's sharp inquiry. The bitter nip in her words was enough to convey that she didn't believe they had any concern for the people of Vanris. "The crown prince's new allies did arrange an attack on the fleet we sent to Thaelis to create a distraction while they fled with hostages, all of whom have fortunately returned to us. How deeply he was involved in those decisions remains unclear, but knowing he was involved at all has prompted us to withhold any offer of support for now. However, King Regent Thrasser has also acted against Vanris recently, rendering his claim to that backing as tenuous as the prince's."

The eyes of several of the men at the opposing table shifted briefly to Veyl, making it apparent that at least some of the mentioned rumors concerned her. How much did they know? They would be naturally cautious, especially now that they knew Vanris was aware of Thrasser's betrayal. The Vanrian side was being wary as well, hiding exactly how much they knew of Jaysen's involvement.

Delaphinian General Lucia's gaze settled on Kassian. "What exactly does your sitting king wish to gain from this meeting?"

Kassian drew a deep breath, his gaze drifting to Veyl again, his focus on her setting her ill at ease until a calming wave moved through her. Not only from Seyn this time. She could feel both wave dancers and Kyril as well. She found in that the boost of confidence needed to meet Kassian's eyes as he spoke.

"King Thrasser believes settling this through combat between him and Jaysen is the wrong way to go about—"

"But is that not how Sarket has handled disputes throughout its history?" Veyl interrupted. "Is it not what the people will expect?"

"Ah… Yes, it is, Khesran. But this is a new age for Sarket. We would like to move on from such barbaric traditions."

She could feel Kassian's discomfort now, too. Not in the same way she could feel Kyril and the wave dancers. This was a sense of foreign emotion, something that wasn't part of her as they were. An insect crawling on her skin. "Now that his life is being called into the ring, the practice is barbaric. What a convenient time to change his stance on the subject. He must believe Prince Jaysen will win."

The sense of discomfort from the other table flared, as if a swarm of insects was now biting at her skin.

"Easy, Khesran," Nevias whispered, touching her arm again.

Veyl moved her arm above the table, setting her elbows upon it and steepling her fingers as her mother often did. A posture considered offensive in Sarket, at least when assumed by a woman.

Kassian's brows pinched together, and he rubbed at his temple with the fingers of one hand as if his head pained him. "Well, no, he believes it foolish to hang the fate of a country upon a single fight between two men."

Kyril and the wave dancers lifted her, giving her strength and courage. "It was just as foolish back when my father and King Lodmund did it. Is that why he fears it, because he sees how that ended up? Or does he believe Havaad's justice will favor the prince?" She watched with a curious fascination as the man rubbed more intently at his temple, a sense of certainty moving through her. "That is it. Why? Prince Jaysen is younger. Less experienced. I would think someone who fought in the war would have more confidence," she pressed, feeling his tension building toward a breaking point.

"Because the prince trained with Vanris's best fighters," Kassian snapped, his composure faltering. He tore his gaze away from her, and her awareness of his emotional state went with it.

The other Sarketi delegates shifted in their seats, some casting looks of concern or disgust in Kassian's direction. The silence on Vanris's side threatened to throw off her equilibrium. She could feel those around the table watching her, more than a few with a hint of surprise and curiosity. Welcoming in that soothing strength, she pushed ahead with what she had started.

"The king regent fears Jaysen because he trained in Vanris. Now he wants Vanris's backing to protect him from the rightful king of Sarket so he might continue to sit upon a throne he was never meant to keep. And he dares to ask this after breaking his oath of fealty to Vanris. Do I have that correct?"

Another Sarketi representative, a man with neatly trimmed brown hair and a perfectly shaped beard that showed a sprinkling of gray, shook his head at Kassian and faced Veyl. The moment she met his bright blue eyes, she could feel his disgust with General Danovan as if it were her own. "The crown prince has his Thaelian mind-crafters and has now secured the support of the Eydarith. Wilkin fears he will not fight fair."

Wilkin? The man's easy use of the king's first name suggested a strong familiarity. Who was he to Thrasser? Something about him gave her the feeling his slip had not been unintentional. He was trying to deescalate by humanizing the subject of their tense exchange. A clever man to be handled more carefully.

"Apologies. I believe I missed your title during the introductions." She let a sense of expectation hang between them.

"I am Chief General Gregory Harriksen, Khesran."

Thrasser's closest advisor. The man the king usually left back in Andaro to manage military matters when he attended negotiations in person. "Well met, Chief General." She offered him a respectful nod, which he returned in kind. "It is not the Eydarith he worries about breaking the rules of such an engagement. We all know they would stand behind a proper Sarketi trial by combat. He fears the mind-crafters."

"I will not lie to you, Khesran. Though it has been many long years since the war, our people continue to find it difficult to trust those they know can manipulate their minds."

"Understandably so," she answered, catching a disconcerting swell of annoyance and bewilderment from those on her side of the table. The shock of being able to suddenly feel their reactions when she wasn't even looking at them threatened to break her focus. Were the wave dancers responsible for this?

The smallest hint of surprise flitted across Gregory's features. "You show an uncommon grasp of the challenges we face, Khesran." He inclined his head to her. "Your Delaphinian and Fallenese allies are not unexpected, but am I to understand an agreement has been reached between Vanris and Thaelis, excepting, I presume, those who have chosen to ally with the crown prince?"

Veyl felt a flare of tension from Kyril and pushed some of the soothing the wave dancers offered away, urging it back along the connection to him. This was the reason he was here, though she sensed the others were no longer as comfortable with that arrangement as they had been.

"Thaelis's representatives have agreed to our country's annexation into Vanris," Kyril stated, skirting around the fact that Thaelis had not yet established an actual governing body in the council's absence.

A soft murmur moved along the opposite table, and the Chief General's brows rose a fraction. "A significant change in stance since the day you arrived in Sarket's waters all those months ago planning to capture Vanrian citizens for your repopulation efforts."

"We have since realized that we went about accomplishing our goals in the wrong way and now seek to make amends for the harm done to Vanris and her people." Though Kyril's voice was steady, the brief break in his eye contact with Gregory told Veyl that their personal situation had also affected his level of comfort with his role here. What could they expect? He was facing the prospect of severe punishment for his dalliance with her. That had to make it harder to speak on Vanris's behalf.

"Honorable, I suppose, though you have helped to wedge Sarket into an uncomfortable situation here with your unexpected change of heart."

Veyl smiled, infusing no warmth into the expression. "One you would not have found yourself in had the king regent not chosen to act in violation of his oath of fealty to begin with, would you not agree, Chief General?"

Gregory nodded. "Which leads us to where we are now."

Jethan leaned forward. "A place where Vanris and her allies are disinclined to support either claimant to the throne. What does King Regent Thrasser plan to offer us in exchange for our backing against Crown Prince Jaysen?"

The uncomfortable shifting along the opposing side of the table brought a sense of satisfaction to Veyl.

When Gregory's gaze returned to her, she arched one brow to let him know she, too, was eager to hear what compelling offers they had to make. They had intended to ease into the negotiation with a gentler hand, but she hadn't been in that kind of mood. Besides, this was Sarket. They respected aggression, not kindness. That the others had essentially followed her lead was gratifying. Not enough to ease the misery of what would come when this was over, but it gave her something to feel good about for a time.

Kassian sat up straighter. "Vanris stands to gain—"

"I will handle this if you don't mind, General Danovan," Gregory interrupted.

Kassian looked like a child who'd had their hand slapped for trying to take something that didn't belong to them. He leaned back in his chair and crossed his arms over his chest. "As you wish, Chief General."

"We would consider the addition of another Vanrian military base in Sarket and increased Vanrian presence on the king's advisory council. We would also like to reopen discussions regarding changing our current oath of fealty to a proper alliance at a later date, though I recognize we are not in a position to press for that transition right now."

"That's a place to start from," Nevias said. "Explain how he envisions us supporting him, and we can see how much farther you have to go. Does he expect military aid or merely a declaration that we back his claim to the throne? Is his plan to try negotiating with Jaysen, and would he want us there if he were to do so?" She folded her hands on the table. "Please, Chief General, enlighten us as to the role Sarket wishes Vanris to play in your country's future."

For another three hours, they deliberated over what each side wanted from the other in their theoretical partnership, after which, they called a break, allotting two hours for the separate groups to deliberate among themselves away from the meeting room. When they got up to leave the hall, Jethan sent Kyril off with Kince and Darro and waved Veyl over. Her nerves sparked to life. Kyril didn't look at her, but she could still feel him there, almost as if he were part of her. She could feel Seyn and Ceris as well, though the latter wave dancer's presence had faded some.

She didn't allow herself to watch Kyril's group leave as Jethan ushered her out a different exit. "Yes, Uncle Jethan?"

"You may have diverged from the plan in there, but your parents would have both been proud of how well you controlled the conversation. I know I was."

She merely nodded. Without the active negotiation to distract her, the cost of her nocturnal activities fell heavily on her shoulders again, muting any positive effect his praise might have had.

He steered them into one of several cozy, private meeting rooms meant to accommodate smaller side discussions and shut the door behind them. "You made a mistake, Veyl. A big one. There is no getting around that. But you also did extremely well in there. I suggest you focus on that for the moment. There's nothing you can do to fix the other."

"You're right, I can't." She took a deep breath, trying to fight the tightening in her throat. "I love him."

"No." Jethan shook his head forcefully, a spark of alarm igniting in his eyes. "Don't start that. Do you have any idea how many stupid things I watched your father do in the name of love? It's a wonder he lived through it."

Veyl walked to the bookshelves that lined the back wall, filled with volumes donated by all four kingdoms. Would there be books from Thaelis here one day?

"Yes, but Father got what he wanted in the end,

didn't he?"

"That's not how this is going to go. I'm sorry." To his credit, he sounded genuinely apologetic. "Kyril is Thaelian, and his status here balanced on a knife's edge before this because of what his fleet did in Deepwater. He dragged our people from their lives against their will, Veyl. He took you. How can you possibly love that man?"

"He knows what he did was wrong, and he is sorry for it and has been working to make amends. Would it have been better if he had never done it?" She turned to face him. "Obviously, but I refuse to let you or anyone else make me regret loving him. My one regret is that he will suffer more for it than I will, and I mean to fight that too."

Jethan's expression turned stony. "This wasn't the first time, was it?" He let out a bitter laugh. "Not even close. I can't wait to be the lucky gentleman to share that news with your parents."

A chill swept through her, and Seyn stepped in front of her as if the wave dancer meant to protect her from him. "Uncle, please."

"Return to your room. As of right now, you are no longer a member of Ahninveth Kyril's unit. I will call on you when it's time for negotiations to resume."

Panic swept around her like a current threatening to pull her under. She focused on the one subject she hoped he would see reason on. "No. You can lock me up, but not Seyn. She needs time outside."

His gaze flickered to the wave dancer. "I'll send someone to escort you out with her shortly. You are to go nowhere near the barracks or Ahninveth Kyril without supervision. Now get out."

"Uncle." She infused her tone with gentle pleading and took a step towards him, hoping he would yield some to the fact that he had raised her almost as much as her own parents had.

"Don't bother. Your father is my tehnaak, and you are forcing me into a position where I will have to hurt him. I have no sympathy to give you right now." He turned and opened the door for her, gesturing sharply for her to leave.

Seyn stayed close to her side as they exited. She went directly to the room she shared with Nevias and sat on the bed. The wave dancer set her large, webbed paws on Veyl's thighs and brought her muzzle up in front of her, staring at her with those bright, sea-foam eyes. Veyl put a hand on either side of the beast's face and sank them into her odd fur. A tear slipped down her cheek.

"We need to protect him, Seyn. I don't know how yet, but we must."

Negotiations throughout the afternoon remained fraught with tension. The delegation from Vanris pressed for more than mere visibility on King Thrasser's private council. They wanted at least three seats with an equal voice in any decisions. Fallend and Delaphine's representatives requested one or two positions each for their countries as well. They would consider coming to an agreement for less, but there remained one substantial sticking point. The allied delegation wanted a detailed explanation of the motives and greater goal behind Thrasser's attempt to rid himself of Jaysen and his invitation to Kyril to return and take more captives from the Vanrian base near the coast in southwestern Sarket. He had hoped to accomplish something when he made those decisions, and they demanded to know what it was.

As the day faded into evening, the Sarketi representatives continued insisting there was no deceitful plot. They had merely made an impulsive decision based on the unexpected opportunity presented by the Thaelian fleet's arrival. One driven by Thrasser's desire to keep the throne and the demands of the populace to get rid of the mind-crafters in their midst.

They paused the fraught conversation long enough for four servants to move through the room and light the sconces, then Veyl jumped in the moment the door closed behind them.

"What kind of opportunity would you consider that, exactly?" she demanded, in no state of mind to keep playing their games. Nor was she in the mood to be a figurehead and hold her tongue for the rest of the day as Nevias had advised her to do at the last break, though she had obliged for a few hours, until it simply became too much to ask. "King Thrasser tried to keep his seat of power by attempting to eliminate Jaysen, but he had to know that helping Thaelis take our people would be akin to declaring war on Vanris. There's something you aren't telling us, and there will be no agreement of support until you explain it to our satisfaction."

Kassian scowled, apparently as fed up with the lack of forward progress as they were. "Did you come here to belabor past mistakes or negotiate a future we can build as allies?"

"We came here to determine if we could trust you enough to even consider working together on a future that includes all of us." Veyl moved her arm above the table the instant Nevias reached over, thwarting the woman's subtle effort to rein her in.

"What's the alternative?" Kassian snapped to his feet. "You kill us in the night and go offer your support to the crown prince?"

Gregory stood and put a hand on Kassian's shoulder. "It is late, and tempers are wearing thin. We should all get food and sleep and resume this discussion in the morning when our minds are fresh."

Veyl stood as well, the rest of the table rising when she did. She felt sorry for the servants who would have to come back in and snuff out the sconces so soon after lighting them, but it was clear there would be no more productive conversation today. "Wise words, Chief General. It seems the opportunity for constructive conversation has passed for today. I know I could use some fresh air, followed by a good night's sleep. I expect the rest of you feel the same."

Gregory met her eyes, as she had hoped he would, allowing her to feel the unexpected sincerity in his next words. "You have the makings of a formidable khevarin when it comes your time to rule, Khesran. I wish you and your accompaniment," he said, sweeping over them all with his gaze, "a pleasant eve."

"You as well," Nevias said, speaking before Veyl could respond, and setting a hand firmly on her shoulder.

With a flare of irritation, Veyl settled for a polite nod and allowed Nevias to direct her from the room. The dhomen continued outside with her so she might give Seyn a chance to run and relieve herself. She spotted Kince and Darro heading out to the barracks with Kyril and Ceris. They hadn't allowed her the opportunity to talk to anyone from their unit. She envied Kyril his chance to spend time among them, though she doubted they were giving him the freedom to speak to the group in depth. Did any of the others know what had happened? Had Tassa adhered to her vow of silence?

They hadn't disbanded the unit, and Nevias said they wouldn't until they reached Etrion. One of several unpleasantries awaiting them upon their return to the black city. Most of them she would do almost anything to avoid, such as the coming confrontation with her parents, resulting in severe discipline for her, and a likely much worse punishment for Kyril. Even if the negotiations here ended well, an outcome she had significant doubts about, it would do nothing to keep her parents from reacting negatively to the news Jethan was going to share with them.

Yet even now, perhaps more so now, she yearned to go to Kyril. She belonged with him. Whatever the connection that had formed between them was, she could still feel his presence. That pull was so much like the draw she had felt to the western coast as a child, only many times stronger. He was not physically distant, though he might as well be among the stars sparkling to life in the darkening sky as far as their chances of getting to spend time together went, but in some undefinable way he was closer than ever.

"Khesran, are we done here?"

The impatience in Nevias's tone inspired an impulse to snap back at her, but Veyl smothered that inclination. The situation was enough of a disaster already. "Yes, Dhomen, I suppose we are."

When they got back inside, Nevias headed toward the small dining hall in that wing of the manor, and Veyl stopped.

Nevias turned and arched a brow at her. "Are you coming?"

"I'd like to eat alone in the room if that's acceptable."

"You will not leave there, and you will not have company." Nevias's flat tone said she would regret it if she did.

Veyl scowled at her. "I wasn't planning on it. I just don't want to be around the rest of you, either."

"Embarrassed?"

Perhaps it was a good thing she no longer had her untamable Frightener ability, after all. Veyl spun and started toward the room.

"I'll have food sent for you," Nevias called after her.

Veyl didn't answer. She returned to the room and threw herself down on the bed. Seyn hopped up on the other side and stretched out alongside her, resting her head on Veyl's shoulder.

"At least they haven't tried to take you away." The wave dancer licked her cheek, and Veyl cracked a reluctant smile. "Thank you. Care to tell me how I'm able to sense people's emotions and intentions suddenly?"

The wave dancer looked her in the eyes, an intensity falling over the beast as if she wanted to answer the question. Frustration charged the air between them for a few seconds, and neither of them moved. Then she licked Veyl full in the face, and her jaw cracked open in a big canine grin.

Veyl laughed and playfully pushed the beast away, though the effort made little impression on her. "Sometimes it's hard to believe you're intelligent at all."

She rolled onto her side, put an arm over Seyn's shoulders, and closed her eyes, letting the beast's calm presence soothe her. Sometime later, she awoke to the smell of food and turned to find a plate sitting on the bedside table. Nevias was across the room preparing for bed. A glance out the window revealed that night had finished settling in while she slept.

The dhomen looked at her and gestured to the meal. "I brought some food by earlier, but you were already sound asleep, and your protector didn't seem to want me bothering you. She snarled at me, if you can believe that. I had the kitchens prepare that fresh."

Veyl sat up, a wash of energy moving through her from Seyn, who looked intrigued by the contents of the plate. "Thank you. I hope you brought enough for two."

"Don't let her lie to you. Just because I didn't wake you up for the original meal doesn't mean it didn't get eaten."

"You fed her my dinner?"

"The first one, yes. I deemed it wise to try getting on her good side. The Break-blasted beasts are as disturbingly smart as a kanodrak. No disrespect intended," Nevias added when Seyn growled softly.

Veyl shook her head at the animal, though she breathed a small laugh at the hopeful gaze the wave dancer turned on her food. "She may need to go outside again before I settle in for the night."

"I expected as much. I told the guards standing at the two entrances that one of them was to accompany you if you went out with her."

The orders were undoubtedly more specific, ensuring she did not speak to anyone or visit the barracks. She wanted to argue that she didn't need to be watched every minute like a child but ultimately erred on the side of restraint instead of going digging for an argument. She would have much bigger battles to fight when they returned home. It made sense to save her energy for that.

"Thank you, Dhomen."

Nevias stood staring at her for a few seconds, as though unsure of her next words, before she finally spoke again. "We all make mistakes, Khesran, but what—"

"Please." She looked up, catching a glimmer of sympathy when she met the woman's eyes. "Can we not talk about this right now?"

Nevias nodded. "It may be best to leave it for when we get you home anyhow. Make sure you're rested by morning. I am afraid tomorrow's negotiations won't be any easier."

By the time Veyl finished splitting the meal with Seyn, the dhomen was sound asleep and silence had fallen over the manor and grounds. It was later than she had realized. Nevias and the others must have stayed up talking for some time. She would have liked to hear their thoughts on the discussions with Sarket, but the certainty that her recent transgressions would come up as a topic of conversation had been enough to discourage her from joining them. Had Kyril eaten with them? Or had he taken dinner in his room as well? Would they have allowed him to eat with his unit in the barracks?

As she got up to leave, her thoughts wandered to the company from Sarket and her brother's childhood fear that the Sarketi people would one day seek vengeance for the death of King Lodmund. She didn't believe her father's defeat of the man would be the reason they turned against Vanris—the former king had not been that well-loved—but that didn't mean she trusted them not to do so.

Careful not to make any noise, she picked up her sword belt and buckled it on. So armed and with Seyn at her side, she stepped out into the hall, easing the door shut behind her in an effort not to wake Nevias. Her gaze flickered briefly to the room Kyril was in, but even in the empty hallway, merely looking his way felt risky. She hurried toward the doors that would take her outside, away from the barracks. She didn't want an escort. What she longed for was a few minutes with no one else there to remind her of what she had done wrong, but that was unlikely to happen, so she took a deep breath and opened one of the double doors.

Two guards bowed to her as she emerged, and one of them stepped forward. "Khesran Veyl, it will be my honor to accompany you."

When she met the woman's eyes, the outpouring of genuine pleasure and pride from her came as a surprise. She meant what she said. Veyl always assumed most of the guards found their royal charges tedious. Though she had befriended many city guards, she hadn't ever gotten to know most of those who worked within the palace. They rarely indulged in conversation while on duty. And yet, even if this woman was happy to fulfill her assignment, Veyl would much prefer she didn't.

Embracing that intense desire to be left alone, she held the eye contact, focusing not on her own emotions, but those she was receiving from the woman. She tried to project agreement and a lack of concern as she said, "I appreciate your offer, but there's no harm in giving your khesran a moment to herself to reflect upon a trying day, is there?"

The woman's brow crinkled slightly as if something in Veyl's words confused her. "No… I suppose there isn't, if that's what you would prefer, Khesran."

Veyl's pulse quickened. She met the eyes of the other guard as he took a step forward, daring to hope, and yet afraid of what it might mean if it worked. "You agree, don't you? As your khesran, I ought to be allowed a moment alone. It's not as if I plan to wander far. Just out to let Seyn stretch her legs."

He reversed his step, returning to his post. "It is as you say, Khesran. You should have time to yourself."

"Thank you."

She turned and strode swiftly away, her pulse racing wildly, afraid to linger in case they came to their senses. She didn't slow until she had rounded the corner of the building and could no longer feel their eyes upon her. It surprised her to see someone else out in the night standing beside the war memorial tower and gazing up at its impressive height. The man glanced over his shoulder when she drew near, his gaze settling on her for an instant before he turned back to the monument, his hands clasped behind him.

"Chief General Harriksen," Veyl greeted as she approached.

"That is a mouthful, isn't it?" He glanced down at her when she stepped up beside him. He was taller than she had realized when speaking with him from across the table, with a broad chest and bulky musculature adding intimidation to his presence that she refused to let discourage her. "We are embraced by the ease of the night, Khesran Veyl. I do not mind if you prefer to use Gregory."

"If you would consent to using simply Veyl."

A subdued smile tugged at the corners of his mouth, mostly hidden by his precisely trimmed facial hair, as he turned his attention back to the tower. "I would not dream of doing so."

"Then I am afraid we are at an impasse, Chief General."

"Not for the first time today." He chuckled, though there was a hint of bitterness in the sound. "I see your mother's influence in how fiercely you defend your country, Khesran. I always admired that in her."

Veyl turned toward him. "This is the first time I have ever seen you in negotiations."

He mirrored her motion, facing her as well. Subtle mimicry was a common tactic for creating rapport. She couldn't help wondering if he did it intentionally or if it might be instinctive. As a negotiator, he would have had training in how to put people at ease, but the action didn't strike her as forced or calculated.

"This is the first one I have come to in a long time. As I understand it, you only started attending such affairs in recent years, so it is of little surprise that our paths have not crossed before."

"True." She glanced up at the tower now, aware of Seyn trotting off to relieve herself. The wave dancer's lack of concern allowed her to relax some in his company. If he harbored any ill intentions, the beast would never have left her side.

"It is rather late for you to be out wandering on your own, Khesran, if you don't mind my noticing?"

"While you are noticing such things, you might also observe that I am neither alone nor unarmed, but I did not feel the call of sleep, and Seyn needed time out of doors."

He peered out into a night lit more by stars and moonlight than by the feeble light from occasional torches around the grounds. His gaze followed the shadowy form of the wave dancer as she all but vanished in the dark. "Such an unusual creature. By all accounts, you are not a mind-crafter, yet you appear to share a bond with that beast like one of your Ferals. How is that possible?"

She wasn't a mind-crafter, but she was feeling the emotions of others that she should not be able to, and it certainly seemed as if she had influenced the guards to let her come out here alone. Was that Seyn's work too, somehow? "You understand correctly. The bond was Seyn's doing. The wave dancers have remarkable skills. If I may ask, what call brought you out into the night?"

"You may have noticed that today's discussions were not especially productive. Contemplating the possibilities for moving forward kept me from sleeping. I came out here to this symbol of remembrance and unity to see if it might inspire me."

Veyl kept her eyes on him now, finding that, though he wasn't looking at her, she could still feel a sense of melancholy and regret from him. Curious. "And have you been inspired?"

He faced her again, his brows pinching together. "I did not find inspiration here, but I think it may have found me."

She took a slight step back from him. Though she got no sense of threat, his intense regard left her a touch unsettled. When her hand sank to her side, Seyn was immediately there, offering the protection and comfort of her presence. "In what way?"

"You have nothing to fear from me, Khesran. It merely occurs to me that you might be just the person to help me solve the problem of how to reach a place of agreement between our delegations."

A crackle of unease raced along her nerves. How long would it be before someone noticed she was missing? If she awoke, would Nevias assume the guards were keeping watch over her, or would the dhomen come looking? She met his eyes, searching for understanding. "Until you explain what Thrasser hoped to gain by getting rid of Jaysen and offering our people to Thaelis, how can you expect to move forward? Those apparent acts of treason built the wall that stands between us now. You must realize that. How can Vanris commit to a king who, by all appearances, was plotting against us and may still be doing so behind our backs even as he asks for our aid?"

He met her eyes, a disconcerting certainty in his. "We have reliable sources that say the crown prince took you hostage and tried to compel you to marry him. Is that true?"

How did he mean to use that information? To convince her Thrasser was the better option, no matter his deeds? "Prince Jaysen…" A sense of alarm drew her attention to Seyn, who was peering at the southwest wing of the manor. She stood alert with her tail high and ears perked forward, practically vibrating with intensity. "That wing is where Sarket's contingent is staying, isn't it?"

He glanced from her to Seyn, then to the building, his hand coming to rest on the hilt of his sword. "She senses something amiss?"

"Yes."

"Return to the safety of your room, Khesran. I will investigate."

"No, I'm coming with you at least as far as the entrance. I need to know that all is well." Not giving him a chance to protest, she strode toward the building, watching and listening for anything that might explain Seyn's tension. The wave dancer trotted out in front of her, alert for danger.

Gregory joined her, his long legs helping him get a step ahead. "I would argue if it were not a waste of time, but if something is wrong, I expect you to get away from there and go for help."

Veyl didn't respond, her gaze going to the double

doors as they walked around toward the side entrance. "Shouldn't there be guards?" she asked in a whisper.

"Yes." A low growl added threat to his voice as he quietly drew his blade.

Veyl reached urgently out through her sense of Kyril and Ceris, comforted by the calm she received from the other wave dancer and the answering hint of concern from Kyril. The two were awake now. That meant they would be alert if danger came their way.

She eased out her swords as they approached the abandoned entry. Gregory glanced at the weapons and gave a slight shake of his head. He put his arm out to stop her and cautiously moved ahead to ease the left door open a crack, leaning forward to peek inside. A mere inch of flickering light from a hall sconce showed in the gap before the door on the right flew open, slamming into him and sending him staggering back with blood gushing from his nose.

The attacker burst out in a flash of blades, one of which bit into the chief general's sword arm. The other barely missed Veyl's face as she twisted out of the way. A snarl from Seyn startled the man, drawing his attention to the lunging wave dancer and giving Veyl the opening she needed to drive a blade into his side. The weapon tore through his gut as Seyn pulled him to the ground, her slender, powerful jaws closing on his throat.

With blood streaming from his nose and one hand clamped over the deep cut in his arm, Gregory sneered at the fallen assailant. "He's Sarketi." He spat red to one side. "The crown prince is behind this."

Throwing caution to the wind, the chief general charged into the building. Two dead guards lay inside the doors, their throats cut. A pair of Sarketi men in light cloth and leather garments, designed more for quiet movement and low visibility in the dark than for protection, emerged from a room to the left, blood on their bared blades. Another man, this one in Eydarith armor, stepped through the doorway across the hall. One of the first two charged at Gregory. The second raised a loaded crossbow and aimed it at Veyl. Gregory moved to engage the man running at him. Seyn burst into action, sprinting at the one about to fire on Veyl. The Eydarith warrior reached the man first, grabbing his arm and twisting until he dropped the crossbow. Then he released him and stepped back, allowing Seyn to take the man down.

The Eydarith looked at Veyl and offered a slight bow of his head before ducking into the closest room. Darting clear of the fight between Gregory and the other man, Veyl sprinted down the hall after him, but another door flew open in her path and a man lunged out at her. Veyl engaged him, knocking his axe away with one sword and swinging at him with the other.

A sense of dread rose in her when two more darkly armored men emerged from a room near the end of the hall. How many were there? The man she was fighting dodged the tip of her sword. She lunged in after him, recognizing that she had little time to solve this problem before the other two reached them. Then the entry doors at the far end of the hall flew open, and Kyril and Ceris burst in with one of the tethdraks and two Sarketi guards behind them.

Turning all her attention to the man in front of her now, she feinted as if moving to counter his attack, then twisted clear instead and swung with her other hand. The weapon skimmed across his leather pauldron and found purchase in his neck. He dropped his axe, grabbing hold of her blade as if to stop her from pulling it free and releasing that flow of precious blood. Veyl yanked it back, cringing as the sharp edge severed several fingers from one hand.

When he fell against the wall, making a desperate

effort to stop the bleeding at his throat as he sank to the floor, she saw that the two at the far end were also down. Gregory had moved up next to her, and more of the Vanrian contingent was arriving. Some of Sarket's soldiers from the barracks were entering through the doorway behind them, and Gregory immediately ordered them to check the rooms for survivors. Kyril and Ceris strode toward them while the Sarketi soldiers rushed off in pairs.

Veyl glanced into the nearest room, spotting General Kassian Danovan lying on the floor in a pool of his own blood. They would find no one else alive in this wing. Of that, she had little doubt. The killers had wasted no time in dispatching the sleeping representatives.

Gregory spat more blood at the body of the man she had killed. "It would appear that someone told the prince about our meeting."

Kyril walked up and handed the chief general a cloth as he looked Veyl over. "You aren't hurt, are you?"

"No."

"You should be." Gregory wiped at the blood streaming from his nose. "Why did the Eydarith attack one of his own allies to protect you?"

"I imagine because Wavelord Kronach believes I am favored by their god. Something to do with the wave dancer's affinity for me, I suspect." That wasn't the entirety of it, but it seemed safe enough to admit and, hopefully, adequate to appease him for the moment.

"Then the crown prince did take you hostage." He looked around. "Where did that Eydarith bastard go? Check the grounds!" he shouted at a group of soldiers as he stormed down the hall. "See if you can find any of them still alive."

"I'll have the tethdraks look for him as well," Kyril called after the man, getting a grunt of assent in answer. He turned back to her and whispered. "You sent for me?"

She didn't know how to respond to that. Somehow, she had. Her connections to him and the wave dancers were changing and strengthening. She didn't know what to make of it. All she knew for certain was that Jaysen had effectively ended this round of negotiations.

hninveth Kyril," Darro called, coming down the hall to join them with Kince and Jethan close behind. "Take your unit and help search the grounds. The tethdraks should be able to track down anyone still lurking in the area."

Kyril's eyes met hers for an instant, the intensity of his affection and accompanying frustration hitting her with the force of a physical blow before he faced the approaching trio and inclined his head slightly. "Yes, Dhomen Darro."

Jethan stepped around him as he turned to leave, looking her over much like Kyril had just done. "Are you all right, Veyl?"

She bent down to wipe her blades clean on the dead man's clothing. As she straightened, she spotted Nevias heading their way with a dark glower. Avoiding the woman's eyes, she sheathed her swords and focused on Jethan. "I am fine, Uncle."

Jethan scowled at Dhomen Nevias when she joined them. "I thought we agreed not to let Khesran Veyl wander alone."

"We did. We need to talk in private." Her eyes met Veyl's, a wariness and concern in them that told Veyl she must have spoken to their guards. "You as well."

Jethan nodded. "Kince, Darro, you two stay here and see what we can do, if anything, to help the Sarketi company. We'll be back in a few minutes."

Steeling herself against what was certain to be an unpleasant encounter, Veyl walked with them into the central meeting chambers and across to the wing Vanris had claimed. Once there, they closed themselves up in the cozy meeting room she and Jethan had met in before.

When Jethan opened his mouth to speak, Nevias barreled over him. "Before you object to my handling of the matter, I told the guards to accompany Veyl if she took Seyn outside, and I confronted them about their failure to do so promptly upon discovering her absence. When I demanded an explanation for how she came to be wandering the grounds alone, they appeared confused and disoriented, unable to state clearly why they had not done as I ordered. If I didn't know better, I would say someone had Charmed them."

Jethan considered Veyl, his eyes narrowing a fraction. "Would you care to explain that, and while you're at it, tell us how Kyril knew where you were and that you were in danger? He woke me and said you needed us in the southwest wing right before sprinting off in that direction."

Veyl glanced toward the door. "There are more important matters to—"

"Humor us," Nevias snapped.

Veyl sank her hand into Seyn's glossy black fur, focusing on the sensation of the thick strands sliding between her fingers. Would it work if she tried to influence them to let this go? Perhaps it was best not to try. This was going to come up again soon, and it would make the situation far worse if she attempted to manipulate them and failed. "I don't know. During the day, I started being able to feel people's reactions and intentions during the meeting. When I went outside earlier, I desperately wanted time alone to clear my head.

I got the strange impression that if I tried to use that new sensitivity to convince the guards to let me pass, it might work, and it did."

"And Kyril?" Jethan prompted with a look of concern that now matched the one Nevias wore.

She brushed back a strand of hair that had fallen into her face, wishing she had braided it earlier after helping Nevias with hers. "It began with an awareness of Seyn that I assumed was because of the bond she forged between us. But then it expanded to include Ceris and Kyril as well. I hadn't tried to do anything with that new bond until tonight." She shrugged. "It must have something to do with the wave dancers we're both connected to. I honestly don't understand it myself. All I know is that this might have ended a lot differently if Kyril hadn't shown up when he did."

They both looked down at Seyn, but a knock at the door headed off any thoughts they might have been inclined to share.

Jethan walked over and yanked it open. "What is it?"

The unusual sharpness in his manner and tone exacerbated the dread growing in Veyl. Her father's tehnaak rarely showed his temper. The events of the last two days were clearly breaking down his typically easygoing nature. Recognizing that made everything worse at a time when things were bad enough already.

The Vanrian guard outside offered a partial bow. "Pardon, Lord Jethan, but Chief General Harriksen requested your presence as soon as possible." He straightened and glanced around the room. "All of you. Khesran Veyl in particular."

Jethan and Nevias shared a wary look.

"We shall continue this discussion later." Nevias gestured for Veyl to accompany them as they headed out.

Gregory awaited them in his room in the southwest

wing. Dailan sat next to him, stitching the wound in his arm. His nose was no longer actively bleeding, though there was drying blood in his beard and mustache and down the front of his clothes. It looked straighter than it had when last she had seen him—something else the healers must have tended to—and more swollen, with bruising spreading out from the bridge down under his eyes. Feyd leaned against one wall, his expression dour and arms rigidly crossed. The four Sarketi guards in the room watched the two Vanrians with open mistrust.

"Did you not think to bring healers of your own?" Nevias asked in a tone Veyl deemed unnecessarily harsh.

Gregory looked past the dhomen at Veyl before responding, his voice altered by the injury to his nose. "Ahninveth Kyril sent these two. They pointed out the indisputable fact that your healing salves are more effective and your healers renowned. It seemed prudent to accept his offer to make use of their skills." His gaze hardened when it moved to Feyd. "Though I will not have a Havaad-cursed mind-crafter working on me."

The Dampener's lips twitched as if he were considering saying something, but Jethan shook his head to discourage him. "You wished to speak with us, Chief General?"

The injury to his face made the man look that much more intimidating when he turned his hard gaze on Jethan. "This room is mine. It is now the only one among those occupied in this wing without a dead body in it. The attack was extremely efficient, and they did not target the Vanrian company or any Sarketi soldiers in the barracks. They came here for the king's delegates. It is fortunate for both of us that Khesran Veyl and I could not sleep. Had your khesran's beast not alerted us to something amiss, you might have found us all dead by morning, and Vanris would be among the prime suspects, particularly since this was supposed to be a clandestine meeting." He glanced at Dailan, a slight tightening of his jaw the only outward sign that the healer's work caused him pain.

"You believe they meant to kill the representatives from Sarket and leave them to be discovered in the morning?" Nevias nodded thoughtfully, not giving him time to answer. "That is how I might have done it, had I wanted to pit our two sides against each other. There is plenty of suspicion among our people to take advantage of."

"Whoever exposed this gathering to Jaysen, they had to have been Sarketi," Veyl remarked. "There wasn't enough time between when we received King Thrasser's missive and our arrival here for someone from Vanris to have gotten word to the crown prince and for him to have acted upon it."

Gregory drew a deep breath and blew it out. "I fear you are right, Khesran." He watched Dailan secure a wrap over the wound, then glanced around at them. "I would like a word alone with Khesran Veyl, if I may."

Jethan shook his head. "I'm afraid that's unacceptable."

Gregory's flat look said he didn't plan to take that as the final answer.

"There's no harm in it. I am qualified to represent Vanris. More so than most." Veyl gave Jethan a look she hoped would make him realize that this might be the perfect opportunity to gain useful information.

Jethan stared at her for a second. Then he drew a deep breath and blew it out, much in the way Gregory had done. A reluctant admission of defeat. "All right. You have five minutes, and we will be right outside."

Dailan handed the chief general a damp cloth with which to wipe the remaining blood from his face, then everyone left the room, including the Sarketi guards. Everyone except Veyl, Gregory, and Seyn. The wave dancer's presence made her a lot more comfortable with the arrangement than she might have been otherwise and almost certainly played a part in Jethan's capitulation.

Gregory wiped at his face with the cloth as he stood and walked to the window, gazing out into the night where soldiers could be seen searching the grounds. "Some of these men were good friends of mine."

Veyl's chest tightened with a pain that was only partly empathy. The rest was his sorrow, piercing through her like an icy breeze. "I am so sorry. I cannot imagine how hard this must be."

"You and your wave dancer are why I am not lying dead among them. The least I can offer you in return is the truth, so you might understand why I have been loath to share it." He faced her after a moment, a hint of moisture in his eyes and anger in the tension of his jaw. He was standing on a precipice, surrounded by the bodies of friends and peers, about to tell her something he clearly expected her to find objectionable. "Sarket has been helping to supply the anti-mind-crafter activists in Vanris. We have been providing them with funds, information, raw materials for forging weapons and armor, anything we could offer that would empower them to strike out against your mind-crafters and leadership."

Veyl's stomach twisted. She wanted to ask why they would do such a thing, but she got the sense he had more to say, and it wasn't all that hard to answer her own question if she considered the source.

"Wilkin hoped it would lead to full-on civil war in Vanris. A war that would target mind-crafters from within and leave you vulnerable to outside threats. When the Thaelian fleet arrived seeking to steal Vanrians, mind-crafters specifically, it was as if a gift had landed in his lap. Another opportunity to weaken and distract Vanris while also removing the crown prince."

A wave of dizziness swept through Veyl, and she set a hand on the side table next to her. "Is this still going on?"

He looked exhausted when he met her eyes. "It took us a few years to find the right connections and establish some alternating supply routes that could escape Vanris's notice. Every part so meticulously arranged that most of those benefiting from it don't even know Sarket is involved. At this point, it has taken on a life of its own. Such a complicated and delicate web will be as difficult to unravel as it was to create. So yes, it is still active."

Something occurred to her that sent a flash of disgust through her. "The queen's death. Thrasser was behind that too, wasn't he?"

Gregory said nothing. He didn't have to.

"And you have the nerve to look us in the eyes and ask for our help while you are actively undermining us from within?"

He wiped away more blood, the rag now pink with it. "I have the knowledge and resources to help you dismantle it, but we need to work together to do so. Wilkin won't like it, but he will go along with it if it secures your aid in dealing with Prince Jaysen and his new allies. However, we cannot afford to commit time to that effort while the crown prince is trying to take Sarket from us."

"Why should we care? You have spent years trying to destroy us from within. Why shouldn't we leave you to deal with your own problem? Jaysen is the rightful heir, after all."

"Because you need the information I can give you if you want to take down that network without it leading to civil war." There was shrewdness behind his narrowed gaze that she disliked. "And Jaysen has made himself a threat to Vanris as well. Not just to Vanris, but, as I understand it, to you personally."

"Calloch." Seyn's growl echoed the insult. "Would you have told us any of this if Ahninveth Kyril hadn't chosen to expose Sarket's activities?" She almost wished the others would come back inside now. They would soon. She could tell Gregory was aware of that as well by the increased frequency with which his gaze flickered toward the door. Yet, he had requested to speak with her alone about this for a reason. She could not help wanting to know what the reason was.

"I was under strict orders to keep this a secret, but your Thaelian allies changed the situation. You are justified in your anger, Khesran. We have sabotaged your country from within. If it means anything, I advised Wilkin not to move forward with that course of action, but I admit to following his orders when he proceeded against my recommendations. I am offering to help right our wrongs, something you appear to be allowing Ahninveth Kyril to do, but we require your aid in handling the crown prince now, before he persuades anyone else to join him." He took a step closer. "I must return to Andaro and deal with the fallout of this mess. You can go back to Etrion and work on convincing your parents that an alliance between us is the best solution to our problems."

She held her ground. "You want me to do the hard part for you?"

With a low growl of frustration, he threw the bloody cloth onto the bed. "There isn't time to do this any other way. It is painfully apparent that Prince Jaysen is growing bolder. Now that he knows Wilkin reached out to Vanris, he will not be content to sit back and wait any longer. Look at what he did here." His voice rose to a shout at the end that brought Nevias and Jethan abruptly back into the room.

Veyl held up a hand to calm them. "Everything is fine. The chief general is understandably upset by the events of this night."

"You've had more than enough time to speak with Khesran Veyl alone," Jethan stated.

Veyl sensed the faint soothing from him that told her he was using his Charmer ability. She gave a tiny shake of her head, hoping he would heed her discouragement. When the sensation faded, she addressed Gregory. "Will King Thrasser support you in undoing the damage these actions have caused?"

His lip lifted in a slight snarl. "I believe I have taken away his choice in the matter by admitting all of this to you, Khesran."

That was the type of reaction she was looking for. Something to show that he was fed up with his king's deceptions and ready to move forward. "Might I offer a suggestion, Chief General?"

"Make it quick. My company is leaving tonight."

Jethan and Nevias looked as surprised as she was by this revelation.

Holding a hand out low in a subtle gesture for them to wait that she hoped they would notice, she continued. "There must be an officer you can trust to bring news of this to Andaro for you. Perhaps a few riders who can travel at speed and avoid drawing attention."

His brows pinched. "What are you proposing, Khesran?"

Jethan and Nevias were now looking at her with the same question in their eyes.

"Come with us back to Etrion and present your case before my parents yourself. Show them you are willing to work with us to fix this. I believe that would go much farther than sending me to speak for you."

Gregory shook his head as the other two looked on with more than a little curiosity and confusion. "You may be right, but I have a duty to my king."

"You have a duty to your country," she countered, "and an opportunity to help determine its fate."

A Sarketi soldier stepped into the doorway Jethan and Nevias had left open. "Chief General."

Gregory pulled his troubled gaze away from Veyl after a moment. "What is it, Captain?"

The soldier gave a stiff, partial bow before speaking. "We've searched the grounds and surrounding area. If any assailants survived, they have escaped."

"Were there any Eydarith among the dead?" Gregory asked.

"No, sir."

"Then at least one did escape," he snapped. "I don't suppose we took anyone alive?" He eyed Veyl as he spoke, thoughts churning behind his eyes.

"Apologies, sir. The Thaelian Feral has his tethdraks working to pick up the Eydarith's scent now, but they've had no luck. We tried to save one man in the hall who was still breathing, but his wounds were too severe."

Gregory nodded, as if he had expected as much. "Gather the men in the barracks. I wish to address them."

"Yes, Chief General." The man gave another bow and left them.

Wariness rose in Gregory's eyes when he turned to Veyl. "The crown prince desires your hand in marriage. That Eydarith, one of his allies, protected you. It occurs to me you might merely wish to see me punished for my part in this."

"That is not my goal, and I can assure you I will never marry Prince Jaysen. I choose to believe that you advised King Thrasser, as you say, which in my mind suggests that you are at least a reasonable man. Someone who might put forth the effort necessary to secure a true alliance with the strongest kingdom on Pandrea for the sake of his country."

His jaw tightened, probably fighting the urge to argue against her assertion about Vanris's might, given how proud a people the Sarketi were. He took a deep breath, his jaw gradually relaxing. "I will take your suggestion under consideration, Khesran. If you will all excuse me, I must speak to my soldiers."

The moment he left the room, Jethan and Nevias were at her side.

"What are you doing?" Nevias demanded.

Veyl glanced around, noticing Gregory's saddlebags on the floor by a chair with a change of clothing draped over the back of it for the morning. She gestured toward the door. "We should speak somewhere more suitable."

When they walked out, most of Kyril's unit was there helping move the fallen Sarketi representatives from their rooms. Gannon spotted her and took a step in her direction, but she discouraged him with a shake of her head and followed Jethan and Nevias back to the other wing. Kince and Darro met them in the hall there and joined them in the small meeting room. When Darro shut the door behind them and opened his mouth to speak, Jethan cut him off, his demanding gaze focused on Veyl.

"Would you care to explain what happened back there?"

She glanced around at them, uneasy with their expectant looks, but she was a khesran. If she couldn't handle this, she would never be a good khevarin. "Chief General Harriksen revealed that Sarket's leadership has been supporting the anti-mind-crafter activists in Vanris for a few years now, providing them with supplies, funds, and information. They were also behind the attack on Queen Astrid and Prince Jaysen when he returned to Sarket."

"That miserable pile of stinking sheyvyosk," Kince spat out, following it with a string of other curses, expressing the rage she saw in all their faces. A fury she could fully comprehend.

"You understand that stinking sheyvyosk is a redundancy, right?" Darro asked. "Stinking, stinky smegma is—"

"Got it," Kince snapped. "And I stand by those bastards deserving the extra foulness."

Darro arched a brow at his tehnaak as though to ask if he had finished. When Kince nodded, he said, "If this is true, there is no way we can back Thrasser's claim to the throne."

"We should—"

"I don't think we have to," Veyl said, speaking over Jethan. She gave him an apologetic look, though she still didn't allow him a chance to say his part. "The chief general claims that he advised Thrasser against those actions and that he has the knowledge to help us dismantle the supply chains they established. He expressed a willingness to work with us to do so in such a way that we can hopefully avoid setting off a civil war in Vanris."

"You think we should support Thrasser because his chief general is slightly less of a calloch than he is?" Kince gave her a cross look that held a string of yet unspoken curses behind it. "I understand Jaysen betrayed us, but what Thrasser—"

"You don't know half of what Jaysen has done." Veyl didn't hold in the swell of pent-up fury and heartache, and Kince retreated a few abrupt steps. He wasn't the only one. The others shifted back from her as well, though they weren't the targets of her outpouring. She drew a deep breath and reached out to Seyn, welcoming the wave dancer's calm assurance to help her rein in her emotions. "What I am trying to say is that I think we should encourage the chief general to go before my parents and present his case. Not because we intend to support Thrasser, but because it is possible that we might find in Gregory Harriksen an alternative candidate for the Sarketi throne."

A weighty silence filled the room. The four individuals, whom she had known all her life staring at her as if she had told them the sun was green.

It was Jethan who finally spoke, though his words weren't what she expected. "You really did Charm the guards, didn't you?"

They stayed there a while longer, mostly questioning Veyl about her unprecedented new abilities that appeared to share traits with both the Charmer and Evoker mind-crafting disciplines, as well as her connection to the wave dancers and Kyril. None of which she could offer much insight into. After that, they had her recount her conversations with Gregory at the memorial tower and later in his room, picking apart every detail.

Eventually, the chief general arrived to inform them he had sent out two riders to Andaro to report the attack and two more to gather reinforcements from the nearest watchtowers along with wagons for transporting the dead home. After a brief discussion, he stated he would retire for the night and meet with them regarding next steps in the morning. It took little effort to convince him to move into an empty room in the Vanrian wing with a few Sarketi guards for extra security, in case the Eydarith or any other assassin who might have gotten away opted to come back to finish the job.

Once Gregory left them, Jethan suggested trying to get some sleep in what remained of the night. Veyl agreed, though it didn't escape her notice that the others lingered after she left, nor that Nevias returned to their shared room an hour later, as Veyl lay staring at the ceiling with Seyn stretched out next to her. She feigned sleep, not ready to hear what they might have discussed in her absence, and genuine sleep found her while she was waiting for Nevias to settle into her bed.

Morning came too early again with a firm knock on the door.

The dhomen answered it, trudging over with drooping eyelids that Veyl could commiserate with.

"Dhomvalen Arhk is here," Kince announced at the door.

That snapped Veyl awake. She dreaded her grandfather learning of her entanglement with Kyril, but the prospect of seeing him excited her all the same. Seyn hopped off the bed, bright and alert in a way Veyl wished she could be, but two nights of not enough sleep weren't conducive to it. Still, she hastily cleaned up and dressed for the day, hurrying out with the hope of at least having a chance of influencing the message her grandfather received from the others.

When she rushed out on Nevias's heels, Arhk was striding into the building with Darro alongside him and his trio of elite guards following, the three ahnvaris all wearing their signature black and dark metal armor that matched his. Even with his advancing age and the healing burn scars, he maintained a powerful presence that drove people out of his path with no more than a glance. He was one of the most feared men in Vanris, and she wanted nothing more than to run up and throw her arms around him. She resisted the urge, given the setting.

His gaze flickered to her as Jethan emerged from his room and fell into step alongside him. Arhk beckoned her with a curl of his fingers while he exchanged a few words with the men on either side of him. Then Gregory came out of the room he had used for the night, and Arhk's group halted, allowing the dhomvalen to take a step forward alone and offer a respectful nod to the sole surviving representative from Sarket.

"Chief General Harriksen, I understand your company suffered considerable losses last night. We received a missive from the crown prince that made it clear he was aware of this meeting, hence my arrival, but it appears my warning comes too late. I am pleased to see at least one of you survived. You have my condolences and those of the khevarin and khemron for your losses."

The stiffness in Gregory's bearing was enough to tell her he was struggling with anger and sorrow, even without the new insight she had into his emotional state. "Thank you, Dhomvalen Arhk. I wish you had arrived sooner, but at least Khesran Veyl helped to save one life." His gaze flickered to her as she approached.

"Is that so?" Arhk arched a brow at her.

"I would certainly be among the dead now if she and her wave dancer had not been there." He offered Veyl a nod of greeting, which she reciprocated, before he turned back to Arhk. "There is much I would like to discuss with you, if you are willing, Dhomvalen, and I would be interested in learning more about this missive you received."

Arhk's discerning gaze picked at Veyl's guarded expression, and she got the faintest hint of curiosity from him. "I would like an opportunity to speak with Vanris's delegates alone first. We will gather in the central meeting hall in half an hour, if that is acceptable, Chief General."

Gregory offered a partial bow. "Until then, Dhomvalen."

Arhk glanced over his shoulder at his Speaker. After a second, the man nodded and strode away. Whatever had passed between in that silent exchange excluded everyone else, not that doing so appeared to give Arhk even a moment's pause, but she noticed a slight tightening around Gregory's eyes. Then the dhomvalen glanced expectantly at Jethan, who took the hint and led the group down the hall toward the smaller meeting room. Darro moved over to let Veyl walk beside her grandfather, and Nevias fell in with them next to Jethan. As soon as they were secure in the private space, Arhk faced them.

"A great deal seems to have happened in a brief time. Tell me exactly what occurred last night, including the details of the chief general's revelation that you hinted at." His gaze settled on Darro. "Someone had also best enlighten me on these complications you mentioned with Khesran Veyl."

Veyl's gut turned at that, but there was little point in fighting it. The truth would come out, but she would be here to speak in her own defense. Not that her actions were especially defensible. At least not those involving Kyril.

They recounted everything in the order requested, beginning with the events that unfolded during the night, which inevitably led to the subject of her unexpected new abilities and connection to the wave dancers and Kyril. Those revelations ignited a spark of interest in him, though she sensed it was more of an analytical curiosity than an emotional reaction.

"Is that all?" he asked when they finished.

Kince's snort said he thought that was plenty.

"Not entirely." Jethan glanced in her direction, not quite looking at her.

"We have no time for evasiveness?" Arhk snapped, a hint of impatience in his sharp regard that the healing burn scars made more unsettling somehow.

"Khesran Veyl has been…" Nevias paused, her scowl telling Veyl how much she resented being put in the position of revealing this to him. And yet, Veyl got a flicker of anticipation from most of them. Perhaps they hoped that, by putting this burden on the dhomvalen's shoulders, they could be free of it. "She has been intimate with Ahninveth Kyril."

"I see." His gaze settled on her, infuriatingly unreadable. "Is this true?"

She forced herself to stand tall before him. "It is."

"Careless of you." His remark furrowed brows
around the room, but a knock on the door kept them
from questioning it. "Come in, Ahninveth."

They all looked as taken aback as she was when Kyril
and Ceris entered the room in the company of Arhk's
Speaker, though she doubted any of the others shared
her carefully concealed delight at seeing him.

Arhk met the Thaelian Feral's eyes as the Speaker
shut the door. "You have been intimate with my granddaughter?"

For a heartbeat, she could see the flicker of alarm
in Kyril's eyes, but he straightened and stood tall as she
had when confronted with the same question, the reaction forcing her to fight back a fond smile. "I have,
Dhomvalen."

"I assume you understand the myriad ways in which
Khesran Veyl was an inappropriate choice of companions?"

Kyril nodded, though she didn't think he looked at
all sorry. A little defiant, if anything.

"Then I can trust that you two, having acknowledged your mistakes, are capable of working together in
your unit without another such incident?"

"We removed Veyl from the ahninveth's unit," Jethan
said.

Arhk scowled at the Charmer. "And I am reinstating
her, effective immediately. Crown Prince Jaysen is aware
of this meeting, and he has made his displeasure quite
plain. People are dead. A little impropriety is not worth
risking her life, especially given that she only recently
escaped him. For now, she will continue to travel with
the unit she is familiar with. Changes to that assignment
can wait until we are all safely back in Etrion."

A little impropriety?

His choice of words earned more than one set of raised brows again.

"Of course, Dhomvalen." Jethan inclined his head, a hint of flush in his cheeks.

"Now, I would like to speak with the khesran alone. We will join you in the meeting hall momentarily."

Veyl dared a glance at Kyril when he turned to leave with the others. Did he also notice that Arhk had not pressed for an answer to his question about them working together without another such incident? He met her eyes, powerful affection and desire crashing over her with that brief glance. How was she supposed to disregard that potent emotion when it reflected her feelings for him?

When they were alone, she faced her grandfather, and he held out his arms in invitation. Veyl walked into his embrace, relief bringing a wave of exhaustion as she leaned against him, finding solace in the welcome of his arms folding around her.

"Are you not angry with me?" If he was, would the lack of remorse in her voice make him more so?

"No. Although I am disappointed in you for not using better judgment."

That answer brought a brief jolt of surprise until a nagging suspicion rose in her. "You already knew, didn't you?"

"You know what I am, Veyl."

She nestled in closer. "An indecently powerful Frightener."

He chuckled. "Yes. I saw him in your fears the day you arrived back in Vanris and broke the Sarketi crew that attacked your ship. You were afraid he might be dead because of what you had asked him to do. When you learned he was alive, that changed. You became terrified that we would find out about the two of you.

More than that, you feared what would happen to him if we did." He drew back, sliding his fingers under her chin to make her look up at him. "Now you must face that fear."

"If you knew all this, why didn't you ever say anything? Why allow me to keep that secret?"

"Because I wanted to give you the opportunity to sort out your own mess."

She still didn't fully understand. Perhaps she should be grateful. If he had said something before this, they would have surely put Kyril to death for it. Although she wasn't entirely confident they would spare him now. Tears stung her eyes. How weary she was of that fear. "I can't let them hurt him. I need to..." she trailed off when he shook his head.

"That can wait. Right now, I would like to understand these powers that are manifesting in you. They sound unrelated to your broken Frightener ability."

"I think they are something else. I can feel people's emotions. At first, I had to meet someone's eyes to sense anything, but now it seems to be growing stronger. When I wanted a few minutes alone last night, I was able to influence the guards the way a Charmer would. I also have a constant awareness of Seyn and Ceris all the time now. And Kyril too." She lowered her gaze. "That is becoming stronger as well. It may have something to do with the wave dancers. I'm not sure what else it could be."

He let go and stepped back from her, that distant, analytical curiosity still the clearest emotion she could get from him. "Is there anything else you have noticed? Anything at all?"

"I..." She didn't want to share more with him, but it might be relevant. "When Kyril and I were..." She made a joining gesture with her hands, abruptly dropping them to her sides as she realized what she was doing, her cheeks blazing hot. "When we were… intimate, he shared my memories of…"

The faintest hint of an amused smirk tugged at Arhk's lips. "Continue."

"He was able to experience our first time together as I remembered it. An encounter Jaysen's Evoker had stripped away from him."

His brows pinched, his gaze turning inward. "Fascinating. There are elements of some different mind-crafter abilities, but this is like nothing I have ever heard of. What of the Eydarith wave-touched and Qwilki Seh'hali aspects? Two geographically unconnected cultures treating you as special. Do you believe there could be anything more to that?"

Veyl rubbed her arms as a chill moved through her. "It's nothing more than religious conceit, like Havaad or the Tempest. They say Kyril is also a child of the ocean and wave-touched…" She trailed off when his brows crept up a fraction.

"And both of you bonded with intelligent, oceanic creatures. You shared memories without speaking and called him to you through your connection to him when you were in danger last night. Quite obviously there is nothing to it." He breathed a soft laugh as if his own sarcasm amused him. "You should consider that, before our people came to Pandrea, the natives here would have deemed it foolish fancy if someone told them about mind-crafting." He turned and walked to the door, stopping with his hand on the handle to look back at her. "Come, we have a meeting to attend. I would like to see how effective this ability of yours can be in a political setting."

"Finding uses for your aberrant granddaughter already?" With a resigned sigh, she followed him. "I suppose that shouldn't surprise me."

"My extraordinary granddaughter." He placed

a hand on her shoulder and leaned in closer as they walked out, whispering, "Never squander an advantage, Khesran."

Veyl didn't need any ability to feel the discomfort coming from Gregory when they entered the meeting room. The man could not have foreseen that he would end up representing Sarket by himself before one of the most feared mind-crafters in Vanris. His uneasy gaze fixed on Arhk for an instant, then settled on her, his distress lessening a fraction with the change in focus. She had earned his gratitude during the night, and apparently some level of trust.

The representative from Delaphine was already there with Nevias, Darro, and Kince. Jethan entered after them along with Kyril and the representative from Fallend. As the others took seats, leaving the center two open for Arhk and Veyl, she stopped, still standing behind her chair, and considered the man across from them.

"There are smaller meeting rooms if you would be more comfortable, Chief General."

A faint tension rippled through those who had already sat in anticipation of a potential change in location.

Gregory met her eyes, a glimmer of gratitude in his regard, but he pulled out his chair. "Thank you, Khesran Veyl. I appreciate your consideration, but perhaps it is better that those lost in the night have their presence preserved here in memory." He gestured to the empty chairs on either side of him.

"Perhaps it is." She sank into her seat, and the rest of the table settled in.

"Chief General Harriksen," Arhk began, a ripple of pressure sweeping through the room that sparked alarm in Gregory and many of those on their side too, though the dhomvalen's tone remained calm and level as he spoke, "do you have any concept of how much damage

Sarket has done to Vanris by supporting the internal strife in our country? Do you comprehend how significant a breach this is of the oath of fealty King Thrasser signed his name to?"

The muscles in Gregory's jaw jumped as he clenched his teeth, a hint of remorse coming off him, though Veyl couldn't discern whether he regretted what Sarket had done or merely regretted telling her about it. "I do, Dhomvalen."

"Last night, you told Khesran Veyl you would work with us to dismantle this supply chain you have created. Do you stand by that statement?"

He drew a deep breath and let it out. "I do."

Arhk leaned forward a fraction. "You must realize we cannot support the king regent's claim to the throne after learning of this."

Gregory's face reddened, a tremor of anger in his voice when he spoke. "So, you would support the man whose allies attacked your people in Thaelis and who tried to force a political marriage with Khesran Veyl?"

Arhk smiled, though the expression lacked warmth. "No."

Panic spiked in the man sitting across from them. He pushed all the way back in his chair, as if trying to put distance between them. Despite his visible alarm, Veyl received another, more subtle emotion from him. A wary curiosity. She offered the barest hint of a nod when Arhk discreetly glanced her way.

"What are you trying to get at, Dhomvalen?" Gregory demanded, his hands gripping the arms of the chair, looking ready to push himself up and leave if he disliked the answer.

"I am saying it would please us to consider putting forth a third candidate for the throne, should there be someone willing to work with us to create a true alliance between Sarket and Vanris."

Gregory's hands tightened, and he lifted a fraction. His eyes met hers, and she did her best to convey a sense of calm. A heartbeat later, he settled back into the chair. "What would become of Wilkin should you choose to move forward with this scenario?"

Arhk folded his hands before him. Veyl still received almost no emotion from him. He was calm and focused. A shrewd strategist who would give nothing away without getting something in return. A man who had grown up in a world of Evokers and Charmers and perfected the art of keeping things hidden. "Given the king regent's crimes, there must be punishment. I imagine there would be room to negotiate the severity of that punishment."

Gregory met the dhomvalen's eyes and held that engagement this time. A feat few seemed able to manage, knowing the man had sent companies of more than a hundred soldiers fleeing in terror without lifting a finger, sometimes permanently scarring their minds with his Frightener ability. "What was in this missive the crown prince sent to Vanris?"

A hint of darkness showed at the edges of Arhk's eyes, his lip curling in a slight sneer. "Crown Prince Jaysen informed us he was disappointed to see Vanris, his childhood home for so many years, turning against him to court a man who has no right to hold on to Sarket's throne. He also extended an invitation for all interested parties to meet and discuss the situation should we care to do so openly. Nothing in the missive offered clarity regarding how he learned of this gathering, only that he deemed it appropriate to send a few representatives of his own to express his displeasure at being excluded. Given the threat in his words, we thought it wise to try heading off an incident. We did not expect him to lash out this swiftly or violently."

Veyl's stomach turned. How could the boy she had held so dear have grown into this loathsome man? One who had arranged an attack against the Vanrian people who helped raise him and ordered the cold-blooded murder of his enemies in their sleep? A man willing to kidnap his own tehnaak and…

A shudder moved through her with the memory of his hands on her body, his lips crushing hers. Suddenly, she could feel the cool edge of his blade pressing against her neck that night in Vanris when she lay sedated in her bed, helpless to fight him. Her breath caught, her chest constricting with remembered fear as his fingers touched her thigh, sliding up the hem of her sleeping gown. What might he have done to her if he had been further along in his descent to madness that night?

Seyn pushed her nose up under Veyl's arm, eliciting a startled gasp from her as that contact broke through the hold those nightmarish memories had taken.

Arhk looked at her, concern furrowing his brow. "Are you well, Khesran?"

Everyone focused on her, and the need to flee their curious gazes sent her pulse racing. "I am sorry. I must step out for a moment. Please excuse me."

She didn't wait for her grandfather's response before standing up and hurrying from the room with as much composure as she could manage. Ceris and Kyril lurked at the edges of her awareness, but she couldn't bring herself to let their offered support in. She wanted to run and hide somewhere far from everyone and everything. How could her tehnaak have done that to her? Fury burned away the tears that stung her eyes. When she turned down the hall her shared room was in, Gannon came storming through the doors at the far end, Ahrin and Iyvalin racing after him.

"Gannon, you're being unreasonable. I'm sure she's fine, she…" Ahrin trailed off when he spotted Veyl.

"Clearly, she isn't fine." Gannon broke into a jog.

Veyl continued toward them, suddenly needing the

rough, crushing hug he pulled her into. She let him hold her, not returning the embrace, but simply leaning against him and squeezing her eyes shut as if that could somehow keep out the memories. How could she let Jaysen's actions still haunt her with such intensity?

"Your heart's pounding," Gannon said softly. "Are you all right?"

"I don't know. I want to fight, and scream, and..." She drew a shuddering breath and whispered. "This resentment burns me up inside. I wish I could be free of it."

He squeezed her a little tighter and murmured, "I know. We'll find a way to make it better. I promise."

hat happened?" Iyvalin asked tentatively, coming up beside them. Concern pinched her delicate brows.

Ahrin hung back, waiting for Kitria, who hurried inside after them.

Veyl stood in Gannon's protective embrace a little longer, not meeting Iyvalin's eyes, though the other woman attempted to meet hers. All she wanted right then was for everything to make sense for once, but it only got more confusing by the moment.

With a sigh, she pulled away from Gannon and glanced up and down the hall to be sure they didn't have company. Then she looked up at him. "You came looking for me? Why?"

Iyvalin answered for him. "We were talking in the barracks, and he hopped to his feet suddenly and rushed out, insisting you needed him. We told him he was behaving irrationally, but it appears as if we were the ones who erred."

Veyl reached out and took the other woman's hand, giving Gannon a curious look. "How did you know?"

"I felt... It was like..." His brows pinched, a hint of moisture rising in his eyes.

Lorek. She could see the powerful sorrow he carried for his lost tehnaak, but she could feel it even more intensely now as he struggled briefly for control. Her strange abilities might explain away what she was receiving from him, but they weren't tehnaak, so he shouldn't be able to sense her in that way.

Veyl took his hand too. "Let's find a quiet place to talk." She should return to the meeting, but Arhk would smooth over her departure. He had a talent for handling people when he needed to, though he might have a few sharp words for her about it later.

"We can't use the barracks." Kitria took Ahrin's hand as he spoke, and Veyl couldn't help noticing the pleasure that lit his eyes. "I don't know what happened between you and Tassa, but anytime someone mentions your name, she looks like she could bite through steel."

No one had told them yet. Lacking a better option, she led the group to the room she shared with Nevias. She and Iyvalin sat on the bed with Seyn between them as Gannon and Ahrin carried over the bench from the foot of Nevias's bed for the rest of them to sit on.

When they had settled, Veyl placed a hand on Seyn's shoulder and looked around at them, her gaze coming to rest on Ahrin, welcomed by the bright flare of happiness that came from him with Kitria's nearness. "Tassa snuck in here the night before last, planning to invite herself into Kyril's bed. When she saw me leaving his room, she ducked through the nearest door to avoid my seeing her. Unfortunately, that was the room Jethan was sleeping in."

"Why were you in Kyril's room?" Iyvalin asked.

Kitria snorted a laugh. "You're jesting, right?"

Iyvalin blushed. "Ah. That again."

"Ah, indeed," Gannon remarked with a slight edge of bitterness, then his eyes widened. "Oh, shit."

Veyl met his eyes. "Exactly. Jethan learned the truth. Now they all know. That's why they haven't allowed me to return to the unit, although my grandfather overruled that decision."

Ahrin grimaced. "Even the dhomvalen knows?"

Veyl nodded. "Oddly, he was the least upset of all of them." Her focus remained on Gannon, noting the curiosity in his eyes that looked ready to spawn a question.

"But that isn't what had you so distraught earlier," he stated with unnerving certainty.

She swallowed, averting her eyes. "No. They were talking about Jaysen in the meeting, and I remembered some of my recent... encounters with him. The memories were vivid enough that it felt like I was there again. I don't understand why my mind can't break free of him. It's over. He's not here. We escaped."

Iyvalin put a hand on Veyl's arm. "Because someone you cherished, a person you trusted implicitly, betrayed and tormented you. That would traumatize anyone. Give yourself time."

"Iyvy's right, Veyl." Ahrin's smile held an abundance of kindness that flowed around her like an embrace. "And he's still involved in all our lives right now, regardless of how much we would rather he not be. It's hard to move on while being constantly reminded of him and what he's become. Be patient with yourself." His gaze flickered from her to his brother and back. "What I want to understand is how Gannon knew something was wrong."

Veyl met Gannon's eyes. "You don't think..."

He negated her unspoken words with a vigorous shake of his head. "How could it be that? It's not as if we've visited a Bondmaker, and we haven't been around Niske recently for her to have created a tehnaak bond between us."

"Would it upset you if the kanodrak had bonded you two somehow?" Iyvalin asked, a genuine curiosity in her voice.

Gannon stared down at his hands in his lap. "I don't know." No one spoke for several seconds, then his head snapped up, and he looked at her. "Not that I have an issue with you, Veyl."

She forced a smile, trying to hide the ache in her chest. "You only just lost Lorek. I think it's understandable for you to be hesitant about the idea of a new tehnaak this soon. Besides," she added, managing a teasing wink, "given my history with such bonds, I wouldn't want to be my tehnaak either."

Gannon reached for her, and she put her hand out to meet his, feeling a surge of warmth through her as they clasped. "Anyone would be lucky to have you as their tehnaak."

The ache in her chest spread.

Kitria pulled her hand away from Ahrin. "This is all lovely, but what about my brother? What will happen to him now that they know about the two of you?"

"Kit." Ahrin's pacifying tone only earned him a warning scowl from her.

"No, Ahrin, she's right to be angry. This is an extremely dangerous situation for Kyril. Far more so than it is for me. Shielding him from the fallout won't be easy."

Kitria leaned forward. "But you will fight to protect him?"

Veyl met those silver eyes that reminded her so much of her mother's. Not the most comforting association right then. "With everything I am."

"And we will do whatever we can to help," Gannon stated, turning an expectant gaze on his brother.

"Of course we will," Ahrin agreed, though he looked as surprised by Gannon's vehement declaration as Veyl was.

"Thank you." Kitria took Ahrin's hand again, giving him a grateful smile. The look she gave Veyl made it clear she held her accountable for the situation her brother was in now, even if he had been a more-than-willing participant in their folly.

They stayed in the room a while longer, and Veyl told them about the strange abilities she had been experiencing. Kitria was quiet throughout most of the conversation. Perhaps she simply worried about her brother, but Veyl had the impression she was deliberately not saying something based on her uncomfortable fidgeting when they speculated as to the cause and meaning of these recent developments.

As morning crept toward noon, they wandered outside to let Seyn stretch her legs and allow themselves to do the same. They avoided the Vanrian barracks, choosing not to risk a confrontation with Tassa.

The Sarketi soldiers were moving around near their barracks, busily preparing for departure. By noon, a light breeze had come up, making small eddies of red dust dance around the memorial tower and grounds. The meeting had disbanded, and Gregory was nearly ready to leave with the remains of the Sarketi company, along with some reinforcements and a pair of wagons brought in by the men he sent out during the night. He was speaking with those two when Veyl spotted an opportunity to approach him. She watched, waiting until the representatives from Vanris had their attention elsewhere before excusing herself from her companions and walking up behind the chief general and his two soldiers, who were supervising the loading of bodies onto the wagons.

"The two of you have gotten little chance to rest," Gregory was saying. "If you need sleep before we depart, I can arrange for some time."

His words made her like him more. Suggesting him to the others as a candidate for the Sarketi throne had felt rushed, but hearing his concern for the well-being of his men helped chase away some of the uncertainty that had crept in since.

"Thank you, Chief General, but we would both prefer to get on the road home."

As the taller of the two soldiers was speaking, the other nodded his agreement, then he glanced to the side and took a half-step back, distrust in his eyes and in the emotions that flowed from him.

"Chief General, the…" he trailed off as if rethinking whatever he was about to say.

Gregory turned to follow the direction of his gaze and spotted her. The bruising under his eyes was even more apparent in the daylight, making him look older and weary. There was an open welcome in his expression when he met her eyes. No matter how he might feel about the other Vanrians there, it appeared she truly had earned his trust. "Khesran Veyl." He glanced at the two men. "If you would continue to supervise this process, I would like to speak with the khesran a moment."

The taller man bowed his head, but the other narrowed his eyes at her. "Are you certain that's safe, sir?"

Gregory snorted. "Had the khesran wanted me dead, I don't imagine she would have bothered saving my life last night. Carry on." He held a hand out, gesturing away from his men as he turned to her. "It is none of my business, Khesran," he said as they strolled to an open spot away from others, "but you appeared distressed when you left the meeting earlier. Is everything all right?"

"I apologize for leaving so abruptly. It is upsetting for me to see how much Prince Jaysen has changed and to consider that this might all lead to the imprisonment or death of someone who was a dear childhood friend."

"I imagine it is." There was compassion in his regard, but also an underlying anger that she suspected was for Jaysen. "Wilkin and the others might have considered what their poor treatment of the boy upon his return could turn him into."

Then he knew about those things, though his phrasing, if she could trust it, also distanced him from that cruelty. "It must also be difficult for you to consider what all of this could mean for King Thrasser." She infused concern into her tone, though she harbored even less sympathy for Thrasser than Gregory appeared to for Jaysen.

"It is. I do not know that I would call Wilkin a friend to me, but he was a dear one to my father and was influential in my rise to this position. While I have not always agreed with his decisions, I have remained loyal to my country and proud of my service. I am sure you can understand why I might be reluctant to throw that all away."

"If the ultimate outcome is one that is beneficial to your country and its people, it seems to me you could have even greater pride in that accomplishment."

A wry smirk curled his lips. "You are a clever young woman, Khesran. I suspect you will only become more formidable with time."

"Thank you. It is gratifying to hear you say so." She allowed herself a demure smile. "Might I ask what you intend to do now?"

He searched her eyes, indecision clear in the sudden stiffness in his bearing. "I mean to do as I told the other representatives and report back to the king regarding what happened here."

"Will you tell him everything?"

He looked away, though she could still feel the unease in him. "That depends on him and how willing he is to work with Vanris. The crown prince's return has stirred unrest and turned many people against King Thrasser. Not only civilians, but soldiers as well. And Jaysen has mind-crafters of his own now. We would be fools not to seek Vanris's support, but we were wrong to ask for it while secretly violating our oath of fealty. Your new Thaelian allies brought that issue into the open. I, for one, am grateful that Vanris will still consider working with us at all. Regardless of what comes, I am certain we will meet again soon."

He was silent as he watched them place the last body, that of Kassian Danovan, in the back of one wagon, then faced her once more, shoulders sinking as if a heavy weight had settled upon them. "It looks as though we have all our dead prepared for the solemn journey home. I should get my company on its way. May your travels be uneventful, Khesran."

Though she was tempted to press for him to come to Etrion again, he wanted to report to his king before making his decision regarding their proposal, so she merely offered a respectful nod. "Yours as well, Chief General."

Arhk emerged to see them off, waiting long enough for the Sarketi company to start their journey before turning to the Vanrian officers. "We are moving out within the hour. See that your units are ready."

Veyl glanced meaningfully toward Kyril, then looked back at her grandfather in question.

Arhk answered with a curt nod before going to talk with Nevias.

A spark of anticipation lit within her as she hurried inside to grab her few belongings and headed out to the barracks where she might finally get to speak to the Thaelian Feral. She hoped he would go along with making her accountable for initiating their romantic entanglement to secure a better outcome for him. And it wouldn't be untrue. The first move had been hers when she nearly kissed him on his ship. In Thaelis and in Vanris, she had sought him out when they slept together. Even here, she had been the one who requested to speak to him in private in his room. According to stories of her parents' courtship, her mother had been the one to pursue her father despite their relationship being forbidden by the former khevarin. If she could make them see the parallels in their circumstances, maybe they would be more lenient.

The hopeful spark vanished when she arrived to find Kince and Darro at the barracks helping Kyril get the unit ready for departure, as if he needed their assistance. They seemed determined to thwart her in a similar fashion for the entire journey home. If Kince and Darro weren't with Kyril, Nevias or Jethan conveniently showed up to keep Veyl company. The only exception came when Arhk called upon them both to question them regarding Veyl's abilities and the connection between them, but that didn't provide them with a chance to talk to each other.

She had one comfort in that, even when she couldn't be with him, Kyril's presence within her was constant now, just as Seyn's was, and Ceris's to a lesser degree. Peculiarly, she had an awareness of Gannon much of the time now too, though the new link to him didn't feel the same as the one she had with Kyril. At least no one intervened if she rode with him, so she spent her time with the twins, Iyvalin, and Kitria when she could, trying not to bemoan her inability to speak to Kyril alone.

They arrived in the black city of Etrion in the early evening, dusty and tired at the end of their second full day of travel. The towering walls she typically associated with the joy of being home closed around them like a cage. Arhk dismissed everyone except for her and Kyril to give them a chance to clean up before the formal council was called together. Jethan ignored the dismissal, continuing to walk with them as Arhk sent a few attendants in search of her parents to bid them come to one of the smaller meeting chambers.

Veyl's insides writhed like a mass of coiling serpents, twisting in on themselves. This seemed an inopportune time to be sick, but maybe the distraction would give them a brief reprieve. What would her parents say when they learned what she had done? What would they do?

A wave of affection flowed over her that carried with it Kyril's distinct determination and strength. Somehow, that only made her feel worse, knowing she was at least partly to blame for whatever punishment awaited him. She could sense his concern, but he kept it admirably under control. A heartbeat later, a cool surge of comfort and support from the wave dancers hit her. She didn't dare look at Kyril given the level of scrutiny they were currently under, but she let her affection flow to him unchecked as she settled a hand on Seyn's shoulders.

When they were almost to the room, a smaller one often used for interrogating prisoners, Arhk waved a group of four guards over to join them along with another attendant. He said nothing to the woman, but his attention moved to his Speaker. The Speaker's focus turned to the attendant, who nodded and hurried off on whatever secret errand the dhomvalen had passed along. The guards moved ahead to open the room for them, then followed them inside. Arhk turned to the four as soon as the door shut.

"Please escort Ahninveth Kyril to the next room and keep him there until we call for him."

"Dhomvalen." Veyl stepped forward, ready to argue, but Kyril walked obligingly past her with Ceris and the guards, heading for the door at the back of the room to one side of a currently empty fireplace.

"This might be the ideal time to try being cooperative," Jethan suggested, placing himself between her and the departing group.

Veyl said nothing, waiting in frustrated silence for her parents to arrive. When her father entered the room a few minutes later, a flush of alarm swept through her. He had blood on the chest and one sleeve of his jacket, distress apparent in his expression and the turmoil of emotions she got from him for a few heartbeats before the sensation disappeared. That sudden withdrawal confused her until she recalled that his kanodrak, Niskenya, could block out mind-crafters, and while Veyl wasn't sure that was what she was now, the beast's protections apparently still worked against her abilities.

"What's happened, Father?"

He met her eyes, a weariness and heartache in his that frightened her. "Tavin was shot on his way back from the enclosures a short time ago. Based on the information we've extracted so far, the assailant was an anti-mind-crafter insurgent trying to prevent another mind-crafter from being in line for the throne should something happen to you."

Her breath caught. "No."

"Is he alive?" Arhk asked.

"He is, and there is a decent chance he will survive, though the healers are still working on him. Velara's with him now."

Jethan stepped up beside her father and pulled him into a hug. "I'm so sorry, tehnaak," he murmured when Kasiel relented to the show of affection and support for a second.

"This could complicate matters," Arhk commented in a low voice next to her.

She bit back on the urge to yell at him for bringing politics into such a moment because, like it or not, it was all about politics. This would make forging an alliance with the chief general even more difficult. Sarket's meddling had helped enable this. She yearned to run and check on her little brother, but she knew better than to believe Arhk would allow this to delay dealing with the other problems they needed to address.

Proving her right, the dhomvalen took a step closer to the two. "I am sorry to put more burdens upon you at such a time, Kasiel, but there are matters we must discuss."

Jethan stepped back, though he gave Arhk an irritated look as he did so.

Her father nodded. "Tell me, did Prince Jaysen retaliate against our meeting with Thrasser's representatives?"

"He did, but that can wait a moment. There are some complications you should be made aware of before the full council meets."

Her father's brows pinched, and he shifted back a fraction, as if wary of what lay ahead. Then his gaze moved to her. She wished she could legitimately take insult from the dread in his expression, but he was right to suspect this involved her, so she couldn't muster the refreshing anger that might drown out her misery.

"Tell me."

"There are two things." Arhk spoke quickly when Jethan opened his mouth to answer, maintaining control of the conversation in his usual way. "First, your daughter is manifesting new powers that are not quite like any single mind-crafter ability I know of, and this seems to come along with a strengthening connection of some kind to the wave dancers and to Ahninveth Kyril. She has also been engaging in intimate activities with the ahninveth."

At first, her father's brow furrowed with curiosity and concern. By the end, he had somehow gotten taller, and a storm cloud had fallen over him. "Exactly how intimate?"

Arhk pulled something from a pocket and tossed it to Kasiel. Veyl's stomach clenched as her father caught the vial of contraceptive elixir she had brought along. He looked at what he held in his hand, then his narrowing eyes focused on her. Holding it up between his thumb and forefinger, he took a step toward her. Next to him, Irith cowered, his bonded companion's anger with her distressing the cliff cat. Seyn pressed closer to Veyl, a soft growl rising in her throat.

"You planned this?"

Veyl stood her ground. She hadn't truly expected to sleep with Kyril, though she had brought the elixir hoping an opportunity arose. This presented a clear path toward making it clear Kyril had not forced her into anything. "I hoped to be alone with him, yes."

"It was not the first time," Arhk added unhelpfully.

Veyl resented him for how casually he dropped the accusation. Throughout her life, her grandfather had stood by her in her worst moments in a way he had not done for anyone, not even his son. That he had already known about their entanglement and said nothing until someone else discovered the truth made it more of a betrayal. That he would also choose to abandon her now, when so much was at stake, was hard to stomach.

"You lied to me," Kasiel stated, taking a few steps closer. "You lied to both of us."

"Father, I—"

He turned away from her. "Where is he?"

"He's..." Jethan paused when someone knocked at the main door.

"Enter," Arhk called, ignoring her father's negating head shake.

The woman who came through the door had the milky white eyes of a Bondmaker, and she looked as surprised as everyone else when Gannon charged in behind her. He strode swiftly to Veyl, casting a glower around the room as he did so.

When he met her eyes, his distress crashed into her. "Is something wrong?"

"Explain this interruption, Inren Gannon," her father demanded.

"If I may, Khemron..." When their attention turned to the Bondmaker, she faced Veyl and Gannon, her brows rising as she considered them. "It appears this young man is your daughter's tehnaak, though there is something unusual about the connection. It's uncommonly robust for a fledgling bond and bears some of the same energy as her bond with the wave dancer."

Everyone was staring at the two of them now, more so at her than him. Whatever was going on, it was unfortunately quite clear that she was at the heart of it.

Her father closed his eyes and took a deep breath, the toll all of this was taking making him look much older at that moment. Enough so that Veyl suffered a twinge of guilt for having added to his troubles. He opened his eyes, focusing on the Bondmaker. "Could the wave dancer have done this?"

"I'm not certain. Like most bonds, it has equal weight on both sides, but the thread that completes it, the part that resembles her bond to the wave dancer, appears to originate from Khesran Veyl."

Gannon's intense gaze pinned the Bondmaker. "Are you saying Veyl finished the bond herself? She made us tehnaak?"

"It shouldn't be possible, but it appears so."

Gannon turned on Veyl, his face twisted with a rage that drove her back a few steps, providing Seyn space to move protectively in between them. "You didn't even ask," he shouted before storming from the room and slamming the door behind him.

"Gannon." His name fell from her lips, little more than a heartbroken whisper.

Why did such strange things keep happening to her? Nothing with her ever worked like it was supposed to. First her unconventional tehnaak bond with Jaysen, then her dangerously powerful Frightener ability, and now this chaos, whatever it was, changing her and her relationships with the people she cared about. Would nothing in her life ever be normal again?

They all stared at the door for a moment, silenced by the weight of Gannon's outrage, except for Arhk, who eyed Veyl like a fascinating puzzle he could not wait to solve. She shifted her feet, his interest drawing forth the feeling that she belonged among her own people even less now than she had when her Frightener ability refused to be controlled. An abomination.

"That's not all," the Bondmaker ventured, her tone picking up a wary hesitancy now.

Arhk nodded encouragement, eager for another piece of the puzzle. "Please continue."

"I don't know who or what is in that back room, but there are two threads extending in that direction. One similar to that connecting her to her wave dancer, though less intense. The other, while it carries some of that same energy, is far stronger and appears much like a..." she paused, clasping her hands as she glanced uneasily at Kasiel.

"Like a what?" her father pressed.

"It looks much like a tehanyehn, a love bond."

Kasiel's jaw muscles jumped when he clenched his teeth. Veyl could see his chest rise and fall a few times in quick succession, as if he were trying to hold in a potent anger. Irith sank to the ground next to him, laying his head on the floor between his broad paws, his bright blue eyes shifting to Veyl as though seeking reassurance.

"That is enough for now, but I require your silence regarding this matter."

The Bondmaker bowed. "Yes, Khemron."

"Thank you. You are free to go."

As she left the room, his gaze snapped back to Veyl. "Ahnvaris Yserra is outside the door. She will escort you to take Seyn to the enclosure. From there, you are to return to your rooms and stay there until we call on you."

Veyl lifted her chin. "I will not."

A wild light lit her father's eyes, and he tipped his head down slightly, looking suddenly much like a predator poised to attack, the furious energy coming off him alarming enough that Seyn and Irith both moved between them. "Your brother may be dying as we waste time discussing your poor judgment and inability to control yourself. I'm not in the mood to indulge impudence."

She refused to believe Tavin was going to die. He couldn't. "Then let me check on him with you. Send Ahninveth Kyril to his rooms in the palace and leave him there under guard until tempers have cooled, and we can address this rationally. Please."

"That is not how this is going to go." He turned to Arhk. "Strip Kyril of his rank and send him to the deeps. I'll take care of my daughter."

"I won't..." She started to object, but as her father faced her again, she caught a subtle head shake from Arhk over his shoulder. Could she trust her grandfather to have her best interests at heart? What about Kyril's? How could she allow them to lock him away in miserable isolation? She could try pointing out that Arhk had been aware of her forbidden activities with the Thaelian Feral long before this and had therefore been complicit in their continuation, but it wouldn't matter. It was Arhk. Somehow, he would suffer no repercussions for his actions, as always.

"Come with me." Her father gestured firmly toward the door.

"What about Ceris?"

"I will ensure he goes in the enclosure with Seyn," Arhk offered.

Somehow, those words hammered home the hopelessness of the situation. There was no talking her way out of this. She closed her eyes for a second, swallowing against the sting of defeat. For now, she would have to accept her father's judgment and try to come up with a plan for undoing some of the damage she had done. She dreaded the idea of being parted from Kyril and the wave dancers, but ultimately, they couldn't fully separate her from the three now that the bonds had formed. Not unless they severed them, and she refused to believe her own parents would be that cruel.

Would they allow her to speak with Kitria and the others?

She had hoped that by saying he would take care of his daughter, her father meant he would walk her to the enclosure himself, giving her a chance to appeal to him, but that wasn't the case. Once outside the door, he put her in the care of Yserra and two additional guards, as if he genuinely believed she might fight them. As if she would be that much of a fool.

"Please let me see Tavin."

He wouldn't look at her. That hurt far worse than any angry words he could have cast at her. "The healers are with him. I'll send an attendant to update you when we know more." He strode swiftly off down the hall, abandoning her with her keepers.

Veyl went with them, reluctantly leaving Seyn in a sectioned off area of the cliff cat habitat. Knowing the wave dancer would have Ceris for company soon made it a little easier to walk away, despite the beast's sorrowful whining. Dark was falling by the time her father's Evoker and the two palace guards escorted her back to her room. Along the way, she saw Kyril and Ceris amidst four guards walking to the enclosure they had just left. The thought of him locked in a dark cell in the deeps made her chest hurt. Like her father, he never looked her way, and the connection between them, while still present, had a dormant feel to it the way her tehnaak bond with Jaysen had after he returned to Sarket when they were younger. Was Kyril upset with her? Was that what this was? If so, he was far from the only one.

The two guards remained outside her door once she was in her rooms. She retreated to the bedroom and sat on her bed, pulling her knees in and leaning back against the headboard. She hated that the first thing that came to mind sitting there was how she and Jaysen used to visit one another by climbing through each other's windows when they were young. How often had they sat on this very bed, talking late into the night? He had ruined those memories when he woke her with a knife at her throat. Countless treasured moments shattered like glass upon the unforgiving reality of a cruelty she hadn't known he possessed.

An attendant delivered a meal to her sitting room at one point, but she didn't bother to investigate. In the distance, she could hear the occasional loud roaring of a kanodrak. It wasn't uncommon for them to announce their presence to the city that way now and then, but this was more frequent than usual. A few of the beasts were upset about something.

She had focused her full attention on the sounds, counting the seconds between roars to distract from her troubled contemplations, when a knock at her window made her jump. Heart pounding, she turned to see Gannon perched on the sill. He looked irritated enough, with his brows pulled sharply down in the center, that she considered leaving him out there, but he had gone to some trouble to reach her, and she needed to talk to him.

She unlatched and opened the window, offering him a hand as he climbed in that he spurned, nearly falling into a chair by the bed in his effort to avoid accepting her aid. "What are you doing here, Gannon?"

"We asked Dailan to check in at the healer's building after we heard about Tavin. You might like to know that they think he'll pull through."

"Thank you." She drew a deep breath, allowing a moment of relief to wash over her. "What's going on with the kanodraks?"

"Oh, that. Feyd did some asking around about it. Apparently, the one Kyril started working with is making a fuss since they carted him off to the deeps. Niskenya joined in, so your father is trying to deal with it. With that keeping him occupied, it seemed a safe time to drop in."

Veyl managed a faint smile at that. Her father held Niskenya's opinion on matters in the highest regard. If the kanodrak believed the other beast had a valid reason to complain about their treatment of Kyril, he would take that into consideration when deciding how to handle the ahninveth's punishment going forward.

"Anyhow, Avris said Merrin heard from Yserra that you were confined to your rooms. We figured you might need a report."

Veyl breathed a soft laugh. Her father's tehsheyn loved him, but they looked out for his children in ways she suspected he didn't always appreciate. "I'm glad you came, and not just for the update about Tavin. I'm not sure if I can make things better between us, but I want to apologize—"

"You don't have to. Ahrin and Iyvalin talked sense into me, like they usually do. I know you didn't do this on purpose…" He trailed off, giving her a shrewd look. "You didn't, did you?"

"No. I would never do that to you, even if I knew how to. I don't understand any of this any better than you do."

He nodded as if he had expected as much and put an arm around her shoulders. "We'll figure it out. I suppose I should consider it a compliment that you chose me, even if it wasn't on purpose." He managed a strained smile.

"If you want the Bondmaker to reverse it, I'm certain they would be willing." Oddly, offering that option brought forth a surge of apprehension. She wasn't sure if she would have ever chosen to take Gannon as her tehnaak before, but now that he was, she dreaded losing that new bond more than she would have expected.

"Why don't we take a little time to think it over first?"

The door to the sitting room opened, and they both froze, staring like startled rabbits as her mother walked in. Velara's typically meticulous hair, the same blood red as Veyl's, was in slight disarray, with several strands pulled loose from her braids, and her eyes, rimmed in red, widened a fraction when she saw them. Her gaze shifted to the open window and back to them.

"Gannon, what are you doing here? Veyl is not to have any company right now."

"She's my tehnaak," he answered, tightening the arm that rested around her shoulders. "You won't keep me from her."

Her mother brought her hands up and rubbed her brow and temples as if trying to chase away a headache. "I understand that development is new and unexpected, but this has not been a good day."

"How is Tavin?" Veyl asked, finding she appreciated the support of that steady arm around her shoulders.

"He lost a lot of blood. They were able to stop the bleeding and repair most of the damage, but he is still in a precarious state." She brushed away a tear that slipped free. "If he makes it through the night, his odds of surviving increase significantly."

Veyl's stomach clenched. "Can I see him?"

"We've postponed the council until morning, though I believe your father is planning to speak with the dhomvalen regarding the meeting in Crimsondale after he resolves the kanodrak problem. I will take you to see your brother, but there are a few things we need to discuss first." Her expectant gaze settled on Gannon.

"Right. I get it. This part's between you two." He faced Veyl and mustered a smile for her. "If you need me, just panic and I'll apparently come running."

Veyl nodded, blinking back tears of gratitude. "Thank you."

Gannon turned toward the window.

"Please use the actual door this time." Her mother gestured toward the proper exit. "The healers have enough to do."

Gannon smirked and headed for the door, bowing slightly on his way past. "Yes, Khevarin."

When they were alone, her mother led her out into the sitting room and poured them each a generous serving of wine from the carafe someone had delivered. She gestured to the table. "You should eat something."

Though her appetite still hadn't returned, Veyl pulled the cover off the tray and prepared a modest selection of food. Her mother availed herself of some of the fruit on one side of the tray, waiting until Veyl had settled into a chair to speak.

"Am I to understand that you had intercourse with Kyril in Crimsondale?"

Veyl nearly choked on the bite of roast she had taken, washing it down with a large swallow of wine.

"Must you say it that way?"

"How else would you like me to say it?"

"It just sounds so…" Her cheeks were growing uncomfortably warm, so she pushed past that part. "Yes. I invited it. I wanted to be with him."

"And it wasn't the first time?" Her mother's expression remained carefully neutral as she took a delicate bite of evalis fruit.

"No, but it was always my choice."

Velara's brows lifted a fraction at that. "And when was the first time?"

How desperately she wanted to crawl under her bed and stay there for a few years. "In Thaelis, before he returned here to warn you about Thrasser." It seemed prudent to remind her mother that he had come to Vanris to try reversing a little of the harm his people had caused.

She got up and walked to one window, looking out on the mind-crafter academy in the darkness. "I want to be angry with you. I am very angry and deeply disappointed that you lied to us, but somehow it is a little harder to hold onto that knowing when this started."

Veyl set down her plate. "What do you mean?"

When her mother turned to look at her, there were tears in her eyes. "They had you trapped there, not knowing if you would ever come home, and from what you and the others said, they had separated you out because of your bloodline and your ability. I imagine it would have been hard to resist any comfort you could find in the arms of someone willing to hold you."

She could leave it at that. Her mother was offering her at least partial forgiveness because of the circumstances, but that did nothing to absolve Kyril. She got up and went to take her mother's hands, meeting her eyes. "That was part of it. I won't pretend it wasn't. But I need you to understand that it wasn't only that. I love him, Mother."

She shook her head, unwelcome pity in her eyes. "You can't."

"We belong together."

She pulled her hands away, and her expression hardened, edging toward anger. "He is not Vanrian, and he has a long way to go to absolve himself of the crimes he committed against our people, if that is even possible. There's no future in which he is an appropriate match for the heir to the Vanrian throne."

"Then I don't want the throne."

A sudden spike of anger and frustration struck Veyl like a mental slap. "You will stop this now. You stand to lose a lot more than you realize if you continue to fight this."

Veyl stepped back from her. "In what way?"

"When your father and I spoke, he suggested the idea of sending Kitria and both wave dancers back to Thaelis on the next ship."

Panic gripped her. "You can't send Seyn…" Veyl trailed off as it sank in what had been missing from her mother's words. "And what about Kyril?"

Her mother drew a deep breath that struck Veyl as an ill portent. "You are not the only one who lied to us regarding the extent of this relationship, but for him, those lies come on top of the offenses he already committed against our people, you included, as I'm sure you can recall. You must understand we can no longer afford to let him get away with what he has done. He needs to face some punishment for his crimes."

Veyl took a few steps back from her, the room closing in around her. "But…" Emotions surged high, choking off her words. Clinging to a thread of rational thought, she reached out for a lifeline, finding Seyn and Ceris ready to respond with a confident wave of reassurance and calm. She drew a tremulous breath. "We can't punish him. We need a representative for Thaelis here, and he remains one of our strongest assets for gaining the support of the rest of his people. The Qwilki have great respect for him."

Her mother's eyes narrowed, her lips pressing into a fine line. After a second, she shook her head. "Those are fair points, and we are considering them, but this is not a table for negotiation. Why don't we check on your brother? We can revisit these things once we have had a decent night's sleep. There will be many meetings and difficult conversations tomorrow. Rest would benefit all of us."

Veyl desperately wanted to point out that Kyril would not likely get much sleep in the deeps, but she could see in her mother's icy gaze that she wouldn't be sympathetic to that subject right now. There would be no more discussion of it tonight, as far as she was concerned. She might put her new abilities to work to influence some people and try freeing him now, but that path could also lead to more problems, especially if she tried it and failed. No, for now, he would have to suffer a night in the deeps, and she would take up the fight again tomorrow.

•

They went to a large private room on the second floor of the healer's building. Four guards stood watch in the hall, a sobering reminder of the fact that this had been a deliberate attempt to kill Tavin. His lighter red hair, like their father's, lay spread upon the pillow around a youthful face that looked much paler than normal. Veyl sat beside him, watching him sleep, while her mother spoke in a hushed voice with a healer.

"How is he?"

"His pulse is still weak. We are keeping a constant watch over him for any signs of distress, but he seems stable for the time being." The healer was looking at Veyl as he answered. When she reached for her brother's hand, hesitating before making contact, he said, "It's all right. The touch of someone who loves him might help."

Veyl slipped her hand into his and squeezed it gently, the lack of response bringing tears to her eyes. His skin was cool, his breathing shallow. A thick, complex bandage wrapped the right side of his chest just inside his shoulder. "How bad is it?"

The healer walked around to stand across from her, near his head, while her mother came up behind her and set a hand on her shoulder.

"There was severe soft tissue injury, and the bolt fractured his shoulder blade. Because of the angle and location of entry, it slid along the outer edge of his ribs, cracking one, but it missed his organs. We managed to repair the damage quickly enough to keep him from bleeding out, though the loss of blood was still substantial. He is extremely lucky to be alive. The sedative will wear off in a few hours. We'll give him more to ensure he rests through the night without too much pain."

Veyl reached up with her free hand and touched the back of her fingers to his cheek, wishing he felt warmer and more alive. "Tav, I'm here. I have a lot to tell you about, so you need to hurry and heal."

Her mother squeezed her shoulder. "There's not much we can do now. We should get some sleep."

"That sounds like a sensible plan, Khevarin," the healer said, his tone gentle and warm with understanding. "We will notify you if there are any changes."

Veyl didn't look up from her brother's slack features. "Can I stay with him just for a little while?"

"You are welcome to remain if you wish," the healer said.

Her mother leaned down and kissed her on the

head. "Don't stay up too late."

"I won't."

Veyl meant those words when she said them, but a few hours later, she was dozing in the chair at Tavin's bedside when his soft groan jarred her awake. Taking his hand in both of hers, she leaned close.

"Tav?"

He blinked his eyes open, a pained grimace twisting his mouth. "Veyl?" Her name whispered weakly between his lips.

"Yes. I'm here."

Tears spilled down his cheeks, and he squeezed his eyes shut. "The bastard killed Loth."

His companion hound. Nausea bubbled up in her stomach. "Oh, Tav, they didn't tell me that. I'm so sorry."

He pulled his hand away, reaching toward his injury as sobs shook him. The hand stopped short of the wound, balling into a fist. Veyl caught hold of it again, bringing it to her chest and placing her other hand on his good shoulder. She nodded at the healer, who had gotten up from his chair in the corner and stood watching them now. When he carried the painkilling sedative over, she helped calm Tavin and elevate him enough for him to drink it. She could tell when it started taking effect a short time later from the way the lines slowly faded from his brow and he struggled to keep his eyes open.

"I wish..." His voice was quiet enough that she had to lean in again to hear it. "I wish I could be as strong as you."

Veyl forced a soft laugh. "What are you talking about? You are at least as strong as I am."

He started shaking his head, then winced and stilled. "Even after everything you've been through, you're determined to be... part of the fight." He was losing the battle to keep his eyes open now. "I never..."

"Never what, Tav?"

He forced his eyes open, but they drifted shut again. "I have never wanted to fight. I'm… afraid."

Veyl watched him until his breathing evened out. Once it had, she leaned down and kissed his forehead before whispering, "I will fight for you."

"Veyl?"

She got up and turned to face the slender young woman now standing behind her. Tavin's tehnaak, Ellaris. "I'm sorry, Ell, he was just awake, but he was in too much pain. The healer sedated him."

Ellaris gazed down at him with gentle affection in her smile and worry in her eyes. "It's all right. At least he woke up."

Veyl took her shoulder and pulled her into an embrace. They stood that way for a time, the healer quietly checking Tavin's pulse and breathing and looking over the bandages for signs of fresh bleeding. When they parted, Veyl and Ellaris both brushed the moisture from their cheeks and glanced down at their wounded loved one.

"I got a little sleep. I can watch over him now."

Veyl nodded. "I'll rest better knowing he's in your care."

When she left the room, Veyl found an additional five guards waiting in the hall.

One of them stepped forward. "Khesran Veyl, the khevarin sent us to escort you back to the palace."

Given the situation, she should have expected something of the sort, and she was too tired to want to do anything other than return to her room and sleep.

"Thank you." She fell into step in their midst and let them set the pace, only noticing now that the kanodraks had quieted.

orning arrived with an early call to join the council. Veyl dressed and hurried out, hoping her parents might have time to update her on Tavin's condition before the meeting was underway. When she entered the room, several of the usual attendees were already settling in. Most looked tired and troubled, the smiles of greeting they offered one another never reaching their eyes.

Her father glanced from her to Arhk, his brows rising slightly in question.

Arhk merely smiled and inclined his head to his son before turning to her and extending a hand to offer her the seat next to him.

Veyl hurried to accept the suggested chair. She knew them both well enough to figure out from their unspoken exchange that her invitation to this meeting was Arhk's doing and had not come from her parents. Anytime they tried to exclude her from a conversation, it meant she was going to come up among the subjects for discussion. While she knew it came from a place of wanting to protect her, she appreciated that her grandfather often included her despite their wishes. She was beginning to suspect it wasn't always solely for her benefit, though.

Veyl leaned closer to Arhk. "What's..." she trailed

off when her mother walked in. Her parents' eyes met across the room, and Velara nodded. Judging from the way her father's posture relaxed a little, it seemed safe to assume her mother had come back from checking on Tavin and found him at least no worse off than he had been last night.

"A new missive arrived from Prince Jaysen this morning." Arhk said in a low voice, answering her unfinished question.

Would the mere mention of his name ever stop making her stomach twist into knots?

Her mother touched her shoulder on the way past, the simple gesture of affection and recognition easing a little of her distress. When she sank into her chair alongside Kasiel, however, she gave Arhk a chastising look that brought a smirk to his lips.

Veyl leaned close to him again and whispered, "I don't remember you flaunting your position before my parents this brazenly when I was a child."

Arhk glanced at her. "You were merely too young and distractible to notice our unspoken disagreements. It pleases me to have you be a part of them now."

Veyl gave a soft snort. "I think you mean a pawn in them."

Arhk smiled at that, and she noted his lack of argument.

When everyone settled, her mother addressed them. "We received another missive from the crown prince of Sarket this morning. He has requested a meeting in Balarus to discuss a more peaceful solution to our current discord. The message suggested that, among other things, he has information about King Thrasser that we might wish to be aware of before we considered an alliance with him." Her gaze shifted to Dhomen Nevias, then swung over to Veyl and Arhk. "Based on what we learned at the negotiation with Thrasser's representatives in Crimsondale, we suspect he is referring to the king regent's support of the anti-mind-crafter movement here in Vanris. We have spoken with Dhomvalen Arhk regarding these matters, but this morning we would like to hear from the rest of you who were present at those proceedings. Since you are in attendance, Khesran Veyl, perhaps you would care to start this session off by telling us what happened with Chief General Harriksen the night of the attack."

That was information only she could provide. They must have intended to call her in for this meeting at some point, though apparently not right away, begging the question of what they had planned to discuss in her absence. "I will do so, but first I would like to know what else was in the missive." She held her mother's gaze, hoping to convey that she would insist upon it.

Her father leaned over and whispered something to her mother.

For a moment, her mother's lips remained pressed in a stubborn line. Finally, she gave a sharp nod and tapped one finger on the pages of the missive lying before them. "Crown Prince Jaysen specifically requested your presence in Balarus." She looked down at those pages, her lips pressing into a tight line as she found what she was looking for on them. "Per his words, he humbly asked that you attend, stating, 'I had lost my way, but I recognize now that my recent treatment of Khesran Veyl was reprehensible. I would appreciate the opportunity to make amends in person.' He goes on to suggest that the meeting would undoubtedly proceed much more smoothly if we granted this simple request."

"Reprehensible at best." Despite the sharpness of her words, Veyl wished she could believe that madness had released its hold on him, and he had reverted to the boy she once knew and loved. She hastily latched on to her connection with Seyn, recognizing that an emotional response would encourage her parents to decide they had been right in trying to shield her from this part of the missive. "That last bit almost sounds like a veiled threat."

"Yes," Kince agreed. "I imagine he wrote it that way intentionally, attempting to leverage some control over the outcome. He showed us in Crimsondale that he is not above using violence to get his way. We need to tread carefully."

Her father nodded. "Precisely why we have decided that, no matter how we choose to handle this, Khesran Veyl will not be heading to Balarus."

General Lucia was considering Veyl thoughtfully from across the table. "But isn't it possible that we could use her to manipulate the situation to our own advantage?"

Her mother opened her mouth to say something, but her father beat her to it.

"General, you and I have a positive history working together, but if you start looking at our daughter as a means to an end, you will rapidly change that. We have lost her twice already. That is two times too many." When Lucia inclined her head in a show of deference, he turned his attention to others around the table. "We received word from the base north of Deepwater that they have new information regarding a possible center of operations for the anti-mind-crafters. It makes sense to send someone to talk to them and see what we can learn on that front. They have directly attacked the royal family now, which tells us they are growing bolder. None of our mind-crafters are safe."

"The chief general said he could assist us in dismantling the supply chains Sarket helped create." Veyl fought the urge to shrink away when all eyes turned to her again. Did either of her parents ever feel that, or was she poorly suited for this? "Couldn't we make use of that? I got the sense he had a lot more information about their organization and leadership than what he shared in Crimsondale."

For a moment, no one spoke, and unease prickled up her spine like the legs of a large insect. She resisted the urge to try brushing away the sensation, keeping her hands settled on the arms of her chair.

"Now is the time for those of you who were in Crimsondale to share your experiences there," her mother said. "If you would, Khesran, please tell us what occurred the night of the attack, starting with when you went outside and encountered Chief General Harriksen. The Evokers will pay attention to any additional information they can gather from your memories."

Given what had happened with Kyril and with her odd new abilities, the idea of having an Evoker in her mind wasn't that comforting. Although her parents already knew about all of that. Her gaze wandered to a painting of a kanodrak standing on a desert cliff, its rider resting a hand on its shoulder as they stared out toward the setting sun. It made her think of the wave dancers out in the cliff cat enclosure and of Kyril. Was he still locked in the deeps?

Reaching out through the bonds, she received an immediate response from Seyn and Ceris. Kyril, although she could feel their connection, didn't respond to her mental touch along that thread. With a soft sigh, she turned her attention to the night of the attack in Crimsondale and described everything she could remember.

By the time they took a noon break, everyone in the room who had been in Crimsondale had given their accounting of events relating to the negotiations with Thrasser's representatives and Jaysen's attack. Fortunately, those who were aware of them carefully glossed over the subject of her abilities and tactfully avoided her indiscretions with Kyril. She suspected her parents were making a deliberate effort not to let those things become too widely known.

She caught Arhk's arm before he stood up, asking in a hushed voice, "Is Kyril still in the deeps?"

"He is."

Frustration crackled in her chest like evergreen needles in a fire. "Why? What good will come of it?"

"Perhaps you should ask your parents that."

Veyl narrowed her eyes at him and shoved her chair back, hurrying to catch her parents before they could leave the room. The unexpected approval in their expressions when she walked up to them encouraged her to try a different approach than she had with Arhk.

"You did well earlier." Her mother smiled at her, reaching out to brush a lock of hair away from Veyl's eye.

"Thank you, Mother. About Seyn. Can I have her back now?"

Her parents exchanged a brief look, a behavior she always hated, because it immediately made it clear they stood unified against her.

"Veyl," her father began, his tone gentle enough to be discouraging under the circumstances, "we don't yet know if the wave dancers are the ones causing these changes in you. We think it best that you not have contact with them for a while until we can investigate this and make a more informed decision."

"When will that be? After we solve this political chaos. I assume at least one of you will head to Balarus. It would be cruel to leave them locked up until you return. Besides, I'm safer with Seyn than I am without her."

Her mother gave her a discerning look. "Are you?"

Veyl met her father's eyes, then glanced meaningfully at Irith. "Are you safer with or without him?"

"This isn't the same."

"How do you know?" She gave a quick shake of her head and changed the subject before she could give in to the temptation to shout her frustration at them. "Will you bring Kyril into the afternoon discussion to represent Thaelis?"

Her mother's tone picked up a sharp edge. "Regardless of what the council decides, we will not be taking him to Balarus. We all know that would only make the situation with Jaysen more volatile, so there is little reason to involve him in this part of the conversation."

She had a point there. "At least let him out of the deeps. You're hurting him, you're hurting the wave dancers, and you're hurting me."

Her mother's expression hardened. "You might find your argument gains more traction without that last part. It is because of your inappropriate interactions with him that he ended up there in the first place."

Her father set a hand on her mother's shoulder. "We'll move him to a regular cell and allow him daily visitation with Ceris, providing you agree to stay away from him. He will remain under constant guard until we resolve the rest of this chaos."

The scowl her mother gave him was enough to tell Veyl they had not discussed this. "Is that wise? He faces charges that could result in a severe sentence. Giving him access to his greatest weapon under these circumstances may not be the best choice."

It was a step in the right direction. If she could distract her mother, maybe she could keep her from talking him out of it. "Might I be allowed to at least visit Seyn?"

Her mother spoke quickly, perhaps fearing that her father would bend on this too if she gave him the opportunity. "Not yet. Give us some time to consider it."

Veyl wanted to point out that they had plenty of other matters to think about and that one of them might depart soon, but she had gained a little ground.

Now was a strategic moment to show her gratitude for that. "Thank you. Is there time to check on Tavin before we reconvene?"

"Of course." Her mother's expression softened at that. She stepped in and gave Veyl's arm a gentle squeeze as she kissed her cheek. "Take two of the guards with you, please."

"I'm not a mind-crafter," she objected, realizing as she said the words that she shouldn't be arguing this if she wanted to sway them to her side on other topics, "but you're right. Better to be safe." She forced a smile.

"You may not be a target of the group that attacked Tavin," her father said, "but you are solidly in the sights of others who would do you harm."

She didn't have to ask who he was referring to. Jaysen had made it clear he hadn't given up on her. Though if there were truly any sincerity to his words, he had no intention of harming her, at least not in the way the insurgents had harmed Tavin. Still, that wasn't enormously comforting.

Veyl did as asked and called upon a couple of palace guards to accompany her to the healer's building. Tavin was sound asleep when she arrived, deep under the influence of another dose of painkilling sedative. Ellaris was dozing in the chair next to his bed. Not wanting to disturb them, Veyl considered searching for Gannon and the others. It should be easier to do so with the tehnaak bond to guide her, but it would also mean dragging the guards around town with her. Instead, she let them escort her back to the palace and requested a meal sent to her room.

Lost in the frustration of how little control she had over the current situation, she sank into a sitting room chair, leaned her head back, and closed her eyes, hoping to find a solution to her troubles waiting in the quiet darkness.

"Rough morning, Khesran?"

Veyl leapt to her feet and spun to face the bedroom doorway. A woman stood there leaning against the door frame, arms crossed casually before her, with a satisfied smirk quirking up one corner of her mouth. The armor she wore was fitted black and dark blue-gray leather, like what the Eydarith man in Crimsondale had been wearing. That, along with her round ears, warmer skin tone, and the way she had the top part of her thick, dark hair pulled back, told Veyl she was Eydarith as well.

"Who are you? And what are you doing in my rooms?"

"I am Tezaak Amera," she responded with a heavy accent that sounded similar to northern Sarketi, with some slight variances.

As if that explained how she had gotten into Veyl's rooms. The guards would never have allowed someone from Sarket to roam around the palace, even if she appeared unarmed. Especially since her armor provided several places one might hide a slender blade. "Tezaak?"

"It's the Eydarith word for what you would call a tidal wave. It is also the title we give our assassins."

Veyl sucked in a breath and took a step back, bumping into the chair.

Amusement lit the woman's dark eyes. "Do not panic. You are in no danger from me. If you are truly wave-touched, there is no amount for which I would harm you. Wavelord Kronach sent me because he knew I had the skill needed to get close to you and deliver his message."

"You arrived here with Jaysen's messengers?"

She answered with a nod and slow blink that reminded Veyl disconcertingly of a cliff cat.

"Couldn't he have behaved like a normal person for once and sent a written missive?"

Amera grinned. "Someone else might have read it."

It made her distinctly uncomfortable to consider that, whatever the wavelord had to say, he didn't want her parents or anyone else to learn of it. "What is this message?"

A knock at the door startled her. Amera stepped back into the shadows of the bedroom as Veyl called for whoever was there to enter. An attendant came inside with a modest meal that he laid out on the sitting-room table. As he did so, she pondered whether she should use the opportunity to leave with him or somehow make him aware that something was wrong. But then she would never learn what this was about before her parents got involved. Besides, the woman hadn't made any threatening moves yet.

"Can I get you anything else, Khesran?" the attendant asked when he finished.

"No, thank you." She watched him leave with a sense of dreadful apprehension, nearly calling him back at the last minute. Then the door clicked shut, and the assassin stepped out again. Veyl faced her. "Well?"

"Wavelord Kronach invites you to meet with him."

"Where?"

The woman walked to the table and took a wedge of evalis from the platter, eating the juicy black fruit before answering. "In Taro."

Veyl scoffed. "I'm not going to Taro."

"I will ride with you."

She laughed. "That doesn't help. Even if I were willing, the khemron and khevarin would never allow me to put myself back within Jaysen's reach."

Amera shrugged. "Do not ask them. One or both will presumably lead a company to meet with the undead prince in the next few days. He will head to Balarus for that engagement and will not be returning to Taro."

That piqued her interest. "Where is he going after Balarus?"

Amera picked up a few slices of apple and ate them slowly, staring at Veyl, her calm gaze offering no additional information.

Veyl exhaled, trying to let her frustration out. "Tell me everything you know, and I will consider his request."

Amera shook her head, picking up another wedge of evalis. "I have told you what I can. The wavelord has not given me voice to say more."

"I could have you questioned by an Evoker."

"Do you not think he considered that? He gave me enough to entice you. I have his assurance that the information he has could prove valuable to you and your people, but he will only give it to you, Khesran, if you come to Taro. That is all the information I can provide. This could be an opportunity to help your country, but you must handle it discreetly."

"What game is he playing? What does he want from me?"

"If you are truly wave-touched, as he believes, there is no risk. He merely wishes to see if you are worthy of the Tempest's favor. Are you strong enough? Are you bold enough?"

"And what if I am not?"

Amera said nothing, turning her attention to enjoying another bite of Veyl's diminishing meal.

The request was ridiculous. She couldn't run off into the night and travel to Taro without the full support and approval of her parents, the rulers of her country. But what if this could earn them the backing of the Eydarith? If they could steal that powerful fighting force out from under Jaysen, they could also cut off his access to the coast. What if the information Kronach had to share with her was critical to their ending this?

"I cannot sneak off with you alone."

"You may bring a few companions if you feel it is

necessary, Khesran. Merely do not make a large production of it. We must move with speed and discretion." She took one last wedge of evalis, leaving three on the plate, and stepped back from the table. Her dark eyes met Veyl's. "The ocean calls you, Khesran. Will you answer it?"

"Must I answer now?" She couldn't possibly make such a weighty decision in haste.

"Decide your path. Gather your companions if it comforts you to do so. There is a small tavern near the western gate. Have a drink there within the next three nights if you will come. You will not see me, but I will approach you when you leave. If you have not arrived by midnight on the third night, I will carry your refusal to Wavelord Kronach, and you will not get another opportunity to sway him." She bowed her head. "Tempest guide you." With those words, she retreated into the bedroom.

Veyl followed her, watching with a burst of frustration as the woman darted out an open window. She had secured them all. Of that, she was certain.

She strode over to shut it behind the tezaak, picking up a piece of the broken latch from the floor. "Fantastic." She stared at it for several seconds. Was she strong and bold enough? "Am I foolish enough?"

With a heavy sigh, she set the piece on the sill and walked out into the halls to stop the first attendant she spotted.

"Yes, Khesran?" The woman bowed and offered a warm smile.

"Could you send someone to call on my friends Gannon, Iyvalin, and Ahrin, to join me for dinner this evening when the council adjourns? And have a meal for four..." though Ahrin would likely bring Kitria, "for five, sent to my rooms, please."

"It shall be done."

After a long afternoon of occasionally heated discussion, the council determined Dhomvalen Arhk would head west with his elite guards, exchanging the safety of numbers for greater speed, to speak with the officer who had information on the anti-mind-crafters. Veyl's father, as khemron, would lead the company heading south to Balarus to meet with Jaysen. The crown prince had always shown him considerable respect when he lived in Etrion, so they hoped sending him to negotiate with Jaysen would encourage civil discourse. As khevarin, her mother would stay behind and assume full leadership of Vanris while handling any other pressing issues that might arise.

For Veyl, the upside of these decisions and the resulting preparations was that her parents didn't have time to dig more deeply into her relationship with Kyril or her developing abilities. Arhk would depart the morning after next, and her father's contingent would head out by the following afternoon. That meant the council was too busy planning for those missions to waste time on less critical matters. Her mother might still try to corner her on the subjects at some point, but certainly not until after she finished ensuring that Arhk and Kasiel were ready for their critical operations.

At least, that's what Veyl assumed as she left the

meeting room with a small sigh of relief, only to have her mother come hurrying after her, all too eager to prove her wrong.

"Veyl." She placed a hand on her arm to stop her and drew her to one side. "We need to have a conversation about your abilities and the other matter."

She drew a breath and faced her mother. "I know that, but nothing is going to change before Father and Grandfather depart. Would it not be better to focus our energy on ensuring they have everything they need to be successful? Especially Father, considering who he is going to meet with. I'd prefer to devote the next few days to those preparations and supporting Tavin in his recovery." She said a silent apology to her brother for using his injury to delay her own suffering, not that she didn't genuinely want to keep visiting him. "It will calm down some after they're gone. Then we will have time to devote to those conversations."

"I suppose there is a lot going on. Very well. We will dine together after your father and grandfather have departed. Though delaying will not make this any easier."

Veyl nodded, relieved they at least wouldn't be discussing any of that now. Although, despite her mother's words, she hoped a little distance from the incident with Kyril would lessen its impact. "I don't expect it to," she lied. "Is there anything I can do to help with the preparations?" She held her breath, hoping the answer was no, but the implication of an offer would please her mother.

Velara smiled. "I'll let them know you are willing, but I think you should use the time to relax this evening. Just take guards with you if you venture out into the city, all right?"

"I will. I planned to meet up with the twins and Iyvy."

"Hmm. Your new tehnaak." Her mother arched a brow. "Do you two mean to keep the bond?"

Veyl looked away and shrugged. "I know he wasn't ready for it, and I don't know if it's what I want or not. It's not as if we planned it. Less than a year ago, I would never have considered Gannon as my tehnaak, not even if he were available. He has changed, though."

"You both have." Her mother took her hand and gave her a gentle smile. "We can have it undone if the two of you don't feel ready or if you should decide it is simply not the right pairing, but the longer it remains, the more painful it will be if you choose to sever it. You know that far too well. Talk about it between you and do what is best for both of you."

"We will. Thank you." Veyl let her mother kiss her cheek before hurrying off to meet the others.

When she reached her chambers, a message lay on the table inviting her to join them in Kitria's rooms. In a way, that was actually preferable. If her father sent any rodents around to check in on her, he would be more likely to search for her in her rooms. He was busy preparing for his departure, so she didn't expect him to spy, but given that he could control beasts even while fighting, a little extra caution wasn't unreasonable.

Veyl took a few minutes to freshen up. When she opened the door to leave, the very man she had just been thinking of stood there, his hand raised and ready to knock.

"Oh, Father, I..." she trailed off, noticing that he wasn't alone. He had Irith with him, as expected, but he also had Seyn.

The wave dancer leapt forward and reared up on her hind legs, putting one paw on each of Veyl's shoulders, and promptly licked her squarely in the face, her breath smelling oddly of fish and salt. It was disconcerting to discover the lanky beast was several inches taller than her when she stood upright like that. Once she had expressed her pleasure at their reunion, she dropped back to the floor and moved around to stand at Veyl's side, tail wagging.

Kasiel shook his head, a wry smile curving his lips. "I sent for her earlier. I am concerned about the bond and what she might be capable of doing with it, but everything I have seen and what I've sensed from her tells me she will protect you. For now, I consider that what matters most. We will investigate the rest when I'm back."

"I knew you would understand. I feel safer with her at my side, and I know she would never harm me." Veyl wiped at the light deposit of canine saliva the wave dancer had left behind, breathing a laugh, but her next thought banished her humor. "Please be careful out there. I don't trust Jaysen anymore."

His expression darkened. "Neither do I, not after what he did to you and to our fleet in Thaelis. I will not give him another opportunity to harm the people I love."

Veyl stepped in and hugged him. "Your family loves you, too. Remember that. If something were to happen to you, it would devastate us." As much as she wanted to visit her companions and discuss her encounter with the Eydarith assassin, she found herself reluctant to move away from his return embrace. He was heading into a risky situation soon and, though he wasn't aware of it, she might be as well.

He held her for a few seconds longer before disengaging. "Look after your mother and brother for me."

Her throat tightened. She didn't want to lie outright to him. All she could do was nod.

"I'll be back before you have time to miss me." He gave her a confident smile and struck off down the hall with Irith.

Resisting the sudden urge to run after him and beg him not to go to Balarus, she placed a hand on Seyn's shoulder and made herself walk to Kitria's rooms. The four were sitting around a well-laden table when she arrived, the aromas of roasted meat and fresh-baked bread filling the room. Ahrin and Kitria shared the couch, shoulders touching as they split a plate between them. Iyvalin sat leaning forward with her elbows on her knees, long silvery hair brushing the edge of the platter as she pondered the food upon it.

Gannon, reclined in a chair with one ankle crossed on the other leg, abruptly stood when she entered, an immediate alertness in his bearing that saddened her a little. Even though their relationship had developed a new level of connection, he still appeared unable to relax and be himself in her company.

His gaze skimmed over her, lingering for a moment on Seyn. "Are you all right? You look like you just bit into a piece of fruit that turned out to be rotten, but you're considering eating it anyway."

Veyl stared at him for a second. He was also more attuned to her than he had ever been before. As she sat in an empty chair, she said, "An oddly accurate assessment."

He sank back into his seat. "At least they returned Seyn to you."

"Father brought her to me a few minutes ago." She smiled at the wave dancer, getting a wet lick on the arm and a big canine grin in return.

Iyvalin grinned, drizzling savory sauce over half of a plump roll she had piled strips of roast on. A practice she had picked up from Ahrin. "As a fellow Feral, he simply couldn't bear leaving you separated." She nibbled at a chunk of cooked carrot as she sat back with her loaded plate, then nodded to herself, and placed the rest in her mouth.

Veyl shifted in her seat, glancing at Seyn, who reciprocated with her serene gaze. "But I'm not a Feral."

"You're something," Gannon muttered, his attention on his own plate now, though he appeared to be simply poking the food around with his fork.

Ahrin exhaled softly and shook his head at his brother. "Tell us, Veyl. What is this rotten fruit, and do you need help choking it down?"

She picked up a plate and considered the selection of food, trying to keep her tone casual to avoid worrying them. "I had an unexpected visitor in my rooms at lunch today. She—"

"By the Break, you need better locks. Who was it this time?" Gannon demanded.

"If I recall correctly, you were the last unexpected visitor." Iyvalin gave him a chastising look as she filled a mug with mead and passed it to Veyl. "Now let her speak, you calloch."

Ahrin settled back on the couch and slid an arm around Kitria's shoulders. The young woman leaned against him, though she didn't appear as relaxed. With her brother still locked up, that wasn't especially surprising.

Veyl continued. "She introduced herself as Tezaak Amera, sent by—"

"An Eydarith assassin?" Gannon, who had sliced off a bite of pheasant and was bringing it to his lips, stiffened, lowering the morsel toward his plate again. "How did she get into your rooms?"

Iyvalin gave him a sharp look.

He frowned and gestured to Veyl with his loaded fork. "Sorry. Go on."

Veyl stared at him. "How do you know what a tezaak is?"

He shrugged. "I picked it up in Taro."

Accepting him at his word, she began fixing herself a plate and recounted the odd encounter in her room in as much detail as she could recall. By the time she finished, the others had all lost interest in their meals.

Gannon stood and placed a log on the crackling fire that chased away the evening's chill, then turned to face her, leaning back against the black mantle. Veyl met his eyes, surprised by the steely resolve in them. He at least appeared to understand where her thoughts on this lay. Perhaps that shouldn't surprise her.

"Well," Ahrin began, "obviously you're not going with…" He trailed off, glancing from Veyl to Gannon and back. Grimacing like someone had just assigned him cleanup duty in the hound enclosure, he removed his arm from Kitria's shoulder and said, "Not going with her alone, that is." Resignation weighed down his words.

Kitria slid her hand into Ahrin's, pulling it onto her lap as if she meant to hold him back. "This is a bad idea." She met Veyl's eyes, a hint of pleading in her silver ones. "Kronach helped us escape Jaysen, but we both know that wasn't an act of compassion."

Veyl disregarded the comment, something made more challenging by how much Kitria's eyes reminded her of her mother's. "This could be a chance to break a piece of the foundation Jaysen is relying upon. Kronach is a respected wavelord among his people. If I can show him I am strong enough to deserve the Tempest's favor, he could sway the Eydarith to abandon Jaysen. It won't be necessary if my father chooses to support the crown prince, but I don't see that happening."

"Do you honestly think the wavelord could talk his people into allying with Vanris? They are still Sarketi." Iyvalin pointed out.

"He believes I am wave-touched. If we can also convince him that Vanris will honor an alliance with the Eydarith beyond this fight, we might persuade him to rally his people in our favor."

Gannon was nodding, a determined light brightening his hazel eyes. "The Eydarith dominate Sarket's coastal territories. It would effectively cut Jaysen and Thrasser off from the ocean and keep any fighting that breaks out on land where Vanris has the greatest advantage."

"And what will he want in return?" Kitria persisted, firmly pressing the counterpoint. "Use of your mind-crafters? The secret to forging dark metal weapons? Access to the plants and recipes for Vanris's healing salves and sedatives?" She gave Veyl a hard look. "A political marriage?"

An unpleasant taste rose in the back of Veyl's mouth. She swallowed. "We'll figure that part out. We have a few days to prepare and can refine our plan on the journey there."

"I don't see how it matters, Veyl. Your parents will never let you go," Iyvalin said, picking up her plate again and settling back as if she felt that concluded the conversation.

"Who said I was going to ask? In a few days' time, my father and grandfather will both be out of the city. I'll leave a message for my mother, so she knows where I'm heading and why, and not to send anyone after me. This could be the key to outmaneuvering Jaysen and Thrasser both."

Ahrin met his brother's eyes. "It's highly likely our parents will ride out with the khemron as well. They are part of his tehsheyn."

"And mine never pay attention to where I'm at anyhow," Iyvalin added, the faintest edge of bitterness in her tone. "I imagine it will be a few days before they even notice I'm not sleeping at home."

"And my brother?" Kitria pulled away from Ahrin, her tone picking up a sharp edge.

"Kit," he said softly, "they won't sentence him while all of this is going on, and the odds are against our being able to influence his situation right now."

"My parents agreed to let him out of the deeps and

give him visitation with Ceris. It's not much, but it is something. I am supposed to dine with my mother after Father leaves, before I... before *we* head to Taro. I can push her to have him moved to guarded rooms in the palace again, like they did when we were negotiating for Thaelis. There's no guarantee she'll agree, but I can promise to try."

Kitria looked at Ahrin. "And I'm to stay here?"

He folded one leg up onto the couch as he turned to face her, taking both her hands in his. "With Kyril in the position he's in, he may need you here. Besides, if you run off with us without the approval of the khem-ron and khevarin, it could make his situation worse."

"It will anyhow. They'll use Evokers to question me when they learn you're gone. It won't be hard for them to discover that I was aware of your plan to leave ahead of time and didn't speak up."

Ahrin looked at Veyl. "She's right. They know Kit and I have gotten close. They will interrogate her if we disappear."

Veyl took a long drink of the mead and considered them. If she left on her own, all of them would face questioning, but Kitria might get overlooked in favor of the twins and Iyvalin, who she had a more substantial history with. And yet, that wasn't an option she found overly appealing. Heading to Taro with only Tezaak Amera and Seyn would be beyond foolish. Even the Eydarith assassin would expect her to be more cautious than that. Kronach would stack this game against her. Proving herself strong enough to deserve the Tempest's favor would only take her so far if she didn't show that she was smart enough too.

"Do you want to come with us?" she asked.

Kitria gave Ahrin a long look, and he kept a neutral expression before her searching gaze, giving no clue whether he wanted her with him on the road to Taro or safe in Etrion. Perhaps even he didn't know which option he favored. She exhaled sharply and faced Veyl. "I would prefer that, but I worry about my brother."

"If you all choose to come with me, we should be prepared to depart after my father and grandfather have left the city. We'll leave that night as discreetly as possible. I will see if I can do anything to improve Kyril's situation when I dine with my mother."

"I am going with you," Gannon stated. "With our unit disbanded, we can sit around and wait for them to reassign us, or we can act on our own. I'm tired of waiting, and I think this is our chance to influence the outcome of this mess." He turned to eating with fresh enthusiasm, as if the very notion had revitalized him.

Veyl yearned to share her tehnaak's confidence. She did her best to mimic what she felt from him when she looked over the other three. "We don't all have to go. I certainly won't blame any of you for sitting this one out."

Ahrin took a long drink of mead before answering, bolstering his courage. "I'm not letting you and my brother travel to Taro alone."

"And I'm not getting left behind." Iyvalin's hard gaze said she had decided her role, no matter what anyone else had to say. "I'd rather risk my life by your side than sit here and worry about you."

Kitria looked faintly ill, but she twined her fingers with Ahrin's and nodded. "I'm coming."

It was the resolve and affection flowing from her friends that helped Veyl find a confident smile for them. "Thank you."

●

Over the next two days, there were several meetings to decide how they planned to handle talks with Jaysen.

Most of the rest of the time, Veyl split her efforts between helping her father out with his preparations and secretly gathering supplies for her own group's departure. Given her mother's request to dine with her, they would have to leave the city late on that third night if they didn't want the khevarin catching on to her absence too quickly. That would make it more difficult, as they would need horses. Claiming they were heading out on a scouting run would be a more plausible excuse in the daytime, since most of the guards knew her parents didn't want her riding routes at night without at least one of her father's tehsheyn along. She had a few alternative ideas and her new abilities to fall back on, assuming she could control them as needed. It had worked on the guards in Crimsondale, but she hadn't dared to try again since. If it worked as well here, they might slip outside the walls without too much difficulty.

The other trick would be to evade the palace guards now that they were on high alert because of the attack on Tavin, but she had done that plenty of times through-out her childhood without the help of any abilities. It shouldn't be too challenging, since her parents had left the responsibility of taking protection with her outside the palace in her hands. A trust they might be more re-luctant to give when this was over, but she would worry about that another time.

By the third evening, both Arhk and her father had departed on their separate missions. Veyl was ready to head out as well, with necessities packed and passed to Kitria, who would deliver them to the other three along with her own. While Veyl dined with her mother, they would take care of feeding themselves and get the sup-plies and mounts arranged in a stable near the gate.

With both of them worried about Tavin and the rest of their family, the evening meal started subdued. Still, Veyl made a point of eating well, not because she was overly hungry, but because she knew it was the last robust meal she might have for a time, and it seemed wasteful not to appreciate it. Once she finished eating, she sat staring into her wine, lost in contemplation of the coming journey, when she realized her mother was watching her over the rim of her own glass and undoubtedly had been for some time.

"Sorry, Mother, I was merely thinking."

"About?"

About the danger and uncertainty lying ahead, and how it turned her stomach to know she was deceiving the people she loved yet again. What might happen to Kyril in their absence? Would her parents ever trust her again if she went through with this? But if meeting with Kronach carried the slightest chance of saving Vanrian lives, how could she not go?

She met her mother's eyes, confused by the hopeful expectation in them, made sharper by the faint underlying emotions reaching Veyl. What was she hoping for? What was it she wanted to hear?

A soft whine rose from Seyn, where she lay next to Veyl's chair.

"I'm going to Taro," she blurted, panic squeezing her chest the instant the words were out.

Her mother's expression barely changed, but a sense of approval came from her. "I had little doubt you would try, but I am very happy that you chose to admit it."

That was a very different reaction from what she had expected. "I… don't understand."

"I had Merrin watching over the messengers Jaysen sent before she departed with your father. She has useful skills for such a task from her time serving as an assassin. The Eydarith woman appeared to make the two men uncomfortable, as if they did not quite trust her. Merrin spotted her breaking away from them the other day and disappearing into the city, so she followed her. After the woman paid you a visit, she apprehended her and brought her here to speak with Evoker Setera."

There was a powerful sinking sensation in Veyl's chest. They wouldn't be going on any clandestine journeys to aid Vanris now. Would the others be relieved, or would they share her disappointment? "So, you know everything?"

"I suspect I know little more than you do. Tezaak Amera is telling the truth when she says that Wavelord Kronach gave her very few details regarding his intentions for meeting with you or this knowledge he claims to have about Jaysen. He seems to have planned for the possibility that she could face capture and questioning."

"Does Father know, too?"

A soft sigh escaped her mother's lips. "No. I did not wish to risk distracting him from his task. He will need his wits about him."

Veyl swirled her wine, trying to maintain an appearance of casual interest, as if this development hadn't upended her plans and left her feeling like a fool. "So, what do we do now?"

"I assume you assembled at least a partial team for this venture?" Her mother arched a brow at her.

"The twins, Iyvalin, and Kitria were preparing to accompany me," Veyl confessed, hoping it wouldn't get them all into trouble.

Her mother's nod said none of this surprised her. "I want Omren Feyd and Inren Dailan to join you as well. Healers are always useful, and Feyd's Dampener ability could be extremely valuable. Considering the conflict involving Omren Tassa in Crimsondale, she and her tehnaak won't be returning to the unit for this mission."

"Wait." Now that her mother appeared to be supporting her plan, anxiety began twisting her gut into knots in a way it hadn't before, when this was all secret. "You're letting me go?"

"I do not want to. You are my daughter, and I would prefer to keep you safe, but you have shown remarkable resilience in the past months and a keen mind for negotiations. This could be a valuable alliance to make. I imagine you have considered the potential benefits of gaining the support of the Eydarith. At least, I hope that is why you were willing to attempt this subterfuge to meet with them. It seems you are our best chance of swaying them. I have no desire to risk you needlessly, so tell me, do you believe you can win Wavelord Kronach as an ally without making sacrifices none of us would find acceptable?"

Like offering him her hand in trade. Veyl swallowed hard and nodded. "I do."

A wave of sorrowful resignation flowed from her mother, carrying with it a potent pride that made Veyl's throat tighten. "We will try, then, but I will not allow you to embark upon this mission without the best protection I can provide you. To that end, I am assigning three more individuals to your entourage, Khesran. With your father and his tehsheyn gone, I had to consider who would be the most dedicated to your safety." She nodded to a guard standing near the rear door of the dining room.

The guard stepped out, returning a moment later, escorting a man Veyl never expected to see again. She hopped up from the chair and ran over to throw her arms around Jinau's neck in a fierce hug.

"You're alive!"

"Only by the grace of the ocean and your remarkable healers, Seh'hali." He returned the embrace somewhat stiffly as he spoke. "I am sorry I failed in my duty to protect you."

Veyl stepped back from him, looking him over once. "But… the zenyal bond disappeared. I was certain you were dead."

"They severed it intentionally the moment they

attacked. Likely to ease the process of making you zenyal to another. A severed bond is often less resistant to reconnection than one broken by death."

"How did you get—"

"Ahndhomen Jinau showed up unexpectedly this morning," her mother interrupted. Her silver eyes scrutinized the Thaelian Charmer with a dispassionate gaze. "He came to Vanris on a ship bringing some of our people back from Thaelis. The timing of his arrival as you were preparing to depart seemed almost... fated. He and Ahnkreth Kyril with his wave dancer will also accompany you."

A surge of excitement made her mildly dizzy as she glanced toward the back entrance again to see Kyril stepping through the doorway, his expression guarded. Ceris stood beside him, tail wagging tentatively.

How desperately she wanted to run to him as she had to Jinau, but she didn't dare.

Her mother stood and approached her. "This is not permission for any intimate contact between you. In fact, I have tasked Dailan and Feyd with ensuring you don't forget that. And it does not erase what has already happened. I merely want to ensure that the people traveling with you will protect you with their lives, and, regardless of how I feel about the relationships you have formed with them, I believe these two will do so. It has also occurred to me that Wavelord Kronach considered Ahnkreth Kyril to be wave-touched as well. Sending both of you might strengthen your position. Be aware that this is merely a delay of judgment for prior transgressions and misdeeds. How you handle yourselves will have a bearing on the determination of punishment once you return." Her gaze shifted to the two men, settling on Jinau. "Do not fail to protect my daughter again, Ahndhomen."

"Mother!"

Velara's gaze remained on Jinau, her brows rising with expectation.

Jinau bowed. "I will not fail, Khevarin. I am grateful for the opportunity to make amends."

"Nor will I," Kyril added, also offering her a deep bow.

With a firm nod, her mother turned back to her. "Tezaak Amera will meet you outside the western gate. The guards are aware you have my approval to leave the city on a crucial clandestine mission."

Veyl stepped closer to her mother. "Why?"

Placing a hand on Veyl's cheek, she gave her a smile tinged with sorrow. "Because you wish to be part of this fight, and you have earned the right to be. And because I believe you can do this. I am terrified of something happening to you again. I won't pretend that I'm not, but it has become apparent that you are your father's daughter in more than just blood. During the war, he risked everything to protect the people he cared for and this country. Now that we stand on the brink of another war with Sarket, it is clear you will do the same, with or without my permission. I would rather grant it and do what I can to help you than deny it and risk you being hurt because you struck out unprepared." She leaned in and placed a soft kiss on Veyl's forehead. "Thank you for choosing to tell me."

"What would you have done if I hadn't?"

"I would have had you arrested and locked in a cell."

Veyl breathed a little laugh, though her smile faded when her mother's expression didn't soften. "You're serious?"

"Very. You meant to act without the approval of your parents, the rulers of your country. That is not to be taken lightly, particularly in politically sensitive matters. Now, there are a few critical points we must discuss before you leave, and we haven't much time."

She glanced around at them and gestured to the table in invitation. "Shall we?"

After discussing acceptable outcomes for negotiating with Kronach and navigating an emotional goodbye, they left to meet up with the rest of the group. Jinau and the wave dancers walked between Veyl and Kyril, who had yet to speak to her. Veyl lengthened her strides, hoping the confidence in her movement would spread to the rest of her. Leaving this time was understandably more anxiety-inducing after her last two experiences being separated from her family. Something about embarking upon this mission carrying the weight of her mother's expectations on her shoulders also made it harder than when she had committed herself to sneaking away. Although she suspected her return, assuming nothing prevented such, would be less unpleasant this way.

"You can do this, Seh'hali."

Was it wrong of her to resent that those words came from Jinau and not Kyril? Why hadn't Kyril spoken to her yet? For that matter, why hadn't she said anything to him? Why did there have to be a new wall between them when they had only just broken down the last one?

She kept her attention on the path ahead and said nothing. When they walked through the door of the tavern, Kitria sprung up from the table, running over to throw her arms around her brother. She bounced back after a second, claiming one of his hands, and looked from Kyril to Jinau, then to Veyl.

"I can hardly believe you got Kyril freed, but... you also brought Jin back from the dead. How?" she asked as the other three walked up to join them.

Gannon nodded respectfully to both men, though there was a hint of fresh tension in his bearing when he did so, something she might have to discuss with him later. They didn't have time now.

Veyl turned toward the exit. "We can talk about all that on the way. We need to get moving. The rest are waiting."

Iyvalin's brows pinched. "The rest?"

Kyril extracted his hand and put it on his sister's shoulder, turning her toward the door. He held her back for a second, allowing Veyl to take the lead. With a gesture for them all to follow, Veyl stepped past, meeting his eyes for a heartbeat. Those cold silver-blue depths told her nothing. Quelling the urge to call upon her new abilities for answers, she headed out, trusting the others to follow. Out in the street, Gannon fell into step beside her. Iyvalin and Ahrin stayed back with Kitria, who was interrogating Kyril and Jinau about how they had become a part of this.

Kyril's answers were brief and to the point. Not quite curt, but certainly not warm. His recent imprisonment, ending on the condition of his returning to Taro with her, a place filled with awful memories, might not have put him in the best of moods. Did he hold some of that against her? She wouldn't consider him entirely out of line if he did. She had been the one to persist in pursuing their relationship after Jaysen's actions forced them apart. Perhaps he feared she would do so again, despite her mother's warnings, and get him executed by the end of this journey. With how intense the desire to go to him burned within her already, she couldn't confidently claim he would be wrong.

They pulled their mounts out of the stable. Two extra horses waited for Kyril and Jinau, already loaded with supplies for the journey, making it clear her mother had planned on it working out this way. Did that mean she had trusted Veyl to tell the truth?

"Is this going to cause problems?" Gannon asked in a low voice, leaning close to ensure no one else would hear.

"I doubt our escort will like it, but it will be safer."

"I imagine your nights will be warmer too," he muttered.

"Gannon," she hissed under her breath.

They hurried to the gate with their laden horses, and the guards ushered them through without questioning. Outside, Feyd and Dailan waited with their mounts a short distance away from a scowling Amera, whose expression only grew more dour when they arrived.

"There are nine of you?" She did nothing to hide the disapproval in her voice.

"Yes."

"You and I have divergent notions of how to be discreet, but none of this has gone to plan since that silver-haired woman showed up."

Veyl stifled a grin. "Dhomen Merrin used to be an assassin."

"An exceptional one, it seems." There was grudging admiration in Amera's tight-lipped smile. "Let us move."

Amera was thorough. She plotted their course across the Crimson Break with a few alternatives, hoping to avoid drawing attention to their group that was now, admittedly, large enough to make that more challenging. With the khevarin's support, it was not as critical to hide from Vanrian scouts and watchtowers, but they still needed to keep Jaysen and Thrasser from learning of their activities. With that in mind, they held closer to the northern border of the Break heading west, where Sarketi scouts were less likely to be patrolling with the rising tensions between the two countries.

Riding swiftly along in the dark and hiding from watchful eyes took Veyl back to the escape from Taro. It bore other similarities too, in that her relationship with Kyril had somehow regressed again. Her connection to him remained dormant, almost cold. With the importance of the mission, her mind needed to be on preparing herself for negotiations with Kronach, a task the wavelord was certain to make frustrating, but the fresh sense of loss proved a substantial distraction. They needed to talk, but that wouldn't happen while racing through the night on horseback.

They were five hours out from Etrion, with one brief break to rest and water the horses, when Amera turned them down into a slot canyon, winding her way along narrow passages until they reached a place where it widened. She signaled them to stop and swung off her mount within the deep sandstone walls that would hide them from anyone surveying the land above.

"There is a spring near the southwest wall for refreshing your water supplies and the horses. You have three hours to rest before we move on. We will continue toward the coast and take a longer break during the hottest part of the day for the animals. The westernmost Sarketi watchtower is under Kronach's control. We will cross the border there."

Veyl turned her attention to her mount, taking the gelding for a stop at the water before leading him off to one side to remove some tack and give his back a rest. She was about finished with him when she caught Kyril's approach out of the corner of her eye. Not wanting him to see the surge of conflicting hurt and longing that rose in her, she focused intently on smoothing the animal's forelock, putting her back to the Thaelian Feral.

"Veyl." He stopped behind her, close enough that the warmth of his nearness sent a flare of longing through her.

She didn't turn. The dry chill of the desert night pulled in around her, taking over all her senses. She could detect the water from the spring like a spark of revitalizing blue in the arid rust-colored landscape. Swallowing against a sudden constriction in her throat, she asked, "Are you upset with me?"

"How could I be?" His hands slid around her waist at the same moment the connection between them surged back to life, blazing with warmth, love, and a desire so intense that everything else fell away.

Veyl gasped and turned to face him. That bond burned through her like wildfire, and she relented to it, stepping in to slide her hands over his shoulders and meet his lips in a searing kiss. He pulled her closer, his arms enfolding her. Pressing against him, she let herself fall deep into the passion of his embrace.

"Didn't the khevarin ask us to keep an eye on them to prevent exactly what's happening right now?" she heard Dailan asking, a distinct edge of discomfort in his tone.

Amera made a scoffing noise. "Your time would be better spent trying to hold back the tides. They are both wave-touched. You will not keep them apart if the Tempest wants them together."

"Let them be," Gannon snapped, his defense of them coming as something of a surprise.

Still, the brief exchange reminded Veyl that they were far from alone. She drew back from Kyril. "But our bond, how did... I don't understand."

"Ceris helped me suppress it to make it easier for us to navigate the situation while we were being kept apart.

I'm sorry if I hurt you. I hoped it might be less painful this way and remove some of the danger if you had to deal with Evokers."

Evokers. After what Jaysen did to him, she could imagine he'd had more than enough of them. "I didn't realize someone could mute a bond in that way."

A gentle apology softened his smile. "Vanrians don't know everything." He slid one hand along her jaw, brushing his thumb lightly across her cheek. "I truly am sorry if I hurt you."

"I was afraid you were angry with me for getting you thrown in the deeps." An echo of her distress from the last few days brought the sting of tears to her eyes.

"We did that together," he murmured. "We let our passion and our bond lead us to be careless. You can't take all the blame for that."

Closing her eyes, she pressed her cheek into his palm, savoring that touch for a moment. Then she looked up at him again. "Did the wave dancers create our connection?"

"I don't think they did. Initially, I wondered if they might have helped complete the tehanyehn bond between us because we are each bound to one of them, but that wouldn't explain your new tehnaak. We should discuss these matters with Jinau. He knows a great deal about Qwilki lore regarding the children of the ocean and the wave dancers. He might have insight to offer."

"The two are connected though—the wave dancers and the children of the ocean?"

Kyril nodded. "The Qwilki consider my bond with Ceris as part of the proof that I am a child of the ocean. I never took it seriously because, as a Feral, it wasn't particularly surprising that he chose me. After watching the way Seyn has bonded with you, however, I'm questioning my dismissal of it."

Amera stalked past them. "You will regret it if you

do not take the opportunity to rest here."

"She's right," Veyl said softly. "We can't afford to be less than alert if we run into trouble."

"If?" Kyril glanced after the tezaak. "We're returning to Taro with an Eydarith assassin as our escort. I can't imagine not running into trouble, though I fear we are as likely to find it at the end of our journey as we are along the way."

"I'm just glad you're here."

He faced her again. "As am I."

They found a sandy spot and settled in to sleep. Kitria and Iyvalin volunteered to stand watch with Amera, despite the assassin's objection that she could handle it on her own. Kyril stretched out next to Veyl, and she rolled onto her side against him, setting her head on his shoulder. His arm curved around her, his hand coming to rest on her hip. The sky above, visible within the frame of the canyon walls, was clear and bright with countless stars. That beautiful view came along with an icy nip in the air, but with him next to her, she felt warmer, and much less afraid.

Gannon stretched out on the ground behind her. "If you need someone to keep your backside warm, just let me know."

The teasing tone in his voice elicited a soft chuckle from Kyril.

Veyl breathed a laugh. "I'll keep that in mind."

She wasn't alone now. Far from it. This journey she had briefly considered facing by herself had become a group effort. They were here to support her in this endeavor. No matter what came next, she would be stronger for them and because of them.

•

Amera kept them closer to the Vanrian border for much

of the morning after they resumed their journey, turning south when they neared the coast. She gave them a
four-hour rest in the afternoon, when the sun was at its
peak, stopping them along the cliffs of a large plateau
where a vast overhang provided shelter from the sun.
The fast pace they maintained wasn't conducive to an
involved conversation of the sort Veyl wanted to have
with Jinau about Qwilki lore and how it related to her,
Kyril, and the wave dancers. They all had to focus on
riding and watching the horizon for threats.

The two amphibious island canines were out of their
element in the desert. The closer they got to the coast,
with the hint of ocean on the wind, the more animated
Ceris and Seyn became. Veyl started hoping, despite
the need for haste, that their journey might bring them
near enough to the water for the wave dancers to visit
it, if only briefly. Swinging out closer to the ocean also
meant giving a wider berth to Balarus, where her father
and his entourage were to meet with Jaysen within the
next two days. Possibly sooner if they kept as hard a pace
as that Amera had set for Veyl's group.

Arhk would have arrived by now at the coastal base
across the border in Vanris, given that he had the easi-
est roads along a direct route and had been the first of
them to leave Etrion. He also had the smallest group to
manage, with only his three elite guards accompanying
him. Veyl envied him that, though she couldn't imagine
who in this impromptu unit she would have wanted to
leave behind. Dailan and Feyd were the least familiar,
but she couldn't deny the value of having two healers
in the unit, particularly when one was also a Dampener.

On the afternoon of their third day out of Etrion,
Amera stopped them for a break in the ruins of a town
destroyed in the early part of the war. Desert winds had
partially buried what remained under drifts of sand. A
rebuilt wellhouse in the center provided travelers with

a chance to refresh themselves and their mounts. Two of the larger outbuildings were still intact enough to provide shelter from the sun for them and the horses. Spotting an opportunity, Veyl led her horse over beside Jinau's, hoping to get answers to a few of the questions that had nagged at her since she and Kyril spoke.

"Seh'hali," Jinau greeted with a respectful nod. His jaw tightened when his gaze landed briefly upon the light scar on her cheek that she had gotten fleeing Jaysen in Taro. "You have questions."

"Tell me what it means to be a child of the ocean and what the connection is between that and the wave dancers."

He turned his attention to loosening his saddle girth while he spoke. "When our ancestors arrived on the islands, the Qwilki accepted them willingly, in part because the teachings of their faith told of a people who would come from across the ocean to watch over them, like shepherds or guardians. These people would have the power to speak directly to their minds and bring them peace. For obvious reasons, they believed the Thaelians were the ones prophesied, and it is hard to argue otherwise. But it goes beyond that, for their teachings say that among those people there would one day come a child of the ocean. Someone with abilities greater than the others. The ocean's keepers," he paused, looking down at Seyn, "the wave dancers, would come to their aid in times of need."

Veyl glanced at Seyn, remembering the wave dancer who had pulled her out of the ocean the day she saved Nagi from the kel'inuk in Thaelis. "If there is one such person, how can Kyril and I both be children of the ocean?"

Jinau snorted, his gaze moving past the horses to where Kyril was casting periodic glances their way as he cared for his own mount. "This child of the ocean would be born incomplete, missing a part of themselves. They would not realize their full potential until reunited with the one who carried within them that fragment."

A chill moved through Veyl. "This is ridiculous."

"Is it?" He faced her, one hand resting on the shoulder of his horse. "The wave dancers have protected you more than once. Seyn bonded with you. Your Frightener ability was extremely powerful, but now that it is gone, Kyril says you are manifesting abilities similar to those of a variety of mind-crafter disciplines."

Gannon came and quietly took her horse from her, meeting her eyes as though asking if she needed his intervention. When she shook her head, he led the animal to where they were tying the others.

Veyl met Jinau's eyes, disturbed by the conviction in them. "You believe all this?"

"When Seyn broke your Frightener ability to protect you, she may have also begun the process of removing whatever barrier stood in the way of your true potential. You are Seh'hali ne Kunua. Denying it will not change it."

"And the wave-touched? Do you think there is something to that too then?"

He took a step closer. "I know nothing of the lore of the Eydarith, but it makes sense to me that there could be some intersection in their beliefs given that they also look to the ocean for their truth."

The intensity in his tone spoke to how fully he believed in what he was telling her. He might look more Thaelian, but his name and his heart were Qwilki.

Veyl shook her head and turned away. Her gaze caught on Kyril, but she didn't want him at that moment. He was part of this madness. Needing to escape them all, she walked outside the building and found a shady, secluded spot in a partially collapsed house near the edge of the little town. She barely had time to gather her thoughts when she heard footsteps coming up behind her. The bond between them gave her his identity as surely as if she had looked to see who it was. One hand slid around her waist as the other brushed her hair aside, clearing the way for him to kiss her neck. That simple contact ignited every nerve, setting her aflame with desire. She leaned into him, wishing she could give herself over to that fire.

"Seh'hali," he murmured.

The sensation of his lips and warm breath brushing her skin when he whispered was exquisite, but the name itself reminded her why she had wandered off. She pulled away, putting distance between them as she turned to face him.

"I am not this Seh'hali you all want me to be."

The heat in his gaze cooled, a troubled look etching furrows in his brow. "Why do you fight what you are when what you are is extraordinary?"

"Because I don't want to be this," she snapped. Drawing a deep breath, she forced a calmer tone. "I was born a khesran of Vanris, heir to my mother's throne. It wasn't something I wanted, but I grew up understanding it was who I needed to be, and I accepted it. I cannot be both the khesran of Vanris and Seh'hali to the people of Thaelis. It's too much to ask."

He closed the distance, and she considered backing away, knowing he had the power to soothe her even more effectively than Seyn could, but she wanted too much to be near him. His hand slid along her jaw and into her hair, and her defenses crumbled as he leaned down to kiss her. She returned the kiss desperately, voicelessly begging him to take her from all of this. For a few seconds, he obliged, pulling her into a heated embrace. When he drew back a little, his eyes shut and his jaw clenched, perhaps recalling that they had no true privacy here. Then he retreated a step, letting hot, dry air fill in the space between them.

"I will never let them part us again. You won't have to deal with this alone, but you can't spend your energy fighting it. Denying yourself. Think of what you could accomplish, who you could help, if you embraced the full potential of the abilities awakening in you."

She moved away from him. "You can't stop them from parting us any more than you can do anything about my new powers. All you can give me is words, and I have had enough of those for now."

Seyn moved to follow her as she turned from him, and she held a palm up. "No. Stay with Ceris."

The wave dancer's sea-foam eyes gazed up at her, conveying a deep sorrow.

Veyl felt her resolve cracking. "Please."

She hurried away, knowing she would lose the will to do so if she lingered, and found a quiet spot in the shade of the sole remaining wall of a building secured in place by drifts of sand. Settling on the slope, she leaned back against the wall, watching as a small rodent—a sandhopper—darted across the sand, leaving V-shaped tracks in its wake. She was within range now to overhear her companions talking, though not clearly enough to make out their words. Letting her eyes close, she focused on the voices and on the people themselves, on what she felt for them. As she let the rest of the world fall away and homed in on each individual, she started feeling their emotions: fear, resolve, concern, and a surge of intimate desire.

Veyl opened her eyes, cheeks warming. It wasn't as if she had seen anything, but whatever Ahrin and Kitria were doing, she felt as if she had spied on them. Embarrassment aside, she shouldn't be able to sense those things. Evokers and Charmers had to be more directly engaged with their subjects to receive that type of information from them. If she dug deeper, what else might she be able to access? Could she reach beyond emotions to active thoughts? Should she?

Perhaps Jinau and Kyril were right. Maybe she was something different. If so, what did that mean for her future? What responsibilities came with being the daughter of the ocean, and how was she supposed to balance that with the life she grew up expecting?

The sound of approaching footsteps drew her attention. She opened her eyes and looked up at Gannon.

He sank to the sand beside her. "Kyril told me you wanted to be alone."

"I see you listened."

He slid an arm around her shoulders. "I heard him speaking. Can't say I did a lot of listening."

Veyl leaned against him. "You're such a calloch."

etting into Sarket was easy. Kronach's warriors completely controlled the tower where they crossed the border. A few nodded to Amera on the way past, barely glancing at the rest of them. It reminded Veyl of the escape from Taro, when the Eydarith had essentially ignored them as if they weren't even there. It was almost as disconcerting now as it had been then.

From there, the assassin led them along a series of trails near the coastline, staying away from primary roadways to avoid Sarketi patrols that might be loyal to Jaysen. Whatever the Wavelord's intentions were, it was clear he had no interest in sharing them with the crown prince. At least, not yet.

They could hear and smell the ocean, even taste it on the breeze, and somehow its nearness helped soothe a little of the dread that had sunk its claws into Veyl's shoulders upon entering Sarket. She sensed the same seething discomfort coming from Kyril, Kitria, and Gannon, all of them likely haunted as she was by uncomfortable memories of their previous visit here. In contrast, the wave dancers were increasingly energetic and bright now that they ventured closer to their more natural habitat. Their moods helped ease the ill-feeling that returning to Taro brought, at least for Veyl and Kyril.

When they reached the outskirts of the city, Amera took them to the property of an Eydarith family that bred and trained sturdy warhorses. They left their mounts in a stable there. Navigating the city without drawing attention would be easier on foot. Even then, Amera didn't take them on any of the major thoroughfares, opting instead for a brief, steep hike that took them up the mountainside after dark and around through a less frequented gate manned by Kronach's soldiers. From there, they kept to back alleys, traveling along in a couple of small groups with Kyril and Gannon walking alone. If either of them got too far from the others, their connections to Veyl could guide them to her.

The wave dancers might have been a problem, but Ceris and Seyn stayed in the first group with Amera, Veyl, Feyd and Kitria. Feyd used his Dampener ability to obscure the vision of anyone they spotted in the dark, nighttime alleyways. It led to a few residents briefly panicking when they thought they had lost their eyesight, but it made it possible to keep the two canines with them without being seen. If Veyl needed to prove herself worthy of the Tempest, having the ocean beasts there to support her would certainly help.

They passed a young man leaning against a building, smoking. They left him behind dumping the contents of his pipe and muttering to himself about giving it up if it was going to render him blind.

Amera moved close to Feyd and whispered, "You would make a great assassin."

The Dampener looked her dead in the eye and said, "Keep that in mind."

For a second, Veyl found it amusing, but she didn't honestly know that much about Feyd's history. It was counterintuitive for a healer to work as a killer, wasn't it? Although who would know better the ways to kill a person effectively than someone trained to deal with injuries of all kinds and triage them on a battlefield? He would have extensive knowledge of the myriad ways to ensure death. Couple that with his ability to mute the senses, and it would almost be too easy for him.

She glanced at Dailan, and the man answered with a subtle nod that sent a chill through her. Given his sense of humor, he might be teasing her, but it was something to keep in mind.

Before long, the tense journey ended at a side entrance to the castle grounds. More of Kronach's warriors admitted them, and Amera led them through the halls, barking orders to the first few soldiers and servants they ran across in the fascinating blended language the Eydarith used. Veyl caught a few words mixed in that were borrowed from Sarketi or Pandrean Common, but most of it was unintelligible to her ears.

The halls of Kronach's castle were gray stone, built from the rock that formed the closest mountains. Some of the bright white stone from farther up in the moun-tains, heavily used in the Sarketi capital of Andaro, showed up in places in this part of the structure. Pri-marily in small alcove shrines she suspected were once dedicated to Havaad, but that now had shells, pieces of coral, and carved driftwood arranged upon them where the god's statue would have stood.

By the time they reached a long hall full of private chambers, several servants and Eydarith warriors were in attendance. The former tidied rooms and carried in fresh water for washbasins while the latter stood watch over the flurry of activity, intimidating silent sentinels in their chain and blue-gray stained leather armor.

Amera stopped them before one door. "We did not expect to entertain a party of this size, but we can ac-commodate you. This chamber was prepared for you, Khesran Veyl. You will find water to wash with and clean clothing in the wardrobe should you wish to change. The rest of you may make use of the other rooms, though some may need to share. If you require clean garments, the servants will do their best to provide them for you. I will alert Wavelord Kronach of your arrival. He may wish for you to join him for his evening repast."

Behind her, Veyl heard Ahrin translating softly for Kitria, Kyril, and Jinau, who had the disadvantage of not sharing a language with the Eydarith, though Kyril, and Jinau to a lesser degree, had picked up a little Pandrean Common on their prior visit to the continent. Ahrin and Iyvalin had assigned themselves the task early on of including the two Thaelians in conversations with Amera.

Veyl inclined her head to the assassin. "Thank you, Tezaak Amera."

The woman gave a sharp nod before spinning and striding off down the hall. When Veyl turned, she found the others watching her expectantly.

"Well, at least they seem to be hospitable. I feared they might lock us in cells when we arrived here." She forced a smile as if it were a joke. "Let's clean up. It sounds like we may meet with Wavelord Kronach soon."

Gannon started toward her, but Kyril reached her first. Her tehnaak simply nodded and went to claim the room next to hers. The others took different rooms, leaving the one across from hers open for Kyril to take in some unspoken accord.

"Stay alert," Kyril warned. "Just because they haven't harmed us yet doesn't mean they won't."

She took his hand. "Don't worry. I know better than to trust Kronach."

Kyril leaned down and gave her a quick kiss. "Fierce and wise." He smiled and squeezed her hand once before heading to the remaining room.

Unease crept in as soon as she entered the chamber they had given her and closed the door, cutting herself off from the others, at least physically. The space looked far too much like the room she had been a prisoner in previously, the one in which Jaysen had kissed her and touched her as though she belonged to him. In the wardrobe, she found an Eydarith warrior's dress, the skirt made of strips of fabric over a pair of pants, allowing for greater freedom of movement in the event of a fight. The garment showcased the ocean colors they favored—blues, grays, and off-whites—but the craftsmanship was exquisite. The material had a soft, almost metallic luster to it that gave it a luxurious quality suitable for a woman of elevated social status.

Was the fine clothing a show of respect for her station, or did Kronach merely wish to dress her up to suit him? She was here to represent Vanris, but the temptation to put on something clean was powerful. Wearing it would undoubtedly please the wavelord and perhaps provide an opportunity for her to have her own clothes laundered. Showing gratitude for his gift in their first meeting with him, regardless of his motive for giving it, might be a worthwhile strategy for encouraging his cooperation, so the choice had political merit as well.

Once she had decided, it took a few minutes to find the resolve to undress in this strange place that reminded her of Jaysen and of the crushing fear she had experienced there for herself and the others. After she had stripped down and sponged away the dirt from their travels, she slipped the garments on, finding it unsettling how well they fit. Had Kronach remembered her that precisely, or could this have been prepared for her on her previous visit?

Deciding not to dwell on those questions, she finished changing and wove a few new braids along the right side of her head to ensure that her pointed ear showed. She might not be wearing Vanrian attire, but she could at least style her hair in the fashion of their warriors to show that she was proudly Vanrian. She had completed her preparations and was considering going to speak to Kyril when someone knocked on her door.

"Come in."

Amera entered and gave her a quick visual appraisal. Then she approached and boldly reached up to adjust a shoulder fastening from which hung two shorter strips of fabric like those that made up the skirt.

"Like this, with one in front and one behind as you have it, you are saying you have claimed a partner and been claimed in return." She flipped both strips over Veyl's shoulder. "This shows that you are unclaimed."

Veyl thought of Kyril and immediately pulled one strip to the front again.

Amera snorted softly and shook her head. "Come with me. I will show you to where Kronach waits."

Veyl followed her out the door and stopped in the hall. She could feel Gannon and Kyril nearby. "My companions are coming as well, are they not?"

"We have already escorted some to dinner. Others needed a few more minutes. I will come back for them. The wavelord grows impatient."

She considered telling the woman how little his impatience mattered to her, but she was here to make an ally of him. Swallowing her attitude and placing a hand on Seyn's shoulders to help calm her nerves, she nodded to Amera. "Lead the way."

The assassin allowed a brief side trip at Veyl's request to let Seyn relieve herself, taking them to one of the outdoor shrines to Havaad that, judging from the paw prints and slight stench of urine, also served as a place for letting out castle hounds. At least they kept the feces cleaned up, so it didn't reek as badly as it might otherwise. The wave dancer did her business quickly, her displeasure with the space apparent through their bond and in the way she ventured only as far out as necessary.

"Why not repurpose these shrines like the smaller ones inside the castle?" Veyl asked as they followed Amera through the gray stone halls.

"The alcoves are but displays of reverence for the ocean. True shrines to the Tempest must always be in or within reach of the water. To place them otherwise is to invite powerful, devastating waves to come farther inland."

"A tidal wave… tezaak?"

Amera gave her an approving glance and nodded, her gaze lingering on Veyl for a second. "You know the Tempest favors you," she said, facing forward again. "You could be more here, closer to the ocean. The desert is not where you belong."

Veyl was prepared to deny the notion outright, but something gave her a moment of pause. A feeling of power and belonging that hummed softly through her. She had noticed it growing stronger as they approached the coast but had assumed it was coming from Seyn because of the beast's connection to the ocean. Could that assumption be wrong?

"I am a khesran of Vanris." She hoped she sounded more certain in that assertion than she felt. "What else do I need to be?"

Amera said nothing. She led Veyl to a set of double doors with two female warriors standing guard outside. They opened them quickly enough that Amera and Veyl could continue through without slowing their stride. As soon as they were inside, Veyl stopped.

The room was unexpectedly intimate, with a conversation area to one side that included three chairs and a conspicuous couch with a sloped end that appeared more suited to lying down than sitting before the crackling fire. A second fireplace burned on the opposite side of the room, near a table that could seat six people at the most. Right then, it held place settings for only two, both plates already filled with a selection from the aromatic dishes arranged in the center. None of her companions were there, only Kronach and four guards, two flanking a door at the other side of the room, and two inside the entrance she had come through, who closed it behind her.

Seyn's ears dropped back, and she shifted one foot protectively in front of Veyl.

A metallic taste rose on Veyl's tongue. "What is this? Where is the rest of my unit?"

A hint of something predatory came out in Kronach's smile as he nodded to Amera. "Thank you, Tezaak. You may leave us."

"Wavelord." Amera offered the barest hint of a bow and left through the rear door.

"You found my gift." Kronach stood and prowled over, stopping a few feet back when Seyn growled at him. His one good eye appraised Veyl without shame. "The formal warrior garments suit you."

"My unit?" she pressed.

"Your companions are arriving at their own dinner. My people will inform them you are dining elsewhere tonight."

"They are far from helpless. I brought mind-crafters, and they won't stand for you separating us." Veyl reached for the bonds to Gannon and Kyril, but what she found first was something else. The cold, awesome power of the ocean, awaiting her like an unforgiving instructor eager to teach. The sensation, altogether different from what she expected to come up against, left her feeling adrift and out of her depth.

"Yes, Amera told me. A Dampener, a Charmer, and your wave-touched Feral. A fine entourage for one little princess."

"Khesran," she corrected sharply.

"They will stay where they are because my warriors will explain to them that your safety is dependent upon their cooperation. No harm will befall you so long as they allow me to engage you alone this evening. You and I have matters to discuss that they need not be part of." He gestured toward the table. "Shall we?"

She forged her way past that strange oceanic power to the bonds she was familiar with, drawing courage from them while attempting to send reassurance in return. An effort to convince them she was safe, so they wouldn't risk themselves trying to reach her, though she wasn't sure it was true. With Kyril, Gannon, and the wave dancers now bolstering her, she stood straighter and lifted her chin. "I am not helpless either. Who will ensure your safety, Wavelord?"

He chuckled. "There you are." Sitting at the head of the table, he leaned comfortably back in his chair and gestured to the place to his left where the other setting waited. "Unless you prefer something more comfortable." He gestured in offering to the reclining couch.

Veyl hastened to the chair at the table. "This will do." Once she had seated herself, Seyn rested behind her chair, watching Kronach with an intensity that bordered on threat. Leveling an equally stern gaze on him, Veyl asked, "Why do you go to such trouble to vex me?"

"Don't worry yourself, Princess. It is no trouble at all." He picked up a strip of lean meat with his fingers and tipped his head back, dropping it into his mouth. Then he looked at her as he chewed, a spark of challenge in his eye.

Veyl drew a deep breath and exhaled, trying to focus past the frustration his antics brought her. She had never doubted that he would be difficult to work with, which was one reason she hoped to have some of her companions present to help her deal with him. She should have expected he would find a way around that. "Why did you ask me here?"

He took another bite, still ignoring his utensils,

and watched her as he chewed. After a few seconds, he washed it down with a swallow of something that smelled faintly like mead, though she could tell it was stronger than what she was used to just from the intensity of the aroma. He set his mug down and considered her for a long moment. "What was it like to have your Frightener ability broken?"

Veyl tried to hide her surprise, but his slight smirk told her she had failed. How did he know about that?

A soft growl behind her drew his gaze to Seyn, and his expression sobered a fraction. Veyl welcomed the wave dancer's confidence. Using it to help her reclaim her composure, she picked up a fork and knife, cut away a piece of the meat, and placed it in her mouth. The flavor was unexpected, the sauce rich and robust, but earthy, as if they had used some kind of mushroom in its preparation. The meat itself was far more tender than she expected.

"This is quite pleasant," she said after she swallowed, choosing to follow his example and ignore what he asked her.

He gestured to her mug. "Better if you wash it down with the itovanak." When she gave him a questioning look, he added, "It is like the meads you favor, only stronger."

Veyl picked up the mug and tried a cautious sip. Like the sauce, this was rich and robust at first, leaving her unprepared for the burn that hit her full force when she took a bigger swallow. Kronach chuckled when she choked, and Seyn hopped to her feet. Veyl reached out a hand to calm the beast while she struggled to stop coughing.

The wavelord took a leisurely drink from an ornate silver goblet before setting it between them on the table and nudging it closer to her. "Try this. It will help."

Veyl picked it up, giving him a sharp glare over the

rim of the goblet as she took a wary sip. The drink was light, with a hint of delicate sweetness to it. A dramatic contrast to the other beverage. She took a few more sips to cool the burn in her throat.

When she moved to set it down near him, he shook his head. "Take another sip of that and follow it with the itovanak."

"Why?"

"Because you are the guest here, and you should hear the words of your host. Your people are dining upon my best food and staying in the finest rooms I can offer them. Humor me, Princess." The patience in his regard surprised her a little, though it didn't come across as kindness, but rather the tolerance of someone willing to put in the necessary work to achieve the outcome they desired.

She set the goblet on the table. "Perhaps if my host could pay me the respect of my proper title at the very least."

He considered her for a moment in silence, then cracked a grin. "Humor me, Khesran."

It was a tiny victory, and the pleasure he took in granting it to her made it feel like less of one. Veyl lifted the goblet again, more acutely aware of the fact that he had drunk from it first, now that she wasn't choking. Perhaps he had merely done so to show her it was safe, but the intent way he watched her lips touch the rim made her suspect otherwise. As she took a sip, he reached over and moved her mug closer to her. Uneasy with the way his one dark eye followed her every movement, she set the goblet down and lifted the mug to her lips, taking a careful drink this time. His point was instantly clear. Something about the combination enhanced the hearty flavor of the itovanak while also smoothing the passage of the potent alcohol.

Kronach nodded, satisfied with whatever he saw

in her expression, and turned back to his plate. "Eat, Khesran. We will speak after."

Veyl did so. A few days of hard travel had left her with an appetite, and the fare proved worthy of a Vanrian royal banquet. These were not the usual dishes she associated with Sarket. Like their religion and their language, the Eydarith recipes were unique and turned out to be delicious as well. Most of the obvious ingredients were familiar, but the preparations and unusual spices elevated them into something exceptional.

"This is not what we dined upon when I was here before," she remarked after a time.

There was that satisfied smirk again, sending a flare of irritation through her. "I would not waste the best Eydarith recipes on a Sarketi palate. The undead prince and his soldiers would not have appreciated it. You are Vanrian royalty. I know enough of your finer foods to know your palate is more refined."

Veyl considered him for a moment, emboldened perhaps by the drinks that she had tried a fair bit more of since learning the fascinating secret of their complimentary nature. "You truly do not see yourself as Sarketi?"

"We are not Sarketi. The Eydarith may share some similar blood in our ancestry, but our people are children of the Tempest. We are not the same."

Once they finished eating, Kronach filled their two mugs and the goblet, then carried the mugs to the table in the sitting area.

When he returned for the goblet, Veyl snatched it up first. "I would be more comfortable conversing here, if you please."

Kronach placed one hand on the table and wrapped the other over hers on the goblet, leaning unnecessarily close. "This space is for eating, Khesran. That is for speaking. If you do not wish to speak…"

Veyl relented, letting him take the goblet, if for

no other reason than to end that physical contact. She walked over with Seyn at her side and claimed one of the three chairs, ignoring the fact that he had placed her mug in front of the reclining couch. Seyn settled on the floor before the couch with her head resting at Veyl's feet, as if to ensure no one tried to use the questionable piece of furniture.

Kronach moved the goblet and mug closer to her. "I see you did not bring me back my swords."

"I believe I earned the right to keep those blades."

A glint of amusement lit his eyes and enlivened his presence, the first emotion she had gotten from him with her abilities all evening. Was that because he guarded himself that well, or had her anxiety around him somehow muted her sensitivity? If only she understood how her own powers worked.

He sank back with his mug, draping one leg over an arm of the chair. "You wanted something to remember our time together?" He grinned. "Tell me, do you caress the hilts as you drift to sleep at night?"

A few of his guards chuckled, the sound startling her. They had been so still and silent she had all but forgotten they were there. The sudden acute awareness that he and his warriors heavily outnumbered her here made it harder to continue offering reassurance across her links to Gannon and Kyril.

Veyl glared at him, forcing confidence and a scathing tone. "I prefer something with a thicker blade."

A couple of guards openly laughed at that.

Kronach chuckled. "I do enjoy sparring with you, Khesran."

Veyl leaned forward, burying her fear. "If I am favored by the Tempest, should you not show me more respect?"

Kronach took a deep drink, then he turned his head a fraction, making it seem as if that off-white eye amid all the scars was looking at her. "You have been out on the ocean, yes?"

Unnerved by his gaze, she took a drink from the goblet and followed it with a swallow of the itovanak, using the delay to compose herself. "You know I have."

"Was it gentle? Did it coddle and protect you?"

Veyl swallowed. "It was not, and it did not."

"Our god is not kind. If he has shown you favor, then you have great strength within you. You must be worthy somehow. If I am to consider working with you, I wish to know that what I see in you is real—that you have not misled me with Vanrian mind-crafting and a beautiful face. If my bluntness and arrogance are enough to fracture your defenses, you are not what I thought you to be."

"You will never break my defenses, Wavelord Kronach," she snapped. "You asked me here for a reason. Let us set aside these games and get to that."

Kronach smiled. "No. That is not the Eydarith way. Tonight, we dine and drink and speak of other things. Tomorrow, we negotiate." He gestured to the mug in front of her. "What would you ask me, Khesran?"

Veyl narrowed her eyes at him and took another drink, though she had undoubtedly had more than enough at this point. "Very well. Tell me why you think my Frightener ability is broken."

Kronach moved his leg off the chair arm and leaned forward, staring hard at her. Into her. "Because I can feel it."

Veyl's chest constricted, and she shifted back in her chair to put more distance between them. "I don't think..." She trailed off when Kronach held a hand up.

"Do not think, Khesran. Feel. Whether you are worthy of the Tempest's favor remains to be seen, but you are wave-touched. I could not be a wavelord if I were not also. How do you think I knew what you were?" He spoke again before she could respond. "Because I can feel you without needing to touch you. From the moment you set foot in my city, your heartbeat echoed in my mind. I must admit, I love how it quickens when you are afraid, beating fast and fierce as a little mouse's."

Veyl started shaking her head, her heart racing now just as he had described it.

"You Vanrians are so preoccupied with the bonds you hold dear, the threads you can manipulate to connect you to each other, yet you cannot let yourself see that they exist outside your own people. The wave-touched are threaded together as well, though I cannot say how alike those bonds are to the ones your people cultivate." There was something disturbingly intimate about his contented smile when he sat back in his chair and rested one leg over the arm again. "But you are the first wave-touched I have encountered who was not born of the ocean's people."

"What about Kyril?" Veyl asked, trying to move past her initial reaction to his words, which had been to close herself off to everything, silencing all her connections in a way that she hadn't realized was possible before that moment. Knowing that block might alarm the others motivated her to open herself up again, tentatively.

"Your Feral is only part-Thaelian. From learning what I could about the undead prince's Thaelian allies, I have concluded that these Qwilki they share their lands with may also be the ocean's children. Perhaps not favored by the Tempest as the Eydarith are, but of the ocean all the same."

Veyl let down her guard a little at a time, searching for something other than the bonds to Gannon, Kyril, and the wave dancers. The might of the ocean crashed in upon her, fierce and unforgiving. Frustrated, she closed her eyes, reaching into that sensation, struggling her way along it as if she swam through a field of seaweed in a storm, the tendrils snagging her limbs. That presence swept through her in return without reservation, its foreign power threatening to drag her under.

Seyn moved into the storm with her, the beast's remarkable will helping Veyl gradually draw the ocean's might in and find balance with it until she could sort through what she was feeling. With the wave dancer's aid, she found Kronach, a connection different from the others, rough and unyielding like the rocks she had fallen upon when rescuing Nagi from the kel'inuk. His presence was savage and bold. Now that she felt it clearly, she couldn't imagine how she had ever missed it. There were other links too, though they were extremely faint, as if separated by a considerable distance, or simply much weaker.

Kronach was nodding when she opened her eyes, his expression guarded now. "Well done, Khesran. Can you finally feel the power of the Tempest?"

"I feel… the ocean," she answered cautiously, unwilling to commit to the idea of his god being real, but wary of insulting him. "I can feel you… and others." She took a drink from the silver goblet, followed by a longer one from the mug of itovanak that seemed fuller now than she remembered it being a moment ago. Had he filled it again? Was he trying to get her drunk? When he held his silence, she arched a brow and asked, "Do you find me worthy yet?"

"That remains to be seen."

Veyl clenched her teeth, biting back an angry retort. She waited to speak until she had her temper reined in. "What is it you want from me?"

He didn't restrain the intimate suggestion in his slow grin. "Want? I can tell you what I want, Khesran, if you truly wish to know, but you might not like it."

A flicker of alarm constricted her chest, and she drew a breath, placing a hand on Seyn's head for reassurance. "What I mean is, what do you expect to gain by summoning me here?"

He simply stared at her as he raised his mug and took a few long, slow drinks, swishing the hearty liquid in his mouth as though savoring it.

Irritated, Veyl reached for her own mug.

"You have had enough." With a quick snap of his leg, he kicked the mug, startling Veyl and Seyn and spilling what remained across a woven blue and gray rug. He stood and started for the door as if they had concluded their business.

"Kronach!" Veyl snapped to her feet and rushed after him, making it a few strides before the room rocked around her. She reached out, grabbing for anything within range to steady herself and found his arm extended and waiting as if he had predicted her need, or expected it. Taking hold, she glanced back at the mug on the floor, struggling to focus on it, then faced him. "What have you done?"

Seyn was snarling, but Veyl discouraged her from acting, afraid his guards might kill the wave dancer if she attacked him.

Kronach moved closer, taking hold of her arms in a firm grip to keep her upright. Leaning in, he brought his face next to hers and inhaled. "It pleases me to hear my name cross your lips," he whispered.

Longing crashed over her, surging across that newly discovered link, drowning out her repulsion and fury and making his desire hers. He moved his mouth close to hers, and she almost surrendered to that surge of emotion, fighting free of it an instant before their lips touched. She jerked back, nearly falling in her effort to get away from him.

"Calloch," she spat.

"There you are." He grinned and licked his lips, looking unexpectedly satisfied by her resistance. "I only let you drink enough to help you dream in the embrace of the Tempest tonight. Tomorrow, should he see fit to release you, we will speak again."

Veyl's legs gave out, and he caught her, sweeping her up in his arms. "If the Tempest..." She struggled to hold the thought and find the breath to form more than a few words. "Why..."

"You found the Tempest's presence within you, so you have earned a chance to face him, but we do not have the luxury of waiting for you to get there in your own time. Now you must confront him and accept his gifts or fail."

She was vaguely aware of the guards opening the doors and the sounds of several warriors falling into step around them as they went out into the hall. She could feel Seyn's distress and continued to push back against the beast's urge to attack him. He might deserve it, but she would not risk losing the wave dancer when Kronach's actions, however inappropriate and unwelcome, did not appear to be aimed at killing her, at least not as far as she could tell. If only she could get the words past her lips to ask what he had drugged her with.

Her head had grown so heavy it fell against his shoulder. With great effort, she lifted it, resenting the increased contact. It was bad enough being in his arms at all. A few more moments of fighting made it clear she wouldn't win this battle, and her head lolled against him, unwilling to be moved again. Her focus turned to waging a new war over trying to keep her eyes open. She spotted Kyril and the others hurrying down the hall beneath the sinking curtain of heavy eyelids. Weapons sang from their sheaths and people started shouting, though she couldn't focus on the words well enough to make sense of them. Her eyelids finished drifting shut.

•

The ship rocked.

Veyl opened her eyes, staring up at the wood floor of the deck above her. She lay unable to move on a reclining couch that, oddly, sat in the center of the ship's hold full of crates. Waves lapped at the hull, the sound and the movement rhythmic and gentle at first, growing rapidly stronger and more insistent as time crept relentlessly by. The ship started tipping from side to side. Veyl and the couch stayed firmly in their place, as if affixed there while the motion grew steadily more violent, until dangerously powerful waves crashed into the sides, the hull creaking as they threatened to tear it apart. The loud crack of splintering wood assaulted her ears. She couldn't move, couldn't even scream as the ocean rushed in, sweeping around her. It claimed her body in its icy embrace and dragged her down.

The couch disappeared out from under her in the raging waters. Veyl scanned the debris surrounding her, searching for something to grab onto that might help her float back to the surface. The side of a wooden crate swirled within range, but her arms wouldn't respond when she tried to reach for it. Then a new danger presented itself when the fragment swept closer, catching her across the temple with a stinging blow she couldn't defend against. More debris struck her as she continued to sink until she plummeted beneath the roiling, storm-tossed waters into an eerie calm below.

She was breathing. It took a moment for that realization to sink in as darkness folded around her. How was she breathing beneath the ocean? It shouldn't be possible, and yet her chest rose and fell with each inhale and exhale.

Lights appeared in front of her. She recognized the patterns just as whales like those she had seen from Kyril's ship emerged from the darkness, swimming toward her. For an instant, panic gripped her, then, as they parted to go around her, it turned to awe and irritation. Irritation that she couldn't reach out and touch these remarkable creatures. But why couldn't she? What was stopping her? She could breathe here. Why couldn't she move as well?

Veyl focused on the luminescent markings, silently demanding that her body obey, that it respond to her will. She would not be stilled or controlled. The ocean was not her enemy. If what the Qwilki and Kronach said was true, she should be welcome here. This was part of her strength, not a weakness.

Closing her eyes, she focused on the weight of the water, the cold of it, the salty taste creeping between her lips. She reached out. For several heartbeats, it felt as if nothing happened, then her fingertips touched upon something, and she opened her eyes to see her outstretched hand brushing along the side of the nearest whale. The awesome beast sang in strange musical tones, its vast body curving in a gradual arc toward her caress. Turning in place, she watched the magnificent creature, admiring its overwhelming size, tempered by such surprising gentleness.

A familiar voice spoke in the darkness. "Take what is yours, Seh'hali."

Nagi?

Veyl turned, searching for the Qwilki woman and finding nothing but the whales.

"Do not fear the boundless might bearing in on you. Embrace the gift the wave dancer has woken in you and open yourself to all that you must be."

The Qwilki woman was still nowhere to be seen, but her voice came from all directions now. Veyl focused on the whales again, watching the group part to pass around her, reaching out to touch them.

Another creature emerged from the darkness, approaching swiftly, its long body undulating through the water as it wove between the larger beasts. When it drew closer, she recognized the shimmering scales of a ji'ikyan, one of the serpents that had nearly ended her life with its sting.

A jolt of terror brought back the aching cold of the ocean, but she fought it. They both belonged in this place. Why should she fear this creature?

When it was almost upon her, she reached out to it with one hand, inviting it closer. The serpent parted its jaws as if to bite her with those razor teeth. Then it twisted aside, diving over her arm, its smooth scales like silk brushing against her skin as it continued down past her feet. It vanished in the dark below for several heartbeats. Then it came back up, weaving around and between her legs, winding in front of her chest and over her shoulders, bringing her attention to the fact that she wore no clothing. Its body tightened around her, wrapping her in a disturbingly intimate embrace. A strange clicking sound came from its throat now, creating vibrations against the bare skin of her neck and shoulder. The stinger at the end of its tail brushed her leg, moving along the side until it found the location of the previous sting. It stopped there, the point lightly pressing on that spot in threat, or promise.

Veyl tensed, fear threatening to take hold again. Kyril and Ceris had rescued her last time. Who would do so if the beast stung her now?

"Do not fear ji'ikyan." Nagi's voice was gentle and reassuring. "Open yourself to its presence. You will find you and it are kin in spirit."

Taking a calming breath, something that was confusing enough in itself given the circumstance, she spread her awareness in search of her many bonds, not expecting to find them in the depths of the ocean. What she encountered was a series of connections like the one she had to Kronach, only not as strong, reaching from her to the ji'ikyan and the whales too. As she focused on those links, she realized she could feel other bonds as well—to Kyril, Seyn, and Ceris. She was not as alone in these dark waters as she had believed.

Though her heart still raced, Veyl relaxed her body, letting her head fall back and allowing the serpent to hold her in place. She closed her eyes, feeling the vibrations against her neck as the creature continued to make deep clicking noises in its throat. A shock of pain lanced through her leg when the stinger thrust into it. Veyl jerked once with the agony of the fresh wound, then stilled herself again, letting the ji'ikyan cradle her in its coils as the toxin raced into her system, rapidly paralyzing her. Whale song rose in volume all around them. She could no longer move at all when the serpent finally released her, setting her free to sink deeper until icy blackness consumed her.

As she sank, her breathing and heartbeat slowed, becoming sluggish, her thoughts faltering. Her heart stuttered to a stop, awareness slipping away.

A crackle of energy burst within her chest, jolting her heart back to life, and she sucked in a breath of cold water, despite how little sense that made. The crackling raced through her, reviving the sensation in her core, then her hips and shoulders, legs and arms, feet and hands, and finally her toes and fingers. The lightning within didn't stop there. It continued to spread, flickering beyond the boundaries of her flesh, flashes illuminating the dark waters and the myriad strange creatures that had gathered.

Veyl looked around at them, welcoming them. She had never felt so powerful in her life.

•

Someone shook Veyl, and she lashed out, her fist connecting with a satisfying impact against her assailant's jaw. She hoped it would make him bleed. Opening her eyes, she saw Kyril sitting on the bed next to her, bringing his fingers up to touch the bright spot of red beading on his lower lip.

"Oh!" She sat up. "I'm sorry. I thought you were Kronach."

"I should appreciate your reaction then." His lip forgotten, he looked her over with a furrowed brow, the shine of exhaustion in his eyes. Genuine fear flowed off him before she shut it out, not wanting her ability to spy on his emotions without him knowing. "You stopped breathing, and Feyd thought we were going to lose you. I was leaving the room to go find and kill Kronach when you drew in a breath again, and he called me back. I…" His voice caught, and he pulled her into his arms, his embrace painfully tight.

A sound drew her attention, and she looked over his shoulder to see the Dampener slip out the door and ease it shut behind him. Perhaps he went to tell the others she was alive or simply to give them some privacy. Her mother would be deeply disappointed by how much effort the group wasn't putting into keeping them apart, not that she minded.

She tucked her face against his neck, breathing him in. His scent evoked a sense of safety and belonging and sparked a yearning in her. If only she could see a future in which she could continue to enjoy having him close like this.

"Make love to me," she whispered.

He shifted back enough to look down at her. "That bastard drugged you with something that made you stop breathing mere minutes ago. It's not a request I would normally deny, but I'm not sure now is the time."

So he said, but Veyl felt the flare of desire across the thread that bound them when she made the request. She shifted closer until her lips were almost touching his. "But I have never felt so alive, nor so in love."

She kissed him, tasting a hint of his blood from where she had punched him. For a moment, he didn't react. She slid her hands up under his shirt, running them over the hard muscle of his abdomen, then down toward the waist of his pants. His objections forgotten, he kissed her hard, his fingers seeking the fastenings of her dress.

They were both mostly naked when someone knocked, and she heard Gannon's voice outside the door.

"They may need a few more minutes to, ah… talk. Get some sleep."

Kyril pressed his forehead to Veyl's, and they both laughed softly.

"This might take more than a few minutes," Kyril

murmured. "Should I lock the door?"

Unwilling to let go of him, Veyl shook her head. "They'll give us time."

He didn't ask again. Easing her back on the bed, he climbed in with her, sliding his hand up her thigh as he moved in close to her. His silver-blue eyes shone with the pleasure he promised to bring her—pleasure she was more than happy to accept and reciprocate in kind.

•

A while later, when they were both sated, Kyril got up and bolted the door, then settled back in to lie naked beside her. Veyl rested her head on his shoulder and traced a line of his ke'hanoath along his ribs with one finger. His muscles tensed under her touch.

"Does that tickle?" she asked.

"A little, though that's not what caused my reaction."

The tightness of his voice made her grin. "Already? We only just finished."

"Give me a few minutes and I can go for another round. I can't imagine I'll ever get enough of you."

Veyl kissed his chest, and his arm tightened around her shoulders.

When he spoke again, the passion and humor had left his voice. "What did Kronach give you?"

She closed in on herself a little, remembering that vivid experience in the depths of the ocean—disturbingly real and terrifying, yet somehow empowering. "I don't know, but it made me have some exceptionally strange dreams." Were they only dreams? They had to be, didn't they? She was here, in Kyril's arms, not immersed deep in those dark, icy waters.

He kissed her forehead. "We can talk about it more in the morning. I imagine you could use some normal sleep. Do you want me to stay with you?"

Veyl snuggled in, pressing herself against his side. "Do you really have to ask?"

She delighted in the way his chest moved under her cheek with his soft chuckle. "I guess not." He was quiet for a few minutes, his breathing evening out, then, in a sleepy voice, he said, "While I was appreciating all of you, I noticed the scar from the ji'ikyan looks different. Did something else happen?"

A chill swept through Veyl, the strange, drugged dream coming vividly back to her. She forced a steady voice. "It's nothing. Don't worry about it."

When he seemed to have drifted off, she carefully reached down to move the covers off her leg and twisted to look at it. The small circle from the sting had an inch-long horizontal scar across it where they had cut into her leg to flush the poison. That scar, a little darker than her natural skin tone, now had a vertical mark stretching about an inch above and below it that hadn't been there before. The sensation of the ji'ikyan driving its stinger into the old wound flashed through her again, and she flinched. Kyril's arm tightened around her, though he didn't seem to wake.

Covering the leg, she closed her eyes and savored the warmth of the man next to her, but it was a long while before her nerves allowed her to fall asleep.

Pounding on the bedroom door snapped Veyl and Kyril awake early the next morning.

"Khesran Veyl, you and your entourage must come immediately."

Though she felt no particular obligation to indulge the wavelord right then, there was a persuasive urgency in the demand. Kyril got up from the bed, pulled on his pants, and headed for the door. Watching his muscles move as he walked, his long black hair with its blue-stained streaks falling over strong, bare shoulders, was enough to push away some of her initial annoyance with the abrupt awakening. He met her eyes on the way over, waiting for her nod before he answered the door and leaned out.

"Wavelord Kronach wants us?" Kyril managed in passable Pandrean Common.

"Now," the man answered. "You will leave your weapons in your quarters."

Kyril glanced over his shoulder at her, the unfamiliar language still too much of a barrier.

Veyl called, "Give us a few minutes, please."

"I'll give you one," the man snapped back as Kyril shut the door.

Once it was closed, she got up and found the outfit she had worn last night. It was still the cleanest she had. Seyn and Ceris went to sit by the door, waiting for them. When they were ready, Kyril took the two wave dancers for a quick trip outside while Veyl gathered the rest of the unit. The Eydarith warrior who had woken them stood in the hall with two others, all three scowling and shifting as if they had some legitimate reason to be this impatient. Perhaps they did, though she couldn't bring herself to place much confidence in them after their wavelord's treatment of her.

The rest of their company filed out of the rooms looking tired, though several of them brightened when they saw her and offered relieved greetings. Veyl smiled her gratitude to Feyd and answered the others with a solemn nod.

"Kronach better have a valid excuse for this after what he did to you last night," Gannon grumbled under his breath next to her.

"Since he seems to think anything is justifiable as long as it amuses him, I have my doubts," Iyvalin whispered, coming to stand a little closer to them.

Kyril rejoined them, and Veyl nodded to the three warriors. "We are ready."

With a grunt, one of them turned down the hall, his swift strides conveying a sense of urgency. Veyl followed him with Seyn, the rest of the group taking up positions to the sides and behind her. The other two Eydarith fell in at the back as if the three of them could hope to control their nine-person unit should they wish to cause problems.

The lead warrior escorted them to the same throne room where Veyl had first appeared before the wavelord and knelt upon her bloody knee. A vast space, sparsely decorated with weaponry and occasional tapestries bearing mostly depictions of ocean beasts or occasional scenes of battle. The skeleton of a massive sea creature hung high above the throne. Kronach sat there now, as he had before, upon his solitary seat at the front with some of his warriors positioned around the perimeter of the room. Their escort moved to the sides as well, leaving Veyl and her entourage to continue forward alone. When she stopped near the foot of the gray stone dais, the chill of the room amplified by the wavelord's stony regard, she offered the barest hint of a respectful nod, noting that he did not reciprocate.

"A unit of Jaysen's Sarketi and Thaelian soldiers is on its way here now." Kronach dropped the news like a stone at their feet.

Kyril took a few steps forward, threat in his bearing. "You set us up."

Kronach gave a snort. "What sort of fool would I have to be to risk the wrath of Vanris? The Eydarith are a great people, but we are not so arrogant as to believe we can stand against your country. No, this is not my doing."

Veyl wanted to blame him for this, especially after last night, but he had a point, though she suspected it was prudence rather than a lack of arrogance that held him in check. If he was telling them the truth, that meant there was a traitor either among her people or his. She placed a hand on Kyril's arm to keep him from saying more, pleased when he inclined his head to her and stepped back, deferring to her rank. "They are on their way as in, to Taro, or as in, to your throne room?"

Kronach spread his hands, gesturing to the current space.

Nerves dancing, she glanced around them, quickly picking out the other exits. "Could you not hide us? Our mounts are not in your stables. They cannot prove we were here if they never see us."

"Perhaps I could." His brows lifted a fraction. "But now that they are here, I find myself curious to see how this new development unfolds. How will the khesran face her enemy?" Kronach nodded to the guards by the main entrance.

Unarmed, no less. He had deliberately called them here without their weapons.

A searing fury burned through Veyl's fear as she turned to see two warriors opening the doors for a unit of around thirty Sarketi and Thaelian soldiers. When they marched into the room, she walked between her companions to position herself at the head of their group, facing the new arrivals. The Sarketi man in the front, bearing the insignia of a captain on his armor, took an extra step forward and bowed stiffly to her while the rest halted.

"Khesran Veyl, King Jaysen would like you to accompany us to meet with him."

Energy crackled to life in her chest, and she could feel the cold of the deep ocean pressing around her as it had in her dream, only it seemed more protective than oppressive this time. Her companions shifted closer, instinctively reaching for the weapons they had left in their rooms on their host's orders. She held a hand out to discourage them from acting yet.

"You may tell Crown Prince Jaysen that, while I appreciate the invitation, I have other business to attend to right now."

Kronach chuckled, still sitting on his throne, his warriors holding their positions along the walls. It appeared as if he truly intended to stay back and watch how she handled the situation.

"My apologies, Khesran, but I cannot accept that answer," the captain replied.

As he spoke, the soldiers in his unit drew their weapons, tension racing through her companions in response. They were at a distinct disadvantage, a position Kronach had put them in for his own entertainment, but none of them gave any ground. They would fight for her even against these odds. For that alone, she would do everything in her power to avoid making them do so. Once upon a time, that might have meant sacrificing herself for them, but she didn't mean for that to happen either. She sensed one of the Thaelians among the opposing group accessing an ability, though she could not yet tell what that ability was, nor why she could feel it to begin with.

Without warning, her vision went dark. They had a Dampener, which meant Feyd would be the only one unaffected among them. Panic brought every nerve to life, heightening her other senses. She heard the Sarketi group's footsteps as they advanced. In the forced darkness, the serpent coiled around her again, the power of the ocean sweeping in.

A hand touched her arm. "Khesran, I can blind them and challenge their Dampener," Feyd whispered in her ear.

She shook her head, knowing he could see it. "Do nothing yet." Suddenly she could see, though from an unfamiliar perspective closer to the ground. Seyn nudged her hand, encouragement flowing between them, and Veyl let out a bright laugh. "How confident you are now that you have mind-crafters of your own."

A few faltered in their advance, glancing at their captain.

The storm surged. Focusing on the unit through Seyn's eyes, she hit them with a wave of darkness of her own.

"Shit! They have a Dampener too!" the captain shouted.

"No," a Thaelian man near the back countered, the fear in his voice immensely gratifying. "I can't see either. This is something different."

That told her who their Dampener was.

Veyl focused in on him, seizing his fear and transforming it into a weapon against him until he retreated with a cry, scampering back against the wall and falling to the floor where he curled in on himself. She looked around at her companions through her own eyes now, their nods and the wary way they regarded her telling her they could see again. Letting the storm inside drown out the sting of their discomfort, she gestured toward the enemy soldiers with a jerk of her head. Whatever they thought of what had just happened, they didn't hesitate to rush forward and disarm their blinded opponents, holding on to some weapons for themselves and casting the rest away. When they finished, she drew back the Dampener ability, returning sight to Jaysen's soldiers, while exalting in the sensation of lightning flickering out to the ends of her arms and legs.

The might of the ocean still surged in her when she met the eyes of the Sarketi captain, letting her soft words drip like venom from her lips. "Wouldn't you be more comfortable if you knelt?"

He sank to his knees with a whimper.

Walking closer, she glared down at him, Seyn moving up beside her to growl in his face. "Who told Jaysen we were coming here?"

He was trembling violently enough that his voice shook when he answered. "I don't know. A warning came by missive from someone in Etrion the same day Khemron Kasiel arrived in Balarus."

Veyl turned to look at Kronach.

The wavelord rose, wearing a pleased, faintly covetous smile, and gestured his warriors forward. He pointed to Jaysen's soldiers. "Lock all of them up. We will deal with them later." He singled out one woman. "Have my messengers send word to the other wavelords that the Eydarith stand with the Tempest's chosen, Khesran Veyl of Vanris."

"Veyl." Kyril touched her arm.

At the contact, the sensation of the serpent coiled

around her, the cold pressure, and the lightning all slipped away. Veyl sagged against him, the room spinning, sending her stomach into rebellion. Without him to keep her upright, she might have fallen, and the chances of her not throwing up were growing more remote by the second.

He shifted his position to shield her from Kronach's sight with his body and lowered his voice. "Fight it. Don't let him see anything he would consider weakness in you now."

For a moment, anger flared, and she considered throwing up on him. It was easy for him to tell her to fight it. His insides hadn't dissolved into a quivering, rebellious mass. Then she felt strength flowing through her from him and the wave dancers. The more they gave her, the more stable she became.

As the weakness ebbed and her stomach settled, anger crept in again. Kronach might not have betrayed them to Jaysen, but he had set them up by telling them to come here unarmed. She reached along her connection to the wavelord and wrested some strength from him, merely to show him she could do so.

Finding it possible to stand on her own again, she stepped away from Kyril and swallowed back against the last remnants of her nausea before facing their host. When she met his eyes, he bowed his head to her. A small gesture, but one that carried considerable weight.

"You have shown the Tempest that you are worthy of his favor. My people will stand with you. That does not mean I expect to gain nothing in return. Your country will back the Eydarith. When the dust settles and Sarket's next king tries to retaliate against us for supporting you, Vanris will come to our defense. You are the Tempest's child now as much as you are the daughter of your parents. You are his gift to us, and we are his to you."

Were all his people as strange as he was? Was it a product of their religion or simply a quirk of Kronach himself?

Veyl lifted her chin. "Tezaak Amera said you had information for me."

Kronach returned to his throne and sat, tossing one leg over an arm of the large seat. "The undead prince has already taken control of Thrasser and the capital city through him."

Veyl's stomach clenched. "How? Word would have gotten out if he had attacked Andaro."

"He did not have to attack. He snuck some of his mind-crafters into the city and is using them to control the king regent. With Thrasser doing his bidding, he has been able to move in quietly and take over without drawing attention."

"I thought he wanted to kill Thrasser," Ahrin said, stepping closer to the dais.

"He has a new target," Feyd remarked, the certainty in his tone sending a chill through Veyl.

"Vanris." As Veyl said it, Kronach nodded. "Then my father is in terrible danger. Why didn't you tell me sooner?"

"Because you had to find your truth first, and I needed to see if the Tempest would embrace you fully before I could give you our support. It appears he has done so." The lightning started rising in her again, and Kronach held up a hand to stay her. "I also knew we had a little time. The undead prince intends to tell your father Thrasser has agreed to face him in Andaro, and that they both want Vanris to bear witness. Whatever he has planned, he does not mean to do it until he has your father in the capital."

"A trap." Kyril's hands tightened into fists. "How else could he hope to defeat Vanris's greatest Feral?"

Gannon faced her. "I know we have a lot to deal

with and little time, but we should find a few minutes to discuss what happened with Jaysen's men just now. There can be no uncertainty among us if we are to be of any use to your father as a unit."

"You're right." Veyl turned to Jinau. "Would you be willing to question some of Jaysen's men and see if you can learn more?"

Jinau nodded. "I will, Seh'hali, but I do not believe that is the uncertainty your tehnaak wishes to address."

Veyl knew that, but what had happened unsettled her. With that cold power flowing through her, allowing her to wield abilities she shouldn't have, she had felt invincible. She had also felt apart, disconnected from everyone else in the room, even her bonded companions. Now that the power had retreated, an intense sense of aloneness settled in its place, along with a potent fear. When it had only been the Frightener ability, she had broken and hurt many people. What might happen now?

"We need to be comfortable working together to have any hope of success," Gannon pressed.

She looked at him where he stood close to his brother, Iyvalin, and Kitria, all four of them watching her with an almost palpable unease. Dailan didn't appear any less uneasy. Kyril and Jinau proved their long-held conviction that she was something special by stepping in closer to support her. Feyd unexpectedly moved over next to the two Thaelian men, and Veyl gave him a questioning look.

The Dampener shrugged. "Who am I to argue if the Tempest or the ocean itself wants to help us through you? We could use any advantage we can get right now."

"You may be more comfortable with that idea than I am." Veyl looked over them, her gaze settling on the wave dancers, both of whom watched her intently with those ocean-colored eyes. Was some of this their doing?

"I will accompany Ahndhomen Jinau to speak with

our prisoners." Kronach got up and descended from the dais, placing a hand briefly on her shoulder as he walked past in a disconcertingly companionable way.

Veyl watched him for a second, puzzled by the gesture, before nodding to Jinau. When the Thaelian Charmer followed the wavelord, she met Feyd's eyes. She found it hard to trust Kronach, even after he had declared his support for her.

The Dampener bent in a slight bow. "Dailan and I will also accompany them. The captain might speak Vanrian, but Kronach does not, so it may be useful to have us there to bridge that gap."

"Thank you, Omren Feyd."

On the way out the door, Kronach paused and beckoned to one of his female warriors. "Show them to my private sitting room where they can speak among themselves."

Once he and the others had departed, the warrior led the rest of them to a circular chamber on the top floor of the main keep. Every aspect of the space evoked the ocean, and not in a subtle way. From couches and chairs with wavelike curves upholstered in shades of blue, to a marble fireplace with two cresting waves carved up the sides, and a lush carpet the dark color of deep water just before it turned black beyond the reach of light, everything spoke to a pure dedication to the mighty ocean. Paintings and tapestries depicted the ocean and its creatures in a variety of seasons. Shells and pieces of driftwood, some arranged on small piles of sand, sat in displays on the mantle and on each of the tables. Several arched windows on the western side looked out over the city's rooftops onto a stunning view of the coastline.

Feeling a little of the earlier weakness creeping in again, Veyl sank into a chair. Kitria, Ahrin, and Iyvalin took up one couch. Gannon sat in a seat across from her, and Kyril settled on the other couch to her left. Ceris lay between them, and Seyn stretched out on Veyl's right.

"It looked like you Charmed the Sarketi captain back there," Ahrin said, mercilessly diving into the fraught conversation.

"She did a lot more than that," Gannon stated.

Irritation flared in Veyl, and she gave her tehnaak a hard look that he didn't shy away from. He may have felt some of the power she had used through their bond, but did that mean he needed to unsettle everyone more with that information?

Kyril set a hand on her arm. "They deserve to know, Veyl."

She blew out a breath and closed her eyes for a moment. When she opened them again, the others were watching her the way they might watch a volatile stranger. "It wasn't Feyd who took away their sight either," she admitted.

"And the one who acted like a Frightener had gotten to him, was that your doing too?" Iyvalin leaned back a fraction in her spot when she asked, as if instinctively trying to put more distance between them.

Veyl nodded, an ache spreading in her chest.

"How is that possible?" Gannon asked.

Kitria was silent, her troubled gaze focused on her brother's hand on Veyl's arm as though she feared he would contract some illness through that contact.

Veyl wanted to give them an answer that would satisfy them and change the way they regarded her, but she could only shake her head. "I don't know."

"Because she is the Daughter of the Ocean," Kyril stated.

Veyl wanted to slap him for saying it, though she settled for merely pulling her arm away and folding her hands in her lap.

Somewhat surprisingly, it was Kitria who leaned forward and asked, "What does that really mean?"

Veyl gave Kyril a scathing look. "Yes, explain it to us like we're children."

His confident regard offered her no escape from the fate his words imposed upon her. "It means you are gifted. It means the powers of the ocean have chosen you to fight for your people and given you the ability to do so. In this case, that doesn't mean just Vanrians. You fight for the Thaelians, the Qwilki, and perhaps the Eydarith too."

Veyl scowled and turned to look out toward the ocean.

"You didn't break anyone," Ahrin offered, his tone tentative, as if he feared angering her. "That's a positive sign. Do you feel you have more control now than you did when your Frightener ability first awakened?"

"Yes." She looked down at her hands, unsure how to explain that this unprecedented power somehow felt simultaneously more within her control and wholly untamed. "It doesn't feel… the same," she finished lamely.

"So, you're basically manifesting all the mind-crafter abilities," Gannon said.

It wasn't entirely that either, at least not in their typical form. Normally, a mind-crafter with a specific ability could not affect others who shared that ability, but Jaysen's Dampener had deprived her of her vision, and she had done effectively the same to him. Maybe it was best not to make things more confusing at the moment. "I suppose so."

Restless, she got up and walked to the windows.

"Do we go to Balarus now?" Iyvalin asked.

"Yes," Gannon answered immediately.

Veyl gave a slight nod, staring out at the distant waves crashing upon the shore beneath a gray sky. "Yes," she agreed. "I need to meet with Kronach once they're done questioning our prisoners."

Gannon stood when she glanced back at them. "I'll

let him know."

Ahrin also got up, the two women standing with him. "We'll make sure he does so respectfully."

"Thank you." She turned to gaze out the windows again, listening to them leave, all except the wave dancers and Kyril. After a few quiet minutes, he walked up behind her and slid his hands around her waist. She gave in to his gentle pull and leaned back into him. "Why is none of this happening to you?"

"When I was with my partner, Helaya—"

The name surprised her a little. "She was Qwilki?"

"Mostly." He leaned in to press his lips to her head before continuing. "Her mother told me once that I could not stay with her. That I belonged to the ocean and was destined to support and love another. I resented her for that. When Helaya died, I wondered if it was my fault, somehow, because maybe I really wasn't supposed to be with her. I wondered if, had I not loved her, she might have been spared."

Veyl reached down to take his hand and twine her fingers through his, offering silent comfort.

"Nagi told me there would be two of us, and that I was merely a fragment of the greater whole. My role would be to guide, support, and complete the other. To be honest, my pride had a problem with that notion for a long time." He chuckled, the sound bringing a brief smile to her lips. "Then I met you, and I discovered that, if you truly were the Daughter of the Ocean, I didn't mind the idea of being a missing piece of you so much."

He kissed her head again, and she pressed back into his arms more, savoring his strength. Her thoughts drifted to their night together, bringing a delicious warmth that turned to a chill when she remembered the observation he had shared as he fell asleep. "The scar on my leg has changed," she murmured. "In my... dream, when I was under the influence of whatever Kronach gave me, I sank into the depths of the ocean. There were whales there, and a ji'ikyan that embraced me and stung my leg in the same spot again."

He tightened his hold on her a fraction, the force becoming almost uncomfortable, though not enough for her to want to be free of him. "We'll figure this out." He was silent for a few seconds, watching the waves with her, then he said, "What you did in the throne room this morning was incredible, but it took a lot out of you. You should tell the others about that too. You may not always have the wave dancers or me with you to bolster you. They need to know the danger so they can help you if you require it."

Veyl only nodded and leaned her head back against him. When had everything gotten so complicated?

## CHAPTER TWENTY

Veyl stared at Kronach over a horseshoe-shaped table that curved beneath three chandeliers made from the bones of various ocean creatures. She had never been in this room before, though it was familiar in the way it, like most of the rest of the castle, brought the Eydarith devotion to the dynamic world of the ocean inside through the decor. Had the wavelord met with Jaysen for negotiations in this room, beneath these chandeliers? Might the crown prince have sat in this very chair, facing him?

Her former tehnaak, now her enemy in this dangerous political game.

She reached along the link to Gannon, grateful that bond connected her to him now and not the crown prince… The king of Sarket. If Jaysen really had quietly taken over Andaro, that would be his title soon. He was always supposed to assume the Sarketi throne, and she had accepted that for him, even though it meant losing a dear friend. Why couldn't Thrasser simply have let him take his rightful place as planned rather than attempting to have him killed? How much suffering might they have avoided if the king regent had merely followed the plan of succession? That wasn't an option anymore, though. Not now that Jaysen's actions were endangering her family and her people.

She narrowed her eyes at Kronach. "You claim you wish to be our allies, and yet you balk at the first request for aid?"

"My people have not had time to prepare for this."

Veyl sneered. "Horseshit."

Next to her, Gannon snorted a laugh, quickly covering his mouth and turning it into a cough.

Veyl did her best to ignore him, giving more space to the determination coming from Kyril on her other side. "You cannot tell me that you, the cunning wavelord who is always devising ways to manipulate a situation to his benefit or amusement, did not foresee this possibility. I will not believe it. You are merely stalling because you want to watch me fight this battle and see how I do. I will no longer stand for being your entertainment at the expense of my safety and that of my people. This alliance lives or dies with your choice right now, Wavelord. We don't have time to argue with you." Energy crackled within her, and she let a little of it seep out, encouraging it to flow in his direction.

"You don't have time not to, and I enjoy your temper, Khesran." Kronach grinned, his open pleasure making Veyl yearn to strike him in the jaw with the unyielding hilt of a dark metal dagger. His expression sobered after a moment. "Very well, I will send a unit of my warriors with you, but you had best not fail once the public has seen that we are working together."

"Tezaak Amera will also accompany us." Kyril's tone was definitive. It wasn't a question.

The demand surprised Veyl a little, though she didn't let that show, offering a firm nod of support instead. They had to appear united if they were going to make progress with Kronach. The slightest hint of discord in their group would be irresistible to the wavelord.

"Amera is lovely, isn't she?" Kronach asked, apparently still searching for a crack in their rapport to insinuate a wedge into.

"She has skills that could be useful, and she is familiar with our group," Kyril answered, his stony expression hardening even more.

"Valid points, Ahnkreth. She may join you. I have other tezaak if I need such services." Kronach barely looked at Kyril through the brief exchange, his attention staying on Veyl, searching for her reactions. "I advise you to proceed with caution, Khesran. The farther you are from the ocean that feeds you, the weaker your powers may become."

Keenly aware of the presence of the vast expanse of water always in the back of her mind now, she clung to her calm regard, letting Seyn absorb the brunt of her unease at his words. "Do you never have anything encouraging to say?"

Kronach met Kyril's eyes for a moment, then turned back to her. "I will make you strong, Khesran. I will not coddle you."

There was an underlying suggestion of a proposition in his words that she opted to ignore. "At least you are honest."

"My army is yours now, Khesran Veyl, but I will not endanger them needlessly. We will be there when you need us, but until word has reached the other wavelords of our villages along the coast, you must be content with what I give you."

•

"Sheyvyosk!" Veyl kicked the leg of a chair as soon as the sitting-room door closed behind them. The piece of furniture skidded sideways, one leg carving a deep scratch in the beautiful, polished wood floor. The tiny act of destruction brought a glimmer of satisfaction. "Insufferable man. He's like a hound master, doling out treats and expecting me to wag my tail with delight at his attention."

Ahrin calmly shifted the chair back a little from its original placement, and Iyvalin tugged the center rug over, covering the scar on the floor before settling into the seat.

"Couldn't you just Charm him?" Kitria asked, helping Ahrin adjust the position of one couch to match the rug. Once they had it lined up properly, she sank down on it next to him.

"I cannot. Kronach and I share a bond. He would know I was doing it, and that connection might render it ineffective besides."

Gannon's brows pinched as he set his hands on the back of another chair, casually shifting it into alignment with the rug. "Like a tehnaak bond?"

Kyril and Jinau nudged the ends of the other couch with their legs before stepping around to sit on it.

Feyd chuckled.

Veyl couldn't hold back a little laugh at how they had united silently in the effort to cover up for her. "I love you all." She met Gannon's eyes. "No, it's not like a tehnaak bond. Almost more like the connections that link me to the wave dancers, though not as robust. Something to do with being wave-touched, apparently."

"So, what now?" Jinau asked, his intense attention making it clear the question was hers to answer.

Veyl drew a deep breath and looked over them, one hand sinking to Seyn's head. "Kronach asked for an hour to gather the unit he will send with us. We should eat and get ready to depart. I intend to prepare a missive for one of his messengers to take to Etrion. My mother needs to know what is happening in case we run into trouble in Balarus." She bit at her lower lip, stopping quickly when Kyril's gaze focused on the movement and a faint grin tugged at one corner of his mouth, taking her thoughts to the night spent in his arms. Her cheeks warmed, and she looked away from him. "I only wish we knew who the traitor was that told Jaysen I was coming here. Very few were aware of this before my father left Etrion."

"Uh…" Dailan, who had been hanging back behind his tehnaak, took a step forward. "Khesran, I might have a likely suspect."

Veyl arched a brow at him. "Go on."

"After your mother told us to prepare to accompany you, I said something about it to Leath, not realizing that she and Tassa weren't going to be part of the unit this time. It wasn't until I was talking to Ahrin and Iyvalin this morning regarding our mission in Crimsondale that I understood exactly what happened between you and Tassa there." His gaze pulled Kyril in. "Well, the three of you. If she held a grudge and wanted to punish you and Kyril for that, sending Jaysen after you would be an effective way to do so."

Iyvalin frowned at him. "But Tassa and Leath didn't go to Balarus either."

"No," Feyd agreed, "but as an Evoker—"

Veyl instantly saw where he was going. "She would have a unique advantage if she wished to search out someone in the units my father took with him who would be amenable to passing a message to Jaysen's people."

Gannon shook his head, scowling at the floor as if it had wronged him. "The khemron is extremely particular about his soldiers." He looked up at her, a visible tightening around his eyes. "But all she really needed was to find someone willing to pass a missive to Jaysen's messengers before they left the city along with your father's company. In Etrion, that's a lot easier than any of us wants to admit with the anti-mind-crafters about."

Iyvalin frowned, her troubled expression creating a little V between her brows. "But they're still Vanrian, would they really want to help Jaysen?"

Feyd's voice had an uncharacteristic gentleness to it when he spoke, as if he regretted what he was about to say. "The citizens of Etrion don't know of all the recent discord between Veyl and the crown prince. The council has deliberately kept information about his betrayal in Thaelis from becoming widespread. He is the rightful heir to Sarket's throne and, per common knowledge, a dear friend to the khesran. Many who favor Veyl becoming khevarin because they still believe she is not a mind-crafter also think the introduction of non-Vanrian bloodlines could be beneficial to our people."

Veyl recoiled inside. "You're not suggesting they would support a political marriage?"

Feyd nodded. "I am."

The mere notion made her nauseous, and not only because it was Jaysen. She looked at Kyril, who had set his brief fixation on her lips aside for more important matters. He knew firsthand what intermixing would do to the mind-crafter bloodlines, but how did he truly feel about that? Being part-Qwilki, he shared some of their beliefs and supported their people. The woman he had loved before her had been mostly Qwilki. And yet, he had been collecting her people to help strengthen the pure Vanrian bloodlines in Thaelis. But had he really supported that outcome? She supposed it was possible, if for no other reason than to improve their defenses against threats like the Ukhen'kya.

Kyril's brow furrowed as if her prolonged regard troubled him. "We can't know for certain, but it might be worth mentioning these suspicions in your missive to the khevarin. It is hard to commit to making yourself a traitor. If Tassa has taken that initial step, she could prove to be a greater threat going forward. Your mother will have the resources to investigate."

Veyl used the middle finger and thumb of one hand to rub her temples, wishing she could squeeze out the growing headache. "Very well. Make certain we're ready to depart. I will prepare the missive."

Once she had finished that task, she shared a meal with the others, asking Feyd and Jinau to look over what she had written before she gave it to Kronach. When they were ready, they took their few belongings out to the main courtyard, where their mounts were already waiting. Amera and twenty Eydarith warriors, many of whom Veyl had often seen in Kronach's company on her two visits to Taro, were there as well. Kronach himself sat in an elaborate chair made of driftwood on a raised platform overlooking the courtyard.

Veyl strode over to him, waving Kyril and Gannon back when they moved to accompany her. The wavelord stood and waited for her, watching her climb the stairs with Seyn at her side, his subtle smirk giving her the uncomfortable impression that he could imagine too well what she would look like without her clothing. Hammering down the unease that always came with being in his presence, she walked up beside him and turned to scan the unit he was sending with her.

"These warriors…" She glanced at him. "I recognize many of them."

"They are some of my finest."

"Thank you. We appreciate your generosity." She held out the missive. "I have one more favor to ask. I need this delivered to Khevarin Velara as quickly as possible. She needs to be apprised of the situation if she is to be ready to come to my aid, or yours, should things go poorly in Balarus."

He took the sealed letter and handed it to a warrior waiting behind his chair, speaking to the woman in their blended language. When she departed, he turned back to Veyl. "I have never given such gifts to any woman. Are you impressed yet?"

Veyl gave a weary huff. "You know I love another. Why do you persist in acting as if there is some courtship between us?"

"A foolish question, Princess."

"Khesran," she snapped, more annoyed because she had let him get under her skin yet again than by his use of the southern title.

He faced her, somehow moving closer as he turned without visibly advancing. He drew a deep breath, as if inhaling her scent, and a predatory smile curved his lips. "Even were you hideous to look upon, you would remain the most desired political match in all Pandrea. Your kingdom has proven its strength, and you are the heir to that power."

Veyl didn't let herself back away, though it occurred to her that her stubborn will might be compelling her to react exactly as he wanted her to. "Is that it? You desire Vanris's might?"

"I acknowledge it would be beneficial to my people. What I find irresistible is the scent of the Tempest upon you." He leaned close to her ear, his voice lowering to an intimate whisper. "My god has embraced you. His serpent has pressed its length against the warmth of your bare skin. How could I not wish to do the same?"

Veyl swallowed, remembering the ji'ikyan twined around her naked body, that interaction becoming more sensual with the innuendo in his words. How did he even know those details? "I love Kyril."

Unexpectedly, he grinned and shifted back a little, though not nearly as far as she wished he would. "And what benefit is there for your Thaelian Feral if he can secure his claim upon you?"

"Our relationship isn't like that."

Kronach lowered his voice again. "Apologies, Khesran,

I thought he might have gained something from having Vanris's backing. I did not realize he was immune to such temptations. Any advantage your affection has earned him and his people was certainly unintentional."

Kronach moved away, and she wondered if he could feel the gut punch his words had dealt her through their link. If so, he didn't let it show.

She looked at Kyril. He had been part of a resistance movement intending to overthrow the Thaelian council before the Devastation culled their numbers. A man who, with her support, had gained Vanris's commitment to take down that council and help them deal with the Ukhen'kya. Everything he had wanted to accomplish with his weakened rebellion on Thaelis had become attainable again through the power her love gave him access to. Outcomes he still stood to see through once they finished with Sarket. Had he considered all that before he slept with her in Thaelis? Could any of this have occurred to him from the moment he discovered who she was in Deepwater? Might that be why he treated her the way he did on his ship, protecting her while isolating her from the others, making her dependent upon him?

Kyril looked at her, the tightening around his eyes telling her he could sense something was amiss. A rising breeze played with the ends of his black hair, two braids done in the Vanrian soldier style along one side exposing a fine, pointed ear. Those strong features and icy silver-blue eyes made him heartbreakingly handsome. Could he have manipulated her without even needing to involve an Evoker or Charmer?

His brows rose a fraction, asking silently if everything was all right.

If he had an ulterior motive in the beginning, would that matter now? He loved her, didn't he?

"These warriors will see you safe to Balarus and follow your commands," Kronach was telling her. "They are yours as long as you do not ask them to betray our people."

Something in the way he said "our people" made it sound as if he intended those words to encompass her. She couldn't concern herself with that now. These Eydarith fighters were hers to command for the time being. A generous offer considering how he had balked at giving her anything earlier, although it wouldn't surprise her if he had planned this from the start, arguing against it at the table just so he might appear benevolent now. "I would not put them in that position. Thank you, Wavelord," she answered past the constriction in her throat. Never had she wanted to punch the Eydarith leader more than she did right now. "We should be on our way."

"Tempest guide you."

They hadn't escaped the borders of the city yet before Veyl turned in the saddle to give Kyril a scrutinizing look. A light drizzle had started as they left the courtyard, dampening everything beneath the dense cloud cover of a darkening sky. "At what point did you decide to use me to accomplish your political goals? Was it when you learned who I was in Deepwater or later?"

Kyril let out a slow breath and shook his head, his posture stiffening, perhaps because she had put him on the spot with some of their companions in earshot. "This is Kronach's doing, isn't it?"

She faced forward, extending her ability so she could determine how honest he was being without having to look at him. "Please answer my question."

Kyril also stared ahead, his horse moving a little closer to hers. Frustration flowed from him, carried on an undercurrent of regret. "It occurred to me when I learned who you were that if I could get you to trust me, I might eventually sway you against the council. Your support would give us a solid start to earning that of the others we had taken from Vanris, and our resistance would gain a sudden surge in numbers that included more mind-crafters."

"And the possibility that you might get my country to aid you if I spoke up for you, did that occur to you then too?"

He shook his head, a subtle gesture she barely caught out of the corner of her eye. "No. That came later, when the council ordered us to go back for more."

"Before or after you were intimate with me for the first time?" His discomfort and a growing sense of guilt were enough to answer for him, but she waited for him to say it.

"Before," he said, lowering his voice some, "but that isn't why I took you to my bed."

"Really?" She looked at him, burying the hurt deep beneath her anger.

"It was a complicated situation, Veyl." His words brought a sharp flare of dark emotion from Gannon and, surprisingly, from Kitria, who was the closest to them. There was little reaction from Jinau, who rode within listening range as well, which made her suspect he had already known all of this. "You won me over long before I captured your interest, enough so that I hated myself for not being honest with you, but I had to put the needs of my people first. I barely knew you, and yet my feelings for you—"

"Enough." Energy crackled through and around her when she glared at him. "I don't want to hear any more. I was a naïve young woman in a desperate situation, and you took advantage of that."

Recalling how her father talked about using his Feral ability when he told stories of the war to her and Tavin, she focused on her mount and encouraged the animal to go faster. It took less effort than she expected, though perhaps that was because of their proximity to the ocean. The horse broke into a trot, then transitioned to an easy lope. The rest of the party adjusted their speed, keeping her toward the center of the group. Kyril dropped behind, his sister and Jinau falling back with him as the twins and Iyvalin moved up around her. She hoped the moisture accumulating in her hair and on her face would be enough to hide the occasional warm tear that ran down her cheeks.

Kronach was right. Her position made her too attractive a pawn to expect a genuine relationship. If she survived this, there would be suitors aplenty to choose from. Someone would provide a tolerable match if she went into it with her eyes open to the reality of the situation. Besides, Kyril would return to Thaelis in time, and she could not go with him. Vanris was her country. Her home. What she had with him was fated to be brief from the start, no matter what she wanted to believe, even before she knew it was all a lie. Still, acknowledging that didn't make her feel any better about it.

She shook herself and focused on moving the horse a little faster. They might reach Balarus late tomorrow if they maintained a good pace. For now, she needed to keep her mind on the threat to her father. When he was safe, she could worry her silly head over things like childish heartbreak and infantile fantasies of love.

## CHAPTER TWENTY ONE

Veyl watched Amera and Feyd make their way back to where she and the others waited. The outer walls of the keep at Balarus, made from tall, narrow trees that grew in abundance there, rose behind the two. The rest of the company remained hidden off the road in the shadows of the forest.

Not long after leaving Taro, the Eydarith tezaak informed them she spoke passable Vanrian. She had merely chosen not to until Kronach decided whether they would stand with Veyl. As annoying as the revelation was in its way, it was at least helpful in that it created an easier, if still imperfect, bridge in communication between one of the Eydarith and the three Thaelians.

The two riders focused on Veyl now, their mouths set in matching grim lines. It was all she could do not to run out to meet them, but they couldn't risk exposing the rest of the company, Vanris's heir in particular, before they had a thorough understanding of the situation.

Feyd shook his head, his silvery hair, gray eyes, and pale skin making a ghost of him in the fading light. His expression remained dour as their horses covered the last few feet and slipped between the trees to join them. He waited until they had stopped and dismounted before speaking. "Most of Khemron Kasiel's company headed south yesterday morning with Prince Jaysen, supposedly to meet with the king regent. Apparently, he also sent a couple of soldiers back to Etrion to update the khevarin."

"Shit." Gannon's words were adequate to encompass what they were all feeling.

Veyl felt ill, fear for her father and his tehsheyn twisting her stomach into knots. "We have to go after them."

"We should find a place to camp for tonight." Amera cast a meaningful glance toward the darkening sky. "It is overcast. There won't be enough light for us to travel safely once it grows dark, particularly with a company this large."

"And the horses need rest," Iyvalin added, giving Veyl an apologetic look. "We pushed them fairly hard to get here."

Veyl yearned to argue with them, but they were right. They had kept a harsh pace to reach Balarus as quickly as they had, and the horses weren't the only ones worn down by the effort. Come morning, her father and Jaysen would be a full two days ahead of them, but the night promised to be devoid of the light of moon or stars. They wouldn't be able to travel safely.

"We'll still have adequate light for another hour at least," Kyril suggested. "And the horses got a brief rest here."

Veyl nodded, avoiding looking at him. She didn't want him to see her gratitude. "Let's cover as much ground as we can while we have enough light remaining. We'll keep watch for a place to camp."

The company struck out at speed again, though they didn't push as hard this time to avoid hurting the horses. The route to Andaro from Balarus cut east and then south into the mountains along the one reasonably passable road. Any more direct options were steep and rugged enough to add several days and a greater risk of injury to the journey. It was nearing full dark when Torlif, a thickly muscled warrior with shaggy black hair and several braids worked into his beard, led them off the main road to a flatter, less densely forested area where he had claimed to have camped before. With little chatter, they went about settling in for the night.

Too restless to relax after she finished tending her mount, Veyl stood beside the animal, stroking its neck and gazing up at the dark sky through the thin canopy of evergreens. Kyril wandered over, his presence announcing itself across their bond before he reached her side.

"Can we talk?"

Her immediate inclination was to say no. She didn't want to deal with the storm of emotions he inspired right now, but then Gannon intervened by walking up on her other side and taking her horse, a behavior he appeared to be making a habit of. He cast a meaningful look at Kyril before leading the animal off, conveying encouragement for the two of them to work out their issues without speaking a word.

Veyl gestured away from the others with one hand and started walking. Kyril accompanied her, his strides strong, but measured, as if intentionally trying to match her pace.

"It was Kronach who convinced you to question me, wasn't it?" He asked when she stopped them.

"It was." A slight sting of shame came with the admission.

"You know he's only trying to drive a wedge between us so he might convince you he is not such an unpleasant alternative after all."

She nodded, staring at the dark leather armor that covered his chest because she didn't want to sink into his lovely eyes. "Yes, I know that. I just needed him to be wrong."

He put his hands on her arms, preventing her from turning away, and leaned closer. "But you knew he wasn't. You knew I came to Deepwater believing your people were our enemies. Yes, I originally set out to manipulate you, but even after a lifetime of indoctrination against your people, I became unquestionably yours long before we reached Thaelis. I was at war with myself over you for the entire crossing. I would have returned to Vanris to help you regardless, but I came up with a way my growing attachment to you could still serve our cause. Doing so merely allowed me to justify it to myself.

"You threw my life into chaos, Veyl, and I would choose that chaos again at every turn as long as it meant I could be with you." He slid his fingers under her chin, and she gave to the gentle pressure, reluctantly meeting his eyes. "Tell me, when you gave yourself to me in Thaelis, was it truly because you were falling for me or was it a price you were willing to pay to secure my help?"

She breathed a small laugh, aware of how her answer would mirror his words. "I may have justified it by telling myself it would convince you to aid us, but I wanted you to be my first. My last. My only. I chose to believe that you helped me on your ship because it was the kind thing to do. I needed to believe it. The possibility that you could do what you did and see me as nothing more than a means to an end when I was so vulnerable...so close to breaking... It makes me feel like a fool for letting myself fall in love with you."

A tear slipped down her cheek, and she reached up to brush it off, but he caught her wrist in a gentle grip and moved her hand to the side. Then he carefully wiped it away himself.

"I made mistakes. I was so desperate to save my people from the Ukhen'kya and from our own council that I hurt you and yours in the process. The instant I looked into your eyes in Deepwater, I knew my life was about to change, but I resisted it. My people needed me, and I stubbornly refused to believe a Vanrian could be the one to make me whole again." He brushed a tear from her other cheek before continuing. "When I walked into the room they had put you in, I felt something awaken in me. The future I had planned fell apart in a moment. Ceris's instant affinity for you only confirmed it. I unfairly resented you for that, because part of me still believed that if I was meant to be with you, then Helaya's death was my fault."

She desperately wanted to take him at his word, but Kronach had known what he was talking about. All this time, she had been foolish enough to pretend she would find a partner in life and love the same way anyone else would. Like it or not, that wasn't how it worked when your love came with influence over a powerful kingdom attached. "How do I know this is real? Your people still need our help. How much easier will it be to ensure they receive it if you have a khesran of Vanris willing to fight for them with you?"

His jaw clenched, a flicker of frustration in his brief glance away, but his voice was full of conviction when he spoke. "There is nothing I wouldn't do to protect you and see you through this safely. I need you to believe that. I want you to understand that I will fight for Vanris as hard as I do for Thaelis. But you... I would give my life for you, and I will be there for you no matter what we find at the end of this road. If you can't bring yourself to trust my words, then trust our bond."

Veyl gazed into the face of this man she had become so familiar with since that awful night in Deepwater. He was right. The answers she wanted lay within him, and she had the means to find them.

She pressed one palm to the center of his chest and closed her eyes, seeking the bonds that existed within her. How many were there now? One at a time, she suppressed them, silencing the connections to the wave-touched she could still sense, then to Gannon, and Ceris. Seyn whimpered softly when she did the same to their bond. She would have to apologize to the wave dancer later. When she had muted all the other links, she focused her full attention on the one that bound her to Kyril.

What she found was not just a complete love bond, but one that was of equal strength along its full length. If anything, it appeared slightly stronger at his end, as if the weaver of that thread had grown weary when they reached her side. A discovery that surprised her. That wasn't all, however. Some of the cool, calming fortitude that she associated with the ocean and the wave dancers flowed through that link as well, passing between them along the bond.

Veyl opened herself fully to that connection, letting it flow into her, feeling the intricate weave of love, devotion, and underlying power that created as it moved through her. Warmth filled her, banishing the chill of the night. Kyril's presence enfolded her, both a comforting blanket and a steady shield. He became part of her, an inseparable aspect of her being, and yet still a unique and separate entity.

Giving more of herself to that single link, she reached out to his end, inviting him to share the experience with her. Without opening her eyes, she felt an instant of surprise, followed by genuine pleasure. She didn't have to look to sense him moving closer before his lips pressed to hers, bringing their bond to a new level of completion with physical touch in the form of a soft, lingering kiss.

When they parted, she finally opened her eyes. "I should have belie..." She trailed off when he placed a gentle finger to her lips.

"With everything you've been through—everything the people around you have put you through, myself included—you have every reason to be cautious with your trust. You don't need to apologize for questioning me. I merely hope you know you can trust me now. Whatever we face ahead, you can rely on me."

Veyl stepped forward into his arms and leaned against him, resting her cheek on his chest. "I'm tired," she murmured, allowing the other connections to spark to life again when she noticed Seyn still staring forlornly up at her. She held one hand down, and the wave dancer pressed her nose into it.

Kyril wrapped his arms around her and kissed her head. "You should be. I wish I could promise you rest, but I fear that may not come for some time yet."

Veyl nodded. She stayed in his arms for a few minutes before they separated and rejoined the others. The group split up around two small fires, eating a passable meal they had pulled together. Kronach's warriors were skilled in the art of living on the road and put considerable effort into ensuring she didn't have to waste energy on such mundane tasks. In truth, those tasks might have provided a welcome distraction. Still, there seemed little point in arguing with them over it, since their behavior appeared to be couched in respect for her rank and role rather than the usual misguided Sarketi misogyny. The Eydarith, despite being people of Sarket, didn't seem to cater to those divisive notions.

Turning her attention to the others, she watched Ahrin for a few minutes as he stared into the fire, his brow furrowed while his fingers absently worked the bark off a twig. "What's bothering you, Ahrin?"

His eyes snapped up, and he glanced around, looking almost startled at finding everyone else there. "I was wondering…" He paused and tossed aside the twig. "You were in the planning meetings. Do you know who went with your father?"

His question caused a squeezing sensation in her

chest. "Are your parents with him, you mean?"

"I suppose." Ahrin gave a self-conscious shrug. "I knew they were leaving. I just wasn't sure if they both rode out with the khemron or if Father and Kince headed out for the coast again to help the dhomvalen."

Veyl pushed away the slight resentment that rose with the fact that he was asking because they all knew her father was marching into a trap. She couldn't blame him for worrying about his parents, or even wanting to prioritize them, but her own overwhelming fear for her father made it hard to remain objective. "My father took his tehsheyn with him."

Ahrin lowered his gaze, staring into the fire again as he gave a solemn nod. Their father and mother would both be arriving in Andaro with the khemron.

Gannon's jaw clenched. He kept his thoughts to himself, but a sense of distress that mirrored her own whispered across their bond.

"What about his beasts?" Iyvalin asked.

Veyl absently set a hand on Seyn's shoulder where the wave dancer lay curled against her leg. "He left Irith behind, but he took Niskenya and one of the tethdraks."

"They'll have to kill the beasts to get to him," Jinau remarked.

The pop when he snapped a branch in two to add to the fire made Veyl jump, and she blinked against the sting of tears as an unpleasant chill moved through her. Losing Niskenya would be a kind of death for her father. She had to believe they would arrive in time to prevent such an outcome, though it all depended on how quickly Jaysen meant to spring his trap and what he hoped to accomplish by doing so.

"We will not get close to Andaro without being challenged," Amera commented.

It was an unwelcome observation, though no less true for that. Their company was too large to approach the capital without drawing attention, especially during a time of internal strife.

"We have two Dampeners," Feyd offered, glancing at Veyl.

"One and a half," she corrected. "I barely know what I'm doing. But we might have another option." She turned to Amera. "Jaysen sent those men to Taro to collect me and take me to him. Kronach summoning me to Taro while the crown prince was away brings his loyalty into question, but if his warriors were to deliver me to Jaysen themselves, they could claim that was Kronach's intention all along."

"But won't it look suspicious if Jaysen's men don't arrive in Andaro with them?" Kitria asked.

Amera grinned, her nod of approval giving Veyl a spark of satisfaction. "No. The khesran is right. It would be consistent with Wavelord Kronach's ways to hold Jaysen's men back so he might take all the credit for himself."

"Fine, but it would also require us letting Veyl enter Andaro as a prisoner without her unit to protect her," Kyril stated, the tension in his voice enough to tell her he would fight against the idea.

Veyl watched a large owl land in a nearby tree and hoot out into the night, its presence bringing the night-star eagle, Akyla, to mind and heightening her concern for her father. She observed it for a moment, then met Gannon's eyes, knowing he and Kyril would be the hardest to win over. "What if we approached with half of the Eydarith and left the rest back with you? Caution and strategic help from Feyd could get you close without being noticed, especially if we draw their attention to the group I'm with. It would get us into the city, where we could assess the situation. Then Amera or one of the other Eydarith could report back and devise a strategy for bringing the rest of you inside the walls."

"What it would do is give Jaysen another chance to hurt you," Gannon stated, cutting off whatever protest Kyril started making next to her.

"I can handle myself. He doesn't know about my abilities. A little careful Charming should be enough to keep him from doing anything too drastic while we figure out our next move."

"You just admitted that you barely know what you're doing with these new powers. Not to mention, Jaysen has an unknown number of mind-crafters with him. For any ability you use, there may be someone there who can sense it." Kyril placed a hand on her shoulder, drawing her gaze to him. "And if Kronach was right about you being weaker farther inland, what will you do then?"

"I don't have to be as strong as I was in Taro. I am plenty strong enough to deal with him as I am now." She hoped that was true. The abilities she had manifested recently were far from familiar at this point. Counting on them was risky. "I will need Seyn to stay with you, though. He would kill her if I brought her with me."

"Leaving you even more vulnerable," Kyril countered.

How much did her abilities rely on the wave dancer? She forced confidence in her bearing and across her bonds. "Vanris needs my father right now. He and his tehsheyn are heroes to most of our people. Unless we come upon his company alive and well on the way to Andaro, we are going to have to get inside that city. We can charge in blind with all eyes free to fall upon us, or we can send a distraction ahead that will get some of us into the city and give us an element of surprise. One of these options has a much greater chance of success."

"And a greater chance of getting you killed," Gannon snapped.

"Or worse," Iyvalin said, just loud enough to send a shiver through Veyl.

The owl hooted and spread its magnificent wings, launching itself over them to disappear into the night. "I'm going to Andaro for my father, with or without your support. I would much rather have it."

Feyd, who had gotten up and was now standing a little out of the firelight, spoke softly into the silence that followed her declaration. "And what if your father is fine, but fighting breaks out because Kronach's men deliver you to the city?"

That was a possibility she hadn't considered. Her mistrust of Jaysen had become rooted so deeply now that she simply assumed they were heading into a hostile situation.

"That is easy," Amera said. "If there is no sign of trouble when we arrive, the Eydarith enter Andaro as Khesran Veyl's protectors rather than pretending to be her captors. The undead prince may hesitate to make any aggressive moves if he sees that Wavelord Kronach has decided to play a different hand."

"If you have to assume the role of her captors, how do we know we can trust you to help us free her from Prince Jaysen rather than reverting to your prior alliance with him?" Gannon demanded.

"The khesran is more than merely wave-touched now." Amera faced Veyl, a startling reverence in her regard and in the brief gesture she offered, resting her left hand over her right before her and bowing her head, a gesture the other Eydarith mirrored. "The Tempest embraced her and impregnated her with the seed of his power. Kronach has given us to Khesran Veyl. We will not hesitate to lay down our lives for her."

Veyl did her best to disregard the use of the word "impregnated," hoping it was simply a translation issue, though she found her thoughts returning to the serpent that had wound itself around her naked form in the dream. If this power she brought to Andaro with her could help her protect the people she loved, she didn't honestly care how uncomfortable the Eydarith woman's description of it made her. All that mattered was that it could be the answer to saving her father if Jaysen had already sprung a trap upon him and his company.

Amera's last few words sank in then, and Veyl straightened. "Wait. He's given you to me?"

Amera nodded. "Yes, Khesran. You are our wavelord now."

Veyl glanced around at the other Eydarith, all of whom still held the pose with their hands before them and heads bowed. Kronach had given her some of his best warriors. Exactly what did he expect in return?

A shout and clashing of steel in the darkness had them all on their feet in seconds, most, Veyl included, drawing their weapons. Silence followed, carrying with it the distinct overflow of a Charmer's ability to them. A glance around found Jinau missing, along with the expected three Eydarith who were on watch.

Rustling in the bushes to the west of the camp drew their attention, though the lack of concern from the two wave dancers gave Veyl the confidence to gesture for the rest of the group to hold their ground. After a few tense seconds, two Sarketi scouts emerged from the trees in the company of Jinau and one of the Eydarith. The warrior exchanged a few words in their language with Amera, then he glanced at Veyl. She offered him a firm nod upon receiving a more subtle nod of encouragement from Amera, not quite certain what message she was conveying. The warrior disappeared back into the trees, leaving them to handle the scouts.

Veyl strode forward before anyone else could. This was her mission, after all. One of the two Sarketi men was older, his brown hair peppered through with gray, though the deep lines that etched his features appeared to be as much from exposure to the elements as from age. The other was his opposite. Lighter-haired and smooth-skinned, his equipment barely showing signs of use and his youthful eyes bright with fear he hadn't learned to hide.

Four of the warriors, her warriors, circled around behind the scouts, blocking their retreat and allowing Jinau the freedom to approach her. "They were hiding in some bushes watching us. Close enough to over-hear, but wisely downwind." His gaze flickered to the wave dancers, and he nodded solemnly, as if forgiving them for not noticing the intruders. He looked at Veyl. "Would you like me to question them?"

Kyril stepped forward. "No. Let Khesran Veyl do it. She could use the practice, and it will let us see how well her abilities work away from the coast."

Veyl approached the Sarketi scouts, meeting the eyes of each as she drew upon the memory of influencing the guards in Crimsondale. After a few seconds, she focused her attention on the older of the two, finding that she disliked contributing to the fear in the younger man's eyes.

"It is a dark night," she said, letting her ability flow over the man. "A fine opportunity for training. That's why you are out here, isn't it? It would be a shame for that to end with someone getting hurt, wouldn't you agree?"

For a few seconds, she could see him trying to resist her, his brow tightening up into a series of severe ridges. All at once, the tension disappeared, and he nodded. "The boy needs to learn to scout with or without the light."

"How long were you watching us?"

"About twenty minutes."

"Captai—" The boy cut off his protest abruptly when one of the Eydarith touched the edge of her axe to his neck.

Veyl ignored them. "You must feel fortunate to have stumbled upon such valuable information."

"We do." The man grinned as if he still believed he would get the chance to make use of what they had learned.

"We have to kill them," Gannon stated.

Agreement came from most of the others. Moisture sprang up in the young scout's eyes along with a conspicuous darkening at the front of his pants.

Veyl considered the two. The boy looked like he might be around her age, if that. Barely getting started with his life. "We can't just kill them this way."

"What choice have we got?" Gannon countered. "If we take them with us, we risk exposure, and if we let them go, they'll run to the closest barracks for backup and come after us. If we had an Evoker..." He gave Veyl a searching look. "Do we have an Evoker?"

Unease crackled through her, and she reluctantly nodded. "I don't have much experience using it, though."

"Try," Feyd encouraged. "Worst case, you destroy their minds. If it works, they lose some memories of this night and live to see another. The alternative is we put them to death."

Veyl swallowed hard and nodded. "Jinau, will you help?"

The Charmer grunted his assent and came to stand beside her. They escorted the two men farther from the camp, facing away from the others. Jinau took over questioning them, his skill in drawing out the memories she needed attesting to the years he had spent working for the Thaelian council.

The process was strange. When she focused, she could read their memories as if they were playing back in her own mind. At first, they were slippery, like wriggling fish. She had to have Jinau repeat certain questions until she figured out how to take hold of those memories and unravel them, letting them dissipate into nothing like mist before the rising sun. Her nerves were raw when she finally felt safe calling it done, and Jinau used his ability to send them back to their camp to sleep. A few of the Eydarith followed them to ensure they did so, then, despite the inconvenience, they moved their own camp farther away.

They wouldn't get much sleep because of the encounter. It would have been wiser, perhaps, to kill the two, but this might be their last opportunity to solve a conflict without bloodshed. She refused to regret that.

As the white stone city of Andaro came into view, Veyl clung to memories of her goodbyes with her companions. That last impassioned kiss with Kyril, the painfully fierce embrace she had received from Gannon, hugs and words of support from the others. Despite how much she hated leaving them, it was the separation from Seyn that nagged relentlessly at her, a distracting absence that left her more alone and empty than she had felt in a long time. Was it like that for Kyril when they separated him from Ceris or her father when away from his companion beasts?

That sense of power that had grown within her, particularly since her unsettling experience in Taro, seemed to dwindle without the wave dancer there, though she refrained from mentioning that to her Eydarith warriors. They needed to believe in her if she expected them to stand by her through this. She would have preferred to bring Seyn, but if it had gone poorly for her father on his arrival in Andaro, which she feared it had, she didn't doubt Jaysen would take Seyn from her in a permanent fashion. She couldn't risk that. But what if she couldn't save her father without the beast? If that were true, though, Seyn's death would be far more debilitating than merely having this distance between them, which meant leaving her behind was still the right choice.

Interestingly, the wave dancer hadn't put up a fight when Veyl told her to stay with Kyril, as if she had accepted their plan and her part in it. Although she had let out a devastating, mournful wail that was some unsettling combination of a wolf's howl and whale song when Veyl rode away with ten of the Eydarith warriors. That she disliked the separation every bit as much as Veyl did was readily apparent.

Andaro nestled in a river valley high in the mountains of northern Sarket. On the eastern side, the castle pressed up against cliffs of the same white stone that much of the city was built from. The main road and the river both cut through the city, though a branch in the road outside the gate curved around to pass between the mountainside and the wall on the western edge, offering an alternative for those who wanted to avoid the bustle of the city streets. A member of the unit that brought her father back from the southern kingdoms during the war had died fleeing Andaro's soldiers on this road. Not the most comforting association under the circumstances.

When they drew near the closed gates, several guards emerged from the gatehouse, weapons ready. One approached the front of their group, his hard gaze sweeping over the modest company, lingering on her for a second before he spoke.

"What is this?" he demanded.

"Wavelord Kronach sent us to bring Khesran Veyl of Vanris before the crown prince," Torlif stated, carefully avoiding anything that would clarify whether they were acting as escorts or captors. They had decided in advance that the big warrior would serve as leader of the unit escorting Veyl. He had the confidence and bearing to pull it off convincingly, as well as the natural intimidation of his size and musculature.

The guard walked over to consult quietly with two of

his comrades by the gatehouse entrance. The impression Veyl got from the looks they cast her way was that they expected to see her, just not with the Eydarith. A reality that only amplified her growing hatred for Jaysen. At least she wouldn't have to fake her outrage and fear.

After a few minutes, the guard came back, scowling at Torlif as if the man's very existence displeased him. "We'll provide you with an escort to the castle."

As the tall wooden gates groaned open, a presence slammed into Veyl; intelligent, powerful, and bursting with violent rage. It lasted only a couple of heartbeats, but even that brief exposure forced her to grab hold of the saddle pommel to steady herself. There was one creature she could imagine having such a potent mental will. A kanodrak. Niskenya was alive at least, which meant her father must also be, but the beast's fury suggested all was not well.

"Time to move, Khesran."

Amera's tone was sharp, supporting the assumption that Veyl might be their prisoner, but she could feel genuine concern coming from the tezaak. She met the woman's eyes and gave a slight nod to let her know the aggression was appropriate before urging her mount to advance with the rest of them.

People going about their business in the streets paused to watch them pass, their interest rising when they noticed her among the Eydarith. No Vanrians walked openly among them, not like they did in Delaphine and Fallend, but Sarket had never been an ally. They had surrendered and sworn fealty, but that was different. Still, her parents had established Vanrian military bases in the country and installed officials in the capital. The complete absence of pointed ears among the populace struck her as a worrisome sign.

It wasn't until they entered the courtyard outside the castle that it became painfully apparent how bad things had gone for her father's company. On a platform at the base of the steps leading to the main entrance, they had Niskenya on display in a large cage, the kanodrak's silver-gray hide spotted with bloody wounds, either from the steel spikes that lined the inside of the cage itself or spears like those wielded by the twenty soldiers standing guard around it. The spikes forced the kanodrak to crouch uncomfortably or settle on her stomach. She had already worn grooves into the stone by flexing her powerful claws. Seeing her father's magnificent companion, the intelligent, revered beast she had grown up with, caged and tormented was more than she could bear.

"No, Niske!" Veyl swung from her mount and sprinted toward the kanodrak.

The guards turned their weapons on her in warning, but a couple of Eydarith warriors, apparently having anticipated her reaction, caught hold of her before she reached them and dragged her back.

Veyl struggled against them, and they forced her to her knees, twisting her arms painfully behind her. Fury exploded. Were they going to betray her after all? Energy crackled in her chest, burning through the heartbreak and fueling her anger. "Let me go!"

Someone caught hold of her hair and yanked her head back. Suddenly she was staring up into Amera's eyes in a posture all too reminiscent of her capture in Deepwater. "Your authentic reaction supports our ruse," the woman growled in a low voice, "but do not reveal your power now unless you want to doom us all."

Her words cut through the rage, leaving only hollow despair and sorrow behind. When Amera's hand loosened on her hair, Veyl looked at the extraordinary beast caged before her and pushed back against the energy building in her chest. She focused on Niskenya for a moment, cautiously reaching out to her. Mindless fury seeped off the kanodrak, but it became apparent with just the lightest mental touch that she wasn't fully present. Wherever the rest of her was, Veyl was certain she would find her father focusing hard to keep the kanodrak from tearing herself apart to try getting to him.

The two warriors restraining Veyl hauled her to her feet, and the rest closed around her, guiding and guarding her on the way up to the castle doors behind the small Sarketi escort that had brought them from the gates.

They had barely stepped inside the towering white entrance hall when one of the Thaelian councilors, Darith, emerged from a hallway to their left with an accompaniment of four Sarketi soldiers. His smile when he saw her made her long to spit on him. Under the circumstances, it wouldn't be an unreasonable reaction, though perhaps she should wait until she had a better grasp of the situation before inviting hostility. He wore Sarketi noble attire with its square cuts and muted colors, adopting the less ornamental attire to fit in with his new allies. His hair was also down and arranged in such a way that it mostly hid his pointed ears.

He stopped in front of her, far enough back that he must have considered the possibility of her lashing out. "Khesran Veyl, I did not expect to see you again. A smart woman would have avoided putting herself in this position more than once. Rumors reached us that you are not a mind-crafter anymore. While I have never heard of such a thing happening, your current situation tells me it may be true. Fortunate." He grinned. "For us, that is."

Rumors she suspected came through the same channel as their warning that she had gone to Taro. Veyl said nothing. She wanted them to believe she had no power, but being too eager to confirm her vulnerability might draw suspicion. Instead, she focused on her distress over what she had seen in the courtyard and her fear for her father. As far as she knew, Darith was not a mind-crafter, but the councilors had lied about too many things for her to take any chances. The Eydarith with her would have to protect their own thoughts, but Amera assured her that Kronach's finest—now her warriors—could handle themselves around mind-crafters well enough. The assassin claimed they had developed methods for training against them. Veyl intended to ask her more about that if she survived this.

Darith shrugged as if to say her silence didn't bother him. "I have been asked to show you to your chambers. The king will meet with you when he finishes with his other duties."

"I have no chambers here."

A hint of amusement lit his eyes. "I can show you to his, if you prefer."

Veyl's stomach turned. "No."

A few more guards entered the room, and the councilor waved a dismissive hand at the Eydarith. "We will take her from here."

Torlif stepped forward. He was a very large man. Veyl hadn't realized exactly how large until she watched him stare down Darith, his upper arms thicker than the other man's thighs. "Wavelord Kronach asked that we deliver her to the crown prince directly."

Darith's nervous swallow gave her a small glimmer of satisfaction.

"If you must," Darith snapped, turning away. "Four of you may accompany us."

Torlif, Amera, and two others continued with Veyl. The rest would begin the careful process of seeing what they could learn from interacting with the local soldiers. She hoped the tremble in her legs as she walked wasn't obvious to anyone else. The idea of being around Jaysen again made her nauseous, a visceral reaction she hadn't expected would be so debilitating. She wasn't helpless, but the situation was delicate. If she wanted to rescue her father and his company, she had to proceed carefully. Even with all the powers she had manifested, their numbers were too few to engage in an outright assault on the city's forces.

"Where is the king regent?" Veyl asked, finding her voice again. "I'd like to speak with him."

"I'm afraid that isn't possible. He is resting. He has been unwell, and we need him healthy for the coming coronation ceremony. No doubt he will be pleased to hear of your concern."

"Of course." She was confident that whatever was wrong with the regent was no benign illness, but for now, she had little choice but to accept him at his word.

Darith led them up a few flights of stairs and turned down a long, wide hallway lined with statues of warriors, most holding weapons that appeared more decorative than functional. All the decor was militaristic, from the statues to the tapestries and paintings. The only exceptions were occasional hunting trophies displayed on some walls, tributes to a different type of aggression. To her Vanrian sensibilities, the white stone lacked the welcoming ambience of the darker palette that made up much of the palace in Etrion, and it felt colder too, making it seem even less pleasant within than it had been outside in the chilly mountain air.

The Thaelian councilor stopped before a door and waited as a guard opened it for them. He led the way inside a room that, while large and well-appointed, was far less spacious and inviting than the quarters she had in Etrion. An elegant white and gold canopy bed was the centerpiece of the room, with a matching bench at the foot and a few chairs and a table to one side near the fireplace. A large window provided some daylight, though it remained oppressive and inadequately lit within.

"You may await his majesty here with your escort.

I will post guards outside the door should you require anything."

Veyl turned to him. "Am I allowed to leave this room?"

"That will be up to his majesty. Good day, Khesran."

Darith waited for everyone except Amera to leave, then followed them out. The moment he was gone, the tezaak did a thorough search of the room. Afterward, she gestured to Veyl to join her in the corner farthest from the door.

"The others will make inquiries and see what they can learn," she whispered. "They will get word to our group outside the city once they have any useful information. We cannot risk letting you stay here longer than necessary, especially alone. The undead prince and his people do not know me. Tell him Kronach gave me to you as a lady's maid. Sending you here should convince him that Taro's wavelord is still his ally. Until he has this country securely under his control, he will want to maintain that alliance, so he should honor the gift. Assuming the role allows me some freedom within the castle, I can maintain communication between you and your warriors and let them know when you are ready to make your move."

Veyl nodded. The tremble in her legs had spread to the rest of her now. She walked to the window and glanced out, horrified to discover that her view overlooked Niskenya in her cage. She couldn't stand to look upon the honored creature, a symbol of Vanris's might, being treated so cruelly. Jaysen would pay for what he had done. She merely had to figure out how to make that happen without losing anyone else.

It didn't surprise her when the subject of her hatred entered the room about five minutes later. The line about him finishing his duties was all for show. His need to gloat over his victory would be too much to resist.

What did shock her was how he looked when he arrived. Deep shadows darkened the area under his eyes, and his face was gaunt. Anger etched new lines in his features, making him appear much older than he had the last time she saw him. For the briefest instant, a flicker of concern moved through her, quickly banished by the reality of his many betrayals.

"Leave us," he said in a soft voice.

Amera didn't hesitate. She had no authority here to argue without undermining Kronach's apparent display of loyalty. On her way out, she met Veyl's eyes as if reminding her to tell him of her intended role. With Jaysen's attention on her, Veyl couldn't risk any signal that she had gotten the message, so she ignored the look and faced him.

As soon as the door closed, Jaysen strode across the room and seized her jaw in his hand, his grip far tighter than necessary, and turned her head from one side to the other. She resisted, but not too much. Not enough to draw his ire, but just enough to avoid suspicion and give him the satisfaction of feeling like he was forcing his will upon her.

"You look all right. Still a decent queen despite the new scar and those unsightly ears."

This from the man who had once wished to have such ears. She resisted the urge to remind him of that and forced a soothing tone. "Jaysen, I'm not—"

The strike was so sudden that her head hit the wall before she could process what had happened. Her ears rang, and she tasted blood inside her lip. Bracing herself with one hand on the windowsill, she tried to focus past the pain and shock to suppress the power threatening to break free. Gently, she touched the tender spot on the back of her head, feeling a warm dampness there. Her fingertips came away tipped in red.

Jaysen was trembling, his face ruddy with rage.

"Don't patronize me! We will be married, and you're going to keep your mouth shut from now on. I will fuck you when it pleases me to do so, and you will bear me all the children I want." He leaned closer, making his face all she could see. She didn't have to fake the fear that made it hard to breathe. "If they have pointed ears, you can watch while I cut the fucking things off and feed them to my hounds. Are we clear?"

Veyl stared at him. Was he truly this far gone? She couldn't tell if her nausea and dizziness were from the blow to the head or the panic threatening to suffocate her. Her voice shook when she spoke. "Is my father alive?"

He took her jaw in his hand again, his fingers digging into her flesh. Then, with no indication of what drove him to do so, he released her and stepped back, his gaze moving to the window. "Do you like the view? I have the same one. Seeing her there helped me sleep more soundly last night. The most impressive trophy in this city. I've been pondering having her head mounted when this is over."

Veyl held her tongue. Putting voice to any of the things she was thinking would undoubtedly get her struck a second time.

Jaysen waited a moment, perhaps expecting an outburst from her. When it didn't come, he looked at her again. "Yes. Your father is in a pit cell below the central keep. It's a cold, squalid place. I should know. They kept me there for a couple of months when I moved back here after my time in Vanris. I wonder if they would have done so if your people hadn't murdered my mother." He tilted his head to one side. "I didn't tell you about that when I showed you my other scars, did I? I was working up the nerve to, before your Thaelian ahnkreth attacked the city. I figured you would discover them by the time we finished on that rooftop. It was going exactly as I had planned."

"It was your companions who interrupted us first, as I recall," Veyl said softly. She touched the split inside her lip with the tip of her tongue.

He started unfastening the toggles on his coat. "I suppose it was, but we might have gotten back to it once I got rid of them if not for the other interruption."

Veyl opted not to disagree with him, watching as he took off his coat and tossed it on the bed, following it with the surcoat. He started removing his undershirt, and she pressed back against the wall. If he meant to have his way with her right now, this entire plan was going to fall apart because she wasn't about to let him.

He drew the shirt off and discarded it with the rest.

That night in Deepwater, he had shown her a few scars he got during his early years back in Sarket, mostly from attempted assassinations, but what she saw now made it clear he had barely scratched the surface. He did a slow turn, holding his arms up to give her an unobstructed view of the elaborate landscape of scars. A collection of religious and Sarketi symbology carved into his chest, ribs, and upper back like some morbid form of ke'hanoath.

"They said it was a necessary process to negate the influence the mind-crafters had gotten over me during my time in Vanris. At first, I tried to fight them, but it only strengthened their conviction. Eventually, I gave in, hoping that each torture session would be the last. Every day, they took me out of the pit and added to their canvas, praying over me while they worked. I think Thrasser quietly wished it would kill me, but I survived somehow, and the priest of Havaad finally declared me clean of mind-crafter influence, though I haven't a clue what decided him. Maybe he just grew bored or ran out of unmarked flesh to work with. After that, they allowed me to rejoin Sarketi society. This," he paused, gesturing to his torso with both hands, "is my life story."

"No." Veyl drew a shallow breath, her head and cheek throbbing from the blow she had taken. "That is senseless torture." She met his eyes. "Please, I must know what happened to my father and his company."

Jaysen let out a bitter laugh and walked closer. "So much sympathy. Careful, Khesran, your selfishness is showing." He shook his head. "Some of your father's company died when we sprung our trap, but we were cautious. Most survived. Your father should be worth a great deal in negotiations, but his tehsheyn are also folk heroes in Vanris. They ought to add to his value. If the khevarin meets my demands, they may all live through this."

Trying to keep her tone neutral, she said, "You know my mother won't agree to this marriage."

"Oh, I think she will, with the right incentives." He leaned in, clearly intending to kiss her, and she turned away, her chest tightening in expectation of another strike. Instead, he chuckled and pressed a finger against the tender spot on her head, drawing a hiss of pain from her. He wiped blood from the wound on the tip of her nose before going to pick up his undershirt from the bed. "You might want to clean up. I can't have my future bride looking a mess." He pulled the shirt on as he spoke.

"The woman..." Veyl let out another soft hiss, this time from frustration at the shake in her voice. "Wavelord Kronach said I could keep the Eydarith woman out in the hall as an attendant."

"Lady's maid, darling." Jaysen put on the shirt, then grabbed his coat and surcoat and strode toward the door. "As long as she follows my orders, you may have her." He glanced over his shoulder, a smirk curving his lips and a gleam in his eye that she could only see as madness. "It's nice to have you back without your ability, Veyl. It will be better this way. You'll see. I'll have the Bondmaker restore our tehnaak bond tomorrow, and we can start working on a love bond after that."

One of the thousand knots in her gut unraveled as she watched him leave. She leaned against the wall and sank slowly to the floor. Pulling her knees in, she laid her arms across them and rested her head on the table they created, closing her eyes. If he had a Bondmaker try to restore their bond, he would learn that she already had a new tehnaak. Not only that, but a love bond and myriad other connections she shouldn't have.

"Khesran." Amera was suddenly crouched beside her, brushing lightly at her hair to check the bloody spot on her head. She let out a string of what Veyl suspected from her tone and delivery were Eydarith curse words.

"I'm fine." Veyl pushed her hands away. "We must act quickly. Jaysen is not in his right mind, and I don't want to give him time to decide he doesn't need all his captives for negotiations after all. My father is in a pit cell beneath the central keep. The others, I imagine, are in the prison, wherever that is. And the cage…" A wave of nausea silenced her.

"We will discover where your father and his company are. One of your warriors should be able to get close enough to inspect the beast's cage to see if there are any weaknesses we can exploit, like an idiot with keys." She took Veyl's arm and slowly helped her to her feet. "Do not worry. We will kill this man and his allies."

Veyl shook her head gingerly. "You can do as you please with his allies. Jaysen has been dead for a long time. Thrasser tortured him to death. The man who took his name, I will kill myself."

Approval shone in Amera's hard gaze. "There is a reason Kronach calls him the undead prince, and it is not solely because he survived Thrasser's attempt to be rid of him."

Frustration flared in Veyl. If she felt steadier on her feet, she might have kicked something, but she held the urge in. "How is it I have known him much of my life and did not see what the wavelord apparently saw so clearly?"

"Kronach is a perceptive man. It is part of what makes him an effective leader, even though he is, what is your word… a calloch?"

Veyl let out a soft laugh and nodded.

"Also, you were seeing the prince with the wrong eyes." Amera tapped a finger on Veyl's chest over her heart. "You wanted to believe the boy you loved was still there. Now that you see him clearly, we will not stand in your way when the time comes."

## CHAPTER TWENTY THREE

Veyl's warriors wasted no time in gathering information. Technically, the Eydarith were Sarketi, and the crown prince still believed Wavelord Kronach to be an ally. That meant they had few limitations moving around the city and castle. Only Amera received special restrictions because of whose attendant she was, specifically barring her from meeting rooms and private chambers aside from Veyl's. She still had far more freedom than Veyl did, and her unique skills as an assassin got her around many limitations, allowing her to do information gathering of her own and act as a liaison between Veyl and her warriors.

They had arrived in Andaro a little before noon. Within two hours, Amera had knowledge to share regarding the location of the other prisoners, guard patrol routes and rotations, and where to find the keys to the prison cells and the cage Niskenya was in. The Eydarith were impressively efficient, and they already had a few ideas on how to bring the rest of their company into the city as well. The one problem they hadn't made progress on was a way to reach her father. After giving her report, Amera had struck out again to attempt infiltration of the lower section of the central keep.

The other half of their group was closer to the city now. Veyl could feel the bonds to Gannon, Kyril, and the wave dancers growing stronger as they approached, her fear that someone might spot them at odds with the intense desire to have them near. Jaysen had yet to visit again, though she doubted she would be lucky enough that he would leave her in peace for the rest of the day. The Bondmaker he promised to bring tomorrow would discover she was hiding a great deal from him. That meant they needed to make their move tonight, which gave them very little time to figure everything out.

She hated waiting. It was hard not to stare out the window at Niskenya. Even harder not to waste energy trying to get into the beast's head to see if she could reach out to her father that way. The understanding that kept her from doing so was how great a risk it came with. If her meddling upset whatever fragile mental hold her father had on the enraged and wounded kanodrak, Niskenya could end up dead. Losing her might be enough to destroy him. Veyl simply had to trust that if the massive predator wasn't fighting her confinement, her father was still alive. Unfortunately, keeping Niskenya calm under these circumstances would require active effort, which meant her father must be trying not to sleep. How many hours he had stayed awake so far and the condition he was in would determine how much longer he could last. Although his stubborn will and Niskenya's combined had overcome significant odds in the past. She had to hope they could do so again.

Three brisk taps on the door preceded Amera's hurried entrance. The woman shut it quickly behind her, closing out the two Sarketi guards who tried to glance inside. "Khesran Veyl, I acquired clean garments for you," she said loudly enough for them to hear. Tossing a couple of Sarketi dresses on the bed, she gestured to the corner farthest from the door.

Veyl joined her there, eager for news. "What else have you learned?"

"Your father's company wasn't pushing quite as hard as we were to get here, so they arrived in the late afternoon the day before yesterday. A feast was held that night, staged as an opening to discussions between the crown prince and the king regent. Some of the food and drink served at the dinner and delivered to the barracks where they housed the rest of the Vanrian company contained a Thaelian paralytic. They attacked Niskenya with poisoned spears once those drugs started taking effect to keep her from trying to go to your father's aid. The few who hadn't eaten the drugged items or who took longer to succumb put up a fierce fight, both at the barracks and the dining hall. The soldiers say Niskenya slaughtered several Sarketi men before she collapsed. We do not know who in your father's company may have suffered injuries or died in the fighting. Specific questions are liable to draw suspicion. We also learned that many Sarketi officials loyal to Thrasser have disappeared since the undead prince's return to Andaro and that Thrasser fell ill around the time of Jaysen's return."

Veyl reached up to run a hand through her hair, then stopped herself, wary of disturbing the wound on her head that had taken some time to quit bleeding. "What about the tethdrak my father brought with him?"

"They killed the beast. Some soldiers said its head is being mounted to hang in the main dining hall."

A dark, sickening surge of loathing filled Veyl, the crackle of power threatening to rise with it. She would make Jaysen pay for this, him and every Thaelian allied with him. "What about the Thaelian mind-crafters? Were they involved?"

"We know they used a Dampener to help avoid fatalities in the dining hall. The undead prince wanted hostages, not corpses. There is unease among the Sarketi soldiers because of the Thaelians, which has the benefit of making them more receptive to the Eydarith as allies. They don't like this alliance with people who, to them, are no different from Vanrians. They believe there are at least a few Evokers and Charmers among them being used for hunting down those loyal to the regent. A rumor that appears to have some truth behind it. They also don't like you being here. Predictably, the undead prince's intention to marry a Vanrian woman is not popular among his people, though they are only willing to admit it in whispers."

None of that was exceptionally surprising. Sarket had long been a realm ruled by warmongers who hated Vanris. They hated anyone who threatened their power or dared to stand up to them. "And my father?"

Her lips pressed into a line for a moment that Veyl didn't find encouraging. "I located the chamber where they are keeping him. I could see the grates over three pit cells from my vantage. There are four Thaelian soldiers posted in the room."

"Mind-crafters," Veyl muttered under her breath.

"I would assume at least one of them is, yes. There are Sarketi guards posted outside the chamber entrance, but no Sarketi within, just the four Thaelians. If we can get inside, we will have only them to deal with."

Anxious hope sparked in her chest. "How did you get in?"

"I did not. There are two high windows on the back wall of that chamber. I was able to climb to one from another area of the castle to see into where the cells are."

Veyl leaned against the wall and slid down it to the floor, staring in the direction of the bed, though her focus wasn't there. "If we can sneak the others into the city, could we have them infiltrate the prison?"

Amera gave her a curious look before crouching down next to her. "Your Dampener, Feyd, would be especially useful for that, as might your Thaelian Charmer, if you are sure you can trust him."

Veyl chuckled, finding her choice of words oddly amusing. "We can rely upon my Thaelians. We'll have to be more careful with Niskenya. Kyril might be of some help with her. He's worked with the kanodraks a little. I fear they will kill her if they catch us trying to free the others first, so we must endeavor to move on all fronts at the same time if we can."

"And the khemron?"

"You and I will go for him. We can send Gannon with the prison group. My bonds to him and Kyril should make it possible to coordinate our efforts. Dailan can come with us in case my father needs a healer's attention."

Amera gave a firm shake of her head. "No. That one does not have the skills. He will jeopardize our effort. If you are to be the one to signal the others, we must ensure you reach your goal unnoticed."

Veyl hesitated. She would be trusting her life to this woman—Kronach's tezaak. Her life and her father's. She met Amera's eyes, and the woman answered her questioning gaze with a look of confidence and certainty Veyl couldn't help admiring.

A smile curved the other woman's lips. "When it is your job to kill without being seen, you either learn it well, or you live a short life. You are wavelord of this unit now. We will not fail you. I will not fail you."

"A wavelord is an Eydarith leader."

"Yes. This is the gift Kronach has given you. He has granted you standing as his equal among our people. I suggest you accept it and focus on the task at hand."

The door flew open, and they both hurried to their feet as Jaysen stormed in with four guards.

He looked Veyl up and down once, then scowled. "I gave you ample time to prepare yourself."

"Apologies, Majesty." Amera stepped forward, drawing his attention. The sudden meekness in her manner nearly made Veyl's jaw drop, though she caught herself before giving away anything. It was as if an entirely different person stood there from the confident killer she had just been plotting with. "It took me longer than it should have to find suitable garments for the khesran. If you will allow me but a moment, I can have her ready for you."

He glared at Amera as if considering punishing her for having the audacity to speak or perhaps for failing his expectations, then he snorted in apparent disgust. "You have five minutes."

"Majesty," Amera said when he started turning away, and Veyl silently cursed the woman for not letting him leave. The assassin bowed to him when he cast a scathing glance at her and gestured to the bed. "Would the deep blue or the pale gray please you more?"

"Expedience would please me," he growled, but he paused as he turned away again to look at the two dresses. After a moment, he snapped, "The gray," and stormed out.

Veyl let the breath she was holding out and started tugging off her clothes. Amera lifted the selected dress, a full-length gown with a fitted bodice and several layers of fabric in a heavy, flared skirt. A popular Sarketi style Veyl considered inefficient and rather absurd. A style meant to ensure women here didn't try looking or acting the same as men.

"Hide my clothes," she whispered when Amera came to help her into the dress. "I can't free my father in this."

Amera tucked the garments under the mattress, then resumed helping her. As soon as they had her dressed and the tezaak secured the last few fastenings, Veyl turned to redoing the two braids in her hair. She startled when the door flew open again and Jaysen let himself in once more.

"No braids."

For a heartbeat, she almost relented to the desperate need to defy him and kept braiding, but indulging her pride now could have too high a cost. She stopped and roughly pulled out what she had done so far, letting the kinked hair fall loose.

Jaysen gave a curt nod and held his elbow out for her. "Come. There are a couple of people I'd like you to see."

It pleased her that she managed to carry herself with grace and poise when she walked forward and slid her hand into the crook of his arm despite the fist of terror that closed around her throat. His words might have no hidden implication or agenda, but dozens of ways they could be the lead-in to something truly awful flashed through her mind. With her father and most of his *tehsheyn*, people she considered her family growing up, now at Jaysen's mercy, he had too many ways he could torment and hurt her. After the greeting he had given her, there wasn't much she would put past him.

Silenced by fear, she let Jaysen lead her from the room and down the hall, Amera following to her left and a step behind, ahead of six Sarketi guards.

"If you continue to be compliant, perhaps I'll take you on a tour of the castle tomorrow. There are some lovely rooms I think you will enjoy spending time in. It's quite different from Etrion, but you'll adjust." His pleasant tone made it sound as if he truly expected her to live here with him and to like it. "Some lords have been resistant to the idea of having their wives around a Vanrian woman. You can understand why, I'm sure. I promised them you would abandon your indelicate ways and set a proper example."

Indelicate? How she would love to remind him exactly how indelicate she could be. She bit the cut on the inside of her lip to distract from the urge to say as much.

He smiled at her. "See, you're already learning to control your temper."

She had almost lost the battle with that very temper before he stopped and turned them to a set of guarded double doors. Curiosity and dread suppressed the sharp words that had nearly slipped between her lips.

"Lord Darith said you asked after the king regent and desired an opportunity to speak with him."

Lord Darith? He was even stripping the councilors of their Thaelian titles now. How did they feel about that? Were they truly desperate enough for his aid in regaining control of Thaelis that they would put up with such insult?

A guard opened one door, and Jaysen led them inside. King Regent Wilkin Thrasser sat in a chair near the window, his graying beard and hair both in need of tidying, the lines in his face deeper than when she had last seen him in Balarus, and his skin somewhat sallow. A Thaelian woman sitting in the seat opposite him stood when they entered. As if awakened by her movement, Thrasser glanced up at them, his dark eyes empty for a few seconds, then he smiled and rose unsteadily, his expression reminding Veyl disturbingly of a doddering old man.

"King..." He paused, looking puzzled, then the smile returned, and he reached out to take one of Jaysen's hands in both of his, a warm and welcoming gesture. "Crown Prince Jaysen. It's always a pleasure." A flicker of darkness and confusion moved across his features when he turned his gaze to Veyl. The smile hesitantly resurfaced. "You remind me of someone, my dear. Do I know you?"

"Veyl is to be my queen, Wilkin. I told you this." Jaysen extracted his hand and gestured to the Thaelian woman as he faced Veyl. "We have a Charmer here to help Wilkin out with his recent memory issues."

A Charmer. It helped to know what the woman was. Veyl focused on Thrasser for a second, drawing upon the Evoker ability now that she knew the Thaelian mind-crafter wouldn't be sensitive to it. Forcing a gentle smile, she took Thrasser's hand the way he had taken Jaysen's a moment ago. "We saw each other in Balarus, King Regent, earlier this year. It was during negotiations between Sarket and Vanris. Don't you recall?"

Again, that flicker of confusion, but what left her momentarily breathless was the scattered mess of broken memories that struggled to coalesce in response to her words. Brief flashes of images, some of which were from the meetings in Balarus. Others were from unrelated occasions, his mind trying to put fragments together in a way that made sense and largely failing.

Thrasser finally shook his head, a hint of frustration in his furrowed brow as he drew his hand away. "My mind is not what it used to be, I'm afraid."

Jaysen's smile oozed deep satisfaction. "We won't bother you any longer, Regent. I merely wanted to give my bride a chance to say hello." He slid an arm around Veyl's back, settling his hand at her waist, and steered her from the room.

The moment the door shut behind them, she pulled away and faced him. "What happened to him?" It wasn't as if she didn't know, but he would expect her to wonder, and she needed to know how he would answer.

Jaysen grinned. "We needed him to agree to the coronation, so I had an Evoker and Charmer work together to remake his mind."

"Destroy it, is more like it."

His expression darkened. "What does it matter? This solves the problem of who will sit on the throne without Sarket having to go to war with itself. Once the coronation is complete, we'll have no more need of him." He took her arm, the firmness of his grip making it clear her judgment had struck a nerve. "Come. There's someone else I want you to see."

With apprehension turning her legs into lead weights, Veyl let him guide her along several halls and downstairs to another set of doors, Amera and the guards still trailing behind. One man hurried forward to open the door for them, letting them into a formal dining room with a long table in the center, the reddish wood polished to a high shine. It could easily seat sixteen, possibly as many as twenty if the guests were comfortable getting cozy.

An open area to one side near a gaping fireplace, where chairs or couches might normally sit for people to chat and drink before or after the meal, had been cleared of furniture. A pungent man in tattered, dirty clothes knelt there between two soldiers, his hands shackled behind his back and his head bowed. Several alert guards stood around the room, as if they expected trouble.

A wash of relief flowed over her upon seeing it wasn't her father or one of his people. Then the prisoner slowly raised his head as they approached, and her cheeks heated with shame that rapidly gave way to a growing horror. With his face swollen and bruised, and a gaping wound in the place of one eye, she barely recognized Chief General Gregory Harriksen. They had only ever met in Crimsondale, and he no longer looked at all like the proud, robust soldier he had been then.

Veyl stopped. "What is this?"

Jaysen released her arm and moved his hand up to the back of her neck, his painful grip forcing her a few steps closer to the beaten man. "You can guess how surprised I was when the Chief General's memories of negotiations in Crimsondale revealed that Vanris was considering him as an alternative for my throne. You can't possibly imagine how much that betrayal hurt.

If you recall those discussions, you shouldn't have any trouble understanding why."

Crippling fear swept through her, but she fought it, holding her ground. "Then why didn't you just kill him? Why do this?"

The painful pressure on her neck let up when he released her and stepped forward, gesturing for the guards to pull Gregory to his feet. The man struggled to make it upright under at least some of his own power, his remaining eye focusing on her. Jaysen faced her and brushed the back of his fingers across her cheek.

"When the Evoker was sharing his memories, it moved me to hear how impressed he said the Chief General was with you. So much so that I thought he might like to see our wedding. That's why I left him the one eye. Although…" He paused, a malicious gleam rising in his blue eyes. "With so many Vanrians here, I believe we have more than enough guests now, wouldn't you agree?"

A metallic taste swept across her tongue, and her vision tunneled. "Jaysen, no."

He drew his dagger before she finished her protest and rammed it into Gregory's throat. When he yanked it out, blood spurted, some of it hitting the skirt of Veyl's dress and her arm on that side. She reeled back, running into the chairs and table behind her with enough force to shift them a few inches, the noise of wood scraping against the hard floor shockingly loud in a room where the only other sound was that of Gregory's wet choking.

Veyl fought the crackling in her chest. Even with her power, she couldn't be certain of taking out this many guards before they neutralized her, and if she failed, her father and his company would pay for that failure. She turned away from the dying man, unwilling to watch him expire in the arms of Jaysen's soldiers, and they lowered him down to finish bleeding out on the floor.

"What is the point of all this?" She shouted the question, her voice cracking.

Jaysen set the dagger on the table and took hold of her chin, forcing her to look at him, his fingers slick with blood. "I want you to abandon the notion that someone else will take my throne." He rubbed his thumb along her cheek, his gaze following the streak of red the caress must have left there. "You should consider how fortunate you are that I'm willing to forgive you for the things you've done. That I'm willing to allow others to pay the price for your cruelty." His gaze moved to her lips and stayed there. "I want you to kiss me, Veyl." He murmured those last words, but an edge of threat lay beneath them.

She feared she would throw up on him if his lips touched hers. How forgiving would he be of that? "Free my father, please."

He shook his head. "Not while his beast lives. I was planning to take care of her as part of my coronation, but I suppose I could move up the timeline if you wish."

"No." How she hated the desperate breathlessness of her voice at that moment. "No. We can wait. I can't... I'm not ready for that."

He answered her words with a disgusted sneer and wiped one bloody finger over her lips before turning his back on her. For a moment, he stared down at the dead man, then he gestured to the two soldiers. "Get rid of him and have someone clean up this mess." As they moved to obey his orders, he waved Amera and the guards that had been following them forward. "Take my future queen back to her room. I can't have her coming to dinner looking like that." With that, he strode out the door.

Veyl brusquely wiped at the blood on her lips with a sleeve of the dress as the guards closed around her to escort her out. As soon as they were back in the room, she hurried to the basin on the vanity to rinse away the rest of Gregory's blood Jaysen had smeared on her face, her hands trembling. In the mirror, she saw Amera slowly shaking her head at her as though disappointed.

"What?"

"You did well, but you should have kissed him instead of bringing his attention back to your father and his beast."

Veyl spun, fury rising. "I'm sorry, but I would rather fall upon my sword than kiss that man, and I want my father out of here."

"I think a part of you still wishes to find the boy you knew in him. All he can see are the ways people have wronged him. All he can feel is a burning need for revenge. No matter what cruelty broke him, you cannot pity him now, and you cannot give him more opportunities to hurt you. He will use them."

"By the Break," she shouted, throwing up her hands. "What do you want from me? I'm just... I'm not..." Something in Amera's firm, patient gaze silenced her.

The other woman stepped forward and took the damp cloth Veyl was still holding, using it to wipe away the last traces of blood on her face. "You are a khesran of Vanris, a child of the ocean, and a wavelord of the Eydarith, favored by the Tempest. This is your war. Your army may be small, but it is fierce and loyal. You can win this if you can be stronger than any one person should ever have to be. Let go of who you have been and become what you must be to destroy him."

## CHAPTER TWENTY FOUR

Veyl lay back on the bed and closed her eyes, not caring if she wrinkled the deep blue dress she was now wearing. She scratched at her arm, trying to erase the lingering sensation of Gregory's warm blood spraying upon it. At least he would not suffer anymore. What Jaysen had done to Thrasser was arguably worse. She never liked the man, but to see him that way, struggling to make sense of the disconnected memory fragments they had left him… She would rather die than live so broken. Would Jaysen consider doing something like that to her, to make her more tractable?

As much as the idea horrified her, she believed the man he had become would.

Amera was out again, this time to coordinate their plan with the others. Torlif would assume responsibility for bringing the second group into the city. They made a deliberate choice not to discuss the specifics of how he meant to accomplish that. Typically, anyone who could use the Evoker ability should be resistant to others using it on them, but the Dampener had affected Veyl in Taro, and her use of the same skill had blinded him. That suggested that her abilities might not protect her in the expected manner. To be safe, in case there was an Evoker at dinner, she would try to keep certain thoughts in the forefront of her mind to control what they could access and avoid drawing suspicion. The less she knew about what her warriors and unit were doing, the easier it would be to prevent that information from popping up at the wrong moment.

The tezaak returned in time to help Veyl tidy up her dress and hair, delicately brushing over the wound on her head, before guards arrived to take her to dinner. That Jaysen didn't come to escort her himself was both a relief and an undoubtedly intentional slight. Whether he wanted her to lose her temper to provide him with an excuse to punish her or merely hoped to continue breaking down her morale wasn't clear, but she didn't intend to give him the satisfaction of either outcome.

The guards escorted her into the dining hall, this one larger than the one he had taken her to earlier, with three tables set in a squared-off horseshoe configuration. Some of the Sarketi nobles present moved as if to stand, but when Jaysen remained seated, they sank back into their chairs, a few averting their eyes uncomfortably. Many, particularly the Thaelians, watched her walk along the length of the table arrangement with critical regard. She held her head high, knowing Jaysen would grow suspicious if she let herself appear broken this soon. He knew her better than that. And yet, the moment she reached the end and turned, preparing to sit in the open chair beside him, she saw what was hanging above the room's main entrance and felt instantly shattered.

Over the doors she had come through hung the head of the tethdrak her father had brought with him. A beautiful creature with light reddish and tan scales and back-swept horns. A magnificent beast in life. They had to have rushed the process to have it up already, though it was hard to tell with it mounted so far from where she stood. Had Jaysen pushed them to finish it for her sake? One more way to torment her. Was this punishment for escaping him in Taro and supporting someone else to take his throne? It seemed an extreme way to convey that message.

Veyl remained standing.

Jaysen placed his hand over hers on the back of her chair. "I think you'll find it more comfortable to sit while you eat, Khesran."

A few chuckles answered his remark. One Sarketi woman glanced away and dabbed at her eyes with a handkerchief as if the spectacle genuinely upset her. Veyl didn't care. She despised them all.

Jaysen gave her hand a firm squeeze, his tone hardening. "Sit."

"I would rather not."

He lowered his voice. "Would you like something else to look at? I could have a different head mounted, if you prefer."

She recognized the threat for what it was. Who would he choose? One of her father's tehsheyn? Or perhaps he would advance Niskenya's execution as he had threatened to do earlier. It looked as though he would win this confrontation, but she was keeping a tally now, and she meant to return each blow he had dealt her all at once. She would make him feel the pain he had inflicted upon her.

Drawing a deep breath, she pulled out the chair and sank onto the cushioned green seat with all the grace she could muster.

A few things made the rest of the uncomfortable meal tolerable, the first being the fact that Jaysen apparently truly expected her to set a "proper example" for the women of Sarket. That she spoke as little as possible, limiting her interactions to brief polite answers to direct questions, appeared to please him. Throughout the evening, as he indulged in much wine and conversation, she caught him sharing the occasional nod or meaningful look with a few of the Thaelians present. Almost certainly mind-crafters, though she didn't dare use her abilities to confirm as much. She kept her thoughts on her father, his company, and the earlier unpleasant encounters with Thrasser and Gregory, any subject Jaysen might expect to occupy her mind, letting fear and rage war for control of her emotions.

The other thing that helped, though she had to be careful not to acknowledge it in any meaningful way, was the fact that she could feel how close the wave dancers, Kyril, and Gannon were to the city now. Night was falling. If everything proceeded according to plan, they would be inside the walls soon. Gannon would be part of a group in charge of freeing the prisoners. She didn't envy Kyril the task she had given him of trying to break Niskenya out. She could only hope the wave dancers had the ability to soothe the mighty predator and keep her from turning on her rescuers.

As dinner wound down, she noted how often her increasingly inebriated *fiancé* took her hand or distract-edly placed his on her leg. It required an act of will not to pull away, though she had only to look up at the teth-drak head to remember what was at stake. Might she get away with excusing herself and returning to her rooms alone? Would he come after her? Would he expect some-thing if he did?

"Majesty, the hour grows late, and I imagine your future queen might appreciate a little of your more fo-cused attention. Perhaps it is time to move on to other entertainment."

The words turned her stomach. The man who spoke them was one of the Thaelian councilors. Someone she didn't know by name, but his comments and haughty smirk told her he had insight into where her thoughts had wandered. An Evoker. She yearned to dig around in his mind and see if a hidden agenda made him so eager to wrap up the evening. Somehow, she managed not to glare at him, tormenting herself instead with the memory of Jaysen touching her face with fingers covered in Gregory's blood to keep her defiance in check and her fear genuine.

Jaysen looked at her, sliding the hand that was resting on her leg up a little higher. "You may be right." He stood, gesturing for the others to remain seated when they also started to rise. "Thank you all for joining us this evening. You are welcome to leave and indulge your own pleasures or stay and continue partaking of the drink and food. My future queen and I have… plans to discuss." There were a few chuckles as he held his hand down to her.

Did they all know she was an unwilling participant in this? Would any of them care if they did?

Veyl took his hand and let him support her up. He placed her hand in the crook of his arm and guided her from the room. She made a point of holding her head high and not meeting anyone's eyes along the way. She also did not look to see how many guards fell in behind them and whether there were any Thaelians among them. Amera, who had been dining in a side room with other attendants and serving staff, hurried out to join them, her presence bolstering Veyl's nerves just a little.

When it became clear they were heading to her rooms rather than somewhere else where conversation might be the actual goal, she applied a small amount of pressure to his arm, hoping to slow his pace. "What did you wish to discuss, my lord?"

"Nothing." His response was abrupt, his manner that of someone who expected an argument ahead and had already resolved to win it. "I'm not interested in being lied to by you."

She could force herself to endure a kiss the way Amera had told her she should, but how was she supposed to keep it from going beyond that? He wore no weapons, which might suggest trust to someone who didn't know him well, but it was more likely that he was wary of providing her access to them. Probably a smart choice. She wasn't sure how many guards followed them or whether any were Thaelian mind-crafters, and she couldn't check without risking giving her intentions away. Besides, they needed to avoid starting a fight until they had the pieces in place to win. Killing Jaysen might be satisfying, but doing so right now would be apt to get her and Amera executed before they could free her father or any of his company. No, somehow, she had to make it through whatever happened next without turning it into a violent confrontation.

Comfort swept in from Seyn, the beast now close enough to initiate deeper contact and support through their bond. A connection that, like the others, hadn't been created with the aid of a Bondmaker. Veyl suspected Seyn and Ceris were responsible for their bonds to her, but the ones to Kyril and Gannon were at least partly her own doing. Even if she hadn't formed them intentionally, she clearly could do so, and in that she might have a way of handling Jaysen for the short term.

When they arrived at her room, he sent her in ahead of him and turned to block Amera and the guards. "This is between the two of us. I want no interruptions."

He slammed the door in the face of a bowing guard, but not before Veyl caught the two fingers Amera held briefly in front of her thigh. Two Thaelians among those left in the hall who would almost certainly be mind-crafters. A Charmer and Evoker perhaps. Or one might be a Frightener if he had any doubts about her ability truly being broken, assuming the Thaelians had any Frighteners left after the one she had killed in Taro. All that was certain was that the councilors had hidden an abundance of mind-crafters from their populace. A Speaker might be of use to alert him if something was amiss while he was in here discussing matters with her. Without knowing exactly what they were, she would have to continue exercising caution. If she accessed any abilities, she would need to do so subtly. Still, kissing him if she had to was one thing. The way he slid home the bolt on the door suggested this had the potential to escalate beyond that.

He pivoted and strode forward, shoving her back against one bedpost with his palm over her breastbone, his fingers and thumb curving around the base of her neck in explicit threat. The carvings on the post dug into her back, but that discomfort wasn't enough to discourage her from pushing harder against it when he leaned close, bringing his nose beside her cheek and inhaling in a manner that reminded her of Kronach. For once, she would have preferred the wavelord.

He stayed there, a tremble in his hand, and whispered, "I should hate you, so why can't I stop wanting you?"

That was easy to answer. Because he had become fixated on her. He had made her one of the executors of his suffering in his mind. He had also turned her into a condition of his victory. Something to be conquered and owned to prove his power. She couldn't say any of that to him without making her situation worse, however, so she maintained her silence, drawing carefully upon Seyn's presence, not far away at all now.

"Kiss me."

If she had to initiate, even after Amera's earlier comment, Veyl wasn't sure she could have done it at his command, but he didn't wait. He crushed her lips with his in a violent kiss, his tongue instantly demanding entry.

Veyl jerked back, gritting her teeth against the pain when the wound on her head struck the bedpost. His expression darkened, his hand tightening around her neck as anger rose in his eyes.

"Wait." She touched a finger to his lips, the contact distracting him from his fury for a precious instant.

Steeling herself, she moved the finger and leaned in, closing her eyes and pulling Kyril to the forefront of her mind as she touched her lips to his in a soft, lingering kiss. In the darkness behind her eyelids, she reached into him, searching for the severed tehnaak link. Because it had bound them before, it should respond to her presence.

His hand softened, shifting back down to her breastbone as she found that broken thread inside him and tentatively drew upon it. On her side, that link now connected her to Gannon, but she could create a new one. Something not as strong that he would be less likely to notice. When she drew the threads together, she felt the wave dancer's influence moving in her, guiding her through completing the bond.

Jaysen slid a hand around her waist, pulling her closer, his tongue seeking entry between her lips again, but with a gentler inquiry this time. His fury faltered before her tender approach and the inevitable spark of empathy the newly forged bond created. To accomplish what she wanted to, she couldn't continue to hold Kyril in her thoughts, so she let go of him, forcing herself to allow a deepening of the kiss. She drew upon a memory of her past with Jaysen. Of that first kiss they had shared in her room on his last night in Vanris before returning to Sarket. A powerful moment full of trust and vulnerability between two curious youths who were best friends and tehnaak.

She drew back from his kiss, letting her memory of that experience lightly play across the new bond, encouraging him to call up his recollection of the same event. "Do you remember the first time we kissed?" she whispered. "Do you remember the way you slid your finger down the ke'hanoath on my neck, and it made me shiver?"

Jaysen shifted back, suspicion narrowing his eyes. "What are you doing?"

The new bond would make it easier to influence him without the overflow that might alert the Thaelians. That was what she needed.

"I miss the way we were before everything fell apart." She touched his face, her fingertips light upon his cheek. There. A flicker of uncertainty and wary hope in the bright blue eyes gazing into hers. Perfect. She closed the gap he had created between them, letting the bond carry some of her Charmer ability into him without the risk of alerting another Charmer. "This is something you want to remember, to savor, isn't it? Every kiss. Every touch."

"I…" He swallowed. "I do." Still too resistant.

She placed another light kiss on his lips, keeping him focused on the heightened emotions and sensations of these few seconds and nothing else. Making him hers to influence. She drew back and met his eyes again. "You've had too much to drink to do that now, haven't you? You'll forget this. The wine will hamper your ability to appreciate our first joining. An experience we can never have a second time."

He started nodding, though there was still reluctance, his mistrust of her, and of everyone, rooted too deeply. "I don't know if I can stop now. You were supposed to be mine well before this. I've waited a long time." He slid a hand into her hair, his fingers barely missing the wound that she feared might be bleeding again.

She hated his possessive words, his closeness, his smell, his hands upon her. Focusing past all of that, she fed a little more ability through their bond. "Think how much more intense it will be when the tehnaak bond connects us again. Everything precisely as it should be.

Complete together."

That was the key she needed. The tehnaak bond he meant to have restored was a critical piece of their joining for him.

His nod gained confidence, the resistance fracturing. "Yes. That is how I want it. How it always should have been. Perfect." He gave her a deep, messy kiss before stepping back and stroking her cheek, beaming at her. "Tomorrow, then."

"Tomorrow," she agreed.

She held her breath until he stepped out the door and shut it behind him, then she hurried over to take a mouthful of water directly from the pitcher sitting on a side table near the window. When Amera tapped on the door and entered, she had just finished rinsing her mouth and spat the water into the basin.

The tezaak nodded her approval. "Well done, Wavelord. He left looking pleased."

Veyl gave her a hard look. "I bonded him."

Amera's eyes narrowed. "Is that wise?"

"It should allow me to maintain some awareness of him. I'm hoping I'll be able to tell when he's asleep, at the very least."

She moved to the window and gazed down at the caged kanodrak. If only she could create a bond with her father and let him know help was coming. Let him know there was a reason to keep fighting. But the only way was to seek him through his link to Niskenya. Tentatively, she reached out to the beast and had her mental presence rebuffed aggressively enough that she staggered back a step. In the cage below, the kanodrak tensed and snarled, drawing the nervous attention of the surrounding guards, a few of whom turned their spears in her direction. That wasn't the type of help her father needed.

Veyl threw herself down on the bed and stared at

the patterns of gold embroidery in the white canopy above her, focusing on her bonds. Mostly on Jaysen, waiting for the silence that would tell her he had fallen asleep. She passed a sense of patience to Gannon and Kyril, gratefully accepting the reassurance and resolve that answered her.

Eventually, well into the night, the quiet came. When the link to Jaysen settled, it surprised her to find that she could feel some of the other wave-touched in Sarket more clearly, and Kronach foremost among them. She didn't have time to investigate that now. The moment had come to execute their plan.

When Veyl got up, Amera immediately came to help her free of the dress. Sarketi feminine styles were far too complicated for a swift change. That was undoubtedly intentional. When she was far enough to finish on her own, the Eydarith woman pulled her travel clothes out from under the mattress, along with a few items that hadn't been there before.

Veyl stared at the weapons she tossed onto the bed. "When did you... How?"

Amera chuckled. "One day you will recognize I am adept at what I do. The others should be in position to act, but we must get close to your father before you give them the signal to move. There are two guards outside your door right now. How do you wish to handle them?"

Veyl considered her escape from Taro. This time, they didn't know whether the man they wished to save had suffered any injuries that might slow them down, and they wouldn't have local guards willing to ignore them the way Kronach had ordered his Eydarith to. They couldn't afford to be reckless. "We need to avoid raising any alarms for as long as possible. I'll have to Charm them. If they disappear from in front of my door, the next patrol that wanders by is sure to notice."

"You are certain you can?"

"Yes." It worked with Jaysen. She had the advantage of the bond she had created with him to make it easier, but she had successfully Charmed the guards in Crimsondale, and Seyn was close enough to support her now. Besides, their plan depended on her newly awakened abilities. If it didn't work, they had bigger problems.

Amera met her eyes. "The gifts of the Tempest are at your disposal. It is up to you to use them. Confidence and determination will lead you to the victory you seek."

"You may be an excellent tezaak, but you also make a fine adviser."

Amera shrugged and adjusted her sword belt.

Veyl drew a deep breath. Then she gave a resolute nod and faced the door.

The instant her fingertips touched the door lever, an idea struck Veyl, and she drew her hand back. Turning, she hurried to the bed where the blue dress lay and flipped up the outer skirt, using her dagger to cut away the many layers beneath. It was a sloppy job, but it only had to hold up to a quick glance. These men had expectations for how a Sarketi lady was supposed to dress. She only needed their minds to adjust what they were seeing to make it fit that narrative long enough for her to Charm them. Pulling the outer part on over her clothes, she had Amera secure it snugly enough to keep it in place before wrapping her sword belt in a layer of the sacrificed underskirt and handing it to the other woman.

"Stay back for a minute. We need them focused on me."

Amera nodded, stepping off to one side when Veyl returned to the door. The moment she opened it the guards snapped to attention and turned. One lowered his spear in warning and gestured to the room behind her.

"Your maid can leave, but you have to stay inside until the king says otherwise."

Veyl forced a smile she hoped looked adequately meek and vulnerable. "Oh, I didn't want to go anywhere. I was just wondering if you could do me a small favor." As she spoke, she opened herself up more to her connections with Seyn and Ceris, letting their innate power bolster her own.

The guard raised his spear, apparently not threatened by a noblewoman asking for assistance. When he took a step forward, Veyl did the same, drawing his full attention to her, and that of his companion, who hurried to join him. Exactly what she needed.

She had no training with all of this, but she had grown up learning about the different mind-crafter abilities and the basics of how they worked in the academies. That knowledge had helped her to muddle through so far, though she would have appreciated having the confidence of more genuine experience heading into this. Too many lives hung in the balance, relying on unfamiliar powers she had little experience using.

Infusing her voice with her intent and hopefully enough ability to affect them without drawing unwanted attention, she said, "It has been a stressful day. I was going to try getting some sleep and hoped I could count on the two of you to make certain I am not disturbed. That's not much to ask, is it?"

For an instant, their brows furrowed as though something troubled them. Then they both answered with slow nods.

"Of course not, my lady," the closer of the two said, his blue eyes losing some focus.

"Thank you. I heard a noise down the hall to the left a moment ago. You should probably take a thorough look and make sure no one's over there. I trust you to return quietly to your posts when you are confident it's safe." She waited for them to nod again. "Thank you. I'll rest better knowing you are here watching over me."

"Yes, my lady," they answered in near perfect unison before stalking a short distance to the crossing hallway to search for signs of anything amiss.

Wasting no time, Amera slipped out with her and eased the door shut. They hurried in the opposite direction, ducking into a room a few down on the other side that the tezaak had scouted out earlier. It was similar to the one Veyl was staying in, though the bed was less ornate. No one was using it now. The window opened onto a short, sloped section of rooftop that, assuming one didn't fall to their death, provided a precarious way to gain access to a covered walkway on that side of the building, or so Amera assured her. Veyl discarded the remains of the dress, kicking it under the bed, and donned the sword belt.

Amera led the way from there, stepping out onto the rooftop and crouching with her hands pressed to the sloped surface. Veyl's heart jumped into her throat when the woman slid about four feet, caught hold of the eave, and disappeared. An instant later, she heard a tap on the underside of the roof from the walkway below.

This was madness. Not that she hadn't spent her share of time on dangerous rooftops, particularly as a child, but there was nothing to grab hold of at the edge that she could see. Setting aside dignity, she crawled out on her stomach to maximize resistance and inched her way to the edge. When she got there, she reached under and felt for something to hold on to, almost crying out when Amera grabbed her wrist and moved it forward until it bumped up against the top of a post. She felt around for a second more, finding a spot to wedge her hand into where the rafter connected, and, fighting the suffocating ball of terror in her throat, she slid off.

A wild swing put her in position to grab on with her free hand, though it painfully twisted the wrist of the other. Amera watched calmly while Veyl hooked one leg over the railing and pulled herself in. A quick, awkward scramble got her on to the covered walkway. Swallowing hard, she peered over the half-wall at the long drop to a little garden below with three stone benches set around a fountain in the center.

"I may never trust you again," she murmured.

Amera chuckled. "Come. We have no time for sight-seeing."

Her heart still in her throat, she followed the other woman along the walkway, pausing when she did to check at the windows for anyone awake within. Finally, they slipped through a door into a steep stairwell. Amera stopped them every few steps to listen. Veyl itched to get to her father, but the more people they encountered, the greater the risk of something going wrong. She needed to trust the Eydarith tezaak, and she found that, despite her earlier words, she did. The woman had proven remarkably capable and, so far as she knew, had yet to truly lead her astray.

Upon reaching the bottom of the stairs, Amera stood for several seconds with her ear to the edge of the door and one hand resting on the lever. Then she nodded and beckoned Veyl closer, whispering, "Beyond this door, three halls intersect. We will need to head straight across and turn left at the next opportunity. It opens into a small antechamber with a set of doors at the back where the two Sarketi soldiers stand guard. They will have time to raise an alarm to alert the Thaelians before we can reach them."

There were too many ways this could go wrong. "Wait. If there are four Thaelians beyond the doors, they could all be mind-crafters. Using any of my abilities on the guards would be the same as shouting out our arrival."

Amera unbuckled her sword belt and handed it to Veyl. "I will lure the guards out. Stay hidden behind the wall and be ready. Come."

Veyl had questions, but the tezaak was already

through the door and moving quietly forward along the wall. She paused at the intersection to listen again, then peered both ways before crossing. With no other viable options, Veyl followed, calling upon her experiences avoiding guards in the Etrion palace and doing her best to mimic the woman's actions.

It was dark and musty in these halls. A charcoal gray stone made up the walls instead of the white used in the rest of the castle. Combined with narrow passages and sparing placement of torches along the way, it deepened the gloom of the lower reaches. They were a level below ground here. Since Amera had peered in a window to see the grates over the pit cells, that meant the room they were heading for had to be more than a single story tall. The natural light would help make it more tolerable for guards stationed there, though not at this hour. Prisoners couldn't climb out of a well-designed pit cell, so there wasn't much point to putting guards on them unless you were concerned about rescue attempts. Something admittedly more likely when holding a high-profile prisoner, such as a ruler of another country.

Veyl crept along after Amera, pleased with how silently she moved behind the seasoned assassin. Whatever happened once they reached the antechamber outside their destination, she would have to be ready to react, because they could no longer risk speaking.

When they got to the edge of the doorway, Amera signaled her to wait with one hand before hurrying through.

"You can't be down here," a guard stated, his tone a fraction more weary than commanding.

"I'm so sorry." Meek, common, and slightly fearful. It was still hard to believe that voice could come from Amera. "I noticed someone sneaking about the castle when I was out getting sweet wine for my lady. They were acting suspiciously, so I followed them down here.

I lost sight of them a few seconds before…" Her voice started trembling. "I'm so glad I found you. There's a b-body just up the hall. I'm afraid the killer could still be nearby. I don't feel safe trying to make my way back alone."

"A body?" The alarm in the guard's tone said her performance had convinced him.

"That's right. Fresh enough it was still bleeding when I came upon it."

"Show us where."

Veyl carefully set down Amera's weapons and pressed back against the wall, easing her swords from their sheaths, and listening to the approaching footsteps. Amera hurried past, pointing in the opposite direction. The guards kept pace, almost breaking into a jog through the doorway. The moment they emerged, the nearest one caught Veyl out of the corner of his eye and twisted toward her, drawing his sword, his mouth opening as if he meant to shout. She drove one blade in hard between his parted lips and pushed up, tilting his head so she could thrust the second one home into the gap she had widened below his chin and above the upper edge of his gorget.

The man fell forward, the weight of him in his metal armor threatening to bear her to the ground. She gave in and let herself go down beneath him, muffling the sound of his fall with her body, though the impact sent a flash of pain through her back and ribs. His blood flowed hot onto her shoulder as she struggled to wriggle free of him without making a racket. Amera appeared, helping carefully roll his twitching form off her. She gave Veyl a hand up, then looked at the blades planted in the man's mouth and throat. The other guard lay face down in a growing pool of red a few feet away, his own sword covered in his blood on the floor beside him.

"Well done," Amera whispered. "You have the makings of a fine tezaak."

Veyl swallowed, trying not to think about the warmth soaking her shoulder. "Let's rescue my father."

"Mind-crafters bleed like anyone else, but I have no defense against their abilities. You must keep them from influencing me, or you will be alone in there."

Veyl leaned upon the links to Ceris and Seyn, wary of confusing the signal if she reached out to Gannon and Kyril before she was ready for them to move. "I know."

After taking a moment to wipe her blades and put them away while Amera fastened on her sword belt, Veyl stepped into the antechamber. It was about fifteen feet across to the doors behind which she would hopefully find her father. Four statues stood in two pairs along the side walls. All four held weapons in front of them, the killing ends at rest before their feet—a battleaxe, war hammer, a spear, and a greatsword—they had their heads bowed and eyes closed as if in sorrow or shame.

"I'm going to send Gannon in," Veyl murmured, staring at those statues. The khemron of Vanris didn't belong here. Her father, a renowned hero, was far too great a man to be locked up in this place.

Amera stepped up beside her, facing the doors. She said nothing.

Veyl focused on her link to Gannon, trying to pass along a sense of urgency. It was still strange using the bonds this way. It wasn't how a bond typically functioned, but for her, for some reason, everything seemed to work a little differently. A flash of anxiety and determination came back to her that told her he had gotten her message. Drawing a deep breath and stamping down her fear of what still lay ahead, she tried to pass confidence back to him. With Feyd, Jinau, and the larger share of the Eydarith, he had a capable group with him. Kyril's team was smaller. Like Veyl and Amera, they would rely on a great deal of stealth up to the last minute, but until she could guarantee her father's freedom, she didn't dare set them to rescuing the kanodrak.

A flicker of much-needed reassurance came back to her from Gannon.

Amera walked between the statues to the doors with Veyl, and they each placed a hand on one handle.

The most effective abilities for dealing with groups in combat were the Dampener and Frightener abilities, though an Enkindler could also be useful in more subtle ways. If the Thaelians had a Frightener or Dampener of their own behind that door, or both, they should be resistant to her use of those powers, but she had affected the Dampener they faced in Kronach's hall in Taro. She hoped that wasn't simply some inexplicable exception. Unfortunately, there was only one way to find out for certain.

Closing her eyes, she focused on her memories of the ocean, its sound, scent, and the chill of its depths. Ceris and Seyn responded instantly, somehow feeding into the sensation of the power and pressure of water rising in and around her. Even with their help, it wasn't as potent here as it had been in Taro, but she had expected that. It had to be enough.

Veyl nodded. It was time.

They threw open the doors together. She had a brief impression of a tall, dark chamber, lit by several flickering torches, and some chains and ropes hanging from the walls and ceiling. The four Thaelians in the room—a man and three women—reacted reflexively, all grabbing for small pouches at their waists. Veyl slammed darkness and an accompanying sense of despair over them, drawing on two abilities at once. As the first one yanked the pouch clear and hurled it in their direction, confident in her aim despite losing her sight, Veyl recalled the one danger she had failed to account for: Sarket's love of alchemical weapons.

Amera body-slammed into her. The bomb hit the ground in the doorway and exploded, the blast throwing them both to the floor. They flew clear of the worst of the debris, but it still set her ears ringing, and the force of the explosion, even through the woman shielding her, was stunning.

Fury crackled to life in Veyl, and she unleashed another power, one she hadn't fully embraced since its return. Their terror fed into her, pulled from their minds by the Frightener ability. Beneath those Thaelian nightmares, which included Amera's, she came upon a presence with a different feel to it. One so familiar she couldn't have confused it with anything else if she wanted to. Her father's fear at that moment revolved around a growing understanding that he had failed. He did not dread what would happen to him. Never that. His resolve was breaking before the conviction that he would soon lose his hold on Niskenya, and the kano-drak would tear herself apart trying to escape her cage, and before the knowledge that he could no longer help his country, his tehsheyn, or his wife and family. He had failed them all.

But he hadn't. Not yet. And she meant to help him fix this.

Her rage spurring her on, Veyl shoved clear of Amera and got to her feet, letting the lightning crackle through her and out beyond her body, riding with it like a ship on a storm-tossed sea. She kept enough control to exclude Amera and Kasiel from her attack. Then she hit the four with her rage, lashing out at them with all their terror, and the not insubstantial power of her own fears, knowing what could happen if she didn't succeed. The resulting screams fueled her resolve. One woman threw a bomb at something that was only there in her mind. The explosion sent one of the other three flying into the wall hard enough that he crumpled to the floor unconscious or dead.

Another woman turned to flee from her terror, and her leg went through a hole in one of the pit grates. She cried out, flailing in panic for a heartbeat before Amera opened her throat. The tezaak made quick work of the other two as they battled their nightmares. The last one hadn't finished falling when Amera sank to her knees, holding her side.

Veyl struggled to focus on that, on the next steps, on the fact that her father was here in this room, but the storm held onto her, sweeping her up in its power, threatening to tear her apart. She could feel her control fragmenting. Refusing to let her own abilities be the reason they failed, she latched onto her awareness of her father and Amera and followed it until she found her way out of the storm enough to wrestle it back under control.

Releasing a shaky breath, Veyl opened her eyes, her gaze falling upon Amera first. The woman's gasping and her grimace made it obvious she had suffered a substantial injury, though the blood on her clothing didn't appear to be her own.

When Veyl took a step toward her, she shook her head. "The khemron," she snapped.

She required little convincing. Hurrying to the central grate, Veyl knelt and peered into the darkness. "Father, are you down there?"

"Veyl?"

In the strained effort of that one word, she could hear unsettling pain and weakness. He was in that dark, narrow, stinking pit, somewhere beyond the reach of the light, and he was not in good condition. She ran to grab a torch from a bracket and hurried back, laying it at the edge of the grate. The flickering illumination barely pulled his pale features out of the darkness.

"I'm getting you out of there." When she grabbed

hold of the edge of the grate, a second pair of hands joined hers, and she looked at Amera. The other woman had beads of sweat sprouting on her forehead, and blood streaked the back of her hair. "Are you all right?"

"I have been better, but I am all the help you've got."

Given what she knew of the woman, that sounded like a decisive no. It didn't mean she was any less right, however. The two of them were on their own down here. They had to make it work.

With a determined heave, they shifted the grate up and slid it off the top of the cell. She suspected the increased panting from Amera wasn't from fatigue. The woman's hand returned to her side when she stood, grumbling about ladders and ropes, and started for the far corner of the room, walking slightly hunched.

"Don't go anywhere," Veyl called down, relieved to get a pained chuckle from below as she hopped up to help Amera.

One development she took regretful note of as she hurried to grab the rickety, narrow ladder Amera was heading toward, was that Jaysen was awake, fury rolling across her link to him. She had let instinct and anger take over when the Thaelians threw the bomb, casting aside caution. The overflow of her Frightener attack would have alerted anyone in the vicinity that a mind-crafter ability was being used. In fact, most of those sleeping in this part of the castle had likely experienced some vivid nightmares moments ago. They would pay a price for her carelessness, but fretting over that would do nothing to improve the situation. They needed to free her father.

She called for him to move to the side as she began lowering the ladder. The top of the pit was narrow. Wide enough for the ladder and a single person on it. About six feet down, the cell appeared to widen out in a gradual bell shape for another eight or more feet, making it impossible for any unfortunate who found themselves at the bottom to get purchase and climb out. A perfect prison for someone like her father, who might have used rodents to retrieve the keys to a normal cell. They were so confident in the design they hadn't bothered putting locks on the grates.

"Can you climb?" she called down.

"Give me a minute."

The tightness in his voice made her gut clench.

Amera pointed to a rope run through several pulleys attached to a rafter above, clearly designed to use leverage for lifting prisoners, or their bodies, from the pits. "Grab that. I will go down and help him."

"No, you're injured. Let's not put the two most damaged people in our trio to solving a physical problem. Get the rope and lower it in. I'll head down."

Amera answered with a slight shrug and went to do her part. Veyl climbed onto the rickety ladder, trying not to dwell on what would happen if it broke, or she slipped. "Stay clear, I'm coming down."

"You shouldn't be—" His voice cracked, and a fit of coughing interrupted what she suspected would have been a protest of some kind.

Veyl grabbed the torch and climbed onto the rickety ladder. She kept hold of the sides with both hands as she descended, even though the flames from the torch licked up along the rail on one side. The wood was cold and damp. It would amaze her if it even started smoldering. The walls were too close and cramped, their nearness making her skin crawl. Somehow, passing the point where they belled out did nothing to alleviate that claustrophobia.

That her father didn't get up from where he sat near one wall when she reached the bottom told her a great deal about the condition he was in. The torchlight revealed a haggard, unnaturally pallid man, though she hoped that was at least partly an effect of the poor lighting. His clothes were dirty, and the reek of urine and feces shared the air with some other unfortunate stink that made her stomach shrink in on itself. One dark-stained sleeve, torn from his shirt, was tied sloppily around his forearm.

"Is it broken?"

He opened his eyes and nodded slowly, the simple movement requiring great effort. "They dropped me down here while I was still mostly paralyzed." He paused, drawing a shallow breath. "I had enough control by then to try protecting my head, but my arm and collarbone didn't fare so well."

Veyl took a second to focus on her link to Gannon, needing positive news. A sense of tension came back to her, but nothing to suggest that his group had encountered problems yet. "Isn't that the arm you broke on Itana's mace?" She asked, trying to tease out the severity of his condition.

Another weak chuckle. "Not intentionally." He struggled to get up, and she hurried to help him, trying not to breathe in through her nose while she did so. "Tell me you didn't come here alone."

"To Andaro? No. Gannon's leading a group to break the rest of your company out of the prisons. Kyril has another in position to free Niskenya."

The faintest hint of a smile touched his lips. "Have I told you that you're my favorite daughter?"

She breathed a laugh, though the comment brought tears to her eyes. That he still had any sense of humor left after what he had been through was reassuring. "Can you convince Niskenya to work with Kyril?"

"I can try. She's full of rage and in pain, and she feels my condition as well. Persuading her to behave rationally has been an ongoing battle."

His unspoken words hung in the air between them. She didn't need any further explanation to understand that he had very little left to give.

## CHAPTER TWENTY SIX

Veyl nearly leapt out of her own skin when the end of the rope, complete with a complicated harness, slapped down against the ladder next to her. She placed a hand to her chest and drew in a trembling breath.

"Apologies, Wavelord," Amera called down.

Kasiel's brow furrowed. "Your companion's accent and the new title bring up a lot of questions I don't think we have time for right now."

That was fortunate. She opted to ignore Amera's use of the title and his comment. "I can help you put on the harness, but I'll probably need to go up and assist from above. Tezaak Amera's injured, and I doubt she'll be able to put much effort into helping you climb. Can you manage on your own?"

He gave the ladder a sour look. "I don't think I have a choice. This thing won't hold more than one of us at a time. Besides, I wouldn't let you stay down here. You may be my rescuer, but you're also my daughter."

Though she yearned to hug him, his injuries made a poor choice of that idea. Instead, she leaned in and kissed his cheek.

He pulled away. "Don't. I'm filthy."

"Do you honestly think I care? I didn't know if you would even be alive when I found you. A little dirt won't discourage me. Now let's put this on you and get you out of here. Niskenya needs you."

That was all she had to say to focus him. Although with the pain he was in and the blood he had lost, not to mention the fact that she suspected they hadn't given him food or water since dropping him down there, he needed considerable help. The most he could do was try not to make it harder and let her know if she did something that caused too much pain, though she wasn't sure she trusted him to be honest about that.

When the time came to head up the ladder, she was reluctant to leave him, but she had few options, and the situation would only get worse if Jaysen or some of his soldiers showed up. For now, at least, she didn't sense the crown prince coming closer. On the positive side, that meant he probably hadn't figured out where the surge of ability came from. On the negative, if he believed a Frightener overflow could have come from another source, it suggested the Thaelians might have other Frighteners still among their numbers. Either that, or they had discovered the activity at the prison and that was keeping him otherwise occupied for the time being.

She hurried out of the pit, ascending as fast as she dared. It was easier without the torch that she had left at the bottom to give her father light for the start of his climb. Once at the top, she and Amera used the ropes, woven through the system of pulleys for leverage, to help take some of the strain off him as he made his way up. He wouldn't have much chance to rest after he joined them, so any effort they could spare him now would be to all their benefit going forward.

He climbed more slowly than she liked, the minutes ticking by as she paid close attention to her link to Jaysen and those to Kyril and Gannon. Nothing significant had changed that she could feel beyond a faint sense of both frustration and determination from Gannon, but she didn't get any of the panic or desperation that might suggest a significant problem.

When he reached the top, they helped him out together, then Amera sank back against a wall, panting and holding her side again. The sweat standing out on her forehead was decidedly more than their level of exertion could account for, given how fit she was. The khemron was about the same as he staggered over and leaned against the wall next to her, his eyes pinched shut while he struggled to master his own pain. Amera held out a waterskin she must have found in the room, perhaps on one of the dead Thaelians, and tapped his leg to get his attention. He took it with a look of gratitude and drank deeply from it, his thirst confirming Veyl's suspicion that they hadn't given him anything in the pit.

In the slightly better lighting, she could see that his crudely bandaged forearm wasn't straight and the amount of blood staining his clothing was considerable. A flash of fury swept through her upon noticing that they had also cut the Vanrian soldier's braids out of his hair on both sides.

Her father was perceptive enough to figure out what she had focused on. "I survived having my ears cut as a child. At least this will grow back."

"I'll make him a sling for the arm," Amera suggested. "It will take a moment, but it will make the journey out of here easier. Get me a shirt off one of the dead."

Veyl hurried to one of the Thaelians and pulled the woman's shirt off, trying not to think of her as anything more than a resource. She tossed it to Amera.

"Do you—" A flash of alarm from Kyril cut Veyl off.

Recalling the encounter in Kronach's hall, she reached out to Seyn. If the beast was willing, perhaps…

The abrupt transition made her stomach turn. She found herself looking at Kyril through the wave dancer's eyes. He was crouched next to her in the shadow of some columns. The colors weren't quite the same as what Veyl was used to seeing. If anything, they were more vivid, pulling out the deep blue in his hair even in the darkness. A deep longing for the Thaelian Feral rose in her. Not for intimacy, not at a moment like this, but for a chance to be there with him, fighting at his side, helping to ensure they both made it through this.

Seyn turned, her eyes focusing on the cage holding Niskenya in the courtyard beyond their hiding place. She watched as one guard strode forward to intercept an officer jogging out from the castle, who was gesturing toward the kanodrak.

"The king wants that Havaad-cursed beast dispatched now," the officer declared.

"Are you sure? His prior orders were to make certain nothing happened to it before his coronation."

"Do what you're told, Captain. And when you finish here, take your men to the prison. There's a rescue attempt underway. Kill any Eydarith or Vanrians you come across. It appears Wavelord Kronach may have made some new friends."

The captain threw up a hand. "How are we supposed to tell the Vanrians from the Havaad-cursed Thaelians?"

The man from the castle lunged forward, his face flushing, hands clenching into fists. "Figure it out!" With that, he spun and sprinted back toward the castle.

Veyl's heart beat double-time. Both of the other groups were in danger now. She needed to be out there. But maybe she could be, to a limited degree. More so than just using Seyn would allow. With their bonds, and assuming she had access to all the mind-crafter disciplines, she should be able to use the Speaker ability to communicate with Kyril and Gannon, at least one way.

Focusing on her bond with Kyril, she tried thinking to him.

*I have my father. Save Niskenya.*

A flood o f r elief s wept b ack a cross t heir l ink. S he stayed with Seyn long enough to see Kyril and the others with him charge out of hiding. Twenty guards was a lot for the small group to handle, though they had the wave dancers to help, at least. She had to pull away from Seyn to give more attention to Gannon, losing the visual aspect of their connection.

*They know you're in the prison, Gannon. Be ready.*

What she got from him first was a fl are of su rprise, followed by gratitude and a sense of intensifying focus. Gannon wouldn't let the Sarketi win if he could do anything to stop it. She hoped they had successfully freed at least some of her father's company by now. With the Eydarith and Kasiel's more seasoned fighters helping, Jaysen's soldiers would have a brutal fight on their hands.

Veyl dove back in behind Seyn's eyes as the beast took down a guard. The man wasn't wearing a helmet or had perhaps lost his in the encounter. Either way, he paid for that lack now as the wave dancer's long, powerful jaws tore away part of his face, giving Veyl a close-up look at the bone and muscle tissue beneath. She could taste blood when the beast forced her muzzle between his flailing hands and ripped into his throat. Then Seyn glanced up from the dead man, and Veyl saw Kyril rush ahead past a soldier he had cut down and take a mighty swing at the lock on Niskenya's cage with an axe he had picked up somewhere.

Back in the chamber under the keep, she sank to her knees and threw up, the taste of the man's blood still lingering. She wiped her mouth and looked up at her father. "You need to reach Niskenya. Now."

His brow furrowed with effort, his gaze unfocused. "I'm trying. The fighting has her riled."

Veyl turned to Amera, who was adjusting the makeshift sling over her father's shoulder, drawing an agonized groan from him. "We need to get out there."

The tezaak set a hand to her side again with a soft grunt. "Help the khemron. I will lead."

Veyl nodded. Even if her father weren't dealing with severe injuries, he would need someone to guide him so he could focus on Niskenya while they made their escape. Under the circumstances, he would be hard-pressed to walk or reach out to the kanodrak, let alone do both, even with help. At least it felt as if Jaysen had moved further away. Though that might not bode well for her companions, it would give their trio a chance to get out of the keep.

Veyl slipped under her father's good arm, letting him lean some of his weight on her while she directed him. His gaze turned inward, focusing on trying to keep Niskenya from attacking her rescuers in her pain and rage. Veyl yearned to look back through Seyn's eyes, but right now she had to be the eyes for herself and her father.

They had barely stepped out into the first hallway when the sound of people running along another hall in the direction they had originally come from reached them.

Amera scowled. "Follow me." She gestured in the opposite direction with a jerk of her head. "There is another way, but we will have to go to the second floor. There is an elevated outer walkway that extends around to the courtyard."

Veyl nodded, appreciating the tezaak's preparatory efforts now more than ever. Climbing stairs would be difficult, but it was still preferable to being caught down here with a collection of dead guards and an escaped prisoner when only one of them was fit to fight. They turned away from the sounds of approach and hurried, as best they could considering Amera's hunched walk and her father's injuries and distraction, to the next hall. The tezaak took them through a wooden door onto steep, narrow stairs like those they had originally come down.

Grunts of pain from both of Veyl's companions punctuated the frustratingly slow process of ascending. Amera had just eased open a door two floors up when they heard the one at the bottom slam open. She waved Veyl and Kasiel out and hurried after them, gently closing the door behind them.

By now, Jaysen would have sent someone to check on her in her room, but the infiltration of the prison and the attack on the soldiers watching over Niskenya would hopefully keep most of his castle guards busy. This hallway appeared unoccupied for the moment. They crept along the large white-stone passage. The brightness of those walls made Veyl feel uncomfortably exposed after the dark, oppressive halls below, and she became acutely aware of the blood and stink clinging to their clothing. Anyone who spotted them would know they were up to something.

Amera stopped and pulled aside a tapestry to reveal a flush door set in the wall. She leaned against it, listening for a moment, then she eased it open and peered out.

"How is Niskenya?" Veyl asked in a whisper.

Her father didn't respond. The distance in his stare told her he was almost entirely immersed in the kanodrak's mind. That might be for the best, given the amount of pain he had to be in. Not that Niskenya was in fantastic condition herself. Perhaps she could chance a quick look through Seyn's eyes. She was receiving a disorienting blend of ferocity and fatigue from the wave dancer that told her they were still fighting.

"Move."

Amera's hiss snapped her to attention, and she abandoned the idea of reaching out to Seyn in favor of hurrying them out of the open hallway. The exterior walkway was the same in design as the one they used on their way to the pit cells. In fact, it looked as if this might be part of the same structure. It was conveniently too narrow to be a sensible choice for moving groups of soldiers around, but also lacked the advantage of rooms in which they might hide if they heard someone coming.

They had just started moving when the door opened behind them and a guard leaned into the walk. Veyl twisted out from under her father's shoulder, drawing one sword as she did so, and caught the man in the jaw with the pommel using her left hand. She followed through with the right, taking advantage of his unsteady lean to grab him and yank him forward, sending him toppling over the rail. It wasn't clear if he screamed before he hit bottom because her father had staggered into a post when she spun away from him, his cry of pain echoed by a ground-shaking roar from the kanodrak.

"Father!" Veyl rushed back to his side. "I'm sorry."

"You had no choice," he managed through clenched teeth, squeezing his eyes shut. "You handled it well."

Veyl reached out to Seyn, slipping behind her eyes. Pain flashed back at her when the edge of a soldier's blade nicked the wave dancer's shoulder in that instant of distraction. Guilt surged in Veyl, knowing her abrupt arrival in Seyn's head had compromised the beast. Fortunately, her yelp caught Kyril's attention. He ducked under his current opponent's strike and spun around to drive his blade into the side of the man attacking Seyn.

Not ten feet away, Niskenya was free, violently tearing through a unit of Sarketi guards. At least for now, she had an enemy to occupy her. They needed to get her bonded companion to the courtyard before that changed.

Drawing back, Veyl moved into position under her father's arm and guided him forward again. Amera, who was leaning against the next post watching them, nodded and resumed walking, though it took the woman a little longer to get going this time.

They made their way along the elevated walkway toward the castle courtyard as fast as their two injured members would allow. When they came around the corner and were finally overlooking the scene, Veyl let out a shaky breath of relief. The battle was done, and Kyril was down on one knee in a respectful pose before the bloodied kanodrak, with the two wave dancers flanking him. She could hear Niskenya's deep growling, her sides heaving with the effort of the fight, but at least she wasn't attacking.

Veyl felt Jaysen arrive before she saw him, his presence drawing her attention up to a balcony to the left of and one floor above their walkway. The sound of pounding feet on more wooden walkways overhead told her he wasn't alone.

"What are you waiting for?" He shouted. "Shoot the beast!"

Veyl's heart stuttered in her chest at the creak of bowstrings being drawn and the swoosh of arrows releasing. Several projectiles slammed into Niskenya. Kasiel cried out in fury and pain as he shared her experience. The kanodrak roared and lashed out, the swipe of one powerful paw sending both Ceris and Kyril flying several feet. Kyril struck the ground hard, his pain spearing across their link in a flash before it fell silent. He didn't move. The wave dancer let out a sharp yelp when he hit, but he landed and rolled to his feet, darting forward alongside Seyn to stand protectively over the fallen Feral.

"Niske!"

Veyl didn't care to imagine how much it hurt her father to yell that loudly with his broken collarbone, but she was grateful he did so. The kanodrak froze and looked up. She lunged over the two wave dancers and their fallen charge and sprinted across the courtyard. A large group of armed men and women came racing out from deeper in the grounds with Gannon and Torlif in the lead and a group of Sarketi soldiers on their tail. Veyl spotted several of her father's tehsheyn among them.

Jaysen had come to the edge of the balcony above now, and was staring down at her, a molten fury spilling across their link.

An officer stepped up next to him. "Majesty, many soldiers have fled. They refused to fight alongside the Thaelians. Without them, I'm afraid we have lost control of Andaro"

His fury flared brightly within her like an exploding firebomb. He clenched his hands on the balcony rail, looking as if he meant to tear it asunder. "We are not done," he snarled at her. "You will regret this the next time we meet." With those words, he spun and disappeared back into the castle.

As if of its own accord, her tongue sought the cut on the inside of her lip. She turned to see Amera struggling to help her father to a set of stairs descending to the courtyard. Veyl hurried over and intervened.

"You're wounded. Go ahead of us."

The tezaak didn't argue. When they were almost at the bottom, Torlif came up and took over supporting her father down to where the distressed and battered kanodrak waited. Niskenya huffed contentedly when her bonded was finally returned to her, pressing her head to his uninjured side, even with all the arrows protruding from her thick silver-gray hide.

Veyl turned toward where Kyril lay, their bond still silent, but not gone. Ceris stood watch as Dailan knelt beside him, fingers pressing to his neck in search of a pulse. After a moment, he glanced over at her and nodded, confirming that he lived.

Amera stopped beside her, her breath coming in

strained gasps. "You cannot…help your Feral. Only…the healers can aid him now, but…you might still help your people."

Veyl looked around. Her father was leaning against Niskenya's shoulder, eyes closed, his good hand pressed against her neck. The massive kanodrak had her head turned toward him, purring now as if she weren't in a dire state herself from her many injuries. Nerith had come running up from the prison group and was cautiously approaching the two. A brief flash of alarm swept through Veyl at not seeing Healer Tath, the twins' mother, with her tehnaak. Then she spotted the other woman being supported by her father's Speaker and an Eydarith woman. One leg appeared unable to bear weight, but she was alive.

Fighting had broken out between the rest of the group from the prison and their pursuers, but it didn't look as if it would last long. Abandoned by the crown prince, the remaining Sarketi soldiers were trying to flee or surrendering. Seyn sprinted to her and pressed herself against Veyl's leg hard enough that she nearly knocked her over. Setting a hand on the beast's head, she turned her gaze to the front gate. She could feel Jaysen moving away from them. If he escaped, this would not be the last time they fought him and his allies. How much more damage could he do given time to regroup and seek additional support?

It was hard not to run to Kyril, but Amera was right. She could do nothing for him that the healers couldn't do better. If anything, she would only be in their way. What she might do more effectively was end this.

Several people were gathering around her now, their grim, determined looks telling her they shared her line of thinking. She scanned them, her eyes picking out Feyd.

"No. You stay and help Dailan. There are too many

injured. My father is in expert hands, but please make sure Kyril lives through this. I don't want to come back to find him…" She couldn't say it. It felt like speaking the word might invite it to come true.

Feyd hesitated, glancing between her and his tehnaak.

"Don't worry. We'll look after the khesran," Merrin said, as she and Avris joined them.

Feyd eyed the two, then looked at the others that were gathering around Veyl, including many of her Eydarith, Ahrin, Iyvalin, Gannon, and Jinau. He gave a firm nod. "All right. Just make sure you all come back in one piece. We haven't got that many healers."

Veyl glanced over at Kyril again. He still hadn't moved. Kitria was beside him now, looking slightly frantic, but not devastated, which told her he probably wasn't dying, though that could change rapidly if the blow from the kanodrak caused enough damage.

"Min! Yserra!" her father called out. "Take some soldiers and go with Veyl."

Pride burst through her at the fact that he wasn't ordering them to stop her. He was trusting her and giving her more of his people to support her. When the two came running to join her growing unit, she met her father's eyes.

He inclined his head a fraction. A subtle gesture of respect, though worry shone in his eyes. "Stop him, but be careful."

"I will."

She turned and ran toward the courtyard exit with a mixed unit accompanying her that included Vanrian soldiers and mind-crafters from her and her father's companies, as well as her Eydarith warriors and Jinau. Gannon and Seyn stayed close alongside her.

Jaysen had left the castle. Her link to him told her he was moving out into the city. She had to hope he hadn't acquired horses somewhere. Their occupation of the courtyard would have blocked him from the royal stables, but he could always commandeer some from another stable. They had to catch up with him, but she had no way of knowing how many Thaelians and Sarketi soldiers he might have taken with him. All she could do was hope the haste with which he had departed prevented him from organizing much of his remaining force.

Thinking about how she had seen through Seyn's eyes the same way her father could with his beasts, she tried reaching out, to see if she could scout with a bird as he did. Next to her, the wave dancer stumbled. Veyl's effort faltered. Was she doing something wrong? Or maybe connecting with unfamiliar creatures was simply more difficult. They didn't have time for her to figure it out. Jaysen was trying to slip away, and she had no intention of letting him.

Veyl passed through the courtyard entrance with her hastily assembled unit. She was sore, exhausted, the wound on her head was throbbing, and she was worried about everyone she was leaving behind, but those were all reasons to push harder. She couldn't let Jaysen get away. Not after everything he had done. He would remain a threat to her and the people she loved. Now more than ever, she understood why her father had gone to such lengths to end the war all those years ago. Somehow, she would bring this to an end.

"Wavelord." Torlif came up beside her, surprisingly swift and light-footed for a man of his size. "They may try to seize mounts along the way to outrun us, but I lived in this city for two years. I can show you a shortcut to the north gate if you will allow it. We may have a chance of cutting them off."

Veyl glanced over at him, a spark of hope flashing in her chest. "Lead the way."

He turned right outside the courtyard wall and struck off at a jog down a narrow backstreet.

Veyl worked to keep pace with him. "I thought the Eydarith preferred to live along the coast."

He gave her a brief, scrutinizing look, as if trying to determine how much he should tell her. "The ocean is mighty, but so are the mountains. The Eydarith stand between them. We must understand both if we do not wish to be crushed by either."

"Kronach stationed you here to keep tabs on Sarket's leaders," she ventured.

Torlif said nothing, but his faint smirk was answer enough. The wavelord of Taro was a clever man. There was little she would put past him at this point. His efforts to stay one step ahead of events might be admirable, if only he didn't find trying to manipulate her so Break-blasted amusing.

Veyl gave up any further attempt at conversation, opting to save her energy for facing Jaysen and however many soldiers and mind-crafters he had taken with him in his rushed escape. She desperately wished she had a better idea of what awaited them. Had he left any of the Thaelians behind? It seemed unlikely that he could have gathered them all that quickly, and yet, they were the ones whose support had gotten him this far. Would he abandon them so easily in the hopes of finding some other advantage once he was safe?

Torlif turned and used a crumbling brick half-wall to launch himself up onto the low roof of a shed. The action caught Veyl by surprise. Lacking an opportunity to question the move, she maintained her momentum and leapt up after him. Seyn lunged up alongside her. She had to trust that the others could manage. As far as she had seen, none of those who followed her were nursing serious injuries.

"Did this man lose his mind somewhere?" Gannon asked, panting his way up beside her when she paused briefly to pick a landing spot for jumping down on the other side. "I feel like this is some sadistic training course Dhomen Merrin would come up with."

A chuckle behind them told her Merrin had joined them on the roof.

Veyl breathed a wry laugh. "We'd best hope he hasn't."

She jumped, landing a bit too solidly on the packed dirt beyond the shed. The impact jarred her clear up to her throbbing head. Pushing discomfort aside, she broke into a faster jog to catch up with the burly Eydarith warrior.

Torlif ducked through broken slats in a tall fence and cut across the muddy yard behind someone's house, leaping the shorter, intact fence on the other side. Veyl's body yearned to stop and be done with this part. She might be fit and well-trained, but it had been some time since she'd had any proper rest. Dread over whether they would catch Jaysen and what would happen if they did drained her energy almost as much as the chase itself.

"What if someone had repaired that fence?" she asked, trying to take her mind off her uncertainties.

Torlif chuckled, and it gave her some satisfaction to hear that he was beginning to sound a little winded. "I would have made a new hole."

Veyl believed that. She could imagine him plowing through the fence without missing a stride, blasting out the other side like an angry tethdrak breaking free of its enclosure.

Eventually, they cut down a back street heading west and ran out onto the main road through the city, near the northern gate. Jaysen and his followers were in sight, a sufficiently large group that Veyl's heart pounded its way up into her throat. Had she made the wrong decision by coming after them?

Some of them, the prince included, had mounts now and were far enough away that they could still change direction and try a different way around or turn and run for the southern gate. Instead, Jaysen slowed, continuing toward them, and stopped his horse perhaps fifteen feet away from her and her motley unit. Something in his smile as he dismounted sent a chill through her. He strode forward, cutting the distance in half, his mixed Thaelian and Sarketi company following his lead. They outnumbered her group at least three to one.

"Were you upset that I didn't say goodbye, Khesran, or did you hope to come with?"

Words were useless at this point. Trying to gain the advantage of surprise, Veyl slammed darkness over his company with her Dampener ability. A few panicked cries and terrified sobs told her she had probably caught some bystanders up in her effort, but it was challenging to separate Sarketi civilians from Sarketi soldiers. She couldn't worry about that now.

A flash of victory swept through her. She had his company subdued, rendering them helpless with the loss of their sight.

Next to her, Seyn splayed out her front legs as if struggling for balance before collapsing, and the link to the wave dancer fell silent. The bond to Ceris did the same a heartbeat later. With the bond to Kyril already dormant, that left Veyl a lot fewer options for bolstering her abilities. She felt her power faltering—sliding from her grasp like a slippery rope with the lives of her unit hanging from it. The energy required to influence so many depleted what remained of her strength. On her other side, Gannon staggered, shifting into a wider stance.

Horror crept in. Had she been draining them all along, the enormous power of her abilities made possible only because she could pull energy from those she shared bonds with, like some twisted parasite? With Kyril and the wave dancers removed from the pool, Gannon couldn't bolster her alone. A dizzying surge of weakness swept through her, and the landscape tilted. The darkness she had cast her enemies into fractured and dissipated. She tried to draw from Jaysen, but that link didn't work the same, perhaps because she had been so careful to put limits on it when she created it so he wouldn't be aware of it.

A slow, smug smile curved Jaysen's lips.

A Thaelian with the milky eyes of a Bondmaker stepped up beside him and gestured to Gannon. "That one is her tehnaak," he offered in a low voice.

Jaysen's smile broke. Loathing burned behind his eyes as he stalked closer. "You replaced me with this bastard?"

He gestured sharply, and an instant later, an arrow plunged into Gannon's thigh. Veyl gasped as his pain burst across their bond. Jaysen lunged forward and slugged Gannon in the gut. Then he kicked the un-injured leg out from under him. Her tehnaak hit the ground, curling around his stomach and gasping for air, one hand grabbing at the arrow protruding from his thigh.

Before they could retaliate, the rest of her group, except for her father's Dampener Minera, froze in place. A few crouched slightly as if they were no longer con-fident on their feet, signs that at least one Dampener on Jaysen's side had cast them into darkness. In so few seconds, the tables turned completely against them.

The crown prince approached, his strides confident now, and she drew her blades.

He made a beckoning gesture toward his company with one finger. Several archers stepped forward, aiming at her. "You won't come close enough to hurt me, Veyl. Drop your weapons."

Despair swelled within her. She glanced at Minera, the only other among them who could still see what was happening. The moment the woman met her eyes, an arrow slammed into her chest and she fell to her knees. Her tehnaak, Evoker Yserra, unable to see it happen, but able to feel it through their bond, screamed and sank to the ground, crawling toward her sense of the other woman. The archer who had fired the shot nocked another arrow and trained his bow on Iyvalin.

"No!" Veyl dropped her swords, her stomach twisting in knots. Had she led them to their deaths? Would he kill them all one at a time, locked in darkness, while she looked on?

Jaysen came forward and kicked the two weapons away from her before stopping to stare into her eyes, his smug smile returning. "I told you we weren't finished, but I didn't expect you to be this eager to continue."

He reached toward her cheek, and she stepped abruptly back. His fist snapped out, striking a punch to her gut like the one he had delivered to Gannon, knocking the breath out of her. When she doubled over, he caught hold of her hair and pulled her upright, wrapping his other hand tightly around her throat.

She wanted to fight him. She had the training to do so. They both did, but she was still better. Instead, she fought herself. With her unit at his mercy, all he had to do was signal his company, and they would take more down the way they had Gannon and Minera. The crackle of energy that fueled her abilities was silent. Gannon writhed on the ground next to her, struggling to draw a breath, blood spreading around the arrow in his leg. The wave dancers and Kyril were dark voids within her.

Trying to draw air back into her lungs was harder with Jaysen's hand squeezing her throat. Spots flashed before her eyes. She couldn't just let him strangle her, but who would his people shoot next if she fought him? If she could eliminate his Dampener, she could help her unit return to the fight, but that was impossible under the circumstances. Veyl struggled to reach across the bond she had made between them, trying to focus as darkness crept in at the edges of her vision. She could feel his hatred, his fear, and, behind it, an all-consuming despair far greater than her own. Even now, when it looked as though he would win. How horribly broken he was.

A tear slipped down her cheek, and his grip loosened a fraction.

"I'm sorry, Veyl," he murmured, the slight tremble in his voice suggesting he might genuinely believe he was. "But you lied to me again. You let me think you weren't a mind-crafter anymore, and the way you kissed me… Tomorrow, you said. I can't stomach another betrayal." His hand clamped down tighter than it had before.

Her legs trembled, weakening, blood pounding in her head.

Then a burst of strength swept into Veyl, her abilities crackling to life with renewed energy. She recognized the feel of the connection. Kronach. Seizing hold of the offered power, she blasted it over Jaysen's company, dropping them back into darkness and taking away their sense of touch this time as well. To discourage resistance, she used the Enkindler ability to overwhelm them with despair and hopelessness, crushing their spirits. It was their turn to crouch and freeze in panic once more while her unit abruptly recovered. Yserra rushed to Minera, pulling the woman into her arms. Ahrin and Iyvalin ran to Gannon.

Jaysen alone she spared from her assault. He didn't deserve anything so simple and free of pain. He would know the suffering he had caused. She wanted him to feel it all.

Accepting more of the strength being extended to her, she reached across the link, leveraging it to give her greater access to his mind using the Evoker and Charmer abilities. A wave of memories flashed between them of their childhood together; laughing over games of Feral's Folly, dining with her family, sneaking to each other's rooms or meeting on the rooftop to talk through the night.

Jaysen's grip on her hair and throat released, and he staggered back a step, moisture rising in his eyes.

Veyl mirrored his step, staying close, staring into his bright blue eyes as her own began stinging. Those moments were some of the best memories of his life… and of hers. Amera was right. She still yearned to see the boy she had known in him, and that made it impossible to fully hate him even now. It would be so much easier if she did. He had been her tehnaak and best friend. She loathed the people who had etched their hatred in his flesh and twisted him into the vile, joyless creature standing before her.

The day he saved her from falling off the academy rooftop played back in their minds.

*"Jaysen."*

*He froze, staring at the hand that gripped the legs of the statue. "What?"*

*"Thank you for not letting go of me."*

*"I would never let go of you, Veyl."*

She remembered the way something had changed in his bearing when he said those words. And so he hadn't. For better or worse, he had never let go of her.

"I'm sorry," she murmured, a tear sliding hot down her cheek. "I'm sorry for how you lost your mother and how Thrasser and his men treated you. For how they tortured and betrayed you. I wish they had not broken you with their cruelty. I wish I could have helped you back then."

"You—" Jaysen shrank from her as if her words were their blades carving into his flesh all over again. "I loved you." His voice cracked, and he sank to his knees. "I love you."

Veyl sank down with him, letting herself feel the full weight of his misery. "Shh." Pushing deeper into his mind, she seized upon the memories of Deepwater, before his companions found them and Kyril's fleet attacked, when it had only been the two of them on that rooftop. "Do you remember that night in Deepwater?

The way it felt when we kissed?"

He nodded, tears flowing unchecked down his cheeks.

"How we lay under the stars together and rekindled our tehnaak bond?" She drew more deeply upon the Evoker ability now, meticulously taking apart and restructuring his memories, using the persuasion of the Charmer ability to fabricate something new. "The way we held one another, languishing in each other's arms until morning." She stole away his memory of the interruption and the attack, relentlessly tearing apart everything that came after it. "We ran off together after that, didn't we? Just you and me. Going to build a simple life free from all the politics and backstabbing."

He smiled and nodded, his tears coming faster now. His eyes glazed over. His mind eagerly helping her assemble the memories she wanted him to have, using fragments of reality along with fantasies he had made up for himself to create the life he yearned for. She moved closer as if she might kiss him, gently easing a long dagger from his belt.

"You and me, Jaysen. No one else. Building our own family together," she whispered.

"You and me," he agreed, the joy in his smile reminding her very much of the boy she once held so dear, "the way we always wanted."

No. Only he had wanted that.

Veyl put one hand on his shoulder and numbed his physical sensation with the Dampener ability. Then, she drove the dagger hard up into his chest. She held on, his body jerking as she pulled it out to shove it in again, desperate to end it as quickly as possible. The need to see him suffer was gone. She only wanted him to be free of the pain while he still remembered something good, even if those memories weren't real. One last time, she had lied to him.

He coughed blood, his body convulsing as he collapsed against her. A wave of dizziness and the warmth of his life spilling out on her hands turned her stomach. She kept building that false future in his mind as she let him fall to the side, tears streaming down her own cheeks when she staggered to her feet and stumbled back into someone. Whoever it was, they caught her shoulders in a firm grip, but she couldn't react. She had given too much. Now she was drowning, locked deep in the mind of the man dying on the ground before her. Darkness swirled around her, false memories of a life and family that never existed racing through her head. Pain and desperation clutched at her, pulling her down into a place she didn't want to go.

Her legs gave out, the storm swirling her under, her reality threatening to break before the flood of a fabricated truth as his life ebbed.

Someone else's arms drew her into a gentle, but reassuring embrace. Not closing around her physical body, but around the part of her mind that had gotten stuck in the memories she created for Jaysen. She recognized that presence. She loved that presence. Kyril. A blade flashed out in the darkness of her mind, severing the decaying thread that tied her to Jaysen. The pain faded. The storm let go.

•

Veyl gradually became aware of someone behind her, supporting her weight against their hard chest, and the rhythmic movement of a horse beneath her. Her eyes snapped open. She really was astride a horse. Whoever rode behind her had a muscular arm wrapped firmly around her, keeping her upright in the saddle. The courtyard entrance of the castle in Andaro was a short distance ahead of them. She straightened, taking control of her own body.

"Welcome back, Princess."

Kronach. Of course, it had to be Kronach.

"Gannon!" Even before she moved to look, she felt him close by, in substantial pain, but alive. The turning of her head sent the world spinning, and she bent to the side and threw up, some of it spattering her leg and Kronach's on the way down.

"Not the show of gratitude I was hoping for." Kronach shifted his arm to steady her better.

Veyl spat. Then she turned slowly this time, wiping her mouth as she looked around. To the right, Gannon lay on a flat cart. A weary Seyn had availed herself of the space next to him. The realization that she had drawn strength from the wave dancers to the point of their collapse brought a surge of fresh shame with it. Iyvalin and Ahrin were walking alongside the cart, conversing with her injured tehnaak. Trying to keep his spirits up if their brave, though somewhat tenuous, smiles were any indication.

There were many Eydarith now, the smaller group who had accompanied her in pursuit of Jaysen walking among mounted warriors who must have arrived with Kronach, their ranks stretching as far back as she could see from her limited vantage. They were escorting Jaysen's disarmed Sarketi soldiers in their midst. With great care, she turned to the other side, finding more Eydarith and prisoners, along with another cart. This one held Minera's still form. Yserra walked alongside her tehnaak's body, holding one of the dead woman's hands, tears creeping silently down her cheeks, her sorrow so potent Veyl could feel it almost as acutely as if it were her own.

"Her tehnaak is dead because they followed me." A sob caught in her throat.

Kronach shifted her weight in front of him, the

abrupt movement forcing her attention to her balance as they angled toward the castle courtyard. "I suspect the situation would have gotten far worse if you had not stopped the undead prince when you did, Khesran."

She wasn't in the proper state of mind to accept his praise or appreciate that he used her correct title this time. "Where are the Thaelians?"

"Without knowing which were mind-crafters, we deemed it wise to dispatch most of them. Ahndhomen Jinau convinced us to spare a few. They are under his watch farther back with the aid of some of my more seasoned warriors."

Veyl could think of no good reason to argue with that decision, particularly since it was already done, and they had at least been willing to let the Thaelian Charmer have some say in the outcome. "And… Jaysen?"

"His body is behind us. I was deeply connected to you when you killed him. After what you suffered through in that moment, I did not think you would want to look upon his body just yet."

Veyl drew a deep breath, struggling between the depth of gratitude she felt toward his consideration and her unease with his intimate knowledge of what she had experienced while killing Jaysen. "You assisted me back there. How did you have so much power to give?"

"As wavelord of Taro, I am connected to all my people. It is part of what makes the Eydarith strong." He shifted her again, and she had the sudden disconcerting certainty that he was enjoying having her pressed against him in the narrow confines of his saddle a little too much.

"If you do that again, I will stab you. I don't care if you did help me back there."

Kronach chuckled.

"You took from your own people to meet the demands of my abilities?"

"I did. There will be good-natured boasting and arguments later over who gave the most when their wavelord called upon them. It is part of who we are. And you, Khesran, have become the perfect… marriage of Vanrian and Eydarith."

She shrugged off his emphasis on the word, knowing full well he was trying to get under her skin. "But I have no Eydarith blood, nor any Qwilki. I am purely Vanrian."

He slowed his mount as they entered the courtyard, letting the rest of the substantially enlarged company pass around them. "Remember, Vanrians are not the only ones capable of forming bonds. You are wave-touched. Therefore, you have within you connections to other wave-touched. If you were born Eydarith, you would have links to all of us. Our ocean god, the Tempest, granted you a limited bond with his children and unlocked the potential in your Vanrian blood."

"I'm not certain I believe that, but if it were true, why would the Tempest do that?"

"I cannot pretend to know the mind of our god, but the kingdom of Sarket needed cleansing. Through you, the ocean has reached beyond its shores and washed away some of the filth blighting our lands." He brought his mount to a full stop, and the company continued flowing around them like a river parting around a boulder.

Veyl drew in a breath, surprised by the Eydarith swarming past them in even greater numbers than she first realized. "So many?" She breathed the question, certain her words would go unheard, drowned out by the sound of hooves on the courtyard cobblestones.

Kronach leaned close, his chest pressing against her back, and spoke into her ear. "If you succeeded, as I knew you would, Vanris would have taken possession of Sarket's capital. An act of war. With a Sarketi lord present supporting your actions, even an Eydarith one, we might avoid further bloodshed in the wake of these events. The greater the number of Sarket-born warriors seen within these walls as allies rather than prisoners in the aftermath of this, the easier it will be for us to amend the story of what happened here. We can retell it as a combined effort to overthrow corrupt leaders instead of a hostile takeover by another kingdom."

He was right. By coming here with such a powerful force, he was shielding Vanris from the backlash of this. "And what do you hope to gain from your efforts, Wavelord Kronach?"

His lips were close enough to her ear that she felt the brush of his facial hair when he smiled. "There will be time for such conversations later. Let us check in with the khemron." He urged his horse onward again.

That was something she desperately wanted to do. To see to her father, Kyril, and Amera, as well as the rest of those who suffered injuries. She wasn't looking forward to telling her father about Minera, though she suspected she wouldn't have the chance before he learned of it from someone else now that they were trailing behind the others. She noticed that the cart carrying Jaysen still had not passed them. Kronach had his well-concealed thoughtful side.

"I have another question?"

"Yes, Khesran."

"Why did I end up on your horse? I could have ridden on the cart with Gannon. He is my tehnaak, and there was room."

"The khesran of Vanris, transported on a dirty cart?" He leaned close to her ear again and murmured, "I think you know the answer to that." His arm around her tightened a fraction.

"Haven't you got a wife or someone else to sate your needs?"

"Several powerful women have invited my seed.

They now raise our offspring in the cities or villages they lead. But to bring your storm to my bed..." He trailed off, inhaling deeply.

"You are a lewd old calloch," she growled under her breath.

His chest vibrated against her back with a low chuckle. "I take offense at your calling me old."

## CHAPTER TWENTY EIGHT

When they reached the back of the courtyard, all the remaining skirmishes had ended, and they had already moved most of the injured into the castle. Her father sat on the ground leaning against a pillar, watching as Nerith and Tath, the latter with a makeshift brace supporting one ankle, tended to the worst of Niskenya's injuries. With her myriad wounds, they required him to stay awake so he could keep her from lashing out and encourage her to change position when necessary. Deep furrows etched his brow, likely because of her pain as much as his own. No one was tending to him yet, which didn't surprise Veyl a great deal. When Niskenya was stable, he would let them care for his substantial injuries, and not a minute sooner. They wouldn't be able to risk sedating him until the massive predator was calm enough, regardless.

Kronach swung off his mount and helped Veyl down, something she would have preferred not to allow, but she was still unsteady, and it was marginally better than falling on her ass. For the moment, tolerating the wavelord's help and shrugging off his pleased smirk when he steadied her with a hand on her waist would at least let her avoid adding to her father's distress in his injured state.

Despite his condition, her father started struggling

to his feet, and Veyl hurried forward to assist him. The moment he was upright, he pulled her gingerly in with his good arm and pressed a kiss to her forehead.

"Thank you for returning safely to me." The raw edge in his voice was enough to tell her how hard it must have been for him to watch her leave.

"Dampener Minera—"

"Don't, Veyl. Merrin already told me. It isn't your fault." He turned toward Kronach, his arm still around her shoulders, and watched the cart carrying Jaysen roll past behind the wavelord.

Veyl couldn't help but look. Despite the blood that saturated his clothes from the stab wounds she had inflicted, his face appeared serene. She hoped that meant her effort to block his pain and send him to his death lost in pleasant, false memories had worked.

Kronach glanced over his shoulder at the cart. "Your daughter eliminated the undead prince's threat to our countries, Khemron. She has brought great honor to your line with her handling of the situation."

"I never doubted she would do so." Her father was quiet for a moment, his gaze taking in the substantial Eydarith force that filled the courtyard now. "Thank you for supporting our efforts here, Wavelord Kronach. There is clearly much for us to discuss, though it will need to wait until injuries have been seen to."

Kronach bobbed his head in a nod to her father's injured arm, casting a respectful glance at Niskenya. "My warriors can help manage prisoners and aid the wounded in the interim."

"We would appreciate that. Thank you again."

Seyn trotted up as Kronach offered a partial bow to each of them and strode away. The wave dancer nudged Veyl's hand with her nose. Fresh guilt twisted in her chest, and she sank to one knee, a move that put her slightly below eye level with the tall canine. Seyn's membranous ears perked up, and she stepped forward, pushing her head against Veyl's cheek in a vaguely cat-like gesture. Veyl brought her arms around the beast's neck and buried her face in that odd waterproof fur.

"It's still disconcerting to see you bonded with her like a Feral."

The exhaustion and rough edge of pain in his voice caused a twisting in her chest. She lingered with Seyn a moment longer, feeling the weight of the beast's devotion resting heavy on her shoulders. Then she stood and met her father's eyes.

"I am a Feral. I am also an Evoker, a Dampener, a... Well, you get the idea. None of it makes sense, but somehow I can use all those abilities and more now."

He gave her a troubled look, brows pinching. "We need to have a long talk."

Jethan jogged over to them. "Kas, we–"

"Uncle Jethan!" Veyl threw her arms around her father's tehnaak. She suspected he had survived their ordeal, given that her father would be much worse off if he had lost him, but it was comforting to have that confirmed.

The strength of Jethan's return embrace was welcome. He offered her the full hug her father couldn't give her in his condition. When she stepped back, she noted a swollen black eye and an angry cut along his jaw that both needed tending. He hadn't come out un-scathed, but he was alive.

"If I had known you were going to save us one day, I might not have minded what a pest you were growing up so much." He winked in response to her mock glower. "Avris was trying to convince me you used multiple mind-crafter abilities to defeat Jaysen. It hasn't been an hour since it happened, and there are already tall tales going around."

Veyl gave a somber nod. "She was telling the truth,

but you didn't come out here to talk about that."

He stared at her for a second, brow furrowing, then turned to his tehnaak. The unease in the look the two shared caused a sinking sensation in her chest. "Kince and Darro are leading a search of the castle and grounds for any hostile Thaelians or Sarketi still lurking about. We've taken over most of the main entry hall for tending our injured. There's a cot waiting for you, Kas, and enough room for Niske to stay near you. We figured she might be calmer when they put you out to work on that arm if she could watch over you."

Her father nodded, a flood of gratitude in the look he gave his tehnaak. "Thank you. I may have a hard time getting her to let me out of her sight for a while."

"Wait until Mother has you back." Veyl breathed a laugh when he grimaced. "Come on, I can help you inside," she offered, taking a step toward him.

"No." Jethan cut her off and slipped into place under her father's good arm. "Avris said you blacked out for several minutes after killing Jaysen. I think we should let you take it easy for a while."

His stern gaze told her there was little point in arguing. "All right. I'll come inside with you. I need to check on a few people, and maybe I can help care for the wounded."

"So much for resting. You are undeniably Kas's child." Jethan laughed, the sound accompanied by a soft chuckle from her father, probably the most he could manage without hurting himself too much.

Niskenya followed them at some unspoken invitation from her father. Even knowing the beast was his devoted companion, it was a little unnerving having a creature that could kill someone with a swipe of her paw, or literally crush a person's skull in her jaws, walking that closely behind them. Kyril was fortunate to be alive after the blow he had taken from her, but he was alive. If he weren't, he couldn't have come to her aid when she became trapped in the memories she had helped Jaysen's mind create. She could sense him now, though his presence was fuzzy, as if a thick fog had fallen between them.

Inside the entrance hall, rows of cots brought in from somewhere—serving staff quarters or the barracks, perhaps—were arranged in rows to tend the wounded. There were more than she expected. Some were untended injuries from when Jaysen sprang his trap on her father's company. Others were from the fighting through the night, including several among the newly arrived Eydarith that suggested there had been a fair amount of chaos after she blacked out.

She gave her father a kiss on the cheek and a gentle half-hug, then left him in the care of his tehnaak and healers. Walking through the hall, she spotted Gannon first, lying back on a cot, already put to sleep so Dailan could get to work on the arrow in his leg. Iyvalin and Ahrin were beside him, as was Kitria, both of her hands holding one of Ahrin's, supporting him as he fretted over his brother. It worried Veyl that she wasn't with Kyril until a hand settled on her shoulder.

"Veyl."

She turned, a dizzying wave of relief rushing through her. Even knowing he was alive, a part of her feared that the fog between them might mean he was in danger of not being so much longer. Seeing him standing there, with bloodied bandages wrapped tight around his bare torso, was enough to make her giddy with relief.

"You're all right."

"By some standards." His eyes were glassy, and his stance wavered a little. Indications that they had given him something to help with the pain, which would also explain the fogginess of their connection. "Niske didn't seem intent on killing me, but she shredded my armor and did a fair number to the flesh beneath."

And yet, even injured as he was, he had come to her aid. Her words came out in a desperate rush. "I am so sorry. I didn't realize I was draining you, and Gannon, and the wave dancers. I would never hurt any of you on purpose."

He brought one hand up to brush a strand of hair behind her ear. "It's all right, Veyl. We're all right." He gestured to Gannon, then to the wave dancers, who were sitting together staring up at them. "I'm only sorry we couldn't be there for you when you faced Jaysen."

"You have nothing to apologize for. You all gave me so much." She stepped closer and lowered her voice, sinking into the silver-blue of his eyes. "And you were there. When I couldn't pull free of Jaysen's mind, you helped me come back. You were there when I needed you most of all."

She felt the surge of his love an instant before he kissed her. Veyl slid her hands up to his shoulders and stepped closer, wary of his injuries. He reached his arms around her waist, drawing her body against him despite the pain it surely caused, and deepened the kiss. The intensity of their passion swept her in, pure and wonderful after all they had been through.

Someone pointedly cleared their throat next to them, and Veyl startled, pulling away as the reality surrounding them crashed back in.

Feyd was standing beside them, eyebrows raised. "You have an audience, Khesran," he muttered, glancing meaningfully to one side.

Veyl followed his gaze to find her father watching from where he sat on the cot they had set aside for him, looking far from amused. She suspected a strong sedative was the only thing keeping him from making his displeasure more forcefully known, given the way he wobbled where he sat and struggled to keep his eyes open. Tath and Nerith were both encouraging him to lie down.

Feyd put a hand on Kyril's arm. "Now that you've… verified she's still breathing, perhaps we should finally get you stitched up."

Veyl stepped back from the Thaelian Feral, her cheeks blazing hot. She met his eyes, then glanced away, meeting Feyd's instead. "Take care of him. I have a few other people to check on."

"I will, Khesran."

Seyn trotted after her as she hurried deeper into the entrance hall, avoiding looking in her father's direction. Maybe she could convince him it was a hallucination brought on by the sedative, though he was far from the only one who had witnessed the kiss. She scanned for familiar faces, relieved that most of the rest were among the people helping and not those lying on cots. One was still missing, however. Amera had been struggling when they parted ways. Without the Eydarith tezaak, she would never have gotten her father out of that pit. In fact, none of this would have come together as well as it had if Amera hadn't used her skills to pass information between the rest of the unit and Veyl and to scout out the castle and grounds. She had also been the one to push Veyl to be stronger and bolder when she needed it.

"Looking for someone, Khesran?"

Veyl turned to see one of her father's soldiers watching her. "Yes. An Eydarith woman by the name of Amera."

The soldier inclined her head in a gesture of respect for Veyl's station. "Was she injured?"

Veyl nodded, unease twisting in her chest.

"If she is not out here, you might check in there." The woman pointed to a door on their left standing cracked open a few inches.

"Thank you." Steeling herself, Veyl walked toward

the door.

The woman hurried ahead to open it for her. The room wasn't particularly large. They had pushed most of the furniture inside up against the walls to get it out of the way. Five bodies lay on the floor, fully covered with blankets. Yserra was there, sitting cross-legged alongside one, her head hanging. She didn't look up when they entered.

The woman guided Veyl to the opposite corner, where she bent down and uncovered the head of the body there.

Veyl drew a sharp breath, tears springing to her eyes.

The woman nodded solemnly and laid the blanket back in place. "I am sorry, Khesran. She was bleeding internally. The healers could not save her."

The moment Amera threw herself between Veyl and the blast from the bomb flashed back in her mind. She put a hand out, seeking the wall for stability. With everything the assassin had done to help them, why was it necessary for her to lose her life as well? It didn't seem fair. It wasn't fair.

Veyl put her back against the wall and slid down it. She buried her face in her hands, struggling not to cry, not with Yserra sitting there next to her lifeless tehnaak.

"Can I bring someone for you, Khesran?"

Veyl shook her head, not looking up. "No. I just… need a little time." Her voice cracked, and she silently urged the woman to leave, resisting the irrational temptation to yell at her to do so.

Seyn settled next to her, resting her head on Veyl's leg, and whimpered softly. The woman quietly exited the room. A moment later, Yserra got up and left without a word, perhaps not wanting to share the space with the person who had gotten her tehnaak killed. Being alone with just the wave dancer and the dead gave her an opportunity to let her tears fall. Not only for Amera, but for everyone who had died or gotten hurt, for those who had lost someone dear, even for Jaysen. Seyn shifted to a sitting position and pushed her head under Veyl's arm, forcing her way in until Veyl gave up and wrapped her arms around the persistent beast, accepting comfort she wasn't sure she deserved.

Sometime later, someone else entered the room. Veyl dreaded looking up to see who it was for fear they might be bringing another body, but she was Khesran. She needed to be stronger than that. She raised her head to see Torlif walking over to her. He stepped around to her opposite side, letting Seyn keep her place, and crouched down.

"Kronach said I should check on my wavelord. He said your heart is wounded."

He had undoubtedly felt her sorrow through their connection. Veyl hated that he had access to her private moments in that way. Her gaze shifted to the covered body beyond her feet. "I got Amera killed."

"Did you? Or did she choose to die in service to her wavelord?"

Veyl scoffed. "How could she want that? Kronach assigned her to a Vanrian girl playing at being a leader."

"The Tempest does not care about the shape of your ears or the source of your blood. Whatever you are in Vanris, you are wave-touched to the Eydarith. A true wavelord. It is an honor to serve and an honor to sacrifice. You have recognized her contributions with your sorrow. Now you must respect her memory by making the most of the life she died protecting. Come." He stood and held a hand down to her. "It has been a long and difficult night. Even those not injured need rest. When the khemron wakes, he will desire to speak with the wavelords. You will want to be ready."

It was odd to realize that he was grouping her in with Kronach and not with her own people, but she didn't doubt he phrased it exactly as he intended. She took his hand and let him help her to her feet.

•

Veyl changed into clothing scrounged from someone's room in the castle to get out of her bloodied attire, then squeezed in about three hours of sleep before her father and Jethan came looking for her with Tath and Nerith trailing behind. The two healers were firmly voicing their opinions on the topic of her father's health and how he wasn't ready to be up and around yet. Opinions that fell on deaf ears, though she got the impression from his clenched jaw that Jethan quietly agreed with them. Tath was the first to give up when they got to the study that appeared to be their destination, deciding she should spend her time checking on the well-being of her sons instead. Veyl couldn't help wondering if she recognized the irony of her efforts as she limped out of the room on her injured ankle.

"Do you have a message for Gannon or his brother?" Tath asked, stopping in the doorway to look back at Veyl.

"Tell Gannon..." she drew a deep breath. What could she say? "Tell him I'm sorry."

Tath scowled. "Nonsense. You have nothing to be sorry for. We might all be dead if not for your courage. I'll tell him you're concerned about him and will visit him soon." She arched a brow at her tehnaak before leaving the room.

Nerith was still attempting to stare down Kasiel with a glare that would make most people cower. Unfortunately, their long-time familiarity appeared to be working against her. "You need to rest."

"Our position here is precarious." His gaze moved to Veyl. "Less so than it might have been, thanks to the new allies Khesran Veyl brought, but still one that needs to be addressed expediently if we want to avoid more fighting."

"Kas…"

He shook his head, the unyielding expression speaking for him.

Nerith stepped forward and gently adjusted the sling that held his arm, a wedge brace fixed under it to keep his broken collarbone in proper position to heal well. "Just be careful, Kas. If this mends poorly because you refused to listen, I promise you I will re-break it while you're conscious."

He chuckled, the tightening around his eyes betraying the pain that caused him. "I don't doubt you would. Now let me talk to my daughter."

Nerith turned to leave, pausing alongside Veyl and placing a hand on her shoulder. "Thank you. There were few ways this could have ended any better than it did, short of Jaysen regaining his rational mind, and I doubt that was going to happen. All of us owe you a great deal for having the courage to come here."

Would she have been so brave without the remarkable people who stood with her?

Veyl's throat tightened, tears stinging her eyes. She settled for a nod, knowing anything more might set those tears free.

Once Nerith was gone, her father pinned her with a scrutinizing gaze, his tehnaak leaning against the wall behind him, arms crossed, observing them both with unabashed curiosity. "Given what little Feyd could tell me while you were chasing down Jaysen, it sounds like your mother sent you to answer a summons from Wavelord Kronach. A decision I'm not sure I would have supported, not that it matters now. It was the wavelord who told you Jaysen had already taken control of Andaro, is that right?"

"Yes. And had Mother chosen not to send me, you might still be slowly dying in that pit."

Jethan breathed a soft laugh but held his tongue.

Her father's brows rose. "Oh, I am all too aware of that. I would very much like to hear how you won that man over to our side, but what I am even more curious to understand is how your suddenly having a full array of mind-crafter abilities comes into this?"

Veyl twisted her hands together in front of her. A fair reflection of what was happening in her gut. "Honestly, I'm not certain I can answer that part. It should be impossible."

"It should." Catching on to her discomfort, he came forward and put his uninjured arm around her, giving her as much of a hug as he could manage. "We will figure it out. There are several things I'd like to discuss, and I want to hear everything that happened leading up to this, but we don't have time for that now. Wavelord Kronach should be..." He trailed off at a knock on the door. After placing a quick kiss on her forehead, he stepped away from Veyl. "Come in."

She was a little surprised to see Kronach enter alone and clearly of his own volition. He looked confident and at ease. However he felt about throwing his lot in with Vanris, his manner and lack of protection sent the message that he did not fear his new allies.

He offered a slight nod to each of them, the one he gave her a little deeper than the others. "Khemron Kasiel. Lord Jethan. Wavelord Khesran Veyl. It is an honor to be in the company of such accomplished warriors."

She noted the slightest narrowing of her father's eyes in response to the title Kronach gave her, but he merely offered a return nod. "Wavelord Kronach, we are honored to meet with you as well, particularly considering your timely arrival in the night."

His arrival had been timely. Almost too much so.

How had he shown up exactly when she needed him most, and why hadn't she sensed his closeness sooner when he had obviously been almost to the city? Could he have blocked the link somehow, denying her that connection and waiting until the moment was right to sweep in as her savior? She wouldn't put it past him. Perhaps she should call upon her Evoker ability to dig that information out of his head, though their link would likely alert him to her meddling.

A faint smirk curved Kronach's lips in response to her contemplative stare, and he gestured to a chair. "There is much to discuss. Shall we make ourselves comfortable?"

"Yes." Her father turned to his tehnaak. "Would you mind—"

"Checking on the food and drink?" Jethan finished for him. "Not at all."

Once Jethan had done so, they all settled into seats. Seyn placed herself between Veyl's chair and Kronach's, staring at the wavelord as though she felt it necessary to remind him that Veyl was not his to toy with. While she appreciated the effort, she had a feeling Kronach would ignore the message.

"We have a somewhat urgent need to establish command of the capital and the kingdom. The chief general is dead, Thrasser is no longer fit to rule, and Khesran Veyl has dealt with the equally unfit crown prince." Her father glanced briefly at her as he said the last, his gaze troubled. "I had hoped you, as the highest-ranking Sarketi leader here, might be able to recommend some alternatives. Someone reliable to place up on the throne while all of this is being sorted out."

Kronach relaxed back into his chair, a confident, satisfied smile easing across his lips. "I will act as regent."

Her father's brows pinched. "I'm not convinced the people of Sarket will accept an Eydarith as their ruler."

"The Eydarith are people of Sarket," Kronach countered. "As you yourself stated, I am the highest-ranking Sarketi leader here."

Veyl leaned forward. "But most Sarketi follow Havaad. The Eydarith are not known for their tolerance of other religions."

Kronach shrugged as if to say he felt it was not an issue. "I have abided their wrongness as wavelord of Taro. I will continue to abide their wrongness as wavelord of Sarket if I must."

Veyl nearly let out an incredulous laugh until she noticed the thoughtful look on her father's face. Was he taking the suggestion seriously?

"You must," he stated, his flat tone making it clear he really was contemplating the idea. "Vanris will consider allowing you to oversee matters here until a proper candidate can assume the throne, but only if you swear to serve all the people of this country fairly, not just the Eydarith. You must also agree to follow the terms of whatever agreements we reach in the coming days."

Kronach's jaw tightened a fraction. She suspected he didn't like the word "allow" used in that context or the way her father had phrased it as an ultimatum, but a great deal of power lay at his fingertips. She couldn't imagine him turning that down. "So shall it be done."

"Excellent. We have details to work out with a larger assembly and agreements to write up, but..." her father paused as a servant brought in wine along with a platter of cheese, bread, and fruit. Once the woman had filled the goblets and left them, he lifted his wine. "Shall we drink to the start of our negotiations?"

Kronach slowly raised his goblet, the deliberateness of the gesture saying that he refused to let anyone rush him. An explicit statement of his intent to maintain some level of control in the coming discussions. Though some friction electrified the air in the room, they all drank when her father did.

The idea of Kronach ruling Sarket made Veyl distinctly uneasy for several reasons, one of which the wavelord tossed upon the table all too readily.

"Have you considered the possibility of a political marriage to bring unity to our countries, Khemron?" He smirked and raised his goblet to Veyl, the expression and gesture playing the inquiry off as more of a joke, though she had no doubts about his underlying genuine interest.

Veyl smiled sweetly and raised her goblet in return. "It is something to ponder, although I'm not convinced you are my brother's type."

Jethan spat out his drink.

## CHAPTER TWENTY NINE

Over the following two days, representatives from the different groups—including the Eydarith, Thrasser's surviving advisors, Kyril and Jinau on behalf of Thaelis, and several members of the company from Vanris—engaged in extensive discussions. Both Thaelis and the Eydarith offered Veyl welcome at their sides of the table, but she chose to sit alongside her father. Vanris was her home, and the country she would work hardest to serve the interests of, no matter what titles and status the others had given her.

It was extremely unusual to be offered such positions of respect by more than one culture, all of whom would willingly claim her as their own: Khesran of Vanris, Eydarith Wavelord, and Seh'hali ne Kunua of Thaelis. She wanted to be proud of that accomplishment, but it felt like just one more abnormality calling her out for the aberration she was. As rumors of her abilities spread, the wary and sometimes fearful looks she received walking the halls of Andaro Castle did nothing to discourage her from feeling that way.

As soon as her father decided the situation was stable enough for the moment under Kronach's leadership, he turned them home to Etrion. He left some of his company there to act as advisors until he could select new ones, since it turned out Jaysen had executed the previous Vanrian advisors stationed in Andaro when he took control of the city.

Their healers unanimously agreed that her father needed more time to heal before he could safely travel. In response to that judgment, he reminded them he hadn't been in much better condition when he made the journey home to Etrion with a shattered arm during the war, and he had survived that.

Veyl suspected her father's eagerness to leave Andaro had a lot to do with Arhk's unexpected arrival. Soon after reaching the Vanrian base near the coast, a messenger sent by Chief General Harriksen had sought the dhomvalen out. The man brought information regarding supply routes, hideout locations, and names of anti-mind-crafter leaders Sarket had been dealing with, all of which made it quite apparent that he had decided to throw his hand in with Vanris. Unfortunately, the chief general hadn't lived to see what might have come of that choice. Veyl believed he could have been an excellent king. Instead, he had bled out before her eyes, another victim of Jaysen's madness, and now Kronach had control of Sarket's throne, for better or worse.

The dhomvalen and the wavelord were fire and oil. Both powerful men, both skilled manipulators, though Arhk was arguably more subtle, and both used to getting their way. Those similarities weren't the only things that sparked conflict between them. The one time Kronach had the gall to make a suggestive comment about her in her grandfather's presence, she could see his death coming to pass in Arhk's eyes. As capable and respected by his people as Kronach was, she got the uncomfortable sense that her grandfather might have the means to bring the wavelord to his end. Under the circumstances, such an incident had the potential to cause considerable upheaval. Far better if they never found out what Arhk was capable of.

The Eydarith warriors Kronach had given Veyl followed her to Etrion, insisting they belonged with their wavelord. Now, almost a week after arriving in the black city, a couple of her warriors waited outside a meeting room in the palace along with two newly appointed Vanrian guards. An Evoker had confirmed Tassa was the one who sent word to Jaysen of Veyl's journey to Taro. They had apprehended everyone involved and had them locked up awaiting trial now, eliminating that threat, but her parents had more pressing concerns. With Veyl's unprecedented abilities becoming more widely known and the anti-mind-crafter situation not yet resolved, they insisted she keep no less than four guards or warriors with her.

Several Vanrian officers were present at the current meeting. They had matters to discuss that were particular to Vanris before they brought in representatives from Delaphine, Fallend, Sarket, and Thaelis to address more widespread issues. Veyl and her brother, who had recovered enough the healers were now allowing him brief periods of activity, attended too, along with her father's tehsheyn. Kasiel sat amongst his spirit family with her mother on a different side than usual to accommodate his injuries. How comforting it must be for him to have all his family, by blood and bond, around him. With Irith there, only Niskenya was missing, but Veyl understood enough about their connection to know the recovering kanodrak was with him in her way, and probably quite attentive to his every move since the incident in Andaro.

Veyl had only Seyn with her, though she could feel her links to Ceris, Gannon, and Kyril. None of those bonds had been formed in the usual fashion, but they were just as effective as any a Bondmaker could create. There was a faint awareness of the wave-touched as well, particularly her warriors, but Kronach's presence, despite the distance between them, was almost more intense.

She understood now that much of his strength came from the fact that he shared a bond with all his people, a phenomenon her father intended to investigate once things were more settled. The Vanrians had believed that no other culture could form such bonds. Her mother had already suggested sending some Vanrian Bondmakers to meet with the Eydarith and learn what they could about the connections between the wave-touched and their people. She almost regretted that she would miss that discovery process.

Veyl pulled her focus back to the conversation.

"We know who most of the anti-mind-crafter leaders are now. We could target them with elite units or even assassins," Jhanik was saying.

"No." Veyl's firm objection drew all eyes to her. Good. She wanted their attention. This was important. "We can't just use brute force to subdue them. These are our own people. Now that we know who they are, let's invite them to negotiations. Our knowledge of their locations and leadership will shake them and make them more inclined to consider finding another way to handle the situation. Involve them in the conversation. Show you are willing to find common ground, and you will make better progress. We need to work together to resolve these issues, or they will remain a source of conflict within Vanris and weaken us."

A faint smirk curved Arhk's lips, though whether that was because he agreed with her or simply because he enjoyed seeing her knock down Jhanik's suggestion, she wasn't sure. Either way, she had at least gotten everyone to pause and listen, and the proud gleam in her parents' eyes said they approved of her direction.

Arhk spoke into the momentary silence. "Perhaps you would like to help with those efforts, Khesran. We could use someone with a kind heart and a sound mind for diplomacy to take on these complicated matters."

Veyl's nerves danced with a flare of anxiety. It was time to ask for what she wanted or risk being assigned to some other purpose. "No. We have plenty of capable negotiators who are not mind-crafters. We should have at least two mind-crafters involved in these discussions, but I would be a poor choice for this endeavor given my unusual range of abilities." She looked at her parents. "I would prefer to lead our annexation efforts in Thaelis."

This new silence held much greater weight somehow than the one before and drew out longer. She had made the decision that morning, and had, so far, spoken only with the twins and Iyvalin about it. Even Kyril was unaware of the new direction she wished to take.

Her parents locked eyes for a moment, some unspoken agreement passing between them. Her mother swept her gaze over the room.

"We are calling a brief recess. This session will reconvene in thirty minutes." Her attention fell on Veyl as the others rose to leave. "Khesrans Veyl and Tavin, we would like you to remain."

Her father stood and beckoned a guard over, who ducked out of the room a moment later in response to his whispered request. Then he waited by his chair, his useable hand resting on Irith's head while everyone else cleared out. Reassurance flooded into Veyl from Seyn. She nearly blocked it out, unpleasantly aware now of the damage she could do by letting the wave dancer support her too much. Yet, she also knew the beast would be confused and hurt by the rejection, so she shoved down her apprehension and allowed it. She needed it.

When the room was empty, her father pinned her with a demanding stare. "I hope you don't plan to tell us this has nothing to do with a certain Thaelian Feral."

She glanced between her parents, a hint of warmth rising in her cheeks. Though she and Kyril had shared no intimacy since their kiss in Andaro, she had little doubt the incident remained fresh in her father's mind. "No. I respect you too much to lie to you again. Knowing he will be returning to his homeland soon has had some influence on my desire to journey there. But it also has a great deal to do with everything that happened with Jaysen and my abilities. I need to get away and clear my head. Handling affairs in Thaelis would be a way for me to do so while still serving our country."

Her mother's lips pressed into a line, the intention in her troubled gaze holding them all hostage until she spoke. "And what about the fact that you are heir to the Vanrian throne?"

"The question begs to be asked if I still should be."

Her mother's brow furrowed. "Is this your way of refusing the throne?"

Veyl glanced at Tavin, breathing a little laugh when he emphatically shook his head, though the levity didn't last. She faced her parents. "Our people are warring among themselves over the advantage mind-crafters have in this country. You both know that, as word of what I can do spreads, continuing to present me as heir will only make the situation worse. There will be attempts to get rid of me, the ultimate mind-crafter, embodiment of everything they are protesting. Until we make progress toward a peaceful solution, I need to stay out of the way. Presenting Tavin as the potential heir might quell some of the rage the revelation of my abilities is certain to stir up. He is a mind-crafter, but he is a type they understand, and one unable to affect human minds. That will make him a more attractive option now." She offered her brother a gentle smile. "Sorry, Tav."

"Your reasoning is sound, even if I don't love the conclusion." He placed a hand on the shoulders of a young cliff cat Kenna had been bringing to visit with him during his recovery.

Their mother gave him a meaningful look. "Tavin."

"Oh, this is now one of those 'we need to talk to your sister alone' moments. All right. I'm leaving. The healers will come after me if I don't check in soon anyway." He offered Veyl a nod on his way out, a supportive gesture that surprised her a little, given how much she knew he dreaded the idea of ruling Vanris.

When he was gone, her mother tilted her head to one side, considering her. "Do you think your brother is capable of handling that level of responsibility?"

Veyl shook her head. "Not yet, but put in some effort with him. The only reason Tavin isn't ready to be a leader is because you two haven't invested the time in teaching him how to lead that you have with me."

The muscles in her father's jaw tightened, and she could see a hint of moisture rising in his eyes. "I don't like where this conversation is going. It feels as if we're losing you."

Turning away to stare into the back corner, her mother wiped at her face with a handkerchief she had drawn from somewhere.

Veyl swallowed against the tightening in her throat. "I know what it feels like, and I know it hurts. I have no desire to be separated from you again either, but I believe this is the most sensible way to handle the situation. Too many cultures are pulling me between them. I don't know who I am or where I belong anymore. There isn't anyone else like me here. Growing up, I dreamed of being someone special, someone unique, but I'm not that fond of the experience now that it's become my reality. My own people look at me with curiosity and fear. I need to step away from that for a time. Let the situation settle some. This would allow me to do that while still acting as a leader for the benefit of our country. I can guide part of the effort to stabilize Thaelis as a flourishing territory of Vanris and help ensure we thoroughly eliminate the Ukhen'kya threat."

"And Ahnkreth Kyril?" Her mother turned, arching a brow at her. "You want us to send you home with him where you might indulge your adolescent infatuation as you please."

The choice of words sparked a crackling in Veyl's chest. "I know you are both upset that I lied to you about my relationship with him, but it is more than what you just called it. I love Kyril. Nothing you say is going to change that. And don't pretend that what I've done with him is so different from your scandalous courtship with each other. As I recall, Father almost didn't survive that experience."

He frowned. "Our mistakes do not excuse your own."

"Nor do I expect them to, but I will still make them. Kyril, however, is not one of them."

A knock held off any response they might have made, and her father drew a deep breath before calling for whoever was there to enter. When the door opened, the subject of their argument walked in with Ceris at his side. He strode boldly up to the table and faced her parents, despite the flicker of unease Veyl received from him now that she was paying attention to their bond.

"Ahnkreth Kyril," her mother began, "as a citizen of Vanris, I assume you understand that Veyl is your khesran, and not some common woman to indulge your fantasies with. Am I wrong?"

Veyl's shoulders and jaw tightened. It appeared they meant to appeal to Kyril's sense of propriety if she would not listen. The surge of affection that flashed across their link quickly drowned her anger. He wasn't going to let anyone control him in this, not even the rulers of Vanris.

"I do understand that she is Khesran of Vanris. Do you understand she is more than that?" A brief flicker of indignation flashed in her parents' eyes at his words, but they held their silence, allowing him a chance to speak his mind. "She is an Eydarith wavelord, Seh'hali ne Kunua to the Qwilki, and a most extraordinary person in so many ways." He turned to look at her. "She and I are both children of the ocean, both wave-touched, our fates entwined since long before we met. I would never insult that treasured bond by merely indulging my fantasies with her."

Veyl's heart soared with his words, and she couldn't hold back her smile. She could tell by her parents' expressions that they had been pushing for a different response from him, but there was something in the look they shared when he finished that ignited a spark of hope in her.

After a moment of thoughtful silence, her father asked, "Have you considered positioning yourself as a member of the new council in Thaelis?"

A flicker of confusion came from Kyril, but Veyl knew this game well enough to see that her parents were going to grant her request. Unless she misread the goal of that question, they were trying a different approach by nudging Kyril toward making himself a more appropriate match for her. She pushed encouragement to him.

"The possibility has crossed my mind," he answered, interpreting her signal correctly. "I believe it is my responsibility to help establish a new order in Thaelis, given that I played a part in eliminating the previous one."

Her parents shared another look, one with a hint of approval in it, and her father gave a subtle nod.

Drawing a deep breath, her silver-eyed gaze drifting to Veyl, then to Kyril, her mother said, "Before you depart, we will raise you as an ahndhomen of Vanris. You will be Veyl's counterpart in the effort of completing the annexation of Thaelis and ensuring the security of the islands from threats like the Ukhen'kya, if any remain."

"We will expect you to conduct any personal engagements with discretion while acting as a representative for your country, particularly when they involve Khesran Veyl," her father added.

"I understand and I am honored by the trust you place in me." Kyril bowed his head.

"And you…" Her mother turned to her as she and Kasiel walked around the side of the table.

Veyl went to meet them, and they each took one of her hands.

"We believe you are capable of managing affairs in Thaelis," her father said, his gaze full of affection and a respect that had grown noticeably since the events in Andaro.

"But you are still a potential heir to the Vanrian throne," her mother continued. "We expect you to conduct yourself as such."

Veyl nodded, a tear sliding down one cheek. "I will not shame or disappoint you. I promise."

Her mother reached up with her free hand to tidy a strand of Veyl's hair. Then she brushed away a tear of her own. "What of your new warriors and your tehnaak?"

"The Eydarith will accompany me. They have made it abundantly clear that they will not abandon their duty to me. The twins and Iyvalin also wish to come."

Her mother pressed her lips together, but her father nodded as if he had expected as much. "I imagine Ahrin wishes to follow Kitria." He gave Kyril a sharp look as if he shared some responsibility for his sister's deepening entanglement with Ahrin. "Darro and Tath won't be pleased, but they will probably allow it."

"Thank you." Veyl gave them each a heartfelt embrace, being careful of her father's injuries. "I love you both so much."

•

They set sail a week later, leaving Jinau behind to protect Thaelis's interests on the Vanrian council until the yet unformed Thaelian council could designate someone else to fill that role. On the evening of the first night at sea, as the fleet was still settling into the routine of travel, Veyl sought Arhk in his cabin. She had wanted to prove that she could do this on her own and had thought her grandfather would only accompany them as far as the coastal base. His setting sail with them felt like a betrayal of the confidence her parents professed to have in her.

When he welcomed her into his cabin, one slightly larger than her own, he was sipping a dark amber liquid with a bold, yet somehow enticing aroma. He poured her a conservative portion, not bothering to ask first if she even wished to try it, though she was curious. She took a sip, and the fiery fumes of potent alcohol raced up the inside of her nose as she choked it down, desperate not to spit it out in front of him. A few harsh exhales through her sinuses did little to alleviate the sting.

"I advise you to enjoy it in small sips and not breathe through your nose while doing so." The barest glimmer of amusement shone in his eyes. "It has a lovely, smooth finish if you do not abuse it."

"I don't believe it is the one being abused." Another sharp exhale helped a little, or perhaps the sting was simply wearing off on its own.

"What brings you to my cabin, Khesran?"

She rubbed her nose and eyed the drink warily. "Do you enjoy being on the ocean?"

"No."

The abrupt, flat response caught her by surprise. "Then why did my parents send you with me?"

Arhk responded to that with a remarkably dignified snort. Something few people could pull off well. "Why do you think?"

She was going to guess that her parents didn't trust her to manage the annexation of Thaelis after all, but the bitterness in his tone and the blackness that crept in at the edges of his eyes told a different story. Maybe this wasn't about her at all. What reason would her parents have for sending him if not to watch over her? They had two significant tasks to handle. Negotiations with Kronach, which they wouldn't involve Arhk in, given the natures of the two men, and talks with the anti-mind-crafter groups. Having one of the most feared mind-crafters in Vanris handling discussions with people who hated mind-crafters might be no better than having her do so.

"They wanted you out of the way?"

Arhk lifted his glass to her, his lips pressed in a tight line before he took a sip. "Your parents think you are more than capable of taking on Thaelis. That is not why I am here, if that was your concern. It is I who am of no value to them in current political dealings, but rest assured, I will not interfere in your affairs upon this journey unless you ask me to. This is your mission, Veyl, and I am proud to see you taking it on with such confidence. Although I am not above Frightening the Thaelians into submission, should they cause you grief."

A flicker of alarm raced through her. She didn't doubt that he could do so. "Please don't."

Arhk offered a smirk that wasn't especially reassuring. "And I will not stand in the way of your romantic entanglements so long as you do not make a display of yourselves and take precautions. I believe you have earned Ahndhomen Kyril's devotion. You could do far worse." He gestured to the glass she hadn't touched again. "Now, have another drink and tell me about the awakening of your abilities."

Veyl took a wary second sip. That was going to be a

delicate tale to tell, given how much he disliked Kronach. "Only if you tell me a story as well."

"Another tale of your father and the war?"

"Not this time. I want to hear about your life in the years before he returned to Vanris."

Arhk's brow furrowed. "Few of those tales are happy."

Veyl countered with a gentle smile. "Then go farther back. Before he was born, or at least before he was taken. Tell me about my grandmother and your early courtship."

Arhk gazed into his drink for a second, his eyes losing their focus as he looked back at his distant past. "I suppose I could."

Veyl settled in her seat and took another sip of the dark amber liquid. Arhk never spoke of her grandmother, Ellaris, Tavin's tehnaak's namesake. A group from the south had murdered her the night they abducted Veyl's father when he was quite young. It seemed she had caught Arhk in a rare mood, and she meant to make the most of it.

They drank late into the evening, Veyl using some of her recent experiences as currency to coax out tales of the life he never talked about from before he lost his wife and son. The next day, true to his word, anytime someone sought him out with questions, he redirected them to her, making it clear she was in charge of the Vanrian company and their mission. He even shrugged off the Delaphinian fleet commander and sent him her way. She got the distinct impression Arhk got a little too much pleasure from the man's irritation at being dismissed by him. Knowing her grandfather was there if she needed to ask for guidance, but that he did not intend to interfere in the task she had requested for herself, ended up being a source of great comfort.

That evening, with the crew members fully invested in their duties, she would finally have time to visit Kyril on his ship. As she prepared to leave the Delaphinian flagship, her companions joined her in her larger cabin. Gannon and Iyvalin started up a game of Feral's Folly. Kitria and Ahrin had retreated to a corner to talk about some things, though Veyl couldn't imagine they were getting much talking done with their mouths attached in that fashion.

"You are welcome to take your dinner in here if you wish," Veyl offered.

"Thank you. It is much nicer than our quarters." Iyvalin gave her a warm smile.

"We might just spend the night here, since I doubt you'll be back." Gannon glanced at his brother, snorted softly, and looked up at her. "When you and Kyril are talking, maybe don't forget your tehnaak is nearby and make sure you keep the experience from sneaking across our bond."

Veyl's cheeks warmed. "I'll keep that in mind." She met Iyvalin's eyes. "Make sure he stays out of trouble. That leg still needs to heal."

Iyvalin grinned. "Don't worry, he'll be too busy driving himself mad attempting to beat me at Feral's Folly. I developed some new strategies I can't wait to try against him."

"Fantastic," Gannon muttered, though the speed with which he reached for his cards made it obvious he was more eager to play than he sounded.

Veyl gave his shoulder a squeeze and left the cabin.

Kyril's flagship had come to Vanris with the most recent group that sailed across, so he had the comfort of that familiar vessel for the return journey. When she and Seyn boarded his ship, she found him in his cabin, gazing out the back windows with Ceris at his side. She had felt his welcome before she could even knock, so she hadn't bothered to do so. A flicker of unease moved through her when she entered. They hadn't had a chance to really talk since that day in the meeting room. Was he glad she was going with him? Would her capacity as the Vanrian leader in charge of Thaelis's integration cause friction between them?

When she didn't join him at the window, he turned and made his way around the table toward her. Ceris went to lie near the bed, and Seyn trotted over to curl up against him, both wave dancers watching them with those bright, intelligent eyes.

Kyril's brows pinched. "You're nervous. Why?"

"I should have asked you how you would feel about having me as the Vanrian representative for this before I requested the role from my parents. It occurs to me you might not want the woman you love in charge of taking away your country's autonomy."

Kyril closed the remaining distance and set one hand on her shoulder. The other he slid along her jaw. His thumb brushed across her cheek, his silver-blue eyes shining with thoughts and emotions he was currently blocking her out of. "What gave you the idea that I love you?"

Her chest tightened with a knot of dread until a grin tugged at his lip and a glimmer of mischief snuck past the block he had put up.

"Calloch," she growled.

His smile broke free, and affection and amusement surged across their bond. "I'm not sure love is a powerful enough word for what I feel for you." He gave her a soft, sweet kiss, then drew away to look into her eyes. "There is no one I trust more to help me ensure this is a positive change for my country. Together, we can bring Thaelis back stronger than it was before. I believe you will fight to make this work for everyone involved. That's who you are, and I love that about you."

"See, you do love me." Veyl smiled and kissed him again, relenting to the gentle pressure he applied, nudging her back toward the bed. "Are your wounds healed enough for this type of activity?"

"You may have to do most of the work." His throaty laugh sent a delicious shiver through her. "I love everything about you, Veyl," he murmured, brushing her hair aside and leaning in to kiss her neck.

Fire ignited where his lips touched her skin. "Shouldn't we be discussing our plans for when we reach Thaelis?"

"Mm-hmm." One hand slid to her lower back and pulled her against him. "Tell me all of your ideas."

She brought her hands up to work at the fastenings of his shirt. "I think I may need to wear you out first if I want you to remember a word I say."

He chuckled. "I have a feeling we're going to work exceptionally well together."

Waves crashed on the rocks below where Veyl stood at the top of the cliffs. A breeze carried the salt spray up to lay it upon her skin in a fine cloak of mist. It picked up some of her hair, not strong enough to lift the one braid that had a new shell token fastened to it. She closed her eyes, feeling the might of the ocean move through her and the contentment of Seyn at her side. In the distance, she could sense Gannon and the Eydarith warriors in Dagony, preparing for the coming voyage. Not nearly as far away, a warm, confident presence was approaching, Ceris a bright spot next to him.

Veyl waited, letting Kyril walk up behind her.

"I'm surprised Gannon and the Eydarith let you wander off alone." He slid his arms around her waist as he spoke.

"Gannon respects my need for time to myself. He is much the same. And the Eydarith believe I am safe here, surrounded by the ocean. They seem to like it on the island, and they've been trading ocean lore with the tribal Qwilki. I think Gannon enjoys helping bridge the language barrier between them." He settled his hands over her abdomen, and she placed hers on top of them, twining her fingers through his.

"You've been coming up here a lot," he murmured.

"This is where you did your training sessions with Erkhan, isn't it?"

"Mm-hmm." She leaned back into his chest when he applied gentle pressure to bring her closer.

"I wouldn't think those were the happiest of memories for you," he prompted.

"No."

He didn't press, letting her relax into him, giving her the space to decide what she wanted to say and when. She appreciated that about him, though it somehow made her feel more obligated to offer an explanation.

Staring out at the water, she spotted a few fins breaking the surface. Whales. Their presence reminded her of that night on his ship when she had nearly kissed the man who had upended her life. A connection they still didn't fully understand drawing them together.

She took a deep breath and let it out, his stillness telling her he was ready to listen. "Sometimes I remember events that never happened. Memories..." She swallowed, pulling away a little as she struggled with the words to explain it.

He held her a little tighter, his firm embrace reassuring. "The memories you created for Jaysen."

"They live in my mind, as vivid as I made them for him." She sighed, forcing herself to relax again in his arms. To feel how strong and real he was. "Coming to this spot, drawing on the reality of the time I spent here when I had no choice, it helps me remember what actually happened that night in Deepwater." His muscles tensed against her back. "Don't worry. Where we are now has thoroughly overshadowed our tumultuous start there. I never dwell on that."

He kissed her head. "If you wanted to, we could ask an Evoker to remove those false memories."

Veyl's stomach turned, and a shudder moved through her.

Kyril squeezed her hands and pushed comfort to her along their bond. "Or not."

"We've both seen the harm an Evoker can do meddling in someone's mind. After what Jaysen had them do to you and Thrasser... after what I did to him, I don't think I could bear to let anyone alter things in my head. Besides, in a strange way I find it comforting. Changing his memories was wrong, but knowing I gave him a little happiness at the end helps me make peace with killing him."

"I know he was your tehnaak once, but you gave him a better end than he deserved. You shouldn't carry any guilt."

She leaned her head back on his shoulder, listening as a powerful wave crashed against the rocks and waiting until the breeze brought the resulting spray up to them to speak. "There are no excuses for the awful things he did, but he had the potential to become a good man before Thrasser's people tortured him. I couldn't bring myself to make him suffer more."

"You remained true to who you are," he whispered in her ear. "I admire that you have that kind of strength."

"Do you think it will be all right here without you?"

"Without us? Yes. Jinau is going to cover my place on the council, and Nagi seems ready to take yours. Thaelis will be fine."

She was reluctant to leave this spot with the ocean crashing on the rocks below and the arms of the man she loved around her. In the distance, some fishing boats with a few larger ships acting as escorts came into view. They had found the substantial island the Ukhen'kya occupied and eliminated that threat. They brought a fair number of them back to one of the smaller Thaelian islands abandoned after the Devastation, keeping them under heavy guard while working to see if there was hope for integrating them into civilized society. So far, they had proven too steeped in their religion and shared a madness that was difficult to reason with, even with the help of mind-crafters.

They also found a few Qwilki and Thaelian prisoners being kept in pens like livestock on their island, some with parts of limbs missing. Five people from one cage were neither Thaelian nor Qwilki, begging the question of what culture and land they came from. Until they overcame the language barrier, that would remain a mystery, and Thaelis would continue to keep a few guardian vessels watching over the fishing boats.

"Is your fleet ready to depart?"

"It is. I hope you don't mind that I had your belongings put in my cabin."

She breathed a soft laugh. "I would mind far more if you hadn't done so. Is it practical to continue being an ahndhomen, an ahnkreth, a member of the council, and a diplomatic envoy?"

"I don't know, Daughter of the Ocean Wavelord Khesran of Vanris," he said, making it one long, convoluted title. "Is it?"

She turned in his arms, his grin sparking giddy delight in her that she hid behind a forced glower. "Are you trying to annoy me?"

"Always." He leaned in to kiss her.

She gladly reciprocated, marveling that she could still get such a thrill from being on the receiving end of his affections despite waking up in his arms every day. She had a feeling everyone here was aware they spent most nights together now. Probably not what her parents had in mind, but even before he returned to Vanris several months ago, Arhk had said nothing about their expanding relationship as long as they kept their romance separate from official proceedings. She got the impression he didn't object to the match. Would her parents be half as accepting?

"Are you looking forward to going home?"

She smiled, gazing into those eyes that shone with such adoration. The token shell she had given him hung from one of the dark blue stained braids in his black hair, a near-perfect match for the one in hers. "You are my home."

"I'm serious." His brows pinched as if seeking to emphasize the concern in his voice. "You haven't seen your family in a while, yet you seem reluctant to depart."

"I want to see them. Quite desperately, in fact. It's just… Here in Thaelis, I am welcomed as the Daughter of the Ocean. People see my unprecedented powers as proof of that. In Vanris, they fear me for it."

"Then we will show them there is nothing to fear. Jinau said that talks with anti-mind-crafter leaders have been going well. The dhomvalen has even started working with them now. We just need to be deliberate and careful in how we approach the subject."

"Perhaps." She looked into his silver-blue eyes, determined to chase away the worry in them. No benefit would come from them both fretting. "What will we do about my parents in Vanris? You know they won't want us staying together."

He grinned. "Tell them we got married here on the island."

"We didn't."

"We could."

"You're a wicked man. I would much rather have their blessing. Perhaps we can persuade them."

"True, you are a Charmer."

"Shame on you." Veyl smacked him playfully in the chest, breaking out in a laugh when she recalled how often she had rolled her eyes at her parents for just such antics. Maybe they would understand, after all. Hadn't their courtship defied the rules?

"Is there a chance they'll consider me a suitable

match now?"

"Ride that kanodrak, and my father will happily give you his only daughter."

"Challenge accepted." He chuckled and kissed her again, desire, love, and confidence surging across their bond. When they parted, she took his hand and turned toward the town. "We should get going. It's a long journey, and I still need to round up my tehnaak and warriors."

"You mean you have to summon them laboriously with a little tug on those threads that connect us all to you?" he teased.

She grinned and sidestepped around a large rock in their path, keeping hold of his hand. As they navigated the rugged terrain, she reached out along one of those bonds, feeling the slight change in Gannon's presence that told her she had gotten his attention. She avoided tugging on all of them at once. The last time she had done that, the Eydarith assumed she was in danger and came running, weapons out and ready for combat. Gannon was more likely to take his sweet time responding, but at least he wouldn't stir up a panic.

Dagony, as they headed down into the town, had an air of calm about it. Vanrians and Delaphinians walked through the streets alongside the Qwilki and Thaelian natives. There had been considerable upheaval in the wake of the council's departure with Jaysen and the Unclean attack. In the months since, Vanrian and Delaphinian forces had helped weed out those still loyal to the council and assisted the Thaelian fleets in hunting down and dealing with the Ukhen'kya, earning the gratitude and respect of the locals. The populace appeared to be adjusting to the new order, and Veyl had been diligent about ensuring her country didn't overreach. She wanted everyone in Thaelis to feel like this was still their home, even though they had gained additional oversight. The new council was deliberate in its methods, always working toward the goal of giving the people more say in how the islands were being managed than they'd had before. It was going well.

Gannon and the Eydarith joined them along the road to the port. He still had the slightest hitch in his step from the arrow he had taken the night they stopped Jaysen. Today, he didn't come up to walk with her on the other side of Seyn as he typically did. Instead, he ceded that spot to Pera, a lean Eydarith warrior with a thin scar that cut at an angle between her hazel eyes and down one side of her nose. She was fiercely pretty, with her brunette hair bound back and a perpetual challenge in her stare. She offered a respectful nod as she came to walk beside Veyl, staying a half-step behind.

"Pera," Veyl acknowledged with a nod. "Do you need something?"

"I am not familiar with your customs around these matters, Wavelord, so I will simply speak. I wish your spirit brother to know me more deeply. Is this acceptable to you?"

On Pera's other side, a faint grin tugged at Gannon's lips, but it was the oddly smug pleasure coming through their bond that Veyl found most amusing. How tempting it was to deny the request just to see how he would react, but with so much of Eydarith culture still a mystery to her, she didn't want to risk offending the woman.

"As long as he is happy, I support it."

"Thank you, Wavelord. I will ensure he is."

The woman fell back a step and moved to the side, allowing Gannon to reclaim his usual place alongside Veyl. He leaned closer, keeping his voice low. "On the crossing, I don't suppose I'll have—"

"I'll arrange for you to have a small cabin to yourself," Kyril interjected a little more loudly than necessary.

Pera cracked a broad grin, and Torlif, apparently privy to the topic at hand, let out a hearty guffaw.

Veyl laughed softly at Gannon's slight flush and reached over to give her tehnaak's hand a squeeze. "We'll take care of you."

"Thanks," he muttered, though the grateful look he cast Kyril told her he wasn't all that bothered by the teasing.

When they reached the docks, Ahrin, Kitria, and Iyvalin were already on the deck of Kyril's flagship, waiting for them. Jinau stood at the foot of the gangplank, ready to see them off. Veyl and Kyril stopped to speak with him as the rest of the group boarded.

"Is everything in order?" Veyl asked.

Jinau nodded, casting a brief glance at the wave dancers. "Be cautious if you come upon any whales. Remember, you carry valuable trade goods this time, and the wave dancers enjoy riling them up."

In a mirrored motion, she and Kyril both habitually touched the shoulders of their respective companions. She met his eyes, and his fond smile infused her with warmth.

Facing Jinau, she said, "We'll be cautious. Are you prepared to join the council?"

"Such public politics are strange when you are used to working from the shadows, but the khemron and khevarin were very generous with their guidance during my time in Vanris. I believe I am ready." He focused on her. "You should know they were arranging a council to meet with Wavelord Kronach soon after you return."

Veyl heaved a sigh. "Why? Please tell me they aren't reconsidering the political marriage idea."

Jinau chuckled. "Have some faith in them, Seh'hali. They want you there because you handle him well and, as hard as it may be to see, he has great respect for you."

"We'll see about that. They're probably hoping I

can convince him to step down from the throne. They should never have allowed him to assume the role of regent. It will take an act of his god to get him off it now."

Jinau smirked. "Fortunately, the Tempest favors you."

Veyl narrowed her eyes at him. "Don't start."

His answering grin broke through her annoyance, and she smiled, stepping in to give him a warm embrace.

"I look forward to seeing you when we return," she said as she moved back from him.

"Will you be returning to Thaelis, Seh'hali?"

She looked up at Kyril. The might of the ocean swept through her, urging her to set sail, offering her confidence even as it reasserted its claim on her. "There is much for us to do in Vanris. I imagine we will stay for some time, but yes, I believe I will be back."

A short time later, as they headed out to the open ocean at the front of Kyril's fleet, Veyl went to stand at the bow, gazing out upon that vast expanse of water with one hand resting on Seyn's shoulders. There were still challenges ahead. The idea of facing those things didn't unsettle her as much as it would have once. So many supported her now. Kyril, the wave dancers, Gannon, the Eydarith, and others. She wouldn't have to confront any of it alone.

She faced Kyril as he walked up beside her. "I believe I am ready to return to Vanris."

He smiled and leaned in to give her a soft kiss overflowing with love and promise.


**The End.**

## Glossary
### *Vanrian and Thaelian Terminology*

| | |
|---|---|
| **Calloch** | Rank ball of monkey shit. A favored insult in Vanris. |
| **Company (military)** | The units and unions under the command of a single dhomen or ahndhomen. |
| **Crack a stone** | Popular Vanrian phrase meaning to open and drink a stoneglass bottle of Vanrian Black Mead. |
| **Evalis** | Black fruit used to make Vanrian Black Mead. Imported from the original Vanrian homeland. |
| **Ke'hanoath** | Each Vanrian's individual story represented in symbols tattooed somewhere on their person. |
| **Mindcraft** | Unusual abilities possessed by some Vanrians/Thaelians to manipulate the minds of humans or animals. |
| **Mind-crafter** | Someone with a mindcraft ability. |
| **...na sek** | Appended to an officer rank when a promotion is temporarily granted for a specific mission. |

**Sheyvyosk**

Stinky smegma.

**Stoneglass**

A Vanrian light metal alloy that looks like stone and is extremely durable. Primarily used to make bottles for Vanrian Black Mead… naturally.

**Tehanyehn**

A romantic spirit pairing connected by a Bondmaker (considered a deeper form of the marriage vows practiced in the southern kingdoms).

**Tehnaak**

Spirit siblings, bound to each other by a Bondmaker and raised together.

**Tehsheyn**

Spirit family, bound by a Bondmaker.

**The Deeps**

Vanrian solitary confinement in Etrion.

**Union (military)**

A grouping of three regular units combined under a third or fourth level ahninveth or inveth.

**Unit, Regular (military)**

A group of thirty-nine soldiers under a single inveth or ahninveth.

**Unit, Feral (military)**

A group of nine soldiers and up to twenty beasts under a single Feral ahninveth.

**Zenyal**

A type of unequal bond formed by a Bondmaker that gives one half of the pairing a measure of control over the other.

## *RANKS & TITLES:*

**Khevarin**

Ruler of Vanris – the rough equivalent of a king or queen.

**Khemron**

Spouse of the ruler of Vanris, shares some of the leadership.

**Khesran**

Child of the khevarin and khemron – basically a prince or princess.

**Dhomvalen**

Protector or warden. Top Vanrian military leader who answers only to the khevarin.

**Ahnvaris**

Dedicated elite guard to important personages.

**Dhomen**

A Vanrian or Thaelian officer – the rough equivalent of a general in the southern kingdoms. There are four levels.

**Ahndhomen**

A Dhomen who is also a mind-crafter (slightly outranks a dhomen). There are four levels.

**Ahnkreth**

A Vanrian or Thaelian officer – commander of a naval fleet.

**Inveth**

A Vanrian or Thaelian officer – the rough equivalent of a captain in the southern kingdoms. There are four levels.

**Ahninveth**

An Inveth who is also a mindcrafter (slightly outranks an inveth). There are four levels.

**Inren**

A Vanrian or Thaelian common soldier. There are four levels.

**Omren**

A Vanrian or Thaelian mindcrafter common soldier. There are four levels.

**Idrek**

A Vanrian or Thaelian recruit – soldier in training.

**Odrek**

A Vanrian or Thaelian mindcrafter recruit – soldier in training.

### *Other terminology*

**Eydarith**

Culture in Sarket that worships the Tempest, god of the sea. They have a unique language and consider themselves separate from the other citizens of Sarket.

**Havaad**

A god worshipped in parts of the southern kingdoms, particularly in Sarket..

**Hyeralisk**

Qwilki term for a deadly hurricane.

**Itovanak**            Strong alcohol favored by the Eydarith.

**Ket'ta**              The shell of a crustacean in Thaelis. Often used for making cups and small bowls.

**Pandrean Alliance**   An alliance formed between the three southern kingdoms of Delaphine, Sarket, and Fallend to fight Vanris

**Qwe'pi**              Crude Qwilki insult.

**Ukhen'kya**           The Unclean. A cannibalistic culture in conflict with the residents of the Thaelian islands.

**Wavelord**            Eydarith leader. Like a king or queen, but believed to be chosen by their god, the Tempest.

### *Mindcrafting disciplines*

**Bondmaker**           A mind-crafter who can create bonds between two or more individuals by using the life threads that exist within them.

**Breaker**             A mind-crafter whose ability is uncontrolled and powerful enough to "break" the minds of their victims to the point that they have no cognitive capabilities or even the ability to respond to their own needs.

**Charmer**

A mind-crafter who can manipulate an individual or small
number of individuals to go
along with their suggestions.

**Dampener**

A mind-crafter who can interfere with the way people's
minds perceive their senses,
effectively taking away the
sight, sound, smell, and/
or touch of individuals or
groups.

**Enkindler**

A mind-crafter who can
inspire positive or negative
emotions in individuals or
groups.

**Evoker**

A mind-crafter who can see
and sometimes alter a single
individuals surface thoughts
and memories.

**Feral**

A mind-crafter who can
connect with, influence, and
control the minds of animals
or groups of animals.

**Frightener**

A mind-crafter who can access
the fears of individuals or
groups and cause them to see
terrifying visions, sometimes
permanently scarring their
minds.

**Heartsmith**

A blind mind-crafter who
can tap into people's deepest
thoughts and emotions in an
abstract way to read the story

of who they are in order to tattoo it upon their skin.

**Speaker**

A mind-crafter who can speak into the minds of individuals or groups, limited somewhat by range and visibility (less so if their subject is also another Speaker).

### *Unique Creatures*

**Cliff Cat**

Large wildcats native to the mountains in Vanris. Some Ferals use them in combat. They have a deep blue-gray coat with darker blue stripes down the spine along either side of a ridge of longer hair. Their eyes are sapphire blue, and their tails end in a puff of hair the same blue as its stripes. They tend to be around waist high to a man at the shoulder.

**Ji'ikyan**

Large ocean serpents with scales a blend of lavender, pink, silver, and pearlescent white, with a translucent dorsal fin running along their substantial length. They have jaws full of teeth designed to tear apart prey that they first paralyze with a toxin injected through a stinger at the end of their tails.

**Kanodrak**

Impressive Vanrian predators brought to Pandrea from the original Vanrian homeland. Taller than a horse and used as mounts by a few Ferals. Vaguely feline with a silver-grey, scaled hide and milky white eyes. They have bone armor plating that starts at the nose and runs along the spine to the base of their long tail. Their massive front incisors extended well below the lower jaw.

**Kednu**

Large deer on the Thaelian islands that are sometimes used as pack animals and occasional mounts.

**Kel'inuk**

Similar in appearance to a salamander, but capable of growing much larger than a horse, these ocean-dwelling amphibians have no teeth. They crush prey repeatedly in their powerful jaws and swallow it whole.

**Nightstar Eagle**

Large black eagle with gold feathers sweeping back from its eyes and along the lower edge of its wings and tail. Revered by followers of Havaad in the southern kingdoms.

**Sandhawk**

Desert hawks commonly seen in southern Vanris and around the Crimson Break.

**Tethdrak**

Vanrian predators brought
to Pandrea from the original
Vanrian homeland. Some
Ferals use them in combat.
Built a little like a hound, but
reptilian. Adults are mid-rib
high to a man at the shoulder.
The thickly muscled limbs
and torso are covered in light
shades of red and brown
scaling with spiked plates
along the length of the spine
and thick tail. Two backswept
horns extend from the head
and their massive jaws bristle
with sharp teeth.

**Wave Dancer**

Sey'yaluth ayon in Qwilki.
Tall, amphibious canines.
Narrow built with long
slender legs, fishlike, gleaming
black scales over the forehead,
across the front of the
shoulders, and along the back
of the hips. They have odd,
glossy black fur made up of
long, thick strands. The black
ears are partially transparent
like a bat's wings and have
fine ridges at intervals in
the membrane, giving them
the appearance of fins. They
have broad scaled paws, with
webbing between the toes
designed for swimming. They
tend to have eyes of some
shade of blue or green.

## Places

**Andaro**

Capital city of the kingdom of Sarket.

**Balarus**

Large town south of the Break in northeastern Sarket.

**Crimson Break**

War-devastated, desert region between Vanris and the southern kingdoms.

**Crimsondale**

Town where the incident that started the war happened. Now part of the Crimson Break.

**Dagony**

Port city on the main island in Thaelis.

**Deepwater**

Small integrated town on the western coast of the Crimson Break.

**Delaphine**

Eastern kingdom on Pandrea. Home to the Delaphinian people.

**Doran**

The northern capital of Vanris.

**Etrion**

The southern capital of Vanris.

**Fallend**

Southern kingdom on Pandrea. Home to the Fallenese people.

| | |
|---|---|
| **Fernwallow** | Small village in Fallend. |
| **Hellaris** | Town in Sarket. |
| **Kilden Mountains** | Mountain range near the coast in Sarket. |
| **Mukyeny** | Town on one of the islands in Thaelis. |
| **Pandrea** | The continent. |
| **Sarket** | Western kingdom on Pandrea. Home to the Sarketi people. |
| **Taro** | Coastal city in Sarket, mostly run by the Eydarith. |
| **Thaelis** | Island chain about a week west of Pandrea. |
| **Vanris** | Northernmost kingdom on Pandrea. New home to the Vanrian people after volcanic activity drove them from their original island home. |
| **Vareyl's Warning** | Black crags that create a natural border between northern and southern Vanris. Called Vareyl's Gift before the war. |

### *People*

| | |
|---|---|
| **Adnar** | Vanrian ahndhomen / Feral kanodrak rider / Nevias's tehnaak) |

**Ahrin**  One of Darro and Tath's twin sons, named after his mother's deceased former tehnaak / Gannon's brother / Iyvalin's tehnaak

**Allonda**  Delaphinian representative

**Amera**  Eydarith tezaak

**Arhk Cavenos**  Dhomvalen of Vanris / Frightener / Veyl's grandfather

**Avris**  Vanrian inveth and combat instructor / Merrin's tehnaak / part of Kasiel's tehsheyn

**Cordin**  Fish market owner / Quillon's brother

**Darith**  Thaelian councilor

**Darro**  Vanrian dhomen / Gannon and Ahrin's father / Kince's tehnaak / part of Kasiel's tehsheyn

**Eavara**  Thalian Ahnkreth (fleet commander) / Speaker

**Ellaris**  Jethan and Keyla's second daughter, named after Veyl's deceased grandmother / Tavin's tehnaak

**Erkhan**  Thaelian Dampener / part of Eavara's crew

**Fen** — Deck boy / part of Kyril's crew

**Feyd** — Vanrian Healer / Dampener / Dailan's tehnaak / part of Kyril's unit

**Gregory Harriksen** — Chief General of Sarket

**Helaya** — Kyril's former love

**Iyvalin** — Arin's tehnaak / Veyl's friend

**Jaysen Lodmund** — Crown prince of Sarket / son of Roald and Astrid / Veyl's best friend

**Jethan Markanis** — Vanrian ahninveth / Charmer / Kasiel's tehnaak and part of his tehsheyn / father of Ellaris and Veyl's former tehnaak, Minya / Velara's cousin

**Jinau** — Thaelian Ahndhomen / Charmer

**Kasiel Cavanos** — Khemron of Vanris / Feral kanodrak rider / Vey's father

**Kince** — Vanrian inveth / Darro's tehnaak / part of Kasiel's tehsheyn

**Kitria** — Kyril's younger sister

**Kronach** — Wavelord of Taro / Eydarith

**Kyril** — Thaelian ahnkreth (fleet commander) / Feral

**Lanis**    Vanrian attendant who helped raise Veyl

**Leath**    Vanrian soldier / Speaker / Tassa's tehnaak / part of Kyril's unit

**Lorek**    Gannon's tehnaak / Veyl's friend

**Mardi**    Thaelian guard

**Merrin**    Vanrian dhomen and combat instructor /Avris's tehnaak / part of Kasiel's tehsheyn

**Meyla**    Thalian officer / Kyril's second

**Minera**    Vanrian ahnvaris / Dampener

**Minya**    Jethan and Keyla's first daughter who died very young / Veyl's first tehnaak

**Nalika**    Vanrian subordinate ahnkreth / part of Kyril's crew

**Nerith**    Vanrian healer / Tath's tehnaak / part of Kasiel's tehsheyn

**Nichal**    Thaelian soldier / part of Kyril's crew

**Nevias**    Vanrian dhomen / Adnar's tehnaak

**Pera**    Eydarith warrior

| | |
|---|---|
| **Quillon** | Thaelian guard |
| **Rel** | Thaelian soldier / part of Kyril's crew |
| **Roald Lodmund** | King of Sarket / Jaysen's father |
| **Rysek** | Vanrian ahnvaris / Dampener / one of Arhk's elite guards |
| **Setera** | Vanrian ahndhomen / Evoker |
| **Shyall** | Thaelian councilor |
| **Tarik** | Vanrian city guard |
| **Tassa** | Vanrian soldier / Enkindler / Leath's tehnaak / part of Kyril's unit |
| **Tavin** | A khesran of Vanris / Veyl's younger brother |
| **Tath** | Vanrian healer / Gannon and Ahrin's mother / Nerith's tehnaak / part of Kasiel's tehsheyn |
| **Torlif** | Eydarith warrior |
| **Velara Markanis** | Khevarin of Vanris / Charmer / Veyl's mother |
| **Veyl** | A khesran of Vanris / heir to the Vanrian throne / daughter of Kasiel and Velara |
| **Wilkin Thrasser** | King Regent of Sarket |

**Yserra**                      Vanrian ahnvaris / Evoker

**Zafyr**                        Vanrian ahnvaris / Evoker

## ACKNOWLEDGEMENTS

Whether you started with the Warden's Son series or this series is your first adventure in the tales of Vanris, thank you for joining me on this journey. I hope you enjoyed this book and will continue to follow Veyl's story through the third and final book. There are a number of people I would like to offer my appreciation, so I will try to capture them all here.

To my mom, Linda, who has been my alpha reader through so many books and provided so much support and valuable feedback throughout the process. I can't imagine doing this without you.

As always, my best friends and beta readers, Rick and Ann, who somehow continue to stand by me regardless of where my crazy goes. You are now, and always will be, my tehsheyn.

To my additional beta readers, Patrick and Marla, your feedback was invaluable. You are greatly appreciated. And to all the ARC readers who have joined this journey, thank you!

As always, I want to acknowledge the fantastic team who helped me put together the finished book. Robert Crescenzio, my incredibly talented cover artist whose vision helps bring these books to life on the covers. Melissa Nash, the fantastic map designer who helped my vision of the land come to life. Alexander Lockwood, my fantastic editor, fellow author, and now friend. Brian Short, my amazing formatter, whom I would also like to thank for your excellent company on many coffeeshop writing days. I love working with you all.

To my other friends and family, know that I love you and value your place in my life even if I don't call you out specifically here.

Last, but certainly not least, to my readers. To me, a book is a collaborative effort between the author and the reader. Without you, this world would only ever come to life in my head. I hope you enjoy experiencing it as much as I did and will continue to follow me on my next adventure.

## AUTHOR BIO

Outside of my career as an author, I am a professional technical and creative writer, spider wrangler, animal lover, and devoted cat mom. Writing fantasy and science fiction stories has been a lifelong passion for me. I love to draw upon my myriad life experiences for my books, doing everything from wild cave exploration and horseback endurance riding to practicing iaido and archery.

•

Thank you for taking time to read this novel. Please leave a review if you enjoyed it.

•

For more about me and my work visit me at http://elysiumpalace.com.

# OTHER WORKS by NIKKI McCORMACK

**CLOCKWORK ENTERPRISES**
The Girl and the Clockwork Cat
The Girl and the Clockwork Conspiracy
The Girl and the Clockwork Crossfire

**THE WARDEN'S SON**
Child of Vanris
Blood of Vanris
Heart of Vanris
Throne of Vanris

**DAUGHTER OF VANRIS**
Wave Dancer
Wave-Touched
Wavelord

**FORBIDDEN THINGS**
Dissident
Exile
Apostate

**ELYSIUM'S FALL**
Dark Hope of the Dragons
Dark Savior of the Dragons

**SILVERBLOOD RAVEN**
A Path of Blood and Amber
A Path of Secrets and Dreams
A Path of Storms and Reckonings

STANDALONE WORK
Golden Eyes
The Keeper
Making Monsters (short story)
In Silence Waiting (short story)
And they All Look Just the Same (short story)
Warden's Rise: A Tale of Vanris (short story)

www.ingramcontent.com/pod-product-compliance
Lightning Source LLC
Chambersburg PA
CBHW021332310726
48971CB00001B/99